Raluana Lane

Rachel Nightingale

Tarya Imprints

First published in Australia in 2025 by Tarya Imprints.
Bendigo, VIC, 3550
Visit the author website at WWW.RACHEL-NIGHTINGALE.INFO

A catalogue record for this book is available from the National Library of Australia

978-0-9756292-0-8 (ebook)
978-0-9756292-1-5 (paperback)
Book Editor: Angela Slatter
Cover design by Lordan June Pinote
Interior design by Jamie Le Rossignol
Printed and bound in Australia by Ingram Spark

Dedication

For Wilf and Eileen. Though an ocean of time separates us,
my heart breaks for what you both endured.

About the Author

Rachel Nightingale (Dr Rachel Le Rossignol) is an author, educator, actor and award-winning playwright. Her fantasy trilogy, *The Tales of Tarya* is published by Odyssey Books and explores the magic of creativity. She is also the co-author of *Mandala: Journeys Within the Circle*, with artist Karen Scott. Her plays and musicals have been performed in Australia, New Zealand and Manila. Rachel co-wrote and performed in Murder on the Puffing Billy Express, a murder mystery show performed regularly on the iconic Puffing Billy steam train in Melbourne, Australia. She holds both a Masters degree and PhD in creative and professional writing, as well as qualifications in editing, social work and education. An experienced public speaker, she has appeared at numerous writing conferences and festivals. As an educator she has run creative writing workshops for primary school age children in India and Australia, and has taught in the tertiary sector in Australia and Vietnam.

Author's Note

This is a true story. The letters written by Wilf and Eileen are real, and the accounts of certain events are based on their writings, or on extant documents from the time, including letters, diaries, telegrams, interviews and articles.

I have done my best, as far as possible, to stay within the known facts. A number of books were invaluable for establishing the bones of the story; I am especially indebted to the extensive research done by Neville Threlfall, Bruce Gamble and Margaret Reeson for their books (listed in the bibliography). Through my research I found questions and errors in available writing, so at times I had to piece together parts of the story from mismatched fragments. Where contradictions existed, I chose what I considered to be the most likely scenarios. As this is a fictionalised account, the demands of creating a resonant narrative also played a part.

Few accounts include much detail about the local people of New Britain, although they were deeply involved in the events of the time this book covers. My grandparents' writing mentions specific people, including Ainui and Pilip, so I have included them in the story, although I have invented detail about some actions. In not wanting to gloss over the central role of the local community I have, at times, also given names to characters; I have chosen names that appeared in contemporaneous writings.

Finally, in giving my story life and colour there are a small number of scenes that arise purely from my imagination, but where this occurs, I have used known events and available documents to shape the work wherever possible. For example, I can piece together Wilf and Eileen's final conversation from the letter Wilf sent shortly afterwards. The events at the minseibu celebration are on record as occurring, but whether my grandfather was one of the attendees, I will never know. Wilf's experiences as a prisoner of the Japanese are typical of known accounts, but there are no known records of what he personally went through. However, as someone fluent in the language of the region, it is highly likely he would have been asked to act as a translator, and from everything I have learned about him, it is equally likely he would have refused.

There are still unanswered questions about the events that occurred during the invasion and occupation of Rabaul, especially around the fate of the 1053 Australian civilians and soldiers who are said to have died on the Montevideo Maru. I have agonised over my choices in telling this part of the story, taking into account the known behaviour of the Japanese in WWII, the evidence of the time, and the choices we know were made by the missionaries.

Please be aware this book contains some terms now considered derogatory and offensive, in order to be true to the language and thinking of the time and setting.

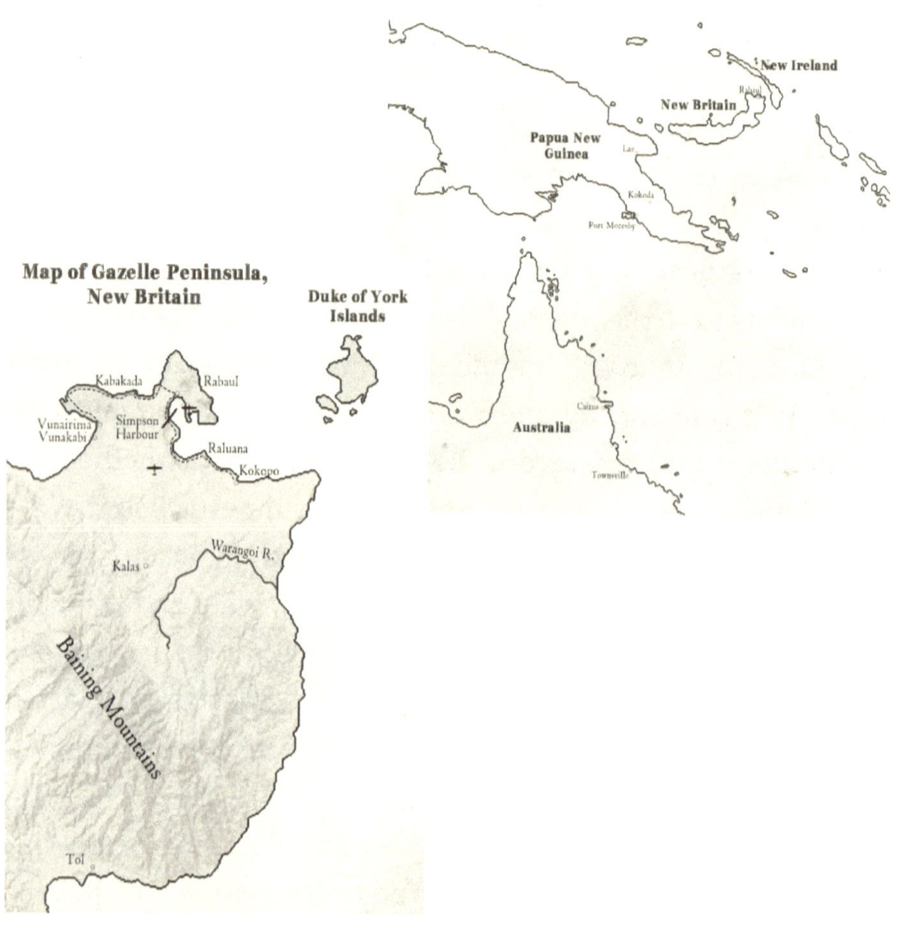

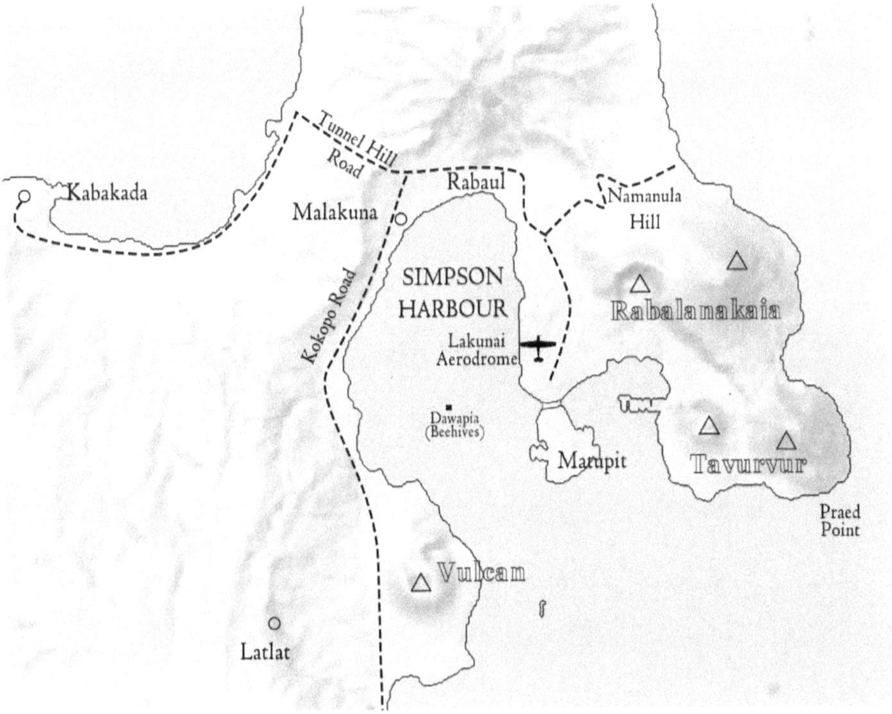

Kabakada
Tunnel Hill Road
Malakuna
Rabaul
Namanula Hill
Kokopo Road
SIMPSON HARBOUR
Rabalanakaia
Lakunai Aerodrome
Dawapia (Beehives)
Matupit
Tavurvur
Praed Point
Vulcan
Latlat

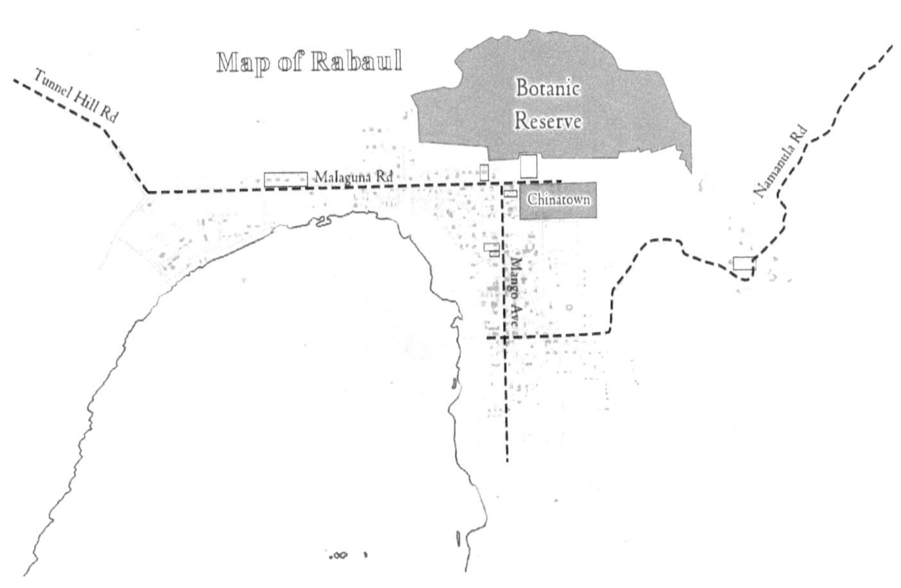

Map of Rabaul
Tunnel Hill Rd
Botanic Reserve
Malaguna Rd
Chinatown
Namanula Rd
Mango Ave

Raluana Lane

Prologue

Eileen

Hobart, Tasmania.

> *The one remains, the many change and pass,*
> *Heaven's light for ever shines; earth's shadows fly;*
> *Life, like a dome of many–colour'd glass,*
> *Stains the white radiance of eternity,*
> *Until death tramples it to fragments.*

Adonais,   48-52
Percy Bysshe Shelley

Lately the smallest things could send Eileen into a reverie. The particular shade of dark blue on her mug as she dropped it into the sink, her fingertips strangely slippery; the fragile winter light streaming through the window, so different to the intense sunlight in the tropical paradise that had been her home. Something triggered her memories now, sending them down pathways long neglected.

Elsewhere in the house an uneven tapping began. Eileen clutched one hand to her heart, gripping the fabric of her dress. It was impossible, yet the tapping had a rhythm so familiar she found it hard to push the thought away.

'Ia Lo.'

She turned, but of course there was no one there, only the shade of memories. Shaking her head, she reached for the secateurs on the kitchen table, and headed for the front door.

Crisp air turned her breath to clouds and brushed icy fingers across her skin as Eileen shuffled from the portico into the garden. Her knees protested as she tentatively took the slight step down to the path. Turning right, she shuffled across the grass towards the roses. Their branches twisted, spiked and bare like arthritic hands, toward the hazy winter sky, kissed with the promise of snow.

The secateurs were heavy in her hand, but she couldn't put the task off any longer. Winter would be over soon. Then it would be too late to prune.

'Good pruning is the secret to healthy blooms, my darling,' Wilf would always say. And she had every faith in his advice because his rose garden was famous throughout Rabaul. No one had managed to grow such flowers in the tropical climate except him. Roses were much more suited to Hobart's cool atmosphere, Eileen thought, as she used both hands to wield the secateurs. Clip. Branches fell. Yet her bushes looked sad and bedraggled despite the appropriate weather.

It's only because it's winter, she thought. They've gone to sleep against the cold. In summer they'll be glorious again.

But not like the gardens in Rabaul. The sweet scent of frangipanis and hibiscus there verged on overwhelming. The coconut trees and mangoes offered endless relief with their shade, branches forming a sweeping canopy over the entire road. A hat was unnecessary even on the brightest days. Try as she might, and with all her expertise as a gardener, Eileen hadn't been able to capture the glory of Rabaul's plant life, made prolific by volcano-fed soil. Too prolific, the jungle always eager to take over the cultivated gardens.

Why was she thinking about Rabaul now? Nothing had occurred to bring it to mind. A thought flashed, *maybe it would.* A shudder of premonition went through her, and she remembered stories of her grandma Emily's sister having the sight, along with other powers that weren't spoken about. As a child Eileen hadn't entirely disbelieved such tales, because she couldn't imagine her perpetually honest grandmother lying about them, but now she was older her faith was the only unseen power she needed. It must be the roses that drew her thoughts to Wilf's long distant garden, far away in the Pacific, where it was warm all year round.

What was left of that garden in Rabaul now? Had it vanished entirely, or did something remain, buried under layers of destruction? Was there life left?

The thought snagged her like a barb and she felt a sharp pain in her chest. Ignoring it, she took to the gnarled spindles of the bush, clipping with a fervour akin to anger. She had pushed these thoughts aside successfully many times. Now would be the same.

Winter-dead branches fell at her feet. She would gather them later. It was more efficient to pick them up in one bundle anyway. After this task was complete, she would water the African violets, then maybe Andrew would be home and he could make her a cup of tea. Or maybe she would get Andrew to water the violets. She was feeling quite tired now. Wielding the secateurs took strength she didn't have. Perhaps it was time for a rest.

Something moved in her peripheral vision, perhaps a visitor. But when she turned her head, it was only Dennis, the big ginger tom. He slunk along the fence line, then strutted towards the back yard, tail proudly upright. There was something in his mouth.

'Oh Dennis, have you been stealing from the neighbour again?'

He turned his head languorously, revealing a small parcel hanging from his maw.

'Put it in the usual place and I'll take it back later,' Eileen sighed. Dennis turned and started towards the front door, as though he understood. He'd leave the parcel on the door mat and return to his patrol. At least it was a better gift than a mouse. Eileen called after him. 'And it's not dinner time yet, so don't start bossing me around.'

It was lucky his mouth was full, or he'd respond to that with a strident mew, no doubt. She returned to the bushes for a final pruning. But her hands didn't seem to be working properly. The rubber handle of the secateurs felt slippery and she watched as, almost in slow motion, they slid from her grip. Another stabbing sensation in her chest made her stagger. Never one to admit weakness, Eileen would have kept gardening, but her legs were suddenly made of jelly. She thought of her chair in the living room, a haven in recent days, with its view over the back yard. The way she felt, it seemed a long way away, but she knew she had to sit, and soon.

Turning, she started for the front door and stopped with a gasp. Someone stood just inside the gate, his face turned away, but his posture infinitely familiar. Eileen took a step towards him, her legs strangely unresponsive. The sound was enough to make him turn. His dear, shy smile beamed at her as he reached out his hand. His crisp white pants and shirt, far better suited to Rabaul's tropical heat than the dying Hobart winter, glowed as if the sun were summer bright. As Eileen approached, reaching to grasp his hand, the glow expanded and became brighter, almost unbearable to her eyes.

'Wilf... oh Wilf. You came home.'

1 – The Eruption

Wilf

4pm, Saturday 29th May 1937. Rabaul.

> Roar of explosion interrupted wedding
> at island mission. Threw confetti as
> darkness descended. Wedding break-
> fast hot soup and quinine.

Headlines, Brisbane Telegraph, Monday 7 June 1937

'I will.'

Jack Trevitt's words were swallowed by a giant bang as the church shook. Beams overhead creaked and cracked. For long seconds the walls moved and anything freestanding wavered, threatening to topple. From his seat in the first row, Wilf Pearce caught a flash of something like fear on the face of the bride, Miss Melville 'Mel' Chaseling. And no wonder. She had only arrived in Rabaul two days before. She wasn't used to the regular tremors, or guria, as the natives called them, that came with living amongst four volcanoes. Wilf had picked her up from the wharf himself, a task he performed regularly with all new arrivals to the Methodist Mission, and seen her initial overwhelm from landing in a completely different climate and culture.

A dozen missionaries were in charge of as many circuits across the Gazelle Peninsula, each circuit encompassing numerous villages. The wives of mission staff were expected to take an active role in the work with native congregations. With all sorts of conventions and rules to follow, there was a lot to learn. As with all new arrivals, Wilf had been reassuring and informative as he helped Miss Chaseling with the important paperwork, outlined the structure and operations of the Mission, and organised for her luggage to be transported to Reverend Frank Lewis's house at Malakuna for the first few days of her stay.

The same Reverend Lewis now seemed to be at risk of being knocked out as a vase of frangipanis and maidenhead fern quavered ominously behind him. Oblivious to the danger, he went on to ask the congregation if they would, by God's grace, uphold and care for these two persons in their marriage. As the joint response rang out, 'we will', Miss Chaseling's bridesmaid, Hazel Jones, was focused on the vase too. Wilf wondered if the quivering of her back was a suppressed giggle. He glanced over at the pew parallel to his and saw Miss Brabin, one of the teachers from the Married Women's School, tighten her lips. Whether this was in disapproval or to suppress her own grin he couldn't be sure. Possibly the latter. Lewis liked things to be done in particular ways, so some of the younger staff considered him a little uptight. No doubt they might enjoy the diversion of a toppled vase on his rigid skull.

Most of those seated in the congregation ignored the guriu and its aftereffects as the service continued. It was a minor tremor compared to the one that collapsed a school in Raluana at lunchtime yesterday. Fortunately there had been no casualties. Another tremor had woken everyone at 5am this morning. Other guria throughout the morning had been brief and far less dramatic.

Mel Chaseling seemed to have recovered her poise, smiling calmly at Jack Trevitt, her husband-to-be, as Reverend Lewis announced the prayer. Wilf remembered she was trained in earth sciences. The day she arrived, she had recognised the volcano formations surrounding Simpsons Harbour, asking Wilf about them throughout the car ride from the wharf. From her seat in the back, Wilf's wife Gladys had laughed delightedly at Mel's enthusiasm.

Weddings were a common occurrence among the staff and Wilf could recite the Methodist order of service by rote, so his thoughts turned to Gladys as the service continued. He hoped she was napping at the Jones' house, and not running about making final preparations for the wedding breakfast at the Mission station. That morning, when he came to pick her and Mrs Lewis up from Kabakada, he had taken one look at the sweat on her forehead and the dark circles under her eyes and suggested she stay there 'to keep an eye on things'.

'And you could always have a little rest,' he had added, trying to make it sound like an afterthought, but he was sure Gladys had seen through his ruse. Still, she hadn't argued. Only a heavy dose of quinine had kept her out of the bed for the last few days of this terrible malaria flare-up. The sheen of sweat told him she might be losing the battle again. She had complained of fatigue and headaches quite frequently in the last few months. The humidity was causing her arms and legs to swell more than usual too, although she was otherwise losing weight, having largely lost her interest in food. To distract himself from his concerns, Wilf forced his attention back to the wedding.

After five years in Rabaul, Reverend Lewis was as familiar as anyone with the regular guria, so Wilf was surprised to realise the Reverend was hurrying through the service rather than savouring the oratory opportunity. Lewis had already moved on to the vows and exchange of rings, and soon drew the bride and groom, and their party, into the vestry to sign the book. Wilf was rattled by Lewis' behaviour and wondered if he had not been paying enough attention to the strange events of the last twenty-four hours. Guria were normal, yes, but that was not all that had occurred.

Yesterday afternoon the water around the island volcano Vulcan, or Rakaia, as the natives called it, had rapidly receded, then risen far beyond its usual level. When it returned to normal, hundreds of fish were stranded on the shore. According to Ainui, the native who often ran errands for Wilf in one of the mission trucks, the mighty kaia who lived in the heart of Rakaia was restless. Then this morning Vulcan had risen out of the sea shortly after 8am, taking on a new conical shape, much to the astonishment of Rabaul's townsfolk. Ainui hadn't been worried though. Wilf was aware of the native saying, 'as long as Father is smoking his pipe, the Mother will be alright', referring to the two largest volcanoes. The Father had certainly been smoking in the last twenty-four hours.

Another sudden explosion disrupted Wilf's musings. The church shook even harder this time. The noise was so loud some of the congregation put their hands over their ears. Maidenhair fern rustled feverishly, a few guests murmured in fear, and something crashed to the floor at the rear of the building. The shaking went on for eternal seconds and most were frozen in their seats, but from his place next to Wilf, Laurie Linggood leapt up, lunged forward, and caught the hand-painted china vase full of frangipani just as it toppled. With a final petulant shake and bang, the noise and movement died away.

Laurie was still standing, flowers in hand, in the now-silent church, when the wedding party returned from the vestry. With a grin, he replaced the floral arrangement, gave the bride and groom a stylish bow, and stepped out of the way to allow the ceremony to finish. Giggles swept through the congregation and Wilf raised his eyebrow to Laurie as he resumed his seat.

Reverend Lewis seemed largely unperturbed by the events, and swiftly concluded the service. Fortunately for the wedding party the church seemed to have stopped its lively dance. As the final words were being spoken, Wilf slipped from the pew and hurried down the centre aisle. He was a keen photographer and relished the opportunity to take some snaps of the happy couple as they left the church. Besides, as officer manager for the Methodist Mission, giving away brides and taking photos of weddings were two of his less official, but no less expected, duties. Laurie was only a few steps behind, his own camera in hand.

Wilf was so focused on positioning himself at the foot of the church steps before the bride and groom emerged, all he initially noticed was the unusual absence of bird calls, and a strange haziness to the light.

'Are you seeing what I'm seeing, Laurie?' he asked as the two men peered through lenses and adjusted settings, hoping to get the best possible pictures.

'It's rather odd light, isn't it? Almost yellow. I don't think I've encountered anything like it before.'

Although Wilf was an experienced photographer, he had to agree. He wasn't quite sure what might work, and making adjustments absorbed his attention until Mel and Jack Trevitt stepped out of the church. They took their position on the stone steps, Jack leaning in a little towards his new bride, lean and lanky and more than a head taller than her. Behind them, Howard Pearson and Hazel Jones took their places as best man and matron of honour. Their grins far eclipsed the more tentative smiles of the bride and groom. Confetti rained down on the new couple, dotting Jack's white suit and Mel's ivory dress with bursts of colour.

As he clicked, Wilf moved in closer, and saw a change sweep over those on the steps. It began with those standing behind everyone else – Reverend Lewis' wife and some of the teaching sisters. Eyes widened, jaws dropped and there were a few gasps, followed by complete silence. Then Hazel and Howard stopped focusing on the photographers and the same expression swept across their faces. Finally, Jack and Mel looked up and outwards, awe and shock replacing their smiles. Wilf lowered his camera and turned to see what had caught everyone's attention.

From the front of Rabaul's Methodist church one would normally see the dazzling blue waters of Simpsons Harbour, the jutting rocks at its centre known as the Beehives, and the lush growth of tropical plants on the surrounding peaks. But now they were blotted out by a column of brilliant white smoke that burst at speed straight upwards from Vulcan. Sparks flickered here and there amongst the billowing curls at the column's periphery. Once the immense pillar reached perhaps a thousand feet in the air, it started veering sideways, as though it had hit a pane of glass. It began to travel in the direction of Latlat, one of the villages not far from Rabaul, dense smoke twisting and churning against the blue sky.

By now most congregants had exited the church and stood in clumps. Wilf guessed many were chatting excitedly about the feast awaiting them at Kabakada Mission House. Mrs Lewis and Gladys Pearce were renowned for putting on a delicious spread, with fruits in jelly, salads, meat platters and of course, an elaborate cake. Gladys was probably whipping up the cream right now to go with the huge bowls of fruit salad that would have been prepared this morning.

As the smoky cloud continued to rise upwards, it began to seethe and darken. Everyone fell silent, staring at the darkening sky.

'Well, the Father is definitely smoking today,' Wilf murmured. Behind him, the celebrations seemed to have resumed with a cheer. He turned to see Jack climbing into the back of the district car. Mel passed her cascading frangipani bouquet to Hazel so she could take her place beside him, then Hazel climbed in as well.

'Time to go, old man,' Howard Pearson nudged Wilf, who hurried round to the driver's seat. Howard slid in beside him.

'See you at Kabakada,' Jack called to the watchers, waving through the window, and everyone cheered as the car rolled away. A jangling sound accompanied them from the trail of empty cans that had previously contained reduced milk. The cans had been carefully saved for the last month by anyone who had received the delicious treat in a parcel from home. Normally these would be attached after the reception, but Laurie hadn't wanted to wait.

The first part of the journey was along Tunnel Hill Road. The road had originally been a tunnel carved by the early German colonists, but this had long since collapsed in on itself, creating a narrow, unsealed pass through the edge of the crater that formed Simpson Harbour. Since the road followed the coastline, they had a clear view of the volcano. Though Wilf was concentrating on driving, he couldn't help but catch glimpses of billowing clouds of smoke.

'Oh goodness!' Mel Trevitt exclaimed only a few minutes after they left the church. 'I've studied volcanoes, but I've never seen a live one. Can we stop for a moment?'

'A pretty exciting start to married life,' Jack chimed in.

Wilf found a spot to pull the car over and they all hurried to the cliff edge to look out at Simpson Harbour. It was still an odd sight to see Vulcan's new cone shape, but the island was becoming harder to make out through the increasingly dense cloud writhing upwards. Where the surface of the harbour was visible, there seemed to be odd movements, like whirlwinds, and the column was shifting colour. At its base a dirty yellow was seeping in, although the top was still brilliant white and spread out so much now the whole thing resembled a giant cauliflower.

Wilf thought he might get a few snaps of the smoking volcano, so he fetched his camera from the car. By the time he rejoined the others, he only managed one shot of the billowing smoke before it began changing again, quickly thickening to a black, roiling mass. Mel was fixated.

'This is incredible.'

One arm around his new wife's shoulder, Jack beamed.

'Quite a show you've put on for us today,' Howard said.

'Only the best for my Mel.'

They fell silent as the volcano continued its performance, ejecting endless black smoke until the sky was filled with a giant, mushroom-shaped mass. Words couldn't capture the immensity of it.

Wilf took another photo, then realised he was out of film. He had left more at Kabakada, to take shots of the reception, but for now all he could do was watch furious smoke fill the sky. It moved with speed across the bay and everyone was shaken out of their awed reverie at the same. Howard Pearson's voice had an almost imperceptible quaver.

'Um… it's coming straight towards us.'

'I know you'd spend all day watching this if you could, Mel, but it is your wedding day if you recall,' Hazel chuckled. 'Perhaps we'd be safest getting to the reception.'

The bride nodded. 'I suppose we should try to arrive before everyone else.'

'They'll take a while,' Jack said. 'Some may have a fresh shirt in their car, but others will have to fetch one.'

Mel's eyes grew round. 'I didn't realise I was marrying into society! I have a going away dress, but nothing new to wear for the wedding breakfast!'

Hazel hooked her arm through the bride's. 'Oh, we're definitely not that fancy – it's the humidity. Everyone carries a change of shirt or they'd end up permanently drenched. Come on, we still have to take more photos of you in that beautiful dress before we get to eat cake!'

With one last backward glance, Mel followed the others back to the car. They continued along the coast road only a little longer, then turned inland on the road to Kabakada. When they hit the next coast road, they were following the outward edge of New Britain, the harbour behind them, so the eruption was no longer in their line of sight, although Wilf could see in the mirror that Mel kept looking out the rear window excitedly.

'It seems to be following us,' she murmured. But all thoughts of the volcano were swept away as they drove up and parked next to the Mission station. Like so many of the church-owned buildings, it was a timber construction raised on stilts, with a wide veranda. Gladys and Mrs Lewis had spent the morning directing the native boys to set up tables on the veranda, with hibiscus and frangipani in vivid sprays of colour on the white tablecloths. White cane chairs were strategically placed for those who needed to wilt in the heat.

Jack Trevitt slipped from the car and offered a hand to his new wife. She climbed out after him and gazed at the lush gardens with a smile. Huge toun trees encircled the area, and brilliant flowers swayed jewel-like in the vivid undergrowth. For someone newly arrived from Australia the vibrant, teeming life of New Britain was beautiful, but could be almost overwhelming. Today the faint scent of copra that often permeated the air was overwhelmed by the acrid smell of sulphur: not surprising given the volcano was belching away only eight miles from the house.

Camera in hand, Wilf gave the newlyweds a moment to drink in the sight of the bounteous feast. The plan was to take photos in the garden, but there was no need to rush. New Britain time was slow, considered.

Howard approached, hand outstretched. 'How about I take a few of the snaps while you check on Gladys?'

They both glanced towards the house before Wilf responded. 'She's supposed to be resting at the Jones'.'

'Well, odds are she's in the kitchen whipping up cream as we speak. I'll wager a tin of butterscotch on it.'

Wilf raised one eyebrow. 'You have butterscotch and you didn't tell me?'

'It arrived with the mail plane this morning.'

Wilf handed Howard his beloved camera. 'Much as I love butterscotch, I'm not going to take that wager because you'll be right,' he called over his shoulder as he started for the house.

Howard was, of course, correct. As Gladys hovered, the houseboy vigorously whipped cream. Wilf stood in the doorway, taking in the absence of sweat on her forehead and the colour in her cheeks.

'Hello, my dear. It looks like the plasmoquin has kicked in?'

Gladys gave him a quick smile and glanced at the houseboy attacking the recalcitrant cream. 'I'm feeling much better and there's work to be done. Can you take those sandwiches out to the tables? You too, Misiel. That cream looks perfect.'

Misiel put down the bowl of cream and sprang into action, hoisting up two large plates and carrying them out of the kitchen, arms teetering like scales finding their balance point.

Wilf approached Gladys cautiously, half expecting to be batted away, but she accepted his kiss on her forehead absent-mindedly as she set to work spooning cream onto scones.

'Don't overdo it, will you?'

'I just need to get these served and I'm done. Then I'll come and join you in the conservatory.'

'Promise?'

She nodded, already half turning away to rinse off the beater. Dismissed, Wilf took the remaining plate of finger sandwiches and headed to the veranda. It took some rearranging, with Misiel's help, to make room for the extra food on the already heavily laden table and they had only just finished the puzzle when cries arose from outdoors.

The bride and groom were posing for gangly Howard Pearson, who stood a short distance away, camera poised. Hazel Jones waited nearby, holding the cascading bouquet of frangipanis, ready to hand it over as needed. But Jack and Mel were not looking at the camera, and their smiles had transformed into open mouths and wide eyes. Heading toward them rapidly was a black, roiling cloud. Before Wilf had reached the edge of the veranda, a strange dark rain began to fall.

The Trevitts, Howard and Hazel broke from their frozen reverie and raced for the veranda steps. Where the rain hit them, it left dark smudges, until their clothes were more grey than white. They reached the shelter of the veranda and stood beside Wilf, watching the air darken. Up close he could see their clothing was not marred by eerie raindrops at all, but clinging flakes of ash.

'Well, this certainly makes for a memorable occasion,' Jack laughed. 'At least we got a few photos before it started.' Howard held out the camera to Wilf, but he didn't take it, his mind already turning to the practicalities.

'You keep it for now. Frank was going to headquarters to change out of his robes after the ceremony and I was supposed to pick him up with his wife, Gil and Miss March once I dropped you all here. If it's this bad here, Malakuna must be seeing even heavier ashfall, so I'd better go get them.'

The others nodded. Jack, Mel and Hazel headed into the house. Howard placed one hand on Wilf's arm. 'Drive carefully.'

'I'll be back soon. Keep an eye on Gladys. She's only standing because the plasmoquin's holding the fever at bay.'

As Wilf turned out of the Mission station, he passed the first of the utility trucks, with Laurie Linggood in the driver's seat.

They flagged each other with a salute, and he kept driving. Visibility was poor and quickly became poorer. The grey ash was falling in clumps rather than flakes now. These clung to the car's windscreen, leaving thick smears when Wilf turned on the windscreen wipers. There was a thud and a crash, and a small stone hit the glass and bounced off without cracking it.

Although he had driven the road between Kabakada and Malakuna many times, Wilf briefly became disoriented as more of the dark slag fell from the sky. It was no longer drifting ash, but denser pumice that clung to everything it landed on. Trees bent under its weight and familiar landmarks were engulfed in smoky grey. Visibility continued to lessen so he flicked on the lights, slowing to a crawl. The other utility passed him at one point, Hazel's husband Albert in the driver's seat. They were making such slow progress, Wilf could see the worried faces of all the women seated in the lorry tray, their best outfits pitted with grey smears.

The car began chugging as debris formed piles on the surface of the road. More stones hit the windscreen, each larger than the previous one. Even inside the car Wilf could smell the biting stink of sulphur. It began to feel like driving through a hellscape.

With a bump the car stalled, run aground on a large pile of ash. Wilf had a moment of indecision as he considered his obligation to Frank Lewis and his fear for Gladys, her health ravaged by so many bouts of malaria. All the particles and sulphur in the air would be terrible for someone whose body was so compromised by illness. If he continued, he might become trapped at Malakuna, the roads unpassable, unable to get back to Gladys. The thought was intolerable. If he went back to Kabakada he could make arrangements to get Gladys further away from the volcano's fall out, then fetch Frank in one of the utilities, which stood a better chance of getting through.

His mind made up, Wilf started the car again, but his first attempt to turn it was unsuccessful. He climbed out, the acrid air searing his lungs. From the boot he pulled a long bandage, which he soaked with water from a jerry can. Long experience had taught all the staff to be prepared, especially on their visits to local villages, where medical supplies and other necessities might be required at a moment's notice. Wringing the bandage out, he wrapped it around his mouth and nose and pulled it into a tight knot. Then he moved boxes and tools around in the boot until he found a shovel.

It took several minutes to relocate the pumice dust that had clumped behind the car's wheels. Though Wilf was the business manager, he was handy with practical tasks, as were all the missionaries. Needs must when one lived in a tropical paradise that nevertheless had limited facilities. Soon the dust was in new piles at the side of the road and his shirt held only the memory of its usual pristine white. Gladys could not complain because he had ruined it to make his way to her!

Stowing the shovel, Wilf returned to the driver's seat. With determined movements he carefully turned the car on the narrow road. There was no other traffic so it didn't matter that it took far longer than usual to make the turn.

With the pumice cloud behind him, he made better progress, though it was difficult to shake off an ominous sensation of being followed. Every time he checked the rear mirror, he saw only a seething mass of black with writhing patches of lighter grey. His native friends would no doubt tell him Rakaia was truly angry now, the great spirit of the volcano letting his displeasure be known through a violent display that spread miles from his harbour home.

Wilf almost missed the turn off to the Mission house. In the increasingly grey terrain, landmarks were gone. Only the sight of a familiar lorry on the side of the road alerted him that he must be close. Several cars and trucks had reached the station by now, so the dust on the road was compressed and he found it easier going as he parked.

A surprising number of guests, mostly Mission folk, had managed to make it to Kabakada. They had all taken shelter on the veranda or inside the house as pumice dust and small rocks continued to rain down. The garden, which had been a glorious feast of colour a mere hour ago, was now bleak.

Laurie, Howard, Jack and Albert Jones were clustered near the steps as Wilf approached. They looked askance at him.

'I couldn't get through,' he began without preliminaries. 'There's pumice piling up on the road.'

Laurie's face fell. 'Essie's on her own at home, apart from Bill and the houseboys of course.'

'The wind's a North-Wester,' Wilf told him, 'so Raluana should be completely clear.' Raluana was south-east of Vulcan. It was probably blue skies and sunlight for Essie, who at nearly nine months pregnant had elected to rest rather than attend the wedding. Laurie didn't look reassured.

'Laurie, can you go and see if Mel and Hazel are ready to leave yet?' Jack asked him. 'I'll fill Wilf in on our change of plans.' Laurie nodded and hurried inside. Jack waited until Laurie was out of earshot.

'He's so stressed about Essie and his little boy, he's been getting everyone worked up. We've been trying to distract him by making plans. We're going to abandon the wedding breakfast. Mel doesn't mind. She's had enough excitement to make up for it. Most brides would be devastated to have their special day disrupted by a volcano, but she's enjoying every minute of it. Says it will give her the practical knowledge she didn't get with her studies.'

The pride in his voice made the others grin.

'The cake and some of the food have already been packed,' Albert Jones said, gesturing to the tables, which looked sparser then earlier, 'so we thought we'd head to the Sisters' House at Vunairima and eat it there where it should be safer. Further from the centre.'

'Did you drop Frank off at Malakuna?' Wilf asked him. Albert nodded.

'We saw Vulcan start to blow just after you left the church. Frank wanted to pack up at HQ so I dropped him there on the way here. The roads weren't bad at that point.'

'They're getting worse now.' Wilf said. 'Even if we're not having the breakfast, I can still collect them and follow you all to Vunairima. I came to get one of the trucks though because the car won't make it. With all this ash Malakuna's probably a nightmare by now. Can you take Gladys to Vunairima and make sure she's looked after?'

Howard shook his head. 'Wilf, you're the backbone of this mission, but for once, how about you forget your duty and take your wife to safety? You're nearly as worried about Gladys as Laurie is about Essie. I suspect it's only a decade of keeping everything running that's stopping you getting into a spin.'

Albert, Jack and Howard all had the same concerned expressions.

'Tell you what,' Howard continued. 'I'm the only single bloke here. Jack gets a free pass because it's his wedding day. I'll take the car back and get the Malakuna mob. You lot head to Vunairima. Get all the girls to safety.'

Wilf was about to protest when he caught sight of Gladys standing in the doorway, watching them. She looked tired. He nodded.

The sky was growing ever darker and cinders were now scattered amongst the pumice and stones. The men leaped into action. Ten minutes later Howard left to battle the ash in the direction of the volcano and everyone else clambered into the remaining lorries and trucks, coughing from the heavy particles in the air. The rotten egg smell was almost unbearable.

Wilf helped Gladys into the front of one of the utes, next to Mel, who had changed out of her wedding dress, and Laurie, who insisted on driving. He took his place in the back next to Jack and the very top layer of the cake, which was draped in netting. Somehow it remained pristine white. The rest of it had been left behind with a large portion of the carefully prepared spread, all now covered in a layer of grey grit. A suitcase of going-away clothes was jammed into the foot well, leaving little room for the two men.

'Driving distracts me from worrying,' Laurie said as he slid into the driver's seat and shifted the truck into gear. The men had conferred and decided since the going would be slow, it probably wouldn't be a problem if he was a little distracted. But Laurie took off at speed, swiftly leaving behind the other utility, which receded into the distance.

Vincent To Papa, one of the native staff, was driving that one, with Albert and Hazel, Ron Wayne, an off again/on again mission employee, and guests Mr and Mrs Atherton with their baby. A convoy of cars followed. Not all the guests were heading to Vunairima. Some were making their way home, wherever that might be, so several cars peeled off in the direction of Malakuna. Others hadn't made it to the reception in the first place, taking the billowing clouds at the wedding as a sign that the day's plans were in disarray. By the time the convoy was on its way to Vunairima, Vincent's truck visible but not keeping pace behind Laurie's, there were only a few cars and trucks remaining. Before long they caught up with other vehicles fleeing the worst of the volcano fallout and Laurie was forced to slow to a more sedate speed.

By now, though it wasn't yet night, the air was dark, choked with thick black pumice. Within minutes a heavy rain started to fall. It was the relentless type of downpour so common in the wet season but made ominous by the pitch-coloured sky. Debris pounded on the car roof, making conversation almost impossible. The pumice dust swiftly turned to mud. Though the truck lights were on, they made no impact on the sheets of silt and rain. It was like driving through thick ink.

Laurie drover slower, then slower again, and finally with a gasp of exasperation he stopped and slipped out into the pelting downpour. Those inside the truck watched him examine the vehicle's lights, then break giant leaves off a nearby tree and use them to do something to the front of the vehicle. Soon the leaves were a sludgy mess and he dropped them at the side of the road. When he re-entered the vehicle, grey mud formed a cap on his head.

'They were coated in pumice,' he explained as he resumed his seat. 'No light coming through at all.'

Their halting, tedious trip continued, but the storm was rapidly increasing in intensity. Soon a reverberating crack broke the incessant pounding of the downpour, loud enough to batter their eardrums. Moments later a giant bolt of lightning broke through the swirling black clouds and soot, searing their eyes with light of such intensity everyone in the car blinked. They sat in silence in the aftershock. As the light faded, the illuminated fury of rain and pumice disappeared in the inky darkness. Laurie was just reaching for the handbrake when another huge cracking noise rent the air, followed by a prolonged tearing. A giant palm tree to the left of the road swayed as though in furious winds then, with a strange grace, fell in terrifying slow motion, landing a mere foot in front of the car.

Raluana Lane

2 – The Storm

Eileen

5:30pm, Saturday 29th May 1937. Vunairima.

As we walked along the road we could not but feel how miraculous it was that we should all have come along that road the night before, and not met with disaster. The road was literally strewn with palms and trees, and was inches thick with rocks that had fallen from the volcano.

Albert Jones, quoted in the Newcastle Morning Herald and Miners' Advocate, Monday 21 June, 1937

Standing behind half the congregation at the church entrance, Eileen, at a little over five feet, couldn't tell what was causing so many gasps and murmurs. Her determination had carried her a long way, from teacher's college in Hobart to her position as assistant head mistress at the girls' school in Vunairima, but now was not the time to employ her teacher's voice to force her way through the eddying crowd. She bit her lip with impatience but kept her manners.

Someone finally called out, 'Vulcan is erupting.'

The horn of the district car tooted, interrupting everyone's exclamations of shock, and for a moment the mood lightened as they all rushed to wave off the bride and groom, headed for Kabakada and the wedding breakfast. Once the car was out of sight people mingled and chatted as though it were an ordinary occasion. Eileen was finally able to make her way down the stairs. The socialising soon stopped as the extent of the eruption became apparent.

A vast, pristine white cloud was shooting straight up from the tip of Vulcan, reaching an enormous height, though its lower stem was a sickly yellow. It started to spread over the harbour, flattening at the top like a giant umbrella until it dominated the landscape. Debris rose from the volcano's conical peak with the smoke, giving the billowing shape darker tones. As the murkier clouds surged upward, they began to curve sideways, forming a canopy with streams of black raining from the underside.

Without warning a fine rain of grey ash began to fall and people ran for cover, either to their vehicles or back up the stairs to the church foyer. Eileen was in the latter group. As a handful of cars and trucks departed, she wondered if they were heading to Kabakada, or whether the feast would be cancelled given the growing gloom.

Reverend Albert Jones, Hazel's husband, strode up the steps towards Eileen. She knew Albert and his wife well, often stopping at their Kabakada house when she made the long trek from Vunairima to Rabaul on her bicycle.

With a glance at the darkening sky, Albert spoke, forgoing formalities because of their friendship. 'Were you coming in the ute to Kabakada?'

'I thought so, yes.'

'Do you mind riding in the back?'

'Of course. Miss March needed a lift too.'

'We'll round up some of the ladies who need a ride, shall we?'

By the time everyone was collected, the ute was well-laden with bags and wedding guests, but no one looked festive. Their fine outfits were smeared with grit, and those who wore hats were continually removing them to shake off fine grey dust built up on flowers and feathers. Nevertheless, they grinned at each other in the truck bed because, despite an edge of unease, this was an adventure of sorts.

For a few minutes the truck didn't move, then Albert came to talk to them again. 'Sorry for the delay, ladies. Reverend Lewis wants to stop at Malakuna. He's worried about the Mission papers and books with all this ash. Wilf Pearce will pick him up from there later. The feast may be a wash out too, so I'm wondering if anyone else wants to be dropped at Malakuna? It might be difficult to get home from Kabakada later.'

Miss March, seated next to Eileen, leaned forward. 'If the stop at Malakuna is only a brief one I do have some school paperwork at headquarters that should be put away. But after that I'll catch a lift to Vunairima. The girls might be worried about Rakaia's anger.'

She glanced up at the sky. The ash fall had become heavier even during this brief delay. 'Miss Brabin, can I rely on you to look after the girls if you get to Vunairima before me? Miss Mills will be able to help you, and Ia Lo.'

'Of course,' Eileen agreed.

'Good. Good. The joys of being a headmistress. Torn by responsibilities! Lovely solo, Miss Byron.' The young lady she was addressing blushed. Miss March had that effect on people.

Eileen smoothed the skirt of her new crepe de chine dress, which had wrinkled a little in the cloying afternoon heat. She had bought it by mail order from Sydney, which was always a risk for sizing, but it fitted well. Focused on her dress, she jumped with shock when Albert Jones banged the side of the ute lightly.

'Well, I think we're all organised. Off we go.'

Though the drive to Malakuna was only short, it took twice the usual time because a line of cars snaked all the way from the Rabaul sportsground to Tunnel Hill Road, everyone apparently having decided escape was a good idea as Vulcan raged. Those seated in the truck tray didn't mind as it gave them plenty of time to watch the extraordinary activity of the volcano. In its swirling depths were occasional flashes of flame. Lower down, the stream of smoke was mostly jet black, fading in an ombre effect to brilliant white at the top, and its long arm continued to extend, twisting across the bay towards them. Even from this distance it was possible to see the objects falling from its underside were becoming larger.

Without warning the ashfall took on a new intensity. Sitting on the open truck tray, Eileen could do nothing but shade her eyes as it landed on her shoulders and knees. Her beautiful new dress was so pockmarked with grey that its original colour, a sunny light blue, was a mere memory.

After the stop at Malakuna they took the Tunnel Hill Road pass through the mountain. Traffic was still heavy with refugees from Rabaul so they moved at a turtle's pace. Facing backwards in the truck, Eileen had a marvellous view of the swirling, ever-darkening clouds that seemed to pursue them as they fled over the hill. The wharf was visible, but barely, whilst the volcanoes around the harbour were hidden in the massing smog.

Once they reached the other side of Tunnel Hill the going was easier. The truck picked up pace along the winding road that usually offered views of Talili Bay on the right, and a parade of villages and plantations, forests, and a backdrop of tall mountains, on the left. But not today. Black smoke pursued them all the way to Kabakada, engulfing all. When they finally reached their destination, Mr Pearce passed them driving the mission car the other way. Eileen wondered whether the road back would still be passable.

The Kabakada Mission House wasn't on stilts, like many of the larger buildings around New Britain. It clung low to the ground, nestled behind trees so only the conservatory, with its many-paned windows, was visible on the far right. A veranda ran across the front and left of the house, allowing plenty of space for a celebration.

Eileen was relieved to climb down from the truck at last. She did her best to brush the ash from her hat, but the dreadful, sticky stuff clung and even seemed to have eaten the straw in places, so she wasn't able to achieve much. She tossed it into the ute, thinking to fetch it later. Shaking out her auburn curls, she made her way to the veranda, looking forward to fine food and conversation. But the heavy grey ash seemed to have clogged everyone's spirits along with their clothes.

'Miss Brabin,' Gladys Pearce approached Eileen, taking her by the elbow. 'I'm so glad you're here. You're a practical kind of a girl. Could you give me a hand packing up some of the food? I don't have enough covers. It will be inedible if we don't do something.'

Eileen followed Mrs Pearce out to the veranda. A moment later two houseboys arrived with a motley assortment of tins, glass containers and tea towels. Gladys began placing tea towels over the sandwiches and scones and passed Eileen a green enamelled tin.

'Start with those.' She nodded towards some delightful petit fours with little iced flowers on top. Eileen began transferring them to the container. Beside her, Mrs Pearce slumped heavily on the table, dropping a tea towel. Eileen knelt to pick it up, noting Mrs Pearce's pallor as she handed it back.

'Are you alright?'

Mrs Pearce nodded, a rather insistent nod that didn't match her drooped posture and shallow breathing.

'I'm fine. It's just the malaria. You know, they say you become more resistant to it the longer you live here, but it's been seven years now and those mosquitoes still love me just as much. You haven't been in Rabaul long, have you?'

'I arrived last August.'

'And have you had the fever yet?'

Eileen shook her head.

'Well, you've been unbelievably lucky. But you know, I don't think we can consider you a real New Britain resident until you've had a bout.' Her smile took the sting from her words. She passed a stack of tea towels to Eileen.

'You know what? I think I need a little rest. Can you finish here?'

'Of course.'

Mrs Pearce looked over at the cake, a delightful three-tiered tower laden with trails of ferns and frangipani. 'Make sure you cover that. It was so much work and it would be a shame if the ash got to it.' She reached out and touched Eileen's cheek, a surprising gesture since she was one of the elder, established mission members whom Eileen felt saw her as a young upstart.

'I hear you're doing good things at the school. We need some youthful energy around here.'

Her hand dropped to her side and she made her way slowly inside, scratching one arm as she went.

Eileen was puzzled. Gladys could only be in her thirties.

Others Eileen's age might consider that old, but she had always preferred the company of older people. They were far less frivolous. It was when they tended towards stodginess that she found them dreary, but many of the missionaries had a lightness of spirit that she found engaging.

Reverend Howard Pearson was one of these. He lingered over the food, a look of longing on his face. Eileen had to bat his hand away from a plate a few times as she continued packing away cakes and slices of fresh pineapple. Soon the containers ran out, but when she checked with the houseboys, they said they couldn't find any more. She almost laughed out loud at Reverend Pearson's evident despondency as anything still uncovered slowly disappeared under the perpetual ash fall.

Her task finished, Eileen thought she might clean up a little. As she stepped into the house, Jack Trevitt began tinging a spoon against a glass.

'Ladies and gentlemen, Mel and I are deeply grateful you're all here to share this special day with us. Unfortunately, Vulcan wanted to come to the party as well and we're finding him a bit of a party pooper. A few of us have conferred and we think it's best to head out to Vunairima – hopefully outrun this blasted ash. For those of you worried about your homes, please don't feel you have to stay. If you live in Rabaul you may wish to come with us. I'm sure between the schools and our home and the Sisters' House we'll be able to accommodate anyone who needs a place. And if you join us, we'll still have some of the lovely wedding breakfast to enjoy. Maybe even cake!'

There was a smattering of applause, and everyone broke into conversation to decide who would go where. Albert Jones was to remain in Kabakada, since it was his home, but Hazel decided to travel on with Mel Trevitt to fulfil her matron of honour duties. Some from Rabaul and Malakuna, including the Pearces, decided to make the onward journey to Vunairima and nearby Vunakabi because of the danger closer to town. Eileen wished Jack might have talked to her before offering up her home for refugees, but she knew it was her Christian duty. And given circumstances here, Rabaul was probably in a dreadful state.

'Miss Brabin,' Dan Oakes, a missionary from the outlying circuits, approached, his English accent crisp. 'You're to come with me and Reverend Lige. Can you find Miss Byron? I promised Miss Chaseling... Mrs Trevitt, that I'd look after her.'

Miss Margaret Byron was a friend of Mel Chaseling – Mel Trevitt now – and had come from Australia with her friend to sing at the wedding. Eileen imagined she was getting far more excitement than she expected from her trip.

Dan Oakes gestured towards the car, and Eileen was relieved to see Osea Lige was driving, since he was the native head teacher at George Brown College, and knew the roads well. In these terrible conditions, his ever-calm demeanour instilled a sense of peace as they began the long drive. The car crawled along the winding coast road of the Gazelle Peninsula to Vunairima in darkness and with ash and rocks falling all around. Miss Byron sat beside Eileen on this leg, as she had on the last one.

Eileen was glad Osea Lige had been at the wedding. She hated the enforced separatism that forbade the natives from entering European spaces. They were even forbidden to sit on benches in the botanical gardens. From her earliest arrival Eileen had found the locals to be friendly, relaxed and full of humour. She had quickly developed an easy rapport with the girls she taught, and friendships with the native staff of the school. Jack Trevitt, as headmaster of George Brown College, had clearly developed the same friendship with Osea Lige, so Eileen thought it would have been terribly wrong if his friend could not attend his marriage.

When rain began to teem, Eileen was glad not to be seated in the tray of a truck. They passed an exodus of people from town, streams of native folk travelling along the side of the road. Their stricken faces and postures suggested the situation in Rabaul was far worse than they had at first thought. Eileen wished they had room to offer them a lift – particularly the small children. More than just smoke and ash filled the air now; a strange sort of grey mud came down in sheets. The sky had darkened to the navy of night, though it was still not even 6 pm, and conditions continued to worsen.

Reverend Lige softly hummed a hymn, punctuating the song with toots of the horn so those walking would know the car was there in the blackness. Soon Eileen was no longer able to hear him as a storm began in earnest, pelting on the roof, with regular bursts of thunder like explosions. Every time a huge fork of lightning streaked down, they could see enough of the road to make out both mission utes up ahead, but Laurie Linggood seemed to have a devil chasing him, because with each new flash of light he was further ahead, with more cars between them. Once Eileen even saw the ute driving along a ditch to pass a large truck.

A particularly loud crack of thunder was followed by a bolt of lightning so swiftly the thunderstorm had to be virtually overhead. The car stopped abruptly, inches behind another vehicle that had been all but invisible in the blackness. Eileen offered a grateful prayer that Reverend Oakes had not been driving or matters might have been different.

The vehicles ahead of them had stopped moving.

'I'll go and see what's happening,' Dan Oakes offered. He was gone a long time. Eileen was pleased that the others seemed to feel no need to make conversation during their wait. Miss Byron had chattered anxiously earlier about the excitement of her trip to New Britain and her nerves about singing at the wedding, but the strange events of the day had finally silenced her. It would have been a struggle in any case to be heard over the heavy rain beating on the roof, and the distant crashes that might be falling trees or thunder or some other disaster – it was hard to tell with so much going on.

Osea Lige left the car briefly to scrape ash away from the lights, ready for when they could continue. Eventually Reverend Oakes returned. His clothes were soaked and covered in a grey mud that looked far heavier than the ash of earlier.

'There was a palm tree over the road,' he said, shaking his head a little as he did so and spraying muddy water around the car. 'It's so dark out, we had to walk along with our hands on the bally thing to see how large it was. Reverend Linggood and Mr Trevitt went to Kabaira and back to fetch axes and we've managed to clear it. We'll be moving again in a minute.'

It could hardly be called moving by the time they began edging their way forward again. Progress was so slow Miss Byron laughed and said, 'I think the trees will get there before we do.'

About a mile further on another opportune flash of lightning gave Reverend Lige enough warning to stop the car when the convoy ground to a halt. Jumpy as a cat, Reverend Oakes hurried off again. This time he returned more quickly.

'Another tree down. There's no moving this one,' he said, once again shaking mud over the car's interior. 'It's too huge. We're going to have to walk.'

Osea Lige took Eileen's hands in his.

'I'm going to stop at some of the villages on the way, so I will farewell you now. My people will be fearful with Rakaia causing so much trouble. I will see you at Vunairima. God be with you as you go, Miss Brabin.'

With a gentle smile he set off, disappearing quickly in the enshrouding darkness.

Under normal circumstances Eileen relished walking, but this was a nightmare trek. All around them coconut palms and mango trees creaked ominously, bowed by the pumice mud that never ceased to fall. More than once the party stopped at the terrible sound, waiting to see whether a tree might come crashing down. Frequently, smaller trees, palm fronds or branches gave up under the weight of piles of ash, and fell to the ground, making the path a terrible obstacle course, made worse by the pitch black. The thick, muddy rain never let up, yet it did little to wash away the pumice that settled on everyone's hair and clothes as they stumbled along. Eileen felt it running over her face and neck. She wished she had not left her hat in the ute.

As if there wasn't enough of concern, unbearably loud roars of thunder startled everyone regularly, followed by lightning that seared the eyes. Several times the lightning hit a tree nearby, causing hellish flames to dance briefly. Cinders began falling all around, which added to the apocalyptic mood. This was no ordinary thunderstorm. Eileen overheard Mel explaining that the electrical storm was a result of all the debris being flung out of the volcano, which was changing this beautiful Eden into something inspired by Dante.

When fireballs began dancing through the coconut trees, Miss Byron, who was walking beside Eileen, spoke plaintively.

'Do you think one of those trees will fall on us? Mel told me I would be having a holiday in paradise. Some paradise! Fire and lightning and volcanoes. I would never have taken time away from my teaching if I'd thought I might die.'

'You're a teacher?'

'Yes.'

Eileen thought of her students, probably huddled together at Vunairima. Jean and Herbert Shelton had arrived from the outlying islands this morning, but had decided not to come to the wedding, since Jean had given birth two days before and was feeling very ragged. She hoped Mr Shelton was helping Miss Mills in looking after her girls, who would need a lot of reassurance during such terrible events.

'Me too. We're on our way to my school now. I'm sure we'll be there soon and we can have a nice hot tea and get comfortable.'

Miss Byron wiped a hand on her dress and offered it. 'I'm Margaret.'

'Eileen.' She didn't want to take the proffered hand, slimy with mud, but she did so, her touch light. Seeing her reluctance, Margaret took her hand back and wiped it again, then examined her outfit.

'My dress is ruined! I bought it specially for today.'

Eileen shrugged. 'I think that's the least of our worries, don't you?'

Before her companion could respond, a horn sounded behind them, and they were caught in the lights of a large copra lorry. A young native man jumped down from it. Eileen recognised him as one of the workers from the plantation near George Brown College, which was not far from the Girls School.

'Quick, sisita, climb in the truck. We will take you to the college.'

Miss Byron looked doubtful. 'Is it safe?'

It was unclear whether she was referring to the men in charge of the truck, or the huge, high-sided lorry. Eileen chose to assume the latter.

'They drive these trucks all the time. They're usually weighed down with heavy bags of copra, so I'm sure a few of us won't be a problem, even with all this extra weight.' She gestured at the coating of pumice mud on her dress, which was starting to harden where the endless rain couldn't reach.

Reassured, Miss Byron allowed herself to be lifted into the lorry with Eileen. Others quickly joined them. Somehow, as though by magic, the native driver found his way around fallen palms the missionaries could never have negotiated. Now and then, when the way became too difficult with the weight of the people in the back, the natives heaved the women out until they found a way to proceed, then hauled them back over the high sides of the truck as though they were bags of copra. Eileen found them wonderfully kind and gentle and mused that given the circumstances she was far happier to be lifted like a bag of copra than walk through the raging storm, which never lessened at all.

Finally, the truck stopped, and one of their native companions spoke to them with an apologetic smile. 'There's no way forward, sisita. But not far now – you can walk?'

And down they were lifted for a final time, to resume their trek through the impenetrable darkness.

It should have been terrifying, yet Eileen felt an extraordinary calmness as she strode along. Though danger was close, she felt a strange sense of calm. Looking around at the people who were beside her, she could see no sign of fear or distress. Their faces were serene, reflecting her own deep feeling of peace and happiness. Despite the thunder and lightning, the falling trees and the endless, heavy downpour of ashy mud, she had the strangest sensation they were being looked after. She felt no fear.

The storm didn't let up for the entire journey. Everyone looked a complete mess by the time they finally reached the Girls' School at Vunairima. Although some of the party lived in the Mission buildings here, by unspoken agreement they remained together initially, crowding onto the veranda and into the living room of the Methodist Sisters' House. Eileen was one of the last to enter, since she had now taken on the role of hostess and let her guests go ahead of her. She had a good view of the crowd from the doorway. The muck that plastered them all was swiftly setting like concrete on drooping hats or hair without the constant rain to wash it away, creating the impression everyone wore old-fashioned cloche hats. Necks and arms, dresses and shirts were the same uniform colour.

'Oh Eileen!' Hazel Jones said, her voice filled with mirth, 'you look like a statue!'

All eyes turned to Eileen, and laughter erupted. With horror she realised her brand-new crepe de chine dress had shrunk with the pumice and was now indecently tight and short. The original colour was indistinguishable.

'I thought we needed a new garden gnome,' she joked. Given her height, it seemed an appropriate comment. Then, wishing to turn the attention away from her greatly reduced modesty, she nodded towards Jack Trevitt, whose hair looked like a helmet.

'At least we can still tell who the bridegroom is.'

All eyes turned to Jack.

'Oh goodness Jack, you still have your buttonhole!' Mel Trevitt laughed. The poor frangipani was wilted and grey, but in place.

Eileen's ruse worked as everyone began examining each other and commenting on their strange new appearance. All except one. Jean Shelton, who had not been outdoors in the storm and so was dry and clean, didn't join in the banter at all. She lay on the cane chaise lounge, feet up, and waved Eileen over to her.

'Miss Brabin, will you fetch me a cup of tea? I've only just got the baby to sleep and I'm utterly worn out.'

Exhausted, damp and indecently dressed, Eileen's ability to embrace proper Mission decorum was pushed to its limits. With three younger sisters and a reputation as a fiery redhead she was used to speaking her mind, much to her father's ire, but she had learned to accept the pleasantries and expectations that kept the Methodist Mission of New Britain running smoothly. Sometimes it was not easy but as one of the younger staff, and not a minister, she knew her input would not be well received. But she was desperate to change, and unhappy at being given a command in her own home.

'I don't think…,' she began. Hazel's hands on Eileen's shoulders stopped her mid-sentence.

'Oh, Mrs Shelton, I'm sure we can rustle up a cup of tea, but poor Eileen here needs to de-pumice. Just give us a moment.'

She steered Eileen away before any more words could be

spoken. As they strode towards the bathroom Alice Mills met them. One of the nurses from the Stewart Hospital, she had been attending to an ill native girl all day. Alice had clearly seen the exchange.

'Don't worry, Eileen, I'll organise the girls to make tea. They've been sheltering in the school hall with Herbert and Jean Shelton and they're quite composed. Happy even, now that you're returned safe and sound. They told me they couldn't possibly sleep because of all the noise and downpour so I think they'll be glad to have something to do.'

Eileen was glad Alice was so level-headed. 'Miss March didn't come with us,' she said. 'It's likely she'll be stuck in Rabaul. The roads are dreadful out there. So, I suppose we're in charge. It might be an idea to put on some soup as well? I won't be long. As Hazel says, I need de-pumicing.'

Alice hurried off to undertake her hostess duties while Eileen and Hazel went to Eileen's room to fetch clean clothes.

'De-pumicing... is that a real word?'

Hazel giggled. 'I just made it up. I could see you were about to blow. Clearly Mrs Shelton hasn't encountered too many redheads before!'

Normally the cold bush shower was thoroughly enjoyable in the tropical heat, but tonight it was unpleasant. However, much scrubbing did the trick and Eileen eventually re-emerged to find all the guests being taken care of. It was a strange sort of breakfast, at nine o'clock at night. People had put out the food rescued from Kabakada and the native girls were busy serving soup. Most people were still there, although Gladys Pearce, who would normally consider it her duty to act as hostess at this sort of gathering, had disappeared, as had her husband Wilf. The mood had brightened considerably now everyone was safely indoors, though the pounding rain and cracks of thunder continued outside.

'Quinine?' Howard Pearson appeared at Eileen's elbow, holding a bottle of the tablets.

'Surely the mosquitoes won't be out in this weather?' she asked, but took the pill anyway.

A couple of the girls from the school came up to her with Ia Lo, the native teacher whose practical, friendly nature had quickly endeared her to Eileen when she first arrived in Rabaul. Ia Lo nodded to one of the girls.

'Sisita Eileen,' the student began, shuffling her feet, though whether from anxiety or excitement it was hard to tell. 'We feel sad for Masta Trevitt that Rakaia made his marriage a big mess. We would like to sing for him and Marama Trevitt.'

Eileen smiled. 'I think that would be wonderful.'

The girls raced off with Ia Lo to organise their impromptu choir. A ferocious storm was not going to dampen their love of singing. A few minutes later they were clustered on the veranda, with the guests watching from doorways and windows as they began.

> Winter reigneth o'er the land
> Freezing with its icy breath;
> Death and bare the tall trees stand:
> All is cheer and drear as death.

'Oh Lord,' Hazel whispered into Eileen's ear. 'Whoever chose the song?'

'They've never experienced winter here. It's either hot and dry, or hot and wet. Maybe they thought this is what winter is like.'

'You could be right. It does look rather like snow out there with everything covered in ash. I'm surprised they even know this hymn though.'

'They're constantly learning something new from the school hymnal. Ssh, I want to listen. They always do such beautiful harmonies.'

The girls had reached the final verse.

So, Lord, after slumber blest
Comes a bright awakening
And our flesh in hope shall rest
Of a never-fading spring.

'Well, I hope there's a bright awakening tomorrow,' Hazel said over the applause, 'but I think we'll be seeing the effects of this eruption for a long time.'

'We've come out of it safely,' Eileen said, 'but I do worry about the local villages close to the volcano. What if people were caught by the ash fall and the storm? I hope Miss March is safe. And what about the Lewises and the Pearces and everyone who lives in Rabaul? How long will it be before they can go home?'

They both looked out into the darkness. There was a tremendous thunder crack, and the dazzling jagged light that followed lit up a shattered landscape. Hazel's eyes darkened.

'The question might be, do they even have a home to go to?'

3 - Warataba: The Thank Offering

Wilf

Tuesday 20th September 1927. MATUPIT.

Each year each group of native churches had a harvest thanksgiving service. For that service, the people from a neighbouring group of churches gathered together in a central church, on a weekday as they liked to make it a fun occasion with native dancing after the church service and some fun also during the service as the presented their gifts to the church.

Eileen Brabin, Memoirs

Wilf drove at speed along the causeway to Matupit, knowing if he went too slowly the car could become bogged. After all, the road had been underwater less than an hour ago and would be again when low tide passed. The first time he had come to this church, shortly after his arrival in Rabaul, over a year ago now, he had thought caution was the best approach despite others' warnings. That had ended with the villagers of Matupit gently chiding him as they worked together to free the Dodge from the dark, sodden soil. Now he knew to go against common sense and keep the vehicle moving. Caution did not always yield the greatest rewards.

Tavurvur, the hornet's nest, as the natives called the volcano Matupit perched on, was smoking today, across the bay from this tiny, but heavily inhabited island. With four volcanoes in close vicinity to Rabaul, steam and sulphur were not unusual.

'Do you think it might ever erupt?' Mrs Platten asked from the back seat. Though her husband, Reverend Gil, had been in Rabaul for three years, she was a recent arrival, and was taking everything in with wide eyes. Gil twisted to face her.

'I believe the last time one of these volcanoes blew was in 1878, so there's a long time between events. I think we're safe for today, my dear.'

'That eruption was when Vulcan first appeared,' Wilf chimed in. 'Before that, that part of the harbour was only coral reef. I've heard the pumice settled on the water so thickly no boat could pass. That was during Reverend Brown's time.'

'Ah, the Methodist Mission's founding father,' Gil said.

'The Tolai still talk about how turtles were cooked in their shells during that event, even though it was so long ago,' Wilf concluded. He met Mrs Platten's eyes in the rear-view mirror, his own twinkling with gentle humour. 'I believe the greater risk today will be one of us exploding from too much food. Probably me. I've been attending Thank Offering services for a week now. One more celebration dinner and I'm likely to balloon up like a turtle myself. But we can't turn down the villagers' hospitality. They take great pride in the annual Warataba. It makes them feel they are really helping the Lotu. And they are. Their contributions are vital to keeping our work going.'

'The Lotu?' Mrs Platten asked.

'The work of the church – it's what the Tolai call it. Here we are!' Wilf fell silent as he concentrated on parking.

'I imagine it came as a surprise to you when you took a job as accountant that your duties included day after day of feasting?' Gil joked.

Wilf murmured assent. 'I suppose I've learned to cope,' he said as he hurried to open the rear door for Mrs Platten.

'Where have you been this last week?' she asked him as they strolled together towards the church.

'Let me see... Nodup was first, then Namali, Ratug... that was an adventure, climbing the mountain, Tavana... and of course Matupit today.'

The native pastor-teacher for the village, Akulia, greeted them in front of the church, arms wide open. 'Welcome, welcome our dear Kuskus, Talatala and Marama. Yuorait?'

Of all the Methodist missionaries, Wilf was the only one the Tolai had given the honorific Kuskus, which meant father. Talatala, the name used for the others, meant teacher.

'We are well and looking forward to today,' Wilf responded to the customary greeting. Akulia clapped his hands together.

'Good, good. We have some big excitement planned for today. Perhaps you will rest at my house until we begin?'

'That would be lovely,' Mrs Platten smiled.

'Mr Cox will be joining us soon,' Wilf said. 'He's coming across on the launch from Malakuna.' Matupit could be reached by road, but taking a launch across the harbour was always an enjoyable mode of travel.

Akulia nodded. 'We look forward to the Talatala's teachings today. If you permit, I'll send one of the boys with the car to fetch him.'

'Reverend Gil will lead the Lotu today. Reverend Cox will only observe. Before I forget, there's a trunk in the boot of the car with some gifts from Australia for the villagers.'

'We'll bring that to the dancing ground.'

Wilf nodded his thanks.

At the teacher's house Akulia's wife, Seita, served them paw paw and refreshing moulie water in a coconut shell so they would have energy for the events ahead. Then it was time for the service. As they made their way to the church once more, they were surrounded by villagers. It seemed in the short time they had been inside everyone who lived on Matupit Island had gathered for the festivities of the annual Warataba.

The missionaries passed the building and made their way to the open land behind it, where a large shade had been erected for the day, the roof of coconut fronds woven together to create excellent protection against the sun. Hundreds of people awaited their arrival: far more than the church could have contained. The women sat on one side of the grounds, adorned with bright, colourful blouses and flowers gleaming bright as gems in their hair, white and yellow and red. The men sat on the other side, most wearing only lap laps tied with vivid sashes, their upper bodies gleaming with oil. Some had dyed their hair shocking yellow with peroxide, or blackened it with boot polish to look their best, and many wore a flower in the tight coils.

Reverend Platten began the special thanksgiving service, using Pidgin throughout. For smaller gatherings, the missionaries around Rabaul used the local Kuanua dialect, but for the annual Thank Offering attendees might have come from further afield, and the number of dialects in New Britain was enormous, so Pidgin was a more inclusive choice.

The first hymn was a raucous affair, with everyone joining in lustily. It seemed not everyone knew the words. Or the tune. But that did not stop their enthusiasm. There was some odd pronunciation of the English words of the song, including the inevitable 'Kong of kongs and lud of luds'. Wilf wondered if a pidgin hymn book might be helpful. His skills at pidgin were growing and it would be a useful contribution to the Mission's work.

Akulia took the lead during the bible reading and prayer. He had a resonant voice and a commanding presence, and had been a keen student during his training at George Brown College. His commitment to his villagers drew great respect from them.

Once the prayer was completed, Akulia gave a simple address about the blessings the Methodists had brought to the people of Matupit and the surrounding area. Then he turned to the missionaries. 'Would you join us inside for the Warataba?'

Reverend Gil looked out at the watching villagers. 'I'll happily do so, but we won't fit everyone in. We could do it out here.'

'I know, I know. But inside is better. Some will come with us. Others must prepare the balaguan and the dancing.'

Seeing Mrs Platten's lost expression, Akulia explained that 'balaguan' was the Kuanua word for 'feast'.

Wilf wondered what the villagers might have planned that required this change from the usual custom of holding the huge gathering outdoors. He sensed an even higher degree of anticipation than usual in the crowd. The Thank Offering was a highlight of the year, with a day-long celebration for each circuit. Although the circuits covered small areas, there were usually numerous tribes within them so the events were well attended and the feasting extravagant. But the sense of excitement here at Matupi was greater than he had seen in a week of attending various Warataba across the Gazelle Peninsula.

A table and chairs had been set up by the altar. Wilf and Reverend and Mrs Platten took their seats as, despite what

Akulia had said, it seemed the entire crowd tried to cram into the pews. The various Luluai, or headmen, of the nearby villages took the front row. On the table was a large enamel bowl, ready for the year's contributions. Akulia banged it on the table. A dull clang rang out. The watching villagers laughed. There was a definite undercurrent of amusement that told Wilf something was going on.

Akulia stood at the pulpit and reached his arms high. 'Let us give thanks through the fruits of our labours, so that the work of the Lotu can continue. People of Matupit, please bring forward your offering.'

Usually, the entire village would stand as their Luluai came forward with the contribution, but this time the only movement seemed to be from one of the men in the first pew. He had barely stood, however, when the doors opened.

'My deepest apologies for my tardiness,' Reverend Cox said as he entered, his voice ringing out. As he made his way up the aisle, congregation members on either side reached to clasp his hands in greeting, making his progress slow. Finally, he reached the table by the altar, where one of the nearby boys had already added a chair for him.

Cox reached across and shook hands with Gil Platten and Wilf, and nodded to Mrs Platten. Then he waved one hand. 'Please continue.'

Often during the offering a local choir would sing, but no one came forward now except the Luluai, shoulders bowed low, one hand clutched at his side. When he reached the table, he half turned so that he was addressing both the missionaries and the watching congregation.

'I am so sorry, we only have a little money to offer today.' He held his hand over the enamelled bowl and opened his grip. Four New Britain three pence pieces clattered into it. 'We do our best,' he continued, 'but all we bring is a few lik lik mark.'

Reverend Gil was about to respond when Wilf placed a hand on one of his, whispering. 'Give it a moment.'

The Luluai bowed his head. 'I know this is not sufficient for the great work of the Lotu,' and he gestured around the building, 'so I send a boy to Rabaul to buy a tin of Bulamakow. Perhaps if you take this meat and sell it you can get some more lik lik mark.'

As he said the last few words the door banged open and a boy of about fifteen came running in. He raced up the aisle and handed a tin of meat to the Luluai, who waved him away and placed the tin in the offering bowl.

Isabel Platten was looking confused, but Reverend Cox had the faintest grin. Under his breath, Wilf urged Gil to pick it up. The Reverend stood and held the tin high, to a round of applause and cheers. Before he could speak the boy came running up again, pulling something out of his pocket. It clattered into the bowl. Gil looked down, frozen for a moment.

'The Lotu will continue through your offering,' he finally managed. Once again, the congregation voiced their approval. He handed the can to Wilf.

'As always, it falls to our accountant to make note of Matupi's contribution.'

Had this been his first Thank Offering, Wilf might have been as confused as Mrs Platten clearly was, but the glint in the Luluai's eye, and the eager focus of the watchers made clear his next step. He reached for the tin opener the boy had belatedly added to the offering, holding it up high before using it to open the tin.

'What's this?' he said, to a round of laughter. His surprise was not entirely feigned, for once he removed the lid, the tin was full of money. He showed the others at the table with him, then held it up for all to see. A roar of approval went up.

Following procedure, Wilf tipped the coins out and swiftly counted them, checking as he did that there were no German ones. It had been five years since the law prohibiting them, but they still occasionally turned up, and even accepting them was illegal. Fortunately, there were none among the pennies, thrupence and sixpences from the tin.

Wilf placed the coins in a small bag and announced the offering total, but he had the sense everyone was waiting for more from him. He was truly intrigued about how they had got the money into the tin, so he was happy to oblige. First, he turned the tin around, looking closely at the label. It was no different to any other canned meat you could buy at the store in Chinatown. When he peered inside, however, there was a clue. The metal was pristine, the meat having been scraped out then the tin cleaned, but he saw a line of solder.

Wilf looked up and smiled. Sliding one finger under the edge of the label, he carefully eased it off, then held it up and received a round of cheers. Next, he made a show of peering inside the tin and then at the outside several times before running his finger over a rectangular ridge on the metal.

Gil was itching with impatience. 'How was it done?'

Wilf stood and held the tin up again, turning it for all to see. 'Your generosity is only matched by this very clever trick,' he said. The Luluai roared with laughter, the entire church joining in. When he sat again, Wilf passed the tin to Gil.

'See this? They've cut a rectangle off the side, then soldered it back on.'

Gil examined the workmanship. 'Neat work. I think this affirms JWB's idea that we should be opening our own technical school.'

There was still a restlessness amongst the watchers that suggested more to come. Whatever it was, Akulia was in on it, because he should have been calling the next village to bring their offering, but he was standing with his arms crossed. The silence stretched out, until finally Akulia spoke.

'Mesek, is there more to your offering?'

The Matupi Lulaui peered at the rear of the church. 'There is, Akulia. They said they would send it. I will look.'

'Maski,' Akulia replied, a phrase that often infuriated impatient Europeans, because it roughly translated to 'no matter how long it takes'.

Fortunately, the wait was brief. The boy who had brought the meat tin came running up again and put a pair of field glasses in Mesek's outstretched hand. Mesek made quite a show of raising these and peering through them at the rear of the hall. Then slowly he scanned upwards. Wilf and the other missionaries looked up to the ceiling, and the congregation spun around to look up as well. There was a curtain strung across the width of the roof, well above head height.

The errand boy had retreated to the rear of the church. Mesek gave a little cough, and the lad reached for a string that hung from the curtain. After a few swift tugs on the string the curtain danced open. There was something hanging from the building's centre beam.

Another smaller boy, who emerged from those crowded into at the back, raced forward and reached for yet another string. Mesek's messenger tried to stop him and cried out in annoyance when he failed and this boy pulled hard on the second string. At first nothing happened, and he tugged the string again. The two boys began a heated discussion about how the string should be handled, which ended with the first messenger pushing the younger one aside and gently manipulating the string. There was movement in the rafters, and something shot down the centre of the church.

A massive roar broke from the crowd. Some reached up as though to catch the flying object but it moved too swiftly. Once it was close, all could see it was an excellent model of a plane. With amazing precision, it glided to a stop just near the table.

With some ceremony, Mesek bent down and picked it up, then placed it carefully in front of Wilf. His eyes sparkled with mirth.

There were several little bags wedged into place along the plane's length and when Wilf pulled the first one out, he discovered it was full of cash, much to everyone's delight. A group of congregants stood and broke into song, allowing Wilf time to empty all the bags and total their contents. There was a substantial sum. When the joyful song was concluded, he stood.

'Many thanks to the people of Matupit for your most generous contribution, which will be of great help in the work of the mission stations. We will use it to buy medicines and to create new buildings to further the work of the Lotu.'

Wilf caught the eye of the messenger boy, who was dancing back and forth on his feet behind the last row of pews. 'Thanks also for the amusement you have given us this morning.' He saw an expression of pride on the boy's face and wondered whether the plane or the tin had been his idea.

The rest of the offerings followed a more usual pattern. One after the other each contributing village stood to sing while their Luluai brought forward the year's offering. There was no more acting or tricks. Wilf counted furiously during each hymn or traditional song. Although there were a lot of small denomination coins, he always succeeding at writing the finally tally in his ledger before the music ended. Gil and Reverend Cox took turns offering thanks for the contributions. Finally, there was no other village to be called. Wilf passed his ledger to Reverend Cox, the most senior missionary present. Cox announced the total offering of each village as well as the figure from the previous year to show the increase that had occurred. After he provided the sum total of this years' contributions, he gave the Benediction and the building quickly emptied. Everyone had much to do to prepare for the afternoon's proceedings.

Akulia ushered the missionaries to his house, which was constructed in native style with palm frond roofing. It was cool and pleasant inside. His wife Seita served them dinner of roast chicken, potatoes and kau kau, the starchy, sweet potato vegetable Wilf had come to love. It was remarkably filling. The chicken was cooked to perfection, with a slight sweetness to the skin that Wilf knew came from rubbing it with pineapple.

They spoke about church business as they ate. Akulia's responsibilities were many, from caring for the villagers' spiritual life through prayer meetings and bible class, to ensuring their physical wellbeing through visiting the aged and sick, as well as teaching them some new practical skills he had learned at George Brown College. In the way he spoke, the missionaries could see he cared deeply for his village and took his responsibilities seriously.

As soon as they had finished their meal there was a disturbance outside the house.

'Now there will be fun,' Akulia said, leading them out to the large open area behind the church where they had begun their morning. The centre of the open space was empty, with villagers arrayed around its perimeter. The missionaries resumed their seat under the shade structure, its wooden poles straight and perfectly aligned. Barely had they sat down when a parade snaked toward them, men carrying long poles from which hung various roasted meats, women bearing banana leaves laden with cooked kau kau and other vegetables covered in a green substance that Wilf knew from experience tasted of coconut. Tiny children carried coconuts or pineapples.

The food was laid down in a long line, starting in front of the missionaries and circling away for quite a distance. Pyramids of bananas were dotted amongst servings of smoked ham and other meats, piles of coconuts, and even sponge cake, no doubt purchased in Chinatown and a favourite of the natives, though slightly stodgy to Australian tastes.

Once the balaguan had been placed in careful order, with much organising and rearranging, the musicians took their spot at the centre of the performance space. They carried a wide range of instruments, including gourds, bamboo tubes, rattles of strung nuts, conch shells and even tin cans. A drummer began the performance with several slow beats on an instrument made of a large hollow log with a lizard skin cover. Others joined in, bamboo flutes capturing the sigh of the wind, which some called the spirit of the bush. There was much use made of coconut shells and it soon became apparent this was to be Matupit's special dance, the kulau dance, which tells the story of the young coconuts.

Dancers made their way onto the field in long grass skirts, each carrying a carved object at least two feet long. Wilf knew these represented the sticks used to open coconuts. Even at this distance it was possible to see they involved extraordinary workmanship. Wilf spotted a curling crocodile, several fish of different designs and various birds among their elaborate ornamentation.

Next to him, Gil sighed. 'This,' he indicated the performers, 'is the sort of thing that makes me wonder if there isn't another way. We come in here and bring our schools and our churches, and expect the natives to learn our way of doing things. That is the easiest road for us, the direct one. But what if we took the winding path? What if we learned about their culture, their way of seeing life? Surely we might learn something from their joyfulness, their ability to relax and celebrate everything?'

Wilf glanced at Reverend Cox. 'There is much to be said for two-way communication,' he said softly. 'An exchange of cultures and understandings. It is so easy to do something a particular way because it's tradition. We're the new guard, you and me. Perhaps if we maintain a mind eager to learn we will see changes.'

'At least we teach them how to minister to their own flock, and give them other skills to improve their quality of life, such as basic medicine. But perhaps our best approach would be to make ourselves redundant by helping them achieve independent management of their lives.'

'Don't let the plantation managers hear you talk like that,' Wilf warned. 'They're on a good wicket with so much cheap labour and a life they couldn't afford in Australia, with servants and houses and views of the ocean. They don't want to hear anything about independence for the natives.'

As the first dance concluded he lowered his voice so only Gil could hear him in the sudden quiet. 'Of course, that's why they hate what we do. We're educating the Tolai and training leaders in the church, which makes them harder to exploit. I wouldn't have it any other way. There's some resistance in the mission, but as more young blood comes in, I hope we'll see a shift.'

The two men sat in companionable agreeance, watching as the first group of dancers left the grounds. Next came a choral performance. Akulia told them the idea behind each piece as it was sung, first a love story, then the traditional victory chant of the Matupi people, and finally a song about the spirits, or kaia, that inhabited this land. With each act the mood of the music changed, from melancholy to defiant to wistful, and different instruments came to the fore.

Then there was another dance, this time a comical telling of a fish hunt, with spears as props and many sudden changes of direction. More singing followed. This pattern of alternating performances was repeated for several hours. The missionaries were amazed at the ability of the musicians to capture the sounds of the natural world: a raging storm, the beating of canoe paddles, the familiar call of birds or frogs – and their ability to keep playing all afternoon. Each dance had its own story and costumes, sometimes incorporating elaborately feathered headdresses or adornments of seashells or coconuts. Often the head dresses were large, unwieldy, and imposing. Some villages had a dance masta who kept the dancers in time, others did not. Without being told, Wilf could tell that one gentle song, with its tide of rising and falling voices and a rattle used occasionally, captured rainfall at sunset.

Fresh fruit and kaluana, the water from green coconuts, were served constantly. As the afternoon wore on the missionaries chatted to the various Luluai, and to the eager young men who came to say hello. Many were keen to work at the Mission, which paid a decent wage and treated its employees with respect, unlike some of the privately owned plantations.

When the musicians took a break, and no choir appeared about to leap in with a performance, Reverend Cox, who had been in conversation with Akulia, stood up. Akulia made a few hand signals to a couple of the nearby native men, and they made their way over to a pile of palm fronds that had been sitting next to the table. Clearing away all the greenery, they revealed a small travel trunk.

Reverend Cox's voice carried across the dancing grounds. 'We are all honoured by the excellent contributions you have made today to continue the work of the Lotu in Matupi and we have had a wonderful time watching your dances and hearing your songs and music.'

Akulia translated his speech into Kuanua, then Wilf repeated it in Pidgin, to be sure all comers would understand. Services were usually only held in Pidgin, but this was a special occasion.

'We send reports to our own country of the generosity of the Tolai people, their hospitality and friendship,' Reverend Cox continued. 'Members of the Methodist Church in Australia, our Lotu at home, are excited to send gifts to help your church to grow.'

This seemed to be the cue for one of the waiting boys to open the trunk. Inside was a range of goods collected from Australian congregations, including bandages and other medical supplies, soap, and notebooks and pencils for the village school. Wilf had previously removed anything unsuitable. People at home had some odd ideas about what might be needed. Woollen scarves and gloves could be put to use in gardens by the resourceful Tolai, holding up running plants, but romance novels and magazines showing the latest women's fashions and expensive household goods were distributed amongst the missionary wives.

There were cheers and clapping as excitement swept through the villagers at the bounty in the trunk. When this died away, there was one final song, which signalled the time to give out the balaguan. Some of the dancers, still in their grass skirts, shell bandoliers across their chest, brought food arrayed on large dark emerald banana leaves to the missionaries and Akulia. Next, they served the Luluai, who promptly took their leaf platters and left the dancing ground. Once they were gone, the villagers began filing past the food, in order, Wilf could see, according to which village had contributed the most to the Warataba. For each village, the men came first, then the women and finally the children. The first arrivals took their serve from the food closest to the missionaries' table but as this was depleted the later arrivals took their serving from further down the line. Like their chiefs, each person took a portion and left the dancing ground.

'They're not eating here?' Mrs Platten asked before tentatively biting into a piece of meat. 'Oh, this is delicious!'

Akulia was the first to respond. 'They will eat in their home. If they eat here and drop food, someone may use it for to puri puri... to make bad medicine against them. There are so many tribes here today. It is safest to only eat with those you trust. We believe in Jesus, yes, but we still have our own beliefs too.'

Before Mrs Platten could voice any sort of response a scurry of movement began around them as a group of men moved to dismantle the structure under which they sat.

'It is time to pack up,' Akulia said. Wilf showed Isobel Platten how to wrap the banana leaf around the food so she could take it home with her. When he turned to fetch his own food, a young boy was standing there, perhaps ten years old. Wilf recognised him instantly as the younger lad from all the theatrics that morning with the tin. His skinny arms were behind his back but as soon as he had Wilf's attention, he brought out the plane from that morning.

'You leave this behind,' the boy said.

Wilf shook his head. 'I didn't leave it anywhere. It's not mine.'

'Yes, it bilongem you,' the boy insisted.

Wilf was about to argue that he didn't recall anyone giving him the plane when he remembered the morning's trickery was a typical native method of passing on a gift. He smiled.

'Did you make this?'

The boy hit his chest twice proudly. 'I make motor-car bilongem Jesus, yes.'

The first ever airstrip had only opened this year, not far from Matupit, and Wilf had been most amused when he learned 'motor-car bilongem Jesus' had quickly become the native term for the first airplanes they had ever seen. He thought it was a perfect name.

'You've done an excellent job. It's incredibly accurate. Are you interested in learning to do things with your hands, like building?'

The boy shook his head. 'I come work for you, drive big car bilongem you.'

'You like the car?' The boy nodded vigorously. 'What's your name?'

'Ainui.'

'Well, Ainui,' Wilf said, offering his hand, 'when you're tall enough to see out the windscreen, and have learned to drive, I'll take you up on that offer. If you can drive as well as you fly a plane, we'll be very lucky to have you.'

Ainui shook the proffered hand vigorously. He seemed to take Wilf's offer of a job in his stride as though it was the only logical answer. He pressed on. 'You have canoe, Kuskus?'

'No, why?'

'Water has come up. Boys left the car other side or it would get stuck. I find you a canoe.'

Ainui ran off to hunt out transport. Wilf explained to the others that the causeway was submerged. They finished their food while they were waiting, then made their way down to the harbour to survey the problem. Ainui met them there just after they arrived, shoulders slumped. Wilf had seen his acting skills this morning, but this time the sadness didn't seem feigned. As he reported his failed mission to find a way back to Rabaul, a few young men came up behind him.

'No canoes.' Like the sun appearing from behind a cloud, Ainui broke into a huge smile. 'I fix you another way across.' He waved one skinny arm at the young men waiting nearby. 'They carry you.'

Mrs Platten looked horrified, but Akulia made it clear there was no other choice, so after farewells were made, one boy picked up Mrs Platten, another pair took the Reverends, and Wilf found himself lifted between the shoulders of two men. At first the carriers were in good spirits. The water was only waist high, and the air warm, the late afternoon sun still wending its way down to the horizon. Ainui hopped along beside them, carrying the model plane and laughing loudly when the men pretended to stumble and almost drop Wilf and Reverend Gil. But the covered causeway was about a hundred and fifty yards long, and by the end the men were not having as much fun.

Safe on dry land on the right side of the causeway, Reverend Cox gave effusive thanks to their rescuers. After handing Wilf his plane, Ainui insisted on vigorously shaking the hands of everyone and extracting another promise about his future job.

'I suspect he'll hold you to that,' Mrs Platten said. Wilf watched the boy wading away until he was just a speck in the distance.

'I hope he will. He's a smart boy. I'm sure he'll be of great help to us.'

Raluana Lane

4 – Arrival in New Britain

Eileen

1:30am, Monday 31st August 1936. Off the coast of New Britain.

Let a girl's education be as serious as a boy's. You bring up your girls as if they were meant for sideboard ornaments, and then complain of their frivolity. Give them the same advantages that you gave their brothers. Teach them, also, that courage and truth are the pillars of their being. There is hardly a girls' school in this Christian Kingdom where the children's courage and sincerity would be thought of half so much importance as their way of coming in at a door. And give them, lastly, not only noble teachings, but noble teachers.

Dorothea Beale, in Australian Christian Commonwealth, 1939

Eileen could barely breathe for the excitement. This was it. She was finally here, and her new life was about to begin. After a year's post-graduate study at Sydney University, she had arrived at her posting in New Britain. For now, all she could see from the porthole was velvet blackness and a shimmering line of stars that must be the harbour lights. But it would be morning soon enough and Rabaul would be visible, with its volcanic mountains and deep harbour.

The voyage had been an adventure in itself: her first taste of the tropics' moist heat, so different to the biting Tasmanian winter she had just left behind. The MV Macdhui, a luxurious liner with all the entertainments one could wish for, from quoits to an onboard cinema, had called in at Cooktown, bustling Port Moresby and the tiny, beautiful island of Samarai, a voluptuous green paradise one could stroll across in twenty minutes. Port Moresby had been interesting, with its busy port and the first natives the missionaries had met, but it had felt industrial. Eileen had much preferred the jeep ride they had taken away from the port, into the jungle. The guides had pointed out birds and butterflies in an endless rainbow of bejewelled colours and she had loved the silence that descended amongst the looming, vivid emerald trees.

Their stop at the island of Kwato had been fascinating mainly because they had visited a mission station, which had given her a clearer picture of what lay ahead. Her least favourite part of the voyage had been a fellow traveller on the ship who had taken it upon himself to teach her patience in the saloon, leaving his wife to bathe their two children, read to them and put them to bed. She particularly disliked that he seemed to think he was doing good by avoiding his family duties in favour of teaching a young woman card games. Mrs Margetts had warned her some women received unwanted attention and even proposals on the ship, usually from unsuitable types, since there were far fewer women in New Britain than men. Things hadn't gone quite that far, but she had certainly received more attention than she was used to. She was not about to lose her head though. Eileen didn't have time for such foolishness.

Knowing how close they were to their final destination, it was impossible to sleep. All she could think of was how different her new life would be from the one she had left behind. Her training had included anthropology, to gain some understanding of the Tolai people and their culture, and Kuanua and Pidgin, so she could begin to speak their language. Eileen considered herself fortunate that her teacher had been Mrs. Margetts, the widow of a former missionary minister from New Britain, who spoke Kuanua like a native. Eileen had come top of her class, so she felt confident she would overcome any communication difficulties quickly. Given they had been told never to speak English to the native people this was going to be important.

Another part of their preparation had been basic medical knowledge and practice, but they had been told they were forbidden to do any medical work. Eileen's best guess was the training was so they could identify problems and make sure those needing help were taken to hospital quickly.

Eileen was not daunted by any of this, nor by the thought of her new responsibilities as assistant teacher at the Methodist Girls School. She enjoyed a challenge immensely and was impatient to begin. She was also eager to be reunited with her devoted Kelpie, Shelley, who had spent the voyage with the crew. At every stop on the way Eileen had taken Shelley onto land and given her plenty of attention, glad she was an intelligent dog who seemed to understand this arrangement was only temporary, making no fuss when they had to be separated again.

The Macdhui steamed on through the night. Since there was no possibility of seeing Rabaul until morning, Eileen took the practical course and dozed until 6am, when she woke to discover they had arrived. Now it would begin!

To her horror, after breakfast in the dining room she discovered they were to have a briefing from a doctor. He introduced himself, but she promptly forgot his name and concentrated on trying to quell her impatience as he droned on about the risks of malaria and tropical ulcers, which could be combatted by taking quinine and wearing stockings or long pants. He emphasised how important it was to be careful to avoid getting dengue fever or blackwater fever, the deadliest form of malaria. None of this was news to Eileen as it had all been covered during her time at George Brown College. After the interminable lecture they were each inspected by the same doctor, to ensure no one was bringing a disease such as measles, deadly for the native population who had not been exposed to European illnesses. Finally they were cleared to disembark.

Allowed to leave the dining room at last, Eileen caught her first sight of Simpson Harbour in the bright morning light. It was breathtaking. The wharf was at the northern tip of the harbour, so looking back she could see a vast circle of crystal water tinged the most extraordinary sapphire, broken at the opposite end by Blanche Bay, which they must have navigated in the dark. A pair of peaked rocks broke the surface of the harbour in the distance. Eileen knew from her training that these were the Beehives, one narrow and the other wider, making her think of Laurel and Hardy. Not far to their right a larger island erupted from the glistening bay, which she guessed was Vulcan, a sleeping volcano, now inhabited by natives. Moving to the opposite side of the ship, she could see a similar island, which she guessed was Matupit.

She surveyed Rabaul itself, clustered around the wharves, then spreading outward for some distance. Beyond the township the land rose gently at first, carpeted in the vivid, shifting greens of the jungle, then swiftly became hilly. To her right, and in the far distance, jagged mountains cut the sky. There was a calm stillness to the air, and a delicious smell, strangely reminiscent of toasted coconut. Eileen felt her stomach growl. She had barely eaten anything during their early breakfast because her excitement was too great. With all the formalities ahead, she might not get to eat for a while and regretted her decision.

At the gangway, one of the crew members waited with Shelley, who greeted her mistress with extreme excitement. Eileen made sure her hat was on straight, picked up her overnight bag with one hand, took the dog lead in the other, and strode down the gangplank to meet her new life.

After a brief ride in the launch, which was made more exciting than necessary through Shelley's wish to leap out and play with the strange, colourful fish that teemed in the perfectly clear water of the bay, she finally stepped onto the wharf of her new home. But before she could reach Rabaul proper there were the usual administrative delays to get through. Customs house, a short distance from the launch, was a strange mix of almost Tudor style external walls, and beautifully carved ornate decoration, with a sunburst over the entranceway, and wishbone-shaped fretwork crisscrossing in semi-circles to form the veranda rail. Eileen was ushered inside by a native man in a blue lap lap and crisp white shirt. He stopped at the entrance and went no further. Another man hurried up as she entered, dressed in white shirt and pants, with sweat stains visible under his arms. In a broad Australian accent he directed her to complete several forms that he handed her, then take them to a table at which another European-looking man was sitting.

Eileen did so and was trying to explain her new role, as a teacher with the Methodist Mission, to the officious Englishman examining her passport, when someone stepped up beside her.

'Miss Brabin?'

His voice was soft, but there was a certainty about it that Eileen instantly liked. His hair was receding at the temples and worn short, so his ears appeared somewhat prominent and both his mouth and eyes had a slight downward turn to them, giving his expression a hint of melancholy. Overall, he was the sort of person who would be described as unassuming. But then he smiled, a gentle smile, and offered his hand. When she took it, he clasped both her hands between his, to Eileen's surprise.

'Welcome to Rabaul. I'm Wilf Pearce, the business manager for the Mission. I hope you've had a pleasant voyage.'

'Most enjoyable, thank you. I'm sorry, I was told you were the accountant.'

'I've been upgraded,' Wilf chuckled. 'If you'll give me a moment, I'll get this sorted for you.'

With another warm smile, he released her hands and turned to the customs officer. His unassuming manner disappeared instantly, and after a brief exchange with the bureaucrat he led Eileen to a bench to wait. He then repeated the process for the other new staff who were arriving. Howard Pearson and Tom Simpson were taking up posts as ministers, and Jack Trevitt was to become the headmaster of the boys' school, George Brown College, which was the brother school to the one Eileen had been posted to. They had all trained together at George Brown College in Haberfield, Sydney, although Howard and Tom's training had been far longer than the one year of postgraduate study for Eileen and Jack. As Wilf Pearce brought each new arrival to Eileen's bench, they struck up a lively conversation about their first impressions.

Finally, they were all collected and Wilf bundled them into a waiting Dodge, with Eileen in the front and the men in the back.

'Don't we need to fetch our bags?' Howard asked.

'No, they'll be collected by Ainui in one of the trucks. He has a boy to help him. They'll drop them off where they're needed. Mr Simpson, you'll be staying with Reverend Lewis, the chairman, for a couple of weeks before your posting so you can acclimatise. Mr Pearson, you'll be working here in Rabaul so you'll be able to move in straight away. Miss Brabin and Mr Trevitt, you'll be taken to Vunairima tonight after a welcome service. But for now, Reverend Lewis would like to meet you all and talk about expectations and so on.'

He glanced at Eileen and winked. 'Don't let all the talk of volcanoes drive you away. The Mother and the Daughters get a little talkative occasionally, but there hasn't been a serious eruption since George Brown's time. There are some real benefits to living in a volcano crater. The soil here is excellent. My roses love it. Reverend Lewis has a good heart but once a minister, always a minister, don't you think?'

This time he looked in the mirror at Tom and Howard. 'I'm sure you're both used to giving sermons, so you'll understand. Reverend Lewis believes it's vital you're fully aware of the cultural aspects of your work and he will spend some time telling you so. From my perspective, and I've been here ten years now, I would suggest the key things to do are to relax and keep your sense of humour.'

The warmth in his voice suggested he held Lewis in high regard, but at the same time his gentle warning that the new arrivals were in for a long morning suggested he might be a useful font of knowledge for how things were run. Eileen smiled to herself. Mr Pearce had certainly succeeded in giving her a clear impression of Reverend Lewis, and of his own sense of humour, which was possibly as sharp as her own.

He drove away from the wharf and through the streets of Rabaul with practiced ease.

'I tell you what, I'll give you a little tour of the place first so you can get your bearings before you're shut away for the morning. There are two streets you need to get straight in your mind – Malaguna Road and Mango Avenue.'

Wilf Pearce drove straight ahead from the Customs House, then turned left. 'This is Mango Avenue. If we'd turned right we would have ended up at Sulphur Creek, and if we'd gone straight ahead, we would have arrived at Government House on Namanula Hill. There's a lookout up there with a lovely view of the harbour, but we're not short on views as a general rule. The European hospital is up there too.'

They passed a squat, symmetrical building painted white, whose only point of interest was a triangular peak above its double door entrance.

'That's the Regent Theatre. The films are mostly from England and Friday night is for natives only. If you don't like the pictures, we've also got baseball and an Olympic swimming pool. And mini golf if you're so inclined. Oh yes, a new tearoom has opened next to the theatre, upstairs in what used to be the German Club. That's the Guinea Drug Store,' he waved a hand. 'It's more like an American drug store than an Australian pharmacy. If the heat gets too much for you, they serve sodas and ice creams.'

Eileen tried to take it all in, but her head was spinning from lack of sleep and breakfast, the humidity, and all the strange sights, and Shelley was overexcited, so she spent a lot of time calming the kelpie. Mango Avenue was wide, with giant trees forming an archway overhead. Profusions of strange new flowers in bright purples and reds, crisp yellows and whites and delicate pinks bordered the road. Many of the buildings were two storeys high, with large verandas. Everything felt expansive and open. Wilf Pearce pointed out the Burns Philps and Carpenter's Stores, for supplies, as well as the New Guinea Club.

'Everyone shortens Burns Philps to Beeps, so if you hear that you'll know what they're talking about. The Rabaul Club is strictly for the posh set,' he continued, 'which is definitely not us mission folk. But I won't lecture you on spending money yet. That will come later, with my official duties. You'll get tired of all the lectures today.' He laughed to take the sting out of his words and continued acting as tour guide. 'The New Guinea Club is for the socialites who don't quite have enough money to make the Rabaul Club set.'

'Social climbers,' Eileen murmured. Her tone made it clear she didn't have much time for those who worried about appearance above substance.

'Exactly!' Wilf said.

A short while later they passed the Cosmopolitan and Pacific Hotels, which Wilf Pearce described as the gateway to Chinatown. This district appeared to be more commercial, with enticing posters on the walls displaying menswear, accessories such as parasols, and other items that, from the car, were impossible to determine.

'Are those stores?' Jack asked from the back seat. Wilf confirmed they were.

'Why aren't there any window displays?' Eileen asked.

'Because of the heat. The sun on the windows would soon spoil everything. Chinatown is a great place to buy souvenirs to send home,' Wilf continued as Eileen twisted in her seat to watch two beautiful Chinese women in elegant silk dresses strolling along, their pastel parasols swirling with hand-painted butterflies and tiny birds. 'You can get men's pants tailored if you need to, but I'm told the results are not so good for the ladies.'

'Probably because they're not used to Australian women's sizes,' Eileen said. She herself was probably no taller than the two women they had passed, but thinking about her sisters in Tasmania, Verna and Jean in particular would seem like giantesses next to the Chinatown residents dotting the streets. It didn't worry her: she had been taught to sew from a young age by her grandmother and everything she was currently wearing she had made herself. As long as she could buy fabric, she would manage.

Wilf slowed the vehicle down at the next corner and pointed off to the right, were there seemed to be a scurry of activity. 'That's the Ra Bung. Whatever fresh food you want, you'll find it here.'

'Can we have a quick look?' Howard Pearson asked. Wilf checked his watch and pulled over. Shelley stayed in the car, head hanging out the half-open window eagerly. As they crossed the road Wilf offered a greeting to the Tolai men who were unloading produce from a red lorry, dressed only in lap laps tied with bright sashes. They responded with familiar smiles and greetings that told Eileen they knew and respected Wilf.

The open-air market was teeming with people, even so early in the morning. The men were not the only ones carrying goods to display – women drew close with slings looped around their foreheads and hanging down their backs, laden with all sorts of fruits and vegetables. Some stall holders had tables but many had their wares laid out on the ground, on glossy green banana leaves. Aside from the men carting wooden crates of pineapples, papaya and sugar cane, there were women squatted next to piles of coconuts, shellfish and leaves wrapped up as little packages. There were flowers, bananas, nuts and fruits such as Eileen had never seen before in profusion alongside eggs, seashells and baskets. Wilf pointed out small piles of a green vegetable somewhat like a miniature avocado pear.

'Don't try those – they're betel nuts. The natives chew them all the time. They say it gives them a feeling of energy and happiness. You'll notice everyone has red teeth from them.'

Weaving amongst the displays were children and babies, some crawling, others suckling on their mothers, a few staring at the new arrivals with huge wide eyes. The women mostly wore calf-length, brightly patterned dresses with puffed sleeves, or similarly cut blouses and skirts, and everyone had flowers in their hair. Eileen was surprised at the variety of hair colours, from black through to a vibrant dyed yellow and even blue.

'We'd better keep moving.' Wilf hurried them back to the car. 'Reverend Lewis will be keen to see you.' The car did a few turns in quick succession until they were driving along a wide road with large, stately buildings and arching trees that met overhead. 'This is Malaguna Road. It's the main thoroughfare through Rabaul, and out of it.'

It ended in a fork, and they veered to the left.

'If you go the other way, it takes you along Tunnel Hill Road, through the mountain and along the coast, until you reach Vunairima. Mr Trevitt and Miss Brabin, you'll be going that way tonight. Mr Pearson and Mr Simpson, as I said, you'll be staying in Rabaul until your circuit assignments are sorted. But time for paperwork and lectures now.'

True to the warning, when they reached the Mission House in Malakuna, Reverend Lewis spent quite some time going over the problems caused by volcano dust, which could turn everything to rust if it was allowed to settle for too long, the need for propriety at all times (with a lingering glare at Eileen, the youngest in the party), and the value of tolerance and acceptance, especially in the light of behaviour that might seem very odd to them. He also spoke about the need for regular showers, pointing out that wearing damp clothes could lead to terrible infection. Most of what he said had been covered in their studies, but Eileen did her best to take it all in, or at least to appear attentive.

As the day progressed, however, her attention waned. There was so much bureaucracy to be gone through. A morning tea and dinner were the only distractions until the early evening, when Reverend Lewis took them to the Rabaul Methodist Church, a lovely little building with a welcoming gothic archway entrance leading to an enclosed porch, many paned windows and lush greenery on all sides. Its steep pitched roof, with a circular window at the peak, reminded Eileen of something out of a story book. She loved it straight away.

After a communion service for the new arrivals, an event attended solely by white people to Eileen's dismay, there was a supper, and far too many new faces. It would take a while for Eileen to learn their names and who was who with the church.

Finally, with night firmly entrenched, a young Tolai man called Ainui drove Eileen and Jack Trevitt the twenty-six miles to

Vunairima, where she caught her first sight of the school compound in the soft moonlight glow. There were clusters of small bamboo huts on stilts, each with a thatched roof of kunai grass and a little bamboo ladder leading up to the door. Ainui waved at them.

'These is where the girls sleep. Eight girls each hut. They all in bed now.' He steered the car towards a two-storey weatherboard and corrugated iron house with a wide veranda running along its entire perimeter. 'This is where the sisitas live,' he told Eileen.

By the time they had parked, an older Australian woman had come down from the veranda. She offered a firm handshake to the new arrivals. 'Mr Trevitt, I presume? I'm Jessie March, your counterpart at the girls' school. Miss Brabin, welcome to your new home.'

Eileen was instantly impressed by Miss March's no nonsense manner. Within minutes, her trunk was moved from the boot of the car to a box room in the far corner of the Teaching Sisters' House by a native boy, Shelley had been given food and water, and Miss March had taken Eileen onto the veranda, forgoing formalities to impart more crucial information. Jack Trevitt left with Ainui to make the short trip to the corresponding native men's school, George Brown College.

'Those are kapok trees,' Eileen's new headmistress indicated the huge, long armed shadows silhouetted against the bright moon. 'See those things that look like long pods hanging from them? Those are actually flying foxes. Well, some of them. Some are actual kapok pods. It's hard to tell them apart. Unless they do that.'

Miss March pointed to where one of the elongated shapes was moving, the upside-down creature turning one bat wing to scratch itself. She led Eileen down the veranda steps and they began a circuit around the house.

'If you hear a banging during the night, don't worry. The flying foxes pick the pods off the tree and throw them at the roof. Since it's made of iron, there's a terrible clatter, but you'll soon get used to it. The girls like to use the kapok to fill their pillows. Some people call the kapok a cotton tree, which isn't technically correct, but it's because the insides of the pods are soft and fluffy. Apparently, they make quite comfortable pillows.'

They continued their stroll. Eileen delighted in the lush fragrance of tropical flowers that scented the night air. She couldn't wait to see this garden during the day. Miss March showed her various plants and explained that gardening was part of the daily routine for the girls of the college. When they completed their circuit and stood at the front steps again, she pointed out the layout of the house.

'All the bedrooms are upstairs, and you enter them from the veranda. You'll want to leave your door open to get a breeze through. But make sure you're completely underneath the mosquito net. The bathroom is at that corner of the veranda, with a bush shower. No electricity here. I'll show you how to use it in the morning.'

A boy came out and told them tea was ready. Miss March introduced him as Samel, then led the way inside and soon they were seated on a cane sofa in the living room, enjoying a cup of tea. Miss March continued speaking as though the interruption hadn't happened.

'You can probably see this room doubles... well, triples really, as a living and dining room and study. Then there's the kitchen and a storeroom through there. But you'll find you spend a lot of time on the veranda. Don't be worried about the black walls in the kitchen – there hasn't been a fire, it's just we use an old wood stove that puffs out soot. No point painting it, it would just get filthy again. Our cook boy is very good.' She suddenly peered at Eileen. 'You do look done in. Take your lovely kelpie and get some sleep. The day starts early, and the girls will be eager to meet you.'

Before Eileen could move, however, there was the sound of tapping outside.

'Is that the flying foxes?' Eileen asked. It seemed too steady a rhythm to be such creatures. Miss March smiled.

'No... no, I think you may have your first visitor.'

The tapping continued, drawing nearer. Someone was walking along the veranda. A moment later a native woman entered the room. Her curly hair was cropped close and her blouse crisp and white. Her face was unlined but Eileen had the sense she was a few years older than she, at the very least. Her most distinguishing feature was that she only had one leg, the other one ending at the knee. The tapping sound had been the wooden cane she carried, knocking on the concrete of the veranda.

'Ia Lo, it's lovely to see you, but what brings you here so late?' Miss March asked. She turned to Eileen.

'This is Ulamila Ia Lo, one of our native teachers. She'll be working closely with you, helping you with the girls. She is excellent with them. Ia Lo, this is Miss Eileen Brabin.'

Ia Lo reached out and clasped Eileen's hands with one of hers. 'Yuorait? I'm so pleased to meet you. I'm here to teach you Kuanua. I want to help you learn to speak it well, so you can start work quickly.'

Ia Lo's English was perfect, and Eileen hoped she could learn to speak Kuanua equally as well. 'That's so thoughtful of you,' she responded, without mentioning that she'd already had lessons from Mrs Margetts, in Sydney. 'But perhaps we could start tomorrow? I've come a long way on a ship today and I'm very tired.'

Ia Lo nodded. 'We can begin tomorrow.'

'What a wonderful idea,' Jessie March said. 'With Ia Lo's expert help you'll be fluent in no time. As I said, she's a gifted teacher. The little ones trail after her like ducklings, they love her so. But Ia Lo, tomorrow we have the welcome assembly of the combined schools, and the drill and rhythm presentations, then lunch. Then the inspection of the schools and student villages and the hospitals, and of course afternoon tea. It's going to be rather a busy day.'

Ia Lo's eyes sparkled with humour. 'That is all true. But the assembly is late in the morning. There is much time before that and learning is important. We can start early.'

Eileen loved her eager spirit. She took the opportunity to ask Ia Lo about the school day and the girls she would be teaching. She was shocked to learn classes usually started at 6am.

Still eager to be of some use that very night, Ia Lo insisted on taking Eileen on a quick moonlit tour around the grounds. Shelley trailed along eagerly, to Ia Lo's delight. It turned out they were only a short distance from the beach. There were lime and cumquat trees along that path, and mango trees as well as the flying foxes' kapok trees at the rear of the house. Hibiscus grew in profusion along the front veranda, and frangipani in the area in front of that. As they completed their circuit of the compound Ia Lo pointed out poinciana trees, with pale green feathery leaves and delicate pink and cream, pea-shaped flowers.

'Those trees are so beautifully dressed,' she said.

Though the colours of the vegetation were muted almost to grey in the night, Eileen found herself falling in love with the garden already. She had high hopes she would enjoy her time in New Britain immensely. But she found she was struggling to keep her eyes open, and Shelley could tell. She began whining as though to say it was bedtime. Ia Lo gave her a pat.

'She is a very clever dog.'

Eileen agreed. 'I'm so glad to meet you,' she said, 'but I must give my apologies. I am so tired. I will see you in the morning for my first lesson.'

They clasped hands again and Ia Lo disappeared into the darkness, the tapping of her cane inaudible once she left the veranda.

After wishing Miss March a good night, Eileen made her way up the wooden stairs to her allocated room on the second floor, which was small but neat and tidy. She found a wooden bed, an alcove hidden by a curtain, with a rail for hanging her clothes, a dressing table and chair. There were lino squares on the floor. Too exhausted to unpack, Eileen undressed and lay down, Shelley in her accustomed position at her feet, and though there were a few clanks on the tin roof that told her the flying foxes were at play, she quickly drifted off.

Raluana Lane

5 – After the Eruption

Wilf

Saturday 5th June 1937. Malakuna.

> Considerable damage personal and Mission property. Unable re-occupy Malakuna or Rabaul. Slight damage Kabakada, Vunairima stations. Natives wonderfully composed despite numerous deaths and demolished villages. Propose establish Chairman's temporary office Raluana when books papers obtainable.

Reverend Frank Lewis, radiogram, 3rd June 1937

Laurie Linggood put his shoulder to the door and gave it another shove. This time it moved, creating almost enough space for a man to slip through.

'Good job!' Reverend Lewis cheered him on.

With one more shove, Laurie widened the gap. 'I think this is as good as it gets. There's something blocking it on the other side.'

'The window must have been left open,' Lewis commented, and slipped through. Watching from beside Howard Pearson, Wilf didn't respond. He knew he had closed the window.

Every item of furniture in Wilf's office was buried beneath a pile of grey pumice dust until only the faintest echo of its shape remained. It was apparent nobody had left the window open. Rather, the branch of a casuarina tree protruded through it, presumably brought down by the weight of falling ash, creating a hole through which the detritus from outside had blown.

In the next room, Reverend Lewis' office, the situation was less dire, especially since the adjoining door had been closed, so it was here they concentrated their efforts at first, collecting papers, ledgers and books into piles. Pilip and Ainui brought in fruit crates, and the four missionary men spent the next hour packing them with crucial documents. The decision had been made to move headquarters to Raluana in the short term as the Mission buildings there were untouched by the volcano, having been in the opposite direction to the prevailing wind that blew rocks, ash and other debris westward across the peninsula.

Lewis focused on sorting the documents while the others packed then carried crates out to the waiting ute.

'What's it looking like in Raluana?' Howard Pearson asked Laurie as they loaded crates into the ute tray.

'We've been lucky. Everything blew in the opposite direction. Essie's been worried about everyone else of course, but for her and the lad life looks pretty normal. What have you been up to?'

'We were stuck at Kabakada initially, and things were looking grim, but they sent the Montoro and evacuated us to Kokopo by sea.' Howard gave his crate a shove, pushing it to the back of the tray. 'There were thousands there, so you can imagine food was short and even with the Catholic mission and surrounding plantations taking everyone in a lot of us were sleeping on floors. My back will probably never be the same! Still, I suppose there are worse things to live through. What about you Wilf?'

The three men turned and went into the building again for another load.

'Vunakabi and Vunairima got a lot of the pumice dust, but not as much as here. The poor air quality has had a terrible effect on poor Gladys. She wants to run around tidying everything up, of course, but she just doesn't have the energy, so she has to be satisfied with organising the boys. They were probably relieved when Frank showed up this morning to take us to Raluana.'

Howard and Laurie smiled. 'I can imagine,' Laurie said. 'Your wife does like to keep things organised. Well, the situation at Raluana will be better for her health, and Mrs Lewis won't let her organise a thing if she's unwell. Did you hear about Tom Simpson's house?'

They had reached Lewis' office.

'The kit house?' Wilf knew Tom had been awaiting its arrival, eager to finally move out to the outlying islands where his ministry would be based. Since the New Hanover circuit was brand new, having never had a minister before, he would have to build everything from scratch.

'That's the one,' Laurie said. 'It hadn't been unloaded yet and the ship it was on sunk during the eruption fallout. His new home is lying at the bottom of the harbour.'

'Which means he'll be with Mrs Lewis and I at Raluana a while longer,' the Reverend joined in the conversation. Howard winked at Wilf. They both knew young Tom, an orphan who had been independent from an early age, was finding Reverend Lewis' preference for doing things in very particular ways somewhat stifling.

'I've got things under control here,' the Reverend continued. 'Howard, if you can give me a hand, Wilf, you might want to get on with packing some of the financial papers.'

Wilf and Laurie returned to the business manager's office, which was now not quite as bleak since Pilip had taken to it with a besom, the native version of a broom, made from the mid-rib of a palm leaf. They began sorting and packing anew.

'Our congregation are coping well,' Laurie began. 'There was only a little damage from the eruptions – a few things shaken apart, but nothing that couldn't be fixed. Everyone's been upset, thinking Rakaia is angry, but we've had some prayer services and spent a lot of time in the villages, and things are settling down. Of course, we'll have to keep an eye on the mosquitos with this never-ending rain or we could see an outbreak of malaria.'

'They've been liberal with the kerosene, but there's so much water around it's not as effective as it should be.'

One of the first things new arrivals learned was to pour a layer of kerosene over the water in tanks, and any standing water in creeks and pools, to kill mosquito wrigglers. Mosquitoes required fresh air to breathe, but the kerosene formed a barrier they were unable to push their proboscises through when they came to the surface, causing them to die.

Wilf began filling a new crate with the contents of a desk drawer. 'That's a concern with Gladys, of course. She's so susceptible, and she's had so many bad bouts of it already. She's been very tired lately and seems to have developed some kind of skin condition, so we're being particularly careful.'

'There have been rumours they might evacuate the women and children if the malaria risk gets too bad,' Laurie said. 'Do these need to be packed?' He indicated a row of archive boxes, each one labelled with a year in Wilf's neat hand, from 1927 to 1937.

'I'm afraid so.'

Laurie began moving them into another crate. 'Well, I hope we never have to pack up the offices again.'

'There's certainly a lot here. We should be fine – it's been...

sixty-one years since the last eruption, so I'm sure once things settle down, we won't have to do this again in our lifetime.'

Pilip skidded into the room on a little pile of ash. 'Kuskus Wilf, Talatala Marmaravut Akulia from Matupit is here to see you.'

Laurie glanced at Wilf with surprise.

'How did he know we were here?'

Wilf shrugged. 'They always know. They have ways of communicating that are much faster than ours. Probably sent a message by drum. Once you've finished with those boxes, I think that'll do.'

He stepped outside and was instantly greeted by Akulia, who clasped his hands and held them for a long moment. Akulia's face was drawn, his customary smile gone.

'Will you walk with me?' he asked and they set out together, through the bleak white landscape. Malakuna was almost unrecognisable. The familiar shapes of buildings were now mounded like strange, grey igloos. Roofs had collapsed from the weight of pumice dust. Palm trees were either stripped bare or their fronds had collapsed so they looked like upended umbrellas that had lost a battle with a hurricane. Which wasn't far from the truth. There were deep runnels in the road from the constant rain. Wilf knew the clean-up in Rabaul had started on Thursday, with hundreds of natives brought in to sweep the ash away, but clearly they hadn't reached Malakuna yet.

'Kuskus Wilf, you have been here a long time. You know the white people who are in charge. The Boss man of Rabaul is saying only twelve people died. This is not true. Near Rakaia, Tavana and Valaur have been destroyed. Many people were gathered to hold a tubuan to calm Rakaia, and many were killed.

Others went to fetch fish that were thrown from the water and they too were killed. There are many more than twelve dead. Their houses are destroyed, their gardens buried. They have no food. They are shocked and grieving. Everything is buried in dust, higher than a person. We need help.'

There was still a strong smell of sulphur in the air, as well as a pungent stink that probably came from rotting food. Wilf found himself coughing before he could reply.

'Akulia, my friend, this is terrible news. I'll talk to Mr McNicoll and see what I can arrange.'

'Thank you, my friend. I wish to show you something as well. One of the boys spotted it.'

They walked through the strange, barren scenery side by side, taking in the devastation in silence. Dotted amongst the piles of ash were bright shreds of colour, caught on broken branches or caught in the solidified pumice. At first Wilf couldn't work out what these were, until he realised they were remnants of banners from the coronation celebrations. Two and a half weeks ago, Rabaul had been festooned with gay decorations in celebration of George VI's coronation. It had been a glorious occasion, with fireworks and processions through the town. Rabaul had been alive with excitement and colour. With most people staying away from the shattered town now, the contrast couldn't be starker.

Wilf thought about the news he had heard from Albert Jones. The natives up in the hills were in the same situation, their gardens destroyed by three feet of ash and their houses collapsed. Jones had journeyed into the hills three days before and returned with reports of natives fleeing to the coast, bundles of whatever they could salvage piled on their heads. Jones had described the villages as unrecognisable, covered in tangles of fallen trees and thick deposits of stones and the clinging grey mud.

Jones had been impressed by the way the native teachers had stuck by their flocks rather than fleeing themselves. Wilf thought that was a good sign that the Methodist Mission was on the right track with their central goal of working towards independence for the Tolai people. Still, the distress and panic caused by the eruption had shown there was still much work to be done to teach them modern medicine and technical skills before the Mission could completely cede management to them. And it was simply not in his nature or his faith to abandon people at a time of darkness and despair.

A few minutes into their walk they neared the beach. There seemed to be less damage here. They stood amongst a stand of coconut trees, where only a few dangling fronds were broken. The rest maintained their fan-like shape. Spiked grass poked through the white dust at their feet, an unusual burst of colour in the ash-strewn terrain. The remains of a woven native hut hung in strips beneath one tree. At first Wilf thought Akulia was showing him the hopeful signs of greenery, but the native pastor pointed upwards, a grin spreading across his face for the first time that day.

Hanging precariously at the top of one of the coconut trees was a model biplane. Wilf's jaw dropped as he recognised the colours. It was the very plane Ainui had presented to him years ago, at one of the first Warataba he had ever attended. For years it had hung on a braided palm rope outside his window, so that when he was working, he could look up and see its shape against the blue sky outside. He hadn't noticed its absence as he packed up his office.

'Well, will you look at that. Ainui's motor-car bilongem Jesus has survived!'

Akulia smiled. 'God is watching over you, Kuskus Wilf. You are a good man. You preach at our native church. You give us many wonderful things. This is your reward. I'll get one of the boys to climb the tree and we will bring you your plane in one piece.'

'And I will do my best to speak with the civil administration and get what help we can for the people around Rakaia. Thank you for showing me this, Akulia, it has lifted my spirits.'

They parted company sombrely. By the time Wilf returned to headquarters one of the trucks was fully loaded with boxes.

'What are you grinning about?' Howard Pearson demanded.

'Do you remember the model plane that hangs outside my window?'

The others all nodded. Most of this generation of missionaries had come long after that exciting Thank Offering, but the story of it was still legendary, and had inspired other tribes to find interesting ways to deliver their annual contribution in the years since, such as by carving out the insides of a pineapple and offering up the fruit with a humble apology. The Tolai loved the humour and theatre of a trick.

'Well, Akulia just showed it to me… stuck up a coconut tree! In one piece. He's going to get someone to fetch it.'

'It wouldn't be headquarters without that plane hanging somewhere,' Howard said.

Laurie Linggood swung into the driver's seat of the second truck to return to Raluana. 'I take that as a good sign,' he said. 'It means we will recover from this. See you all soon. Travel safe!'

Wilf took the wheel for the drive to Raluana, Reverend Lewis and Howard piled in beside him.

At first their conversation revolved around the financial costs arising from the volcano eruptions. The Dodge was beyond repair, having been left at the side of the road, where a huge branch had come down on it. They would need a new car, because the mission couldn't run without one. Even with the two trucks the car was in constant use. Then there would be all the costs of cleaning and repairs. Given the bottom had dropped out of the copra market, the mission plantations were not bringing in the income they once had and everyone had already been asked to find cuts. The economic fallout would only add to their woes.

'I have every confidence in your abilities though, Wilf,' Frank Lewis told him. 'You've turned everything around in the ten years you've been working for us. When I first hired you as our accountant it didn't take long before I realised you could take on the greater responsibilities of business manager, which is why I created the position. I'm confident you'll find a way.'

Wilf diverted the conversation to the greater cost: the deaths Akulia had told him about. 'He estimates hundreds dead. And he said McNicoll has been saying there's a death toll of twelve.'

Reverend Lewis frowned. 'We'll certainly have a lot of work to do with our flock to restore things, but it's crucial Rabaul's administration recognise the native deaths. Akulia's right. Walter McNicoll won't be very receptive. He's already feeling put upon. He thinks everyone's attacking him for his suggestion that we open up Rabaul as quickly as possible. Most of the businessmen think we should move the capital somewhere else, but I don't see that happening any time soon. And then there are all the practical issues to be dealt with. Sanitation, power, clean up and so on. No, I think the best approach would be to talk to Harold Page. He's an active member of our church community and from what I've seen he has a good heart. You get on well with him, don't you, Wilf?'

'I consider him a friend rather than a colleague. I've always found him to be genuinely interested in the welfare of the natives and our work. I'll see what I can do.'

'Wilf!' Howard interrupted.

Wilf barely had time to take in what he was seeing before his instincts kicked in and he slammed on the brakes. Part of the road was washed away. If he had kept a straight path, the car would have slid into a wide ditch. In the two days since the eruptions, the rain had been almost constant, turning the eruption detritus into an off-white mud. Worse still, because all the vegetation had been stripped away by the ash fall, the heavy rains weren't absorbed as they usually would be, causing terrible erosion. A deep gully ran along one side of the road.

Wilf put the car into reverse, but at first nothing happened. The wheels couldn't get traction in the layer of slick pumice. He waited a moment and tried again, barely touching the accelerator. This time the wheels got some grip, and he reversed the utility until he was satisfied he had room to reangle it. Slowly, he drove forward, navigating the edge of the ditch. Nobody breathed as the car inched along. There was an anxious moment as it lost traction again, but then the wheels re-engaged.

Finally, they were past the gully, but for the rest of the trip to Raluana, Wilf was intent on the road. They had to start and stop any number of times. Sections were almost impassable because of piles of pumice, abandoned cars, and fallen trees. The drive that normally took fifteen minutes lasted the better part of an hour. Wilf wondered how long it would take for Rabaul to recover from the devastation of Vulcan's fury.

Eileen

Saturday 12th June 1937. Methodist Mission, Vunairima.

Dear Mum, Dad and Family,

I hope you received my cable and my letter safely.

It was a fortnight yesterday since the eruption, and we have just about got back to normal life out here, having lost most of our refugees. The place looks awful. Nothing but stretches of grey pumice dust. What was formerly dense tropical forest is now merely a jumble of huge branches and dead vines on the ground, and tall naked tree trunks, so that we can now see distances that before we could not. Grass is beginning to break through in scattered shoots in a few places where some of the pumice has been washed off, and some trees are sending up a few new shoots. When the wind rises the whole landscape is nothing but a cloud of pumice dust which quickly covers one's body and one's hair, enters one's eyes and mouth and nose. We have no rain and tank water is getting quite low, but if it comes to the worst we can boil creek water and use it. We are only about 9 or 10 miles from the craters in a direct line (though we are about 26 miles from Rabaul by road), so it is easily understood that we had a pretty bad doing.

Folk are going back to Rabaul now, and trying to dig the mess out of the town and their homes. We are told they had to, or have to, wear masks because of the dust.

On Wednesday Miss March and I expect to walk with some of our native girls up to a native village on a hill from which we can see Rabaul and the craters.

One crater is still puffing a bit, but that is said to be the safety valve. They say that the father mountain down at Nakanai has opened up again. That crater is definitely the safety valve for this whole area. Over Baining a valley is gradually falling in, the hills toppling in all around it. That is in the direct line of weakness through New Britain, and is supposed to have a connection with the eruptions.

Last weekend I spent in bed with my first attack of malarial fever. It was probably due to the extra work and strain, as I did all the outdoor work and the major part of the schoolwork while Miss March took over the housekeeping and cooking for all our refugees. I probably won't have any more fever, and I very quickly recovered from the aftereffects of that attack.

Mrs Trevitt is splendid. I had met her in Sydney, and it seems as if we will be the best of friends up here. It is such a pleasant change to have someone about one's own age here. Our new reverend and his wife, Rev G and Mrs Platten have also arrived, so we have quite a crowd on Vunairima now, seven of us white folk altogether. Mr Platten is mad on anthropology and drags us all along after him. He is starting an anthropological society, meetings to be held once a month on Tuesday evenings, beginning from this week. It should be wonderfully interesting.

Must try to go to bed early.

Love,

Eileen

Eileen put her pen down. Although she had said she should go to bed early, the rain had finally come as she was writing and now clattered incessantly on the roof. She was often able to ignore the sound, but perhaps because it had been dry for so long, it seemed to pound into her brain tonight. Somehow, she sensed sleep would be elusive, and didn't bother to undress.

Instead, she made her way out to the second storey veranda, musing on how inadequate a letter was for capturing the changes the eruptions had wrought. The truth of the matter was that dust had blown in to Vunairima for days, since Tarvurvur joined Vulcan in sending out more ash on the Sunday, creating twice as much fall out. Vunairima's name meant 'the place of the irima tree', but the jungle had transformed into a desert.

It hadn't been all bad. One of the positive experiences to come out of the terrible events was that Eileen had been able to taste 'millionaire's salad', for the first, and probably only, time. Her students had told her it was so rare she might taste it only once in her lifetime, hence its name. It was made from the growing centre shoot of the coconut palm, and since palms were crucial to life and food on the island, they were rarely cut down. But during the terrible storm on the night of the first eruption many trees had fallen, including palms.

Making up the salad was definitely a 'job bilong mari', women's work, but the young men from George Brown College had seen the loss of trees as an opportunity for some easy hunting, since pigs would be simple to spot. They had been successful in obtaining some bush pork and Eileen's students had shown her how to wrap the tough meat in pawpaw leaves and roast it in a hole in the ground filled with hot stones and a bit of fire. Eileen had been amazed at how well the pawpaw leaves tenderised the meat. Their feast, which they called a balaguan, had also included vegetables with coconut cream poured over the top, then wrapped in banana leaves and roasted beside the meat. They told her this particular dish was called punapur. Since meat was a rare part of their diet, the impromptu balaguan had lifted everyone's spirits.

The girls were proud of the beautiful garden they had worked so hard to cultivate and, like Eileen, were deeply upset by the devastation around the compound. When they first saw it, they sat amongst the ash and wept hopelessly. Eileen had resisted a similar impulse. In adjusting to life here, her friendship with her fellow teachers and her girls had given her a sense of purpose, but she relied on the gardens to find a sense of peace. The added responsibilities of the various refugees staying with them from other parts of New Britain had added to the exhaustion brought on by her first, terrible experience of malaria.

Thinking of the girls brought a smile to her face as she leaned on the veranda railing in the dark. Her teaching was another topic she never felt she could describe properly when she wrote to her family. It was easy to describe what they did in the classroom, but difficult to capture the sense of contentment and satisfaction she gained from the work, and the different attitude these students had compared to Australian students. There was an eagerness to learn and a sense of community that made each day a joyful, shared adventure.

With the last of the refugees gone, school had resumed its usual routine. Bookwork was done early in the morning, Eileen in one long indoor classroom and Miss March in the other. Since schoolbooks were in short supply their reading lessons usually involved the bible or Ra Nilai ra Dowot, the school magazine, written in the local dialect. Eileen had just agreed to take on the responsibility of translating English lessons into Kuanua for the magazine and wondered how this would affect her time.

By late morning it was always too hot to concentrate, so they would break for lunch, reading and sometimes a siesta. This was often the time Eileen wrote her letters home. In the afternoon lessons were generally outdoors as the heat of the day reached its peak and they needed the breezes to cool down. During this time the girls learned more practical skills such as gardening, sewing their own clothes or basket weaving.

Ia Lo usually took charge of the weaving as it was a native skill Eileen hadn't yet acquired. Yesterday she had been determined to advance Eileen's abilities, instructing her to sit on the veranda floor with the girls. The pandanus leaves had already been boiled in tubs, then the softened, pulpy part scraped off. Next, they had been left to dry in the heat. Finally, some had been dyed different colours, and others left in their natural glossy cream. Yesterday the students had stripped these leaves lengthwise into the correct widths for weaving. The girls had watched with delight as Ia Lo taught Eileen how to weave the lengths together to create a mat such as the girls slept on, and when she had finally succeeded, they had clamoured to be allowed to claim the mat for their own.

Eileen remembered the feeling of the leaves twisting beneath her fingers and the heat soaking into her blouse and thought how different it all was from George Brown College in Sydney, where she and Jack Trevitt and the other students had wrapped themselves in travelling rugs in front of the large fireplace in the common room, struggling to keep warm. Their training had covered a lot of ground, but it had all been about acquiring knowledge and practical skills. There had been nothing about how the people of New Britain could find a place in your heart with their humour and helpfulness and cheerful spirits.

Eileen missed her family, and Hobart, with its beautiful old buildings, English parks and cool weather, but had grown to love her students and this vibrant paradise. Her heart ached for the deaths and destruction caused by the volcano. Two whole villages had been destroyed, leading Eileen to chastise herself for making a fuss at having to throw out her ruined crepe de chine dress.

During her musings, the rain had slowed. Finally, it stopped, and an unexpected voice carried through the still night air.

'Sisita Eileen!' Ia Lo was standing below and when she realised she had Eileen's attention she beckoned her. Eileen hurried down the wooden stairs to ground level.

'I wanted to show you something, Sisita Eileen.'

'Please, Ia Lo, just called me Eileen. We've been working together almost a year now; I think we can safely say we're friends.'

With a broad smile, Ia Lo looped one arm through Eileen's and they ambled through the dark together.

'You can't sleep tonight either?' Eileen asked.

'No. I feel everything is coming to life again. I wanted to show you. I knew you would be awake.'

They made their way through the compound, past the sad remnants of the school's fruit trees and vegetable patches, beyond a bedraggled strip of jungle, and along the road next to the river.

'Are we going to the cemetery?' Eileen asked. Ia Lo nodded.

Eileen had seen one burial in the last year, a young local student who had died of measles. The girl's family had been proud that she would be buried in the school cemetery. Her body had been wrapped in a woven native mat, this one of an elaborate design with several colours, and after a simple but beautiful service had been lowered into the hole. Then her father and brother had broken off two croton branches from nearby trees and planted one at each end of the grave. Because of this tradition, the cemetery was full of beautiful crotons, with one growing at the top and bottom of every grave.

Eileen had not been back to the cemetery since the dustfall, unable to bear the thought of all the crotons being destroyed. Walking through the grounds, her heart lifted as she saw all the familiar bushes. Though they seemed to have lost some foliage, their long red-orange leaves, with a stain of dark green on each side of the centre, gleamed in the moonlight. Eileen was surprised to see the leaves looking as glossy as ever, given the pumice dust coating everything else.

'The families have come and cleaned them,' Ia Lo told her. 'It is important to honour those who lie here.'

'I'm so glad.'

'I have something else to show you. I hope you are not tired yet.'

She linked Eileen's arm with hers again and took her back the way they had come. There was a bounce in her step that Eileen took to mean her mischievous humour was tickled by whatever was to come. They reached the vegetable patches again, and Eileen saw there were shoots all over the place.

'Oh no!'

'Yes! The older girls know better, but the younger girls thought this would be helpful. They wanted to make everything grow again.'

'If only they'd planted what was here before. It's all hibiscus, isn't it?' Ia Lo simply smiled in response. Eileen shook her head. 'They do love their hibiscus. It looks so pretty in their hair too.

But our vegetable garden is not the place for it.'

Ia Lo fetched a basket woven from coconut fronds that she had placed nearby, and the two women knelt and began pulling out the shoots.

'The soil here is so good they'll grow unmanageable in no time,' Eileen said as they worked steadily. 'Especially with all the rich nutrients from the volcano ash.'

'Soon this would be a hibiscus jungle,' Ia Lo agreed.

'We'd have nowhere to plant our food.'

Pulling out the plants when the girls couldn't see them was the only way. This was not the first time they had done this task, and it wouldn't be the last. The girls thought they were helping, no matter how many times they were asked not to plant pieces pulled off the trees. Eileen and Ia Lo chatted as they worked. Ia Lo was interested in Tasmania, asking many questions about Eileen's three sisters, what they did and how they lived. She particularly loved the idea of butchers' and bakers' shop displays.

'They have lavish displays of fresh, raw meat in the windows, and the colours are so bright.'

The meat sold in Rabaul was kept in a freezer in the Burns Philp store, which Eileen always thought gave it a strange flavour from the long freezing process. There were no shop windows in Rabaul. Eileen wondered whether she should be describing a life that she realised was, in some ways, incredibly privileged, to Ia Lo, who would probably never have the opportunity to travel that Eileen had. But her friend's eagerness to hear everything encouraged her to describe more.

'I always stop and drool at all the delicious pastries on display at the baker's too.'

'You can buy fresh bread any time at these places?'

The notion of being able to buy bread every day must seem so strange. They made their own loaves at the girls' school every Saturday, with flour from Australia and yeast from limes grown in the garden. Big old blackcurrant cordial bottles constantly stood on the big wooden kitchen table, the corks tied on with string to stop them blowing off. Occasionally this wasn't enough and they would erupt during the night, spattering yeast on the smoke-blackened kitchen ceiling. Since no one could reach the ceiling to clean, there were permanent yeast blobs. Because of the humid climate the bread quickly grew mould but they didn't have the time or money to make more regularly. The only solution was to slice the mould off and keep eating the loaf. Eileen decided not to mention to Ia Lo how her mother would throw out their bread after a couple of days, behaviour that seemed extraordinarily wasteful to her now.

Life in Australia, however ordinary it seemed to Eileen, must appear exotic to her Tolai friend, she realised. Some of it sounded like an unlikely story, such as everyone having electricity in their houses. Even the school buildings here didn't have electricity, and household chores were done in the most basic way. Ironing involved placing coconut shell cinders inside a metal box to press clothes, and string was made from plant fibres. Much that Eileen had taken for granted in her old life was not accessible here, particularly twenty-six miles from Rabaul. No wonder Ia Lo found some of her descriptions of stores in Hobart unbelievable, reacting with awe and amazement.

By the time they had cleared the vegetable patch again, Eileen was finally feeling tired. On the surface, it seemed pulling new growth out was the opposite of what was needed, but the hibiscus could take root elsewhere, and it would. They needed this space to grow food for the students. Recovery from the eruptions would be slow, and it would take a lot of work, but the good soil, plentiful rain and endless warmth would soon bring life back to Vunairima, and to Rabaul.

6 – Malaria

Wilf

25th September 1937. Raluana.

It [malaria] takes great slices out of effective life ... It is not only weakening to the body, but depressing to the spirit, and all medical skill seems yet powerless to cope with it.

Dudley Carter (Lark Force), diary, 1942, p. 110

Despite having just completed his shower, Wilf felt his clothes shrink against him, already moist with the humidity. An unexpected spate of storms that had followed the eruption of Rakaia and Tavurvur was well and truly ended now. The dry season at its peak, but you wouldn't know it from the perpetual feeling of dampness everyone carried with them.

When he reached the kitchen, Mrs Lewis had just finished making a pot of tea. She offered him some with a smile.

'You have time for a cup don't you, Wilf? I know Frank is a slave driver but he can't begrudge you a little go-juice to begin your day. Especially with the early starts.'

Wilf accepted a cup gratefully. There was a long day's work ahead. Ever since the eruptions there was the usual business, and the added tasks related to fund-raising and recovery. Wilf often started at 6am and worked late into the night as Gladys dozed fitfully.

Mrs Lewis placed a teacup in front of Gladys, who was seated at the large wooden kitchen table, busy using a dry brush to remove the mildew from Wilf's shoes. He placed a kiss on his wife's forehead and sat next to her. 'What are you doing up at the break of dawn?'

'I couldn't sleep. And you need someone to take care of you. I'm sure without me you'd go to work with mouldy shoes.'

Mrs Lewis placed another cup in front of Wilf. 'I'll leave you two alone.' She stopped at the door. 'Oh, some good news. Frank says the house at Malakuna should be ready for you to move back soon. I know two old married couples sharing is a bit of a drag. And they've finally got rid of all the huge piles of ash along the main streets in town, so it's all starting to look more normal apparently. Well, I must be off. I promised Essie Linggood I'd talk through packing for furlough, since this will be their first one. Now Gladys, you will rest today, won't you? And Wilf, she's still being awfully mean to herself about Tom and Nellie Simpson's wedding.'

Mrs Lewis gave her hat a pat to make sure it was on firmly, and was gone. Wilf turned immediately to his wife.

'What's this about the Simpson's wedding, dear?'

Gladys looked up from her task. There was a fine sheen of perspiration on her forehead and indigo circles made her eyes appear sunken. 'It's nothing, really. I just mentioned how disappointed I was not to be helping out with the wedding breakfast.' She seemed to be struggling to catch her breath. 'You and I... it's what we do. You give the bride away, and I serve up a tasty feast.'

Despite her attempt at a carefree tone, Gladys' shoulders were slumped. Wilf took the shoe and brush from her and placed them on the table, while ignoring her disapproving look, then took her hands in his. They were warm and clammy, but in the endless humidity of Rabaul that was not unusual.

'My dearest, I know it must be frustrating to be unable to do what you're used to doing. You take your Eastern Star vows very seriously. No one would doubt that. You're the heart of kindness and charity. But you've been ill for so long and sometimes we have to put ourselves first.'

Gladys started to speak. Wilf squeezed her hands. 'I know... I know. That is alien to you. But if you wear yourself out, how will you be of service to others?'

A single tear ran down Gladys' cheek. She reclaimed one of her hands and began scratching her arm. 'Oh, Wilf. If I can't be of service, I don't know what to do with myself. You work so hard and I seem to spend all my days resting.'

'Not resting. You're getting well. Your body is working hard to heal itself. That's enough work for now.'

Gladys nodded, though reluctantly. 'Still, when I see you working late into the night on your new project, it makes me feel so guilty to be doing so little myself.'

'I'm sorry if I've been bringing too much work home.'

'Oh, it's not that. You love your work. The idea of a Pidgin hymn book is wonderful. It will be a great help to our Christian work.'

Wilf stood and began to pace the room, unable to hold his excitement in check.

'It will. Laurie's excited about it too now. He's going to spend some time getting printing experience while he's on furlough at the start of the new year, so we can set up our own press. But I can slow down, Gladys.' He turned toward her. 'I'm just choosing hymns at the moment. I don't have to spend every night...'

'Wilf...'

There was something in the gentle way she said his name that made him return to sit beside her. 'My dear husband. When I came here, I knew the risks. Malaria, ulcers, fevers... but I came anyway, because I believed in the work, and wanted to support you. That's what a wife does. Your work is your vocation. However ill I become, I would never want you to give it up because of me. When you resigned in '34, you were miserable. You love it here. It's your home, and you care so much about the people.'

She squeezed his hand.

'You've done so much good for our native congregation. Getting Harold Page to recognise the true numbers of native deaths from the volcano, and organising help for those whose villages were destroyed, was so important. I need you to promise me something, dear.'

'Anything, Gladys.'

'Promise me you'll stay in Rabaul, no matter what.'

Three years ago, when Gladys had experienced a particularly debilitating spell of malaria they had travelled home to Australia. Wilf had resigned from his post, but Gladys had seen how much he missed Rabaul and insisted he return, following him much later.

'Gladys!' Wilf scanned her eyes, trying to understand what was behind such a statement.

'Please, promise me?' He nodded. She leaned in to kiss his cheek. Her cheek felt hot against his. 'You should be getting to work. You know Frank isn't fond of tardiness! At least you don't have far to go these days. Let me get your change of shirt.'

She stood, wavering a little. Wilf instantly stood as well and took her elbow. 'I can do it. You sit back down.'

Gladys' voice became steel. 'Let me do what I can, my dear.'

Wilf released her arm and she turned to leave. But she had taken only a single step when she gave a strange cry and collapsed to the floor. Her face was flushed. Perspiration formed on her forehead and steam rose from her skin. Wilf thought back to the night before. Had he had missed any signs that she had come down with another bout of malaria? When he had gone to bed, she had been restless, turning frequently, but he had been so tired after a long day's work, and extra time spent on his hymn book project, that he had fallen asleep almost instantly. This morning she had been gone from the bed when he arose. The bed clothes had been damp, but that was not unusual in this climate.

'So cold...' Gladys said. Wilf rushed to kneel beside her. Her skin was burning, her clothes were soaking wet. She began scratching her arm urgently and when Wilf took her hand to stop this, he noticed her hands were shaking.

'Oh, my dear. Why didn't you tell me how you were feeling?' Gladys could only shake her head. 'We need to get you to the hospital.'

Wilf picked her up and carried her out to the truck, glad no one had come to fetch it for errands yet today. He glanced at the house, debating for a moment whether to run in and tell Frank what was going on, but he had never seen Gladys so ill. He decided to leave and explain later. After ten years of devoted service the Mission could make a few allowances.

The coast road around Karavia Bay was in its usual condition, easily passable in the utility, though it was not yet dawn, so Wilf flicked the lights on. He had driven this road so many times in the last decade, he knew every curve instinctively and he was able to drive at a decent speed, even in the dark. As he hit the inland part of the journey, west of Vulcan, the trip became less predictable. In the five months since the eruption a lot of work had gone into repairing the roads, but this far out there was still work to be done. All the fallen trees had long been cleared, and some repairs done to the road, but it was narrower than previously, the edges still at risk of further subsidence, so Wilf stayed in the centre. Luckily, he didn't meet any vehicles coming the other way.

Once he hit the coast road around Simpson Harbour, the going was much easier. He turned onto Malaguna Road then took the right onto Mango Avenue to avoid the congestion of the market and Chinatown. He had to slow down driving through Rabaul because even this early in the morning there were people casually strolling from one side of the street to the other.

Gladys was moaning as the car turned onto Namanula Road. When Wilf glanced at her, she was clutching her stomach, clearly in intense pain. Some of what she seemed to be experiencing was not typical of malaria, making him wonder whether she might have blackwater fever, the more deadly variant.

'Watch the road!' Gladys exclaimed. Namanula began as a straight line, but soon started to follow the curve of the hill upwards to the hospital, and as they swung around one bend a bicycle was coming from the other direction. Four young Tolai men were perched on it: one on the basket, one on the bar, peddling, one on the seat as a passenger, and the last on the crown of the rear wheel. Wilf slammed his foot on the brake whilst reaching out with his hand to stop Gladys being thrown forward. She cried out, a sharp, agonised sound. The car slid to a stop on the dirt road and the men waved and continued down the hill, their balance unimpeded by their numbers and the near accident.

Wilf started to apologise, but Gladys silently waved him on. He put the car into gear, continuing their journey. As Gladys started to slump, clutching her stomach with a soft groan, Wilf nearly missed the left turn that led to the top of the hill, but he spun the wheel, sending rocks and dust flying, and pivoted the car in time.

The final section of road leading to the hospital was barely more than a worn track. It gave no clue to the magnificence of the building itself, a sweeping, raised structure with verandas along all sides, including a hexagon portico off the front corner, as well as a double storey tower at the building's centre, and another veranda on the second level. There were several outlying buildings for staff quarters and two enormous palms alongside the front veranda. The hospital dated back to German occupation, having been built in 1909, and mirrored the elegance of nearby Government House.

Wilf pulled to a stop directly in front of the two archways that formed the entrance. He helped Gladys out of the truck. She was hot to the touch and drowsy. Though she had lost weight recently, Wilf was a slim man and he struggled to lift her out of the truck.

'Come on, my dear. We're here now. They'll be able to look after you.'

Fortunately, two Tolai men approached the car, dressed in the white lap laps with crosses painted on them that indicated they were ward boys. One of them turned and raced inside while the other helped Wilf lower Gladys, barely conscious, into the truck's passenger seat.

'Marama, please sit for a moment. We'll get a stretcher. The Sisita will be with you in a moment.'

A moment later the second ward boy returned, carrying a stretcher rolled up. He was followed by a nurse Wilf had met earlier that year, when Gladys had needed hospitalisation for a few days.

'Sister Kruger, she's in a bad way.'

Sister Kruger took Gladys' wrist, then lifted one eyelid after the other. With a nod, she turned and waved to the ward boys. 'Don't worry Mr Pearce, we'll take good care of her.'

Gladys was soon bundled onto the stretcher. Wilf followed Sister Kruger inside. She motioned to a white cane chair on the veranda.

'I'll get the doctor to see her straight away, Mr Pearce, and let you know where things stand.'

'I'd like to stay with her...'

Sister Kruger gently placed herself between Wilf and the door. 'We need to look after her right now, and anxious husbands get in the way. Please take a seat. I'll get one of the boys to bring you some coconut water.'

The wait seemed interminable. Wilf couldn't sit still and found himself pacing the hospital grounds. In the distance he could see the three closest volcanoes: the Mother, and the North and South Daughters. They were giving off gentle, almost reassuring puffs of smoke now, a far cry from the chaos that had come from Vulcan and Tavurvur in May, but the smell of sulphur lingered in the air, as it did throughout the year.

The light was beginning to change, taking on the soft antique gold of dawn, when Sister Kruger returned. 'Mr Pearce, your wife is very unwell. We're doing everything we can for her but I can say at this stage she'll need to be in hospital for quite a while.'

'What's wrong with her?'

'She's had numerous bouts of malaria, hasn't she?'

'There've been quite a few, yes.'

'It looks like those have had some lasting impact on her health. It's possible her kidneys are not working at their best. We'll know more soon, but there's a strong likelihood that even once she recovers, she'll need a long period of recuperation. You'll need to give some thought to ongoing care for Mrs Pearce for a while.'

They spoke for a few more minutes about Gladys' stay in the hospital, then Wilf bid Sister Kruger farewell. He had to discuss the current situation with Reverend Lewis and fetch some things Gladys would need for her stay. But he found himself turning the truck towards the Namanula Hill lookout rather than towards Rabaul. Once he returned to Raluana, work would no doubt take precedence, and he needed time to think.

After parking, Wilf made his way to the edge of the lookout, where, with the growing haze of dawn, he could clearly make out Malaguna Road, a long green line running arrow straight ahead from where he was standing. At the end nearest the lookout was the cemetery and further to the left, Queen Elizabeth Park. Rising into the hills on the right were the spacious botanical gardens, while the left was dominated by the glistening waters of Simpson Harbour. If he tried, Wilf knew he could probably name every building he saw in the rough grid that formed the town, as well as every person who worked in them.

Gladys had been here nearly as long as he, seven years to his ten. But her experiences of this beautiful place were different to his, because she had spent so much time battling illness. Her sense of duty was no less than Wilf's, but lately she had been unable to do everything she was usually driven to do to meet her personal ideals of charity and kindness. Every time she appeared to be recovering, malaria would again lay her low, and lately, in between bouts, she never seemed to overcome a general fatigue. Her weight loss was worrying too.

Though it pained him to think of a prolonged separation, it seemed clear that the time that Gladys had been living in Australia in '34 and '35 was the only period since her move to New Britain when she had really recovered her old spirit, as well as her health. There was nothing for it. The convalescence Nurse Kruger had spoken of would absolutely have to happen in Australia.

What that might mean for the long term, he wasn't sure. Clearly this was not a cycle that could continue, because each new round of illness had a greater impact on Gladys' overall health. Wilf put away such thoughts. Helping Gladys get well was the immediate priority. But he was not due for leave, and Frank was unlikely to allow it anyway. There was so much work to be done managing the rebuilding and recovery from the volcano. A collection was being taken by the Methodist Church of Australia, and a proposal needed to be written regarding the disbursement of these funds. The next Thank Offering would be coming up soon too, although Wilf was worried about collecting from villagers who had faced so much devastation, losing gardens and animals as well as their homes. At the same time, the funds were needed to continue programs of medical assistance and the running of the plantations, which provided work and income. Then there was the purchase of a new car, which was becoming increasingly urgent, as well as other general repair costs.

Last time Gladys had required repatriation to Australia, Ken Allsop had taken over Wilf's position as accountant and manager, and he knew the work of the Mission well enough to take over even with all the extra work. But Ken was in private employment in Rabaul now and wouldn't be able to drop that at short notice. Much as Wilf wanted to go with his wife, he had made a commitment, both contractual and spiritual, to the church, and to the people they served in New Britain.

Bands of vivid orange and yellow were breaking across Simpson Harbour now, reflected in the still waters, and Wilf sat for a while longer, letting the glory of the sunset quell the battle in his heart. Shafts of vivid white burst upwards as the sun broke the horizon, silhouetting the volcanoes encircling the harbour and the Beehives at its centre. As the sun climbed higher, the horizon settled to a soft, glowing white, and the fiery colours faded from the sky and water, leaving them both a dazzling blue. There was no more beautiful place to be in the still of the morning than looking over such peaceful beauty.

Wilf's mind was made up. He would go and discuss the situation with Frank, then have a conversation with the hospital about when it would be safe for Gladys to take a ship to Australia. With luck, she would recover swiftly and return soon. If not, he would join her when it was practical to do so. Decisions about the longer term could wait until they saw what path this illness took.

1st November 1937. Kaukau.

The final words of the hymn were still ringing, 'I know that heav'n is near to me, for there's music in my soul,' when Wilf stepped up to the pulpit. As always, the native congregation sung the harmonies beautifully, although that was partly because their repertoire of hymns was limited and they knew them all very well. He looked forward to working on the Pidgin hymn book that was fast becoming his passion project, since it would allow them to learn many new hymns.

Wilf preached in Pidgin, focusing his message on gratitude for the gifts God provides. Aaron, the native catechist in charge of Malakuna, had already delivered a teaching from the bible, so Wilf's role was to remind the congregation of this message and conclude the service. Although only a lay preacher, he held special authority in the eyes of the members of the indentured labourers' church. As he concluded, they smiled up at him, eyes shining with the joy their Sunday service always brought. They had built this little church themselves, and its simple construction always seemed to Wilf somehow more connected to the values of a simple Christian life than the ornate structures of other church buildings.

As Wilf offered the final blessing, he could sense someone waiting nearby. The service finished, the natives began to file out and Wilf turned, to discover Akulia, his old friend from Matupit, speaking quietly to Aaron. With a nod, Aaron made his way to the church entrance, where he would farewell everyone as they left. Before Wilf could join him, Akulia hurried over. There was sadness in his eyes. He reached to clasp both Wilf's hands in his.

'My dear friend, will you come with me?' Wilf glanced at the front of the church, wishing to fulfil his usual duty of speaking to the parishioners. 'I have urgent news for you. They will understand.'

There was something in his voice that made Wilf turn and

search the native pastor's face. 'What is it?'

'Please, come with me.' Akulia led the way out the side door. The vestry was not, as was usual, a room within this simple church; rather it was a small building, little more than a shed, a few feet away from the side door. Inside it was kitted out with a cupboard, a desk and three chairs. Akulia gestured for Wilf to enter, stopping on the way to request drinks from one of the trainee teachers. Inside, Wilf was surprised to see Frank Lewis already seated behind the desk. He would normally be preparing for the service for whites at the Rabaul church.

Akulia indicated for Wilf to take a seat and he did so. Frank leaned forward.

'Wilf, I'm afraid I have some bad news. We received a telegram at the church this morning. I came straight here.'

Wilf felt a strange hollowness open in his chest. He knew. Before the words were spoken, he knew what they would be, as though this moment had occurred many times before, or as if everything had led to this.

'It's Gladys. I'm afraid she's gone.'

Frank slid a piece of paper across the table. Wilf didn't take it. He stood, as if to leave, glancing at the door, then fell heavily into the chair again. Then he shook his head.

'No. No, that can't be right. She's recuperating. She was doing well. I only received a letter from her yesterday on the mail plane. I was only reading it yesterday. She's getting better.'

'I'm sorry Wilf. You know we're all here for you. Whatever you need.' He stood and came round the table, placing one hand on Wilf's shoulder. 'I'll give you some time.'

Frank left the vestry, murmuring quietly to Akulia on the way. 'I need to get back for the service. You'll look after him, won't you?'

'Of course, Talatala Frank.'

The words washed over Wilf. How could Gladys be gone? In her month in Australia she had made good progress towards recovery. He reached out and grabbed the telegram. His eyes were working perfectly well, but his mind couldn't seem to comprehend what was on the scrap of paper at first. It took him a moment to realise it was from Roy Hardie, Gladys' brother.

'Gladys passed suddenly this am. Funeral tomorrow. Condolences.'

Including the address and names, Roy had managed to come in just under the allowable sixteen words. Gladys had always joked her brother was a man of few words. Wilf laughed bitterly to himself. Where was the detail? How could this have happened? Her letter had been brief, but positive. She had even said she was looking forward to returning to Rabaul.

Akulia placed a teacup on the table, filled with cloudy coconut milk. Surprised that his hands didn't shake, Wilf sipped the cool drink gratefully. Its sweetness was a balm at this strange time.

'Please, my friend, can I do anything to help you? What do you need?'

Wilf looked up at Akulia.

'I don't know Akulia. I don't know.'

2nd November 1937. Raluana.

Wilf,

I hope you received the telegram I sent yesterday and this letter doesn't come as a shock to you. My aim is to send it on the next mail plane, so you should receive it on the 7th. I hope the delay in receiving fuller details hasn't caused too much distress.

First, let me pass on my deepest condolences at the loss of Gladys. I know your love for each other was enduring, and that she was a great help in your work in New Britain. She was a caring sister to me and I'll miss her keenly.

I imagine you're wondering what happened as I'm aware Gladys wrote to you only days before her passing, with news she was recovering. That was true at the time, but she took a turn for the worse on the Saturday just past. It looks like the malaria had a lasting effect on her kidneys. At the end, there was nothing that could be done. Know that she was comfortable and peaceful when she passed.

You may have been surprised to hear how swiftly the funeral was organised. I hope you'll forgive me that you were not able to attend. Knowing the trip from New Britain takes nine days, it was clear you wouldn't arrive in time if you managed to get leave. Gladys also insisted your work shouldn't be interrupted. She was terribly proud of you. For this reason, and because Mother is unwell, we decided a delay would serve no purpose.

As the service was held at the family church in Rookwood, Reverend Poole was able to deliver a most personal and touching address regarding her life and service. He spoke of your marriage and work in glowing terms. Numerous representatives of the Order of the Eastern Star attended. They provided a beautiful wreath of lilies and ferns for the coffin. There was excellent attendance and a number of floral tributes. Gladys was held in high regard by many.

When you have furlough next, I will make myself available to show you where Gladys is buried at Rookwood cemetery.

Know that you were in Gladys' thoughts at the end. She was most explicit that you should continue with your important work, and not spend the rest of your life in mourning.

Sincerest best wishes,

Roy Hardie

For Roy, this was a great many words, but Wilf still wanted to know more. What had the doctors said? Had Gladys been in pain? In the week since the terrible telegram, Wilf had arranged with Frank Lewis that he would take an extraordinary furlough beginning January, so he would take Roy up on his offer as soon as he reached Sydney.

It was beginning to feel real now. Given that initially all there had been to attest to Gladys' death was a brief slip of paper, and all this had happened at a distance, it had been easy to imagine none of it was true, but this letter affirmed reality. Not only was she gone, but her funeral was already over.

Wilf's father had passed four years ago, and now his wife was gone. He felt a hollowness inside, and was glad to be heading home soon. He wanted to see his own family: his mother, all his brothers and sisters – wanted to feel connected to them. At the same time, there was no doubt in his mind he would return to Rabaul after his leave. If family was those with whom you had strong connections, then the Tolai people, Akulia and Aaron, Ainui and Pilip, all the members of the church, they were also his family.

For once, Wilf decided, he would have an early night. There was a great deal to be done in the next two months before furlough, but he felt terribly wrung out, his body heavy. Since he had recently moved back into the freshly cleaned Mission House at Malakuna, he didn't have Mrs Lewis nearby to offer him a cup of tea, and he didn't feel inclined to ask the house boy for one. He made his way to the bedroom, where he removed his shoes and placed them beside the brush. No doubt they would be covered in mildew by the morning.

125

7 - A Foolish Diversion

Eileen

Saturday 19ᵗʰ February 1938. Rabaul.

At that time I developed a queer attitude towards men, except for the missionaries and some others whom I respected. So many others thought that they were specially attractive and appealing. … The white men, apart from the missionaries, adopted that attitude even when traveling by boat between Australia and Rabaul and had to be kept in their place. … It was the more surprising then that I finally allowed myself to be so silly that I allowed myself to become engaged to a young chap in New Britain. We really seriously intended to be married and he gave me an engagement ring.

Eileen Brabin, Memoirs

Eileen pushed open the door to the Rabaul mission house with her hip, since her arms were full with a heavily loaded paper bag. She felt triumphant. The day had begun well, with an easy bike ride from Vunairima to Kabakada, a quick catch up with the Joneses, and the final part of the trip to Rabaul completed by 8am. The Pearsons had still been in bed, but since she had numerous errands to run, they were happy for her to have a bath and change into her shopping clothes, then enjoy a quick breakfast while they had a slower start to the morning.

Things had looked like they might go off kilter, with the rain starting to pour down heavily, and it had been 10:30 before she was able to start shopping in town. Since all European businesses closed at 12pm, there was a risk she wouldn't be able to complete her errands, but in the end, although it was a rush, she managed to do everything. She was in good cheer now, looking forward to visiting with the Pearsons, something she always found enlivening after the excessive sobriety and isolation of life at the girls' school at Vunairima.

Entering the Parsonage, she was surprised to see Eric seated at the kitchen table, in conversation with Howard Pearson. As soon as he saw Eileen, he leaped up and took the bag of supplies from her, placing it on the table.

'Miss Brabin, I've been looking for you! Many happy returns for your birthday yesterday.'

'Thank you, Mr Eriksen.'

'I've told you, Eric, please! We've been seeing each other long enough now to be on a first name basis.'

Helen Pearson had entered the room a few moments before. She cast an appraising look at Eileen, who fought against a blush and cursed her fair skin.

'I don't know if "seeing each other" is the best way to describe it, Eric.'

Eileen accepted his attentions reluctantly, but now she thought about it, spending time with him at the Government Workshops where he worked, or going on a picnic, could probably be taken as encouragement. Not that he needed any. Wherever she turned lately, he seemed to be there. She had explained the situation to Miss March, who had come up with a cunning plan. They had organised a dinner party for tomorrow evening with Miss Beale, Miss Battersby, Mr Beazley (the mission carpenter), Eileen and Eric, and pointedly told Eric that it was an event for single people. Ia Lo was in on the plot, planning to cook native food for the guests, alongside Miss March's famous rainbow cake.

Unfortunately, the subtlety of the idea that Eileen was single, not his sweetheart, seemed to have gone over Eric's head as he chatted excitedly now about the event.

'It's a birthday celebration, isn't it?' He gave a sly grin. 'That means I should bring you a gift.'

'Well, in that case you had better bring one for Miss March and Miss Battersby as well, as we're celebrating their birthdays too.'

She wondered if her response sounded sharper than it should, but she did want to discourage his attentions. This was something she'd become quite practiced at, since she'd experienced several annoying 'issues', such as a plantation owner who called her his 'little bit of fluff'. She was quite forthright at times. But nothing seemed to dampen Eric's enthusiasm.

'So, how was your special day? Did the girls do anything for you?'

'They have a couple of lovely customs. They enjoy decorating everything on every occasion possible, so this time they threaded frangipani onto the midribs of the coconut palms, and made chains of frangipani for the meal table. But I'm afraid their other custom was more problematical. They decided they would sing me out of bed.'

'Sounds delightful!' Helen Pearson said as she supervised the houseboys setting out lunch. Of course she invited Eric to join them.

'Well, yes, they do lovely harmonies, and this time they managed not to begin until 5:30am.'

'This time?' Howard asked, reaching for the bowl of boiled kau kau before it had even hit the table. Helen slapped his hand away.

'It was Miss Battersby's birthday on Tuesday, and the girls were up at 4am to go and sing to her,' Eileen explained.

'Four am? Why so early?' Helen asked as she surveyed the table, which was set with fresh fried fish, the kau kau, condiments and a platter of fruit. Everything looked satisfactory so she took her seat and gave Howard a fond look. He instantly reached for the food.

'Well, it was such a bright moonlight night they had little chance of judging the time correctly, I suppose. They woke me with their noise, and I went out and made them go back to bed before they woke Miss Battersby. They got up a second time at 4.30, but I gave them such a scolding they didn't dare to come out again until I woke them at 5.30am.'

Everyone laughed, and Eric patted Eileen's hand. 'You're such a tiny thing but you certainly have some fire in your engine.'

As always when Eric was around, the conversation was lively. He seemed to know all manner of things about every topic under the sun. Even mouthfuls of fresh fish and kau kau couldn't halt his excited contributions.

Somehow, after traversing a range of topics, including the building of a new aerodrome at Rapindik, the conversation turned to Eileen's return to Vunairima that afternoon. Eric was horrified to hear she planned to cycle home, a journey of some twenty-six miles.

'Oh, you mustn't do that! There was rain this morning and it definitely looked like it was raining over the road to Vunairima. It'll be too bad for cycling.'

'It doesn't look like it's been raining too much. I'm sure I'll be fine.'

'My car isn't running at present, but I'll hire a car and take you home,' Eric insisted. 'After your ride this morning, and all your shopping adventures, I'm sure you'll be too tired.'

Eileen fumed, but bit back her retort that she knew better than he what she was capable of. She took a more diplomatic tack. 'If the road is bad, or if I'm tired, I'll stop at Kabakada for the night and ride on to Vunairima in the morning.'

'At least let me drive you to Kabakada.'

'You can borrow the car,' Howard said. 'Staying at Kabakada tonight sounds like the best plan.'

Pleased to have decided for her, Howard and Erik headed out the door, each to run different errands, leaving Eileen with instructions to be ready at 5:30pm.

'What are you up to this afternoon Eileen?' Helen asked once they were alone.

'I'd like to go to Chinatown to find some silk table napkins for the dinner party.'

'What a delightful idea. Do you think you could fetch a few things for me from the Ra Bung? We need more bananas and taro. I need to go to the church and practice the hymns for this evening's service. I'd be most grateful.'

'Of course!'

'I'll be back here by the time you're done, or you can just let yourself in.'

Helen gave her a short list, and a calico bag, turning it inside out to check for mould first. Then Eileen set off.

During her short walk to the native market, she thought about what to do. Hazel Jones did not know about Eric's amorous designs, and that was how it should be. Eileen did not want everybody in the mission to know he was chasing her around, and if he took her to the Jones house at Kabakada around 5:30pm, the Joneses would feel they had to invite him for dinner. He would undoubtedly say something then to imply a relationship Eileen didn't feel existed. It would be terribly awkward. The only solution would be to complete her shopping quickly and take off on her bike well before 5:30.

The plan seemed to be on track, as she completed her errands and returned to the Pearson's before 2:30pm. Helen was seated on the veranda, a book open in her lap.

'I have your groceries,' Eileen said by way of greeting. 'They didn't just have wudus, they had the nicer bananas too, so I got those for you.' Helen nodded her thanks. 'I'm just going to change into my overalls and I'll be off. If you can let Eric know I wanted to get home quickly...'

'Oh, but you can't!' Helen stood, leaving her book on the table, and took the bag of groceries from Eileen. They went inside together as Helen explained. 'Howard and Eric have taken the valve out of one of the bike wheels. They thought you might be a bit headstrong, so Eric came up with the idea to stop you going.'

Eileen looked out the window, to where she could see her bike propped against a coconut palm. 'Right.' She hurried into the guest bedroom, changed from her cotton frock into her Oshkosh overalls, and returned to farewell Helen.

'Where are you going?

Eileen gave a great smile. 'That silly trick with the valve has reinforced my determination to return home under my own steam. Thank you so much for your hospitality. Please pass on my farewells to the men.'

Astonishment and, perhaps, admiration, battled in Helen's expression. 'Have a safe journey!'

Slinging her carry-all over her shoulder, Eileen fetched her bike and walked it to the Chinese bike shop. It was a matter of minutes to have a new valve put in. Although she was a little upset at having to spend the money, since funds were always tight, she was in great good humour at having defeated Eric's plans.

She made sure to only take a brief stop at Kabakada, determined not to lose her victory. Hazel was delighted to receive the few goods Eileen had obtained for them at the Ra Bung and they shared a quick afternoon tea. It was no time at all before Eileen was on the road. There were no indications of rain and the road was better than it had been that morning. Nor did she feel tired. Elation was giving her energy and as always, cycling made her feel fit as a fiddle.

About two thirds of the way to Vunairima, she became aware of the sound of a vehicle coming up behind her. She pulled over and looked back, surprised to see Eric following her in the car. Her first thought was to give him the same sort of scolding she'd given her singing students earlier in the week, but the expression on his face gave her pause. He left the car and was apologising before he'd reached her side.

'Oh, Eileen, I'm so sorry. So, so sorry. You must be angry at me. It was a very silly trick. Please say you'll forgive me?'

Eric seemed to be in genuine distress. Eileen could only think what a feeble attempt it had been to stop her, and she burst out laughing. For a moment Eric looked shocked, then he laughed too. They stood by the side of the road, palm fronds waving overhead in a slight breeze, unable to hold in their hilarity. Eventually their mirth subsided.

'Well, this has been a funny business,' Eric said. He took Eileen's hand. 'Now that you've forgiven me, please will you let me drive you home? I promise, I won't play any more tricks on you. It's more than my life's worth.'

His hair glowed golden in the late afternoon light and Eileen thought how handsome he looked.

'I suppose you can, since I've made it most of the way on my own. My point has been proven.'

Eric agreed emphatically.

Later that night, Eileen reflected on the events of the day. Eric had stayed for dinner, and recounted the whole story for Miss March and Miss Battersby, with a great deal of humour. He had already won them over on a previous visit because he was capable of a great deal of charm, but Eileen knew good looks and winning ways did not signify a person of good character. At least today's events had revealed he was able to laugh at himself, which did put him in a better light. He had been most enjoyable company that evening, and she found herself looking forward to the singles dinner party the following night. Perhaps she had been too harsh in her dismissal of Eric's attentions.

July 1939. Hobart, Tasmania.

'This is so wicked!'

Marie pulled a face at her sister. 'It's just hot potato chips, Eileen. What could possibly be wicked about it?'

'Well, we're eating them out of a paper cone, for one thing, and we're eating them while we're walking along, for another.'

Marie's look of disdain said it all. Clearly, she thought there was nothing at all wicked about such an ordinary pastime, but for Eileen, after three years in Rabaul, this was a far cry from the sedate behaviour required of all staff. 'You would never eat hot chips in the street?'

'Of course not.'

'Because it's not proper? That's so silly. How do you eat your chips then?'

Eileen took a chip and tapped her younger sister on the nose, replying airily, 'It's far too hot there to eat this sort of food. And there aren't any fish and chip shops anyway.'

Marie wiped non-existent grease from her face and poked her tongue out. They strode down Elizabeth Street, Eileen enjoying browsing all the shop windows. She bit her tongue, thinking if she mentioned the lack of displays in Rabaul, Marie would give her another quizzing. Instead, she focused on the delicious, decadent flavour of deep-fried potato and the comforting warmth of the paper cone in her hands. Winter in Tasmania had come as a shock after the perpetual heat of New Britain. How quickly one adjusted to a different climate.

Distracted by these sensory pleasures, she was startled when Marie suddenly seized hold of her arm.

'Isn't that Eric?'

'You don't need to grab me like that. Where?'

'Going into the Renown.'

Eileen looked across to the other side of the road. The milk bar's door was just closing. 'I've been so terrible – I haven't spent any time with him yet because I've been ill since I got home. We'd better go and say hello. He'll be pleased that I'm well again.'

She looked to the right, checking for traffic. Marie's grip on her arm tightened. 'He was with another woman, Eileen.'

'What? Oh, I'm sure it's just a friend.'

Marie glanced up the street and leaned in conspiratorially. 'How about you go into Soundy's and find yourself that new pair of gloves you were talking about? Eric hasn't met me yet, so he won't recognise me. I'll do a Mata Hari and find out what's going on. I'll come and find you in Soundy's once I know the lay of the land.'

'Nobody wears gloves in Rabaul,' Eileen said. 'It's far too hot!'

Marie gave her a searching look. 'You've retired, remember? You're engaged to marry Eric, so you had to give up your post. You won't be returning. And you were only saying yesterday you had no winter woollies.'

'Of course. It's just, after three years, my thoughts always go to my life there.'

'Is that all? Your letters were perpetually gushing about your work, and your girls, and the beautiful gardens and jungles. Are you sure you're happy to give up your job there to marry Eric?'

Eileen looked across the street to the Renown. 'I think I'll wait to answer that until you report to me, Mata Hari!'

Marie gave her a wink and hurried across the road.

Eileen made her way up Elizabeth Street, crossing over at the next intersection. Soundy's seemed much posher than the Beeps store in Rabaul, with glass and wood display cabinets rather than basic shelves. The wares were vastly different too: dresses and hats of wool, knitwear and embroidered gloves to combat the icy Tasmanian winter, delicate shoes that would cause her to break an ankle if she tried to walk in them on the unpaved roads around the girls' school.

Though Eileen had found herself drooling over window displays of food earlier this morning, what she saw in this department store seemed needlessly extravagant. Life in Rabaul was much simpler, but when she thought about it, she had been happy there. Being home felt strange. Life was overly complicated somehow, with all its social expectations. She missed the genuine smiles of the girls she taught, their weeping at the end of the year when they had to say goodbye to their friends. She even missed making her own soap and bread.

As Eileen wandered through the store, picking up items at random, she wondered what the knot in her stomach was about. She wasn't too worried about what Marie had seen. No doubt there was a reasonable explanation. After all, Eric had been in Hobart six months or so now – he was bound to have got to know people. He was gregarious, keen on regular outings with a large group of friends. Often when they stepped out together in Rabaul he had invited Miss Battersby or Miss Beale from the Stewart Hospital to join them or, in Rabaul, roped in the Pearsons or old Mr Munger. Eileen preferred quiet, one-on-one conversations, but Eric was always happiest at the centre of a gathering.

Perhaps, though, he was having second thoughts? He had been rather ill when he proposed. At the end of a lovely day, he had taken Eileen home, then been overtaken by fever. Seated on the veranda lounge, Eileen had cradled his head and cooled his forehead with a handkerchief dipped in cologne. When he gazed up at her devotedly and asked her to marry him, somehow she had given in. It had all been a rush after that. The malaria had taken him rather badly, and soon after he had flown to Rockhampton to stay with his family until he was better. Once he recovered, he had taken it into his head that they should live in Hobart, near her family, rather than in Queensland, near his, and promptly found himself a job, moving to Hobart just before Christmas.

Shortly after that his letters had become less frequent, but Eileen had put that down to the stress of setting up a new life in a new town, and starting a new job. He had been in contact with her parents, but not as much as one would expect given he was shortly to be their son-in-law and was now living in the same state as them. And Eileen had been terribly ill herself when she arrived home, the fever so bad her sisters had stood in the doorway and laughed at the steam rising from her. No doubt they found it funny because they had often borne the brunt of her steamy temper when they were all younger.

Eileen put down the felt cloche hat she had been turning in her hands for several minutes, realising as she did so that a sales assistant was glaring at her. It suddenly occurred to her that the expectations of good behaviour at the Methodist Mission were no different to here, just more overt. A flood of homesickness overtook her for the freedom of cycling through the jungle in her overalls.

All this subterfuge was foolish, she realised. She was used to managing all sorts of difficult situations in her position as assistant head at the school. Whatever Eric was up to, she would face it head on. Eileen hurried to the entrance of the store, and nearly crashed into her sister as Marie pushed open the glass doors. She took Eileen's arm in hers and hurried her out of the store, turning right up Elizabeth Street, away from the milk bar.

'Let's go home,' she said. Eileen tried to look over her shoulder at the road behind them.

'Was it Eric? I want to talk to him. It's childish not to meet him face to face.'

'I don't think that's a good idea.'

They had passed the Liberty Cinema and reached the corner of the street. Marie continued to hustle Eileen along, practically dragging her across the road. Once they'd reached the other side, Eileen stopped and pulled her arm out of her sister's grasp.

'I am not going anywhere until you tell me what's going on. And why you don't think I should head down this street and talk to my fiancé. Are you trying to protect me? You know I'm stronger than that.'

'Please, let's go home. They've already gone, honestly. They got into a car and drove off. I promise I'll tell you everything on the way.'

'Let's go home then. But you'd better spill the beans!'

Marie nodded and they started up Elizabeth Street again. She immediately began her story. 'Well, when I went in, he was seated in a booth with a girl. She was very fashionably dressed, I have to say.'

Eileen glanced down at her own mismatched and ill-fitting outfit, cobbled together from her sisters' wardrobes since all her dresses were suited to the tropics. She shook her head. 'That's not important.'

'Maybe not to you, but what about to him? Anyway, I heard him call her Mena. And... Eileen, it was definitely a date. He was holding her hand and she popped a chocolate into his mouth.'

Eileen suddenly started going much faster. Marie raced to catch up. 'You're steaming again,' she said when she did. Eileen reached up to touch her face. She didn't feel feverish.

'I don't mean from the malaria,' Marie said. 'I know that look on your face. If we'd gone back, Eric would have been blasted to pieces! Will you slow down? You may be used to walking everywhere, but I'm not!'

Eileen stopped abruptly and turned to face her sister. 'I think it's time I caught up with Eric.'

* * * * *

It turned out Eric had met Mena Sweet because she lived near the Brabins. During a rare visit to Eileen's parents he had seen her strolling down the street and begun a conversation with her. Marie had told Eileen she was pretty, and seemed to adore him. Perhaps that adoration had been what turned Eric's head so quickly. Adoration was not something Eileen had ever given him. She was far too practical.

The conversation to end the engagement had been most civil, despite Jean and Marie's predictions of utter doom for Eric. Eileen had gone into it feeling calm. She was more nervous about contacting Reverend Burton, General Secretary of the Overseas Mission in Sydney, to see if she could have her old teaching post back in Vunairima. Eric had smiled his open, charming smile and admitted he was at fault.

'I find myself in the terrible position of having feelings for you both,' he had said somewhat sheepishly. Eileen had quickly relieved him of this quandary by telling him in no uncertain terms the engagement was over. This was not the reaction he had been expecting, but it had not been a difficult decision. Later, she did not regret it one bit. If fact, when she thought it through, some mad fever must have taken hold of her the night she accepted his proposal, brought about by the tropical night air, the scent of cologne, and his helplessness as he gazed up at her, wide eyes bright with malarial fever. The life she had imagined with Eric seemed to have frozen and cracked apart in the chill of Hobart's winter.

Eileen stood in front of Mena's house now. It was a colonial era house, built of large sandstone bricks in a soft gold colour, with a large bay window and ornate gingerbread ornamentation giving it an air of grandeur. The Sweets were apparently not short on funds, unlike Eileen's own father, who moved the Brabins from one rental property to another as finances required.

Juggling the paper-wrapped packages she carried, Eileen knocked firmly on the door. There was a long delay, but she had caught the flicker of movement from a window and knew someone had to be home. She had no intention of leaving until someone answered. Finally, footsteps echoed on boards, and a moment later the door opened. It had to be the young woman herself. Much as she hated to admit it, Eileen realised Marie was right. Mena was pretty, with big eyes and delicate features.

'Can I help you?'

'Are you Mena Sweet?'

The young woman nodded. Until that moment Eileen had not been sure of the approach she would take, but seeing the trusting expression on the younger woman's face, she let the last wisps of anger evaporate.

'Yes... I am. What can I do for you?'

'These are for you,' Eileen said, and without further ado, she passed the pile of packages over.

'What... I'm sorry... what are these?'

'Has Eric told you he came to Hobart to be married?'

Mena's eyes grew round.

'He... he did?'

'Yes. He did. These are the blankets and linens I prepared for my trousseau. I've called off the engagement and I'm really not going to need blankets where I'm going, so I thought you should have them.'

The young woman looked down at the bundles in her arm, then at Eileen. 'Please, can you give me a moment?' She disappeared into the house, then came out without the packages.

'I suppose I should ask you in for tea?' Her voice came out high pitched. She was so young. It hadn't worried Eileen that at twenty-eight she was three years older than Eric, but seeing this nervous young woman she thought more than years separated them. At times, the decision to push aside her frustration with Eric's immature behaviour had been very deliberate. During a dinner party at the house he shared with two other young men, he and his companions had thought it highly amusing to fire an airgun at mosquitoes. Eileen had left early that evening.

'I don't think that's necessary under the circumstances,' Eileen said. Mena looked relieved. Then confusion crossed her brow.

'Do you want me to pay you for these blankets? I mean, thank you. I don't know what the convention is...'

Eileen waved her hand. 'Oh, the costs are covered.'

Having refused to return the engagement ring to Eric – watching him give it to another woman would have been a step too far – she had taken it to the jewellers that very morning and come away with a tidy sum.

Mena's next words tumbled out in a rush. 'I'm sorry about your engagement, but I didn't know Eric had a fiancée, honestly. We just got to know each other and... well, he's so special, isn't he? He's told me all about his work as an engineer, and shown me his photos from a fancy coronation parade, and he received a medal, did you know? For helping his town when a volcano erupted. I've never met anyone like him.'

One hand was nervously smoothing her skirt as she stuttered into silence. Eileen realised she felt no need to ask any questions about their plans for the relationship. It was no longer her concern. Eric needed admiration, but it was not in Eileen's nature to gush over someone. She exhaled and felt her shoulders lighten.

'It sounds like you'll be perfect for him. It's been... interesting to meet you.'

She turned to leave. Mena seemed suddenly to overcome her anxieties. 'Why are you being nice to me?'

Eileen turned to face her. 'Sometimes fate takes a hand, I suppose. And one can't rail against fate.'

She held out one hand. Surprised, Mena took it, and gasped when Eileen gave her the Tolai double hand clasp rather than a handshake.

'Good luck,' Eileen said with a genuine smile. After Mena had withdrawn and closed the door, she wondered whether she should have said anything about Eric being an unreliable young man, then dismissed the thought. Mena would form her own opinions.

143

8 – Snapshots of a Courtship

Eileen and Wilf

I had always had a strong admiration for Wilf Pearce. He was a widower who had no children, but he was a very kind and gentle person and everyone liked him. He was about 10 years older than I was, but I was tired of younger men by then and I gradually became more friendly with him. He began to make frequent visits to Vunairima in his little car and my kelpie dog who was very jealous, hated him and tried hard to prevent him from coming anywhere near me.

Eileen Brabin, Memoirs

She had no photos, in the end. Just memories, fragments of happy moments.

25th December 1939. Raluana.

'This pudding is absolutely delicious! How ever did you find the time?'

Essie Linggood dug her spoon around for the last morsels of Christmas pudding. Ken Allsop picked up his bowl and shamelessly licked the brandy sauce. Wilf was too busy enjoying his own pudding to add a compliment. Seated next to him, Netta Pearce, Wilf's younger sister, batted her spoon at Ken, who poked his tongue out and gave the bowl another swipe. Netta shook her head.

'Honestly, Ken Allsop, I don't know why I'm marrying you! Eileen, you only got in yesterday morning. That's not enough time to make pudding. You brought it with you, didn't you?'

'I should have done that! I did make one in Hobart, but my sister Jean insisted I leave it behind for them. No, I made this one yesterday. The boat always gets in so early,' Eileen explained. 'And since it's not my first time here, I didn't need the whole lecture on how the Mission works and so on. Just a small amount of paperwork to sign. A new contract, as I'm taking Jessie March's position as headmistress. I'm so glad I had a job to come back to. With Elsie Wilson taking my job I wasn't sure I would.'

'We're glad to have you,' Essie said as she scooped a tiny serve of pudding into her toddler's mouth. It would soon be time for the children's afternoon nap, and they were getting crotchety. Christmas lunch with a group of adults was not a lot of fun.

'Mac doesn't give a lecture to anyone when they arrive,' Wilf said. 'He trusts everyone's been given the appropriate training in Australia, and anything they don't know they'll pick up on the job. He knows what a helpful bunch we all are.'

Reverend Lewis had retired while Eileen was in Hobart, and Reverend Laurie McArthur had replaced him. Eileen already thought of him as Mac, since that's how everyone referred to him. He was not new to the Methodist Mission, having spent five years here, first as Principal of George Brown College, then as the first Superintendent of Education for New Britain, in the early '30s, before family health issues had caused him to return to Australia.

'Well, not spending all day in the Chairman's office gave me plenty of time, and Mr Pearce...'

'Wilf, please. We've known each other more than three years

and it's Christmas. I'm sure we can forgo the formalities.'

Eileen smiled at him and he gave her a shy smile in return. '... Wilf took me shopping for ingredients.'

'It was worth it! This really is delicious!' Wilf said.

'It should normally have a month to cure, but I didn't have the time, of course.'

'Well, perhaps next year you could make it for me again and we can see whether that improves the flavour? Although how it could possibly be any better, I don't know.'

'Of course.'

They smiled at each other. Glancing across the table, Wilf caught Netta watching him. She had come to Rabaul after Gladys' death, ostensibly to look after him. The speed with which she had taken up with Ken Allsop had been a point of contention between them. But who was he to argue against her future happiness? Grief had hit him hard, particularly because he had not been there at the end of Gladys' illness, so he had thrown himself into work to cope. And, despite all the married couples and young families around, he had been content with that. But spending yesterday with Eileen had been like a breeze sweeping the corners of his mind clean. Dare he say he had even had fun?

'Did you get the camera equipment you were after at the photography shop?' Netta asked her brother.

Eileen and Wilf exchanged a look and both laughed.

'That didn't quite work out!' he replied. 'The shopkeeper wanted a ridiculous price for the special lens. When I asked him why it cost so much, he said so many people examined it, it had been damaged several times, and every time he had to send it to Sydney to be repaired...'

Eileen picked up the story seamlessly.

'And he calmly said that the cost of the repairs had to be added on to the price, as he was sure we would understand. I suppose I must be terribly silly because I didn't understand that reasoning!'

Wilf held her gaze.

'You are one of the least silly young women I know. Anyway, it will cost me less to buy the lens new from Sydney, including freight and insurance.'

'Well, I hope your camera is working without a new lens,' Laurie Linggood said. 'We really should take some snaps today. How about we take our coffee and fruit as a picnic and get a Christmas photo?'

As Essie organised the children for their nap, the others gathered up the remnants of their Christmas feast. The Linggood's houseboy fetched a mat woven from banana fronds so they would have something to sit on, and they were soon set up at the beautiful spot where they often had picnics, only a few hundred yards away from the mission house, overlooking the ocean. With the breeze blowing and the water glinting a pure aqua, it was a magical end to the afternoon.

Netta caught up with Wilf as he was carrying a tray of pineapple pieces down the stairs of the veranda. 'Do you have a Christmas gift for me?'

He looked at her in surprise. 'Yes, of course I do. I thought we could exchange gifts this evening.'

'Is it something suitable for...' she glanced over at the others, seated on the matting, 'say, another young woman of a similar age to me?'

'I don't think that would be appropriate.'

Netta tugged his arm to stop him getting too close to the

others, so their words wouldn't be heard. 'Forget appropriate. You are such an accountant! Do something spontaneous and fun for once! What is it? Tell me.'

'It's a shell brooch, in the shape of a seahorse.'

'Well, I'm sure I would have loved it, but you know what would be a better gift? Seeing you happy.' She reached out and took the tray from his hands. 'Go on, go and get it. You can take her on a little stroll along the cliffs.'

'Netta, she's quite a bit younger than me.'

'I know that. But she's intelligent and mature and honestly, Wilf, I haven't seen you smile so much in a long time. You need to bring someone to my wedding, so why not her?'

Wilf looked across at Eileen, her auburn hair glowing with fire in the afternoon sun. She exuded vibrant energy. He pushed his glasses up his nose. 'I don't think so. I'm not her type. I'm far too serious, and old.'

'Are you referring to the handsome young man she went off to marry as her type? Clearly, he wasn't. Trust me, Wilf. I know people.'

Netta was a good judge of character, that much was true. But more importantly, she wouldn't leave him alone until he did what she wanted. That had always been her way, ever since she'd been a small child, her big eyes and round face reminding him of an adorable little pixie. Though he'd been a serious teenager when she was little, she had always been able to lure him away from his books and study, to play amongst the roses. He wouldn't be able to escape her persuasion now.

As the afternoon wore on, Wilf tried to think of a way to give Eileen the gift, but nothing came to him and the little box was a weight in his pants pocket. Finally, Netta sidled up beside him.

'Give it to me.'

He knew better than to argue, handing his sister the box with the brooch. He watched as she drew Eileen away, to admire the view. They had a brief conversation, and the brooch changed hands. Eileen was smiling as she admired it. Then she said something to Netta, and came over.

'Thank you so much for my welcome gift. It's beautiful. Very unexpected, but I do appreciate the sentiment. I'm glad to be back. I was wondering if you'd like to come for dinner, next time you come to Vunairima? Miss March used to hold dinner parties, and since she's gone, I suppose it will be my responsibility now. We feel isolated out there at times, so the company would be wonderful.'

Wilf felt a strange lightness in his chest. 'Of course! Jack Trevitt has been asking if I'd come and deliver some teaching to the men at the college in Pidgin. Would a Saturday suit? It's the only day I can get away.'

They arranged the details, and Wilf promised to speak with Jack soon. Laurie approached just as they were finishing the discussion.

'Wilf, you did say you brought your camera, didn't you? We should get a photo of us all, to remember this lovely Christmas picnic.'

Wilf went to fetch his camera from the house, his step light. When he returned, he arranged everyone in a group, seated on the matting, with Eileen at the centre. Just as he snapped the photo, her hand reached up unconsciously to touch her new brooch, and a smile teased the corner of her mouth.

9th March 1940. Vunairima.

'Anybody home?'

Eileen and Ia Lo looked up from their preparations and smiled at each other. Their dinner party was about to begin.

'In the kitchen, Mel.'

Eileen quickly removed her apron and dropped it over a chair. She hurried out to the veranda. Their house boy had set the table perfectly, with all the best china and lovely ceramic teacups from Chinatown, painted with delicate brushwork.

Mel and Jack Trevitt, and Wilf Pearce, were standing at the top of the steps. They looked fresh, their clothes dry, and Eileen guessed they must have showered and changed after their afternoon's work. When she first arrived in Rabaul she had been astounded at how often people did this, but now it was just part of life in the tropics.

'Take a seat!' she told her guests, gesturing to the table. 'Miss Beale is unwell, so she's not able to join us, but Miss Wilson will be down in a minute.' She hurried to light the kerosene lamps, completing the picture-perfect table with soft lighting.

'I hope Ia Lo will be having dinner with us?' Wilf asked. In Rabaul, such a thing would not be permissible, but here in Vunairima Miss March had always bent the rules with gusto around socialising with the natives, especially Ia Lo, who had been teaching at the girls' school for well over a decade now, so Eileen felt no compunction about continuing that tradition. Ia Lo was a dear friend and co-conspirator for tonight's events.

'Of course. She's cooked us a traditional punapur to go with the duck.'

'Duck?' Jack said. 'One of your flock made the ultimate

sacrifice, did he?'

Eileen nodded solemnly. 'I'm afraid so. We had to have something special for an esteemed guest from the Rabaul circuit. How did your afternoon go with the men?'

Jack glanced at Wilf. 'Extremely well, of course. They love that Wilf is fluent in pidgin and Kuanua, so they can ask him all kinds of tricky theological questions and get a far more detailed answer than I can give.'

Mel looped her arm through his. 'Oh Jack, you do yourself a disservice. You're not so bad. You've been here coming up to four years now.'

'Ah, but Wilf is an old hand.'

'Less of the old, my friend,' Wilf said, while Eileen protested, 'Not old! Just more experienced.'

They glanced at each other and laughed. Their gaze held after the laughter had died away.

Elsie Wilson arrived, breaking the moment. 'Oh, so lovely to see you Mr Pearce! Hello, Mel and Jack.'

Even quiet Elsie enjoyed visitors to Vunairima, though she didn't miss socialising as much as Eileen did.

'Well, now we're all here, how about we take a seat?' Eileen ushered them to the table, just as Ia Lo came out onto the veranda carrying a parcel of banana leaves.

'The duck is ready, Eileen.'

Eileen smiled and hurried inside, plating up the drake and some crispy, golden baked potatoes. It had taken a while to get used to the old cast-iron wood stove, but she felt she had mastered its quirks now. She drained the peas, unfortunately tinned, not fresh, and by the time she had placed them in an enamel bowl, Ia Lo had returned.

'I have organised everyone at the table,' she said, giving Eileen a wink, before taking the bowl and heading outside. Following her with the heavy plate of duck and potatoes, Eileen protested.

'I don't know what you are talking about.'

At the table, Jack and Mel were seated on one side, with Wilf and Elsie on the other. Ia Lo took the remaining seat at the same end as Elsie, leaving Eileen to sit diagonally next to Wilf. They had just finished grace, and Eileen was asking Wilf to carve the duck, when they were interrupted by a raucous barking. Shelley, Eileen's kelpie, came running up the steps and ran straight to Wilf. Bouncing up and down, she barked furiously. Wilf reached out a hand to pat her but she stepped backwards and kept barking, her tail wagging at high speed.

'You'd think she'd be used to you by now,' Jack laughed. 'After all, you have been coming out here more frequently of late. I can't think why!' Mel glanced at Eileen, who cursed her pale skin as she blushed. 'But the students at the college are always glad for your visits.'

'Shelley, go to bed!' Eileen ordered, and the kelpie gave one final bark then trotted off to the stairs. 'I'm sorry Wilf, it's not that she doesn't like you. You saw how her tail was wagging. She's just jealous. She wants me all to herself.'

'Well, she might have to learn to share,' he said. Another silent communication passed between them. Eileen, realising the others were watching, reached for the tongs and began offering everyone potatoes. Ia Lo reached out and unwrapped the banana leaf parcel that was her contribution to the feast. Inside was taro soaked in coconut milk and baked to creamy perfection.

'Oh, Ia Lo, that looks absolutely delicious!' Elsie gushed.

As they ate the conversation ranged across many topics, from the running of the school and plantation at Vunairima to the six men who had recently begun their training as pastors. There had been more eruptions on the third of this month, but everyone agreed they were nothing like the eruptions of '37, which of course led to Elsie being told the story of Jack and Mel's dramatic wedding experience.

'Well, let's hope nothing like that happens during Netta and Ken's nuptials in a fortnight,' Wilf concluded.

'I'll certainly know better than to wear a crepe de chine frock on that occasion,' Eileen said, then had to explain to Elsie the disaster of her shrinking dress. Jack took Mel's hand.

'We were so glad none of our party were hurt,' he said, 'and that we can look back and laugh about it now. I think the shared travail brought everyone together, but I wouldn't want to go through anything that catastrophic again. We're so lucky the war is so far away.'

The others agreed, and the conversation turned, as it inevitably did nowadays, to the terrible conflict in Europe. As they discussed the news that arrived regularly in the papers, Eileen and Ia Lo cleared the table and fetched lemon meringue pudding from the kitchen. Last time they'd had a similar dinner Miss March had cooked and iced a rainbow cake and made cheese tarts, but this time Eileen's pudding would have to suffice, although she had made cheesy biscuits to finish with.

'You should play some music, Eileen,' Ia Lo told her. 'Here, let me take the pudding out while you set up the gramophone.'

Eileen only had a few records. She chose the Moonlight Sonata as that seemed to fit the current, slightly sombre mood and the gentle spill of light across the garden. She wound the gramophone by hand, since there was no electricity, and the flowing notes of Beethoven drifted through the darkness. The soft lamplight made for a rather romantic setting, and when she took her seat again, she locked eyes with Wilf, and felt her stomach flutter.

After pudding Ia Lo brought out the biscuits and Schweppes cordial. Ia Lo gave Eileen a knowing look and said she would go and check on the girls' quarters, wishing everyone a good night. Mel quickly made her own apologies, begging tiredness. When Jack made no move to join her, she laid one hand on his shoulder.

'Can you take me home, Jack?'

'Oh, I'm not quite...' He stopped and glanced at Mel's hand on his shoulder. 'Right, yes, we should be getting home. It's quite late, isn't it. Wilf, you can come over when you're ready, no rush. Just let yourself in.'

Elsie seemed slightly alarmed to find herself with much diminished company. She had only arrived a few days previously and was still in that awkward stage of getting to know everyone. She quickly made her excuses. And then it was just Eileen and Wilf.

'Well, that was a delicious meal. You know, Eileen, it's the highlight of my week when I get to come to Vunairima. Work has been calling me out this way a lot lately.'

'I did notice that.'

They smiled.

'Would you like to take a walk with me? I had something I wanted to ask you.' He glanced upwards. 'You know, the moon is so bright tonight I think I'll bring my camera. I might be lucky and get a decent photograph or two.'

Eileen quickly cleared the table as Wilf fetched his camera. Then they set out across the school garden, making their way towards the river. Around them, the cultivated plots gave way to luxuriant grass and clumps of bamboo, then taller trees twisting around each other, the moonlight making a glorious picture of the dense, tall tropical forest with all its shadows and curls. When they reached the river, it was a still, deep pool, its dark, unmoving depths in stark contrast to the white trunks of fallen trees spanning it.

They chatted about their work for a while. Wilf was making great progress on his Pidgin hymn book. With Eileen's interest in grammar they discussed some possibilities for the hymn he was currently working on. Eileen spoke of how the girls were going with their lessons, and how much she had learned from them in her time in Rabaul. As they walked alongside the river the conversation flowed easily from one topic to the next. They were both passionate about their teaching and held the local people in high regard. Around them, fireflies danced through the trees like luminous stars come to earth.

Finally, they reached the beach. From Vunairima the road followed the water's edge around the bay for a great distance, so their view was of a great sweep of ocean glistening with streaks of moonlight. Overhead, the moon was huge and golden, the navy sky sprinkled with a few glimmering dots of light. Across the bay they could see dark blue mountains which, even in the night, were capped by masses of white clouds. Eileen didn't suffer from homesickness much since she loved her work, but the mountains made her think of Mount Wellington in Hobart and for a moment she was overcome with longing.

'Eileen,' Wilf said softly. She turned to him, thinking how much she admired his gentle nature. He was well respected by all the staff. Even his admonishments, when ministers hadn't done their financial record keeping correctly, were kind but firm. And he knew everything, and everyone. The entire mission relied on him. Eileen realised she had drifted into her thoughts, and brought herself back to the present, focusing anew on Wilf's words. 'I wanted to ask you if you would accompany me to Netta's wedding? I mean, not just... giving you a lift in the ute or... I mean, actually... attending together... um, sitting together and...'

Eileen thought it was adorable that someone so competent and experienced could be so tongue tied. She had to put him out of his misery. 'Oh, you silly thing. Of course I will. There's nothing I'd like more.'

'Really?'

She nodded.

'Well, Netta will be pleased.'

'Netta will?' It came out sharper than she intended.

'Oh... I'm not asking you because Netta wanted me to. Although she does. But only because she wants to see me happy.'

Eileen reached a hand up to his cheek. 'I want to see you happy too.'

He placed his hand over hers, then leaned in. Their lips met, and the fluttering returned to Eileen's stomach. This felt right, and magical. More than that, it felt inevitable. She felt like she had come home.

They lingered in the moonlight a long time, side by side, talking of everything and nothing, sharing a few more gentle kisses. It was a perfect night and Eileen wished it could go on forever. But tomorrow and the next day would bring more perfect moments.

'We should get some sleep,' Wilf finally said.

'You haven't got your photo! You should take one of the moon. It's so huge and beautiful tonight.'

'I can think of something more glorious,' he responded, brushing her hair away. 'Let me take a photo of you in the moonlight, so we can keep this memory forever.'

Eileen stood where Wilf asked her to, with the bay behind her and the golden moon, almost as bright as day, catching her smile and giving a glint of ruby to her hair. Eileen laughed just as he snapped the photo, her heart brimming with joy.

20th May 1940. Vunairima.

Eileen My Dearest,

It's only a couple of hours since I finished off my last scribble to you my Darling but since Ainui is to come in and collect the truck to bring Mrs Trevitt to Rabaul, I'm going to make sure of having something ready to send out to you my precious. You must get so disappointed Sweet one when you get a letter such as I had to send out to you today. But Darling I do have to work sometimes and today seems to be one of these "sometimes". On the other hand some of our workers seem to think that when they have nothing at all to do – the very best place to do it is in my office (that's the penalty of being so popular). Now if you were to come into my office to fill in some of your spare time I'd be thrilled to bits or if Mr Oakes had chosen a time when I wasn't wanting to write to you, it wouldn't have been so bad darling. However that's the joys of being a secretary sweetheart. You'll probably learn lots more about that later on.

You know you are such a lovely sweetheart. You write

such wonderful letters it makes me feel positively ashamed of the notes that I have sent out to you. I even forgot to say thank you to you Darling for the plants that you gave me on Saturday night; in fact now that I have time to think, I don't seem to have said anything in that letter except that I was busy. Still, I'll try and make up for it this time precious.

I forgot to say, Dearest, that I am real pleased that you told Mrs Trevitt how things stood. They are so jolly nice that it seemed a pity not to give them some hint of what was going on.

I must have a very bad influence on you, Darling, or is it just that you are seeking relief from my pesterings, that you have started drinking. Even if it is only tea Sweetheart. It's wonderful of you to want to do that for me, my precious, but don't you think that it would be much easier for you to teach me to drink coffee? I sometimes think I could learn to like coffee just as much as I like tea, particularly coffee as you make it. Still, here's Pilip with my afternoon tea now, so I won't give up drinking tea just yet.

Now that has put the show away. I'm letting you see that you are taking me away from my work. Spend half the morning trying to write to you, and then as soon as the Chairman leaves in the afternoon, I start another letter to you. Still, you are well worth it Darling and when you come to live in Rabaul, I'll be dodging in every now and then throughout the day just to see how my darling little sweetheart is getting along.

Yes sweetest, if you get word from your Dad on Saturday that he is quite agreeable, I'll certainly tell Nan, but I'm not too sure that the following weekend would be the best for you to come to Rabaul, particularly if you want to spend any time with me. Of course I may be wrong in thinking that should be one of your reasons for coming to Rabaul for a weekend. I have been asked to preach at George Brown College Vunairima on the morning of Sunday the

2nd June and also to spend the weekend at Vunairima. I haven't really accepted yet, but I had almost made up my mind to accept. You would hardly believe, Sweetheart, how the invitations to spend weekends away from Rabaul have been pouring in, lovely, and they all seem to lead me in the one direction. I have been asked to spend the next weekend at Vunakabi. If your Dad says "Yes", I think I'll accept – that is if you think you could put up with another weekend like the last one when I was out that way. If your Dad says "No", I suppose I should decline all invitations and spent Saturday and Sunday at the "Pacific" or the "Cosmopolitan".

I don't know that my sister is in a position to say anything. In the first place she came up here to spend a holiday with me and ran off with another man and then she has been so busy looking after him since she came back, that she has almost forgotten that she has a brother. Not that I blame her Dearest. I don't – I'm just beginning to realise what it is like to be perfectly in love with the sweetest girl in the world, and to know she is really in love with you.

That was indeed very nice of Mrs Trevitt, Sweetheart, I'm afraid I shall be availing myself of her often, very often if the answer on Saturday is "Yes". I can't understand though Darling – why she should even guess you were really proud of me. You are not really proud of me are you Pet? What foolish ideas some folk get. It's me who is very proud of you and proud to be able to call you my own Darling Sweetheart.

Well precious, I have quite a break away from this letter. I went and planted out the peanuts we got on Saturday, then had a bath and some tea and now here I am back to spend a few minutes with you before I get down to study.

I am real pleased Darling to know that you are feeling so happy, calm and contented. I want you to be that way always Dearie. I am so sorry Darling that I did not notice that you were so tired out on Saturday night. I'll have to be more watchful in future and not stay so long when you are not up to the mark. Anyhow Sweetheart you must not let yourself get so tired. You've got to remember Darling, that if we are to be married in six or seven months' time you've got to be in perfect health. So Darling, you just look after yourself for a little while longer and then I'll take over and do all the taking care that is necessary. I'm glad to see you have made some good resolutions for this week. Now you just see you carry them out. Early to bed every night – There is no need to worry about me, Darling, there isn't any mental strain for me in what we were talking about. It was merely that I wanted to make sure about you, my precious little Sweetheart.

I'm so glad that you started off so well last night Dearest and went to bed early and had a real good night's sleep. You need it darling, after all those nights when you were not able to get to sleep.

Well Dearest, the "Macdhui" came in about 8.30 pm on Saturday night and all the folk look remarkably well. Mr and Mrs Oakes and family go on to Kavieng tonight, and as the boat is going direct this time they should be home in a day or so. Miss Jenkins looks well although is still the same. I think she had planned to go to Kaukau with Miss Beale on Sunday morning but I went along about 8.30 to see if one wanted her luggage and they mentioned they were going to Kaukau, so I said "Oh you can't do that, I'm preaching." So Miss Jenkins wouldn't – or didn't come – Said something about one shouldn't go if the preacher didn't want them to.

There wasn't any mail at all on the "Macdhui" as it left Sydney the day after the E & A Boat which means that I will have to wait for the next E & A about the middle of June for my rose plants. I thought I'd be able to get them in this week, however they should still be blooming nicely when I bring my *little wife home in a few months' time.*

Oh Darling Eileen, I do love you so much. The days seem to just drag slowly by when we are apart and yet Saturday afternoon and evening go that quickly – I hardly seem to be with you before it's time to go home again. Gee I'll be glad when there isn't any more need to leave you. You don't realise Sweetheart how much I love you or what you really mean to me dearest. I just live for the weekends with you and the thought of having you constantly by me makes me wish that I could just go to sleep one night and wake up to find it was November or December with all the synod work completed and you and I on our way to home and perfect happiness.

I'd just love to go on writing to you my darling, but I must do some study tonight. You are my own Darling little Sweetheart, Eileen and I love you far greater than I have ever loved anyone. You are just everything to me lovely.

Look after yourself Precious and off to bed early each night till Saturday when I will be able to bring you some very joyful news.

All my love to you Eileen, my own Darling Sweetheart and a great big kiss sweetie.

From your Dearest

Wilf

Eileen carefully folded the letter and held it close to her heart for a moment. Typical Wilf, to joke about people not coming because he was preaching. Those who didn't know him well assumed he was a typical accountant, with no sense of humour, so they took his comments seriously. Eileen loved his ability to keep a completely straight face under those circumstances. She would have to set Miss Jenkins straight and encourage her to hear Wilf speak on another occasion. He had the gift of being authoritative but gentle: an excellent preacher.

The letter was a wonderful reminder of the special weekend just past. Though she cherished every moment they spent together, she ran over these recent memories in her mind often, smiling to herself as she stored them in her memories as though wrapping them in tissue paper to be preserved forever. Last Saturday Wilf had picked her up in the car and taken her to Rabaul, where they had gone shopping at the Ra Bung for fresh fruit, and at the Beeps store for an assortment of biscuits, tinned pork and cordial to make a strange sort of picnic. Then they had driven to Raluana. The Linggoods were out at the baseball for the afternoon, so Eileen and Wilf had the stunning view over the bay all to themselves as they enjoyed a late picnic, or an early supper. After they had eaten, Wilf had seemed strangely shy and Eileen teased him about it. Finally, he admitted what was on his mind.

'Eileen, my darling, I can't believe you've come into my life, and that you love me. I know it's only been two months since we first spoke of our feelings, but at the same time it feels like the time between then and now is an eternity because we've had to be apart so much. I don't want to be apart from you anymore.' He had knelt, the sunset forming an extraordinary palette of rose and amber behind him. 'Will you do me the honour of being my wife?'

With Eric, Eileen had put off even accepting a relationship, and with hindsight she recognised her reluctance around wedding planning should have been a clue that her feelings remained ambiguous. Breaking off the engagement had been a relief. With Wilf, she accepted instantly.

'Yes! Of course, yes!'

Wilf had surprised her then, holding out a string of tabu, the Tolai shell money used not only for trade, but for special occasions. 'These are usually given to the bride on her wedding day,' Wilf told her, 'but Akulia said it would be acceptable to use them as a stand in for an engagement ring.'

He had placed the tabu around her neck, and they had stood together watching the sun set over the paradise they called their home, painting the sky in exquisite, fiery colours so that the crystal sea seemed half aflame. Then Wilf had fetched a newspaper from the car, to Eileen's confusion, until he showed her advertisements for rings they could order from Sydney. They had spent some time choosing one, and discussing how Wilf should approach Eileen's father, Claude. Wilf was eager to send a telegram to ask him for permission to marry as soon as possible, but Eileen warned that Claude wouldn't waste money on a telegram in return, so his reply might take some time to arrive, by letter on the mail plane.

Neither of them had felt the need to wait a long time to be married, and even now, days later, Eileen felt no concern that their engagement would be a short one. There was no question in her mind that she and Wilf were well matched: equally passionate about their work with and fondness for the Tolai, both with a love of languages, music and gardening. Her temperament was decidedly fierier than his, but his gentleness was a blessing in her life, she decided. She had always appreciated the way her sister Verna had been the water to her fire growing up, and she admired Wilf's calm, organised energy enormously.

Eileen picked up the envelope the letter had come in, drawing out the photos it contained. Wilf must have had them developed during the week, because she had only posed for them on the weekend. Both showed her in her light blue going-to-town cotton frock, with its lovely, flared skirt, and her best hat, freshly decorated by Ia Lo with hibiscus. Shelley had been dancing round her at the time, eager to claim her attention, and in both photos, Wilf had captured the kelpie standing on her hind legs, paws against Eileen's hands.

'I hope Shelley learns not to be jealous,' Wilf had said afterwards. 'We'll be spending a lot more time together now.'

'She's a smart dog,' Eileen said. 'I'm sure she'll realise if we're married she'll get twice as much attention. Don't worry – she'll come to love you as much as I do.'

9 - Wedding and Work

Eileen and Wilf

Saturday 1ˢᵗ February 1941. Hobart.

JAPAN'S NEW TONE.

Mr. Matsuoka's statement, to Press correspondents in Tokyo this week is being received with widespread interest in Britain and America. Compared with that of earlier utterances from himself and other spokesmen in Tokyo, especially since the signing of Japan's treaty of alliance with Hitler, its tone is one of modulation to fit a diplomatic uneasiness. The Japanese Foreign Minister disclaims any desire on Japan's part for "conquest, oppression, and exploitation," and he regards as "unfortunate" that some of his country-men advocate those things. His assertion that the whole of Japan's Greater East Asia programme is entirely removed from territorial ambition would carry greater weight if Japanese troops were not still concentrated in Formosa and Hainan, and were not continuing their activities in Indo-China; and it totally ignores his Government's having pledged itself to Hitler's cause.

The Sydney Morning Herald, Thursday, December 12, 1940.

Eileen's mother gave her daughter's cheek a powdery kiss.

'You look so beautiful,' she whispered, clutching Eileen's hand for a moment. 'It makes me so happy to see you like this.'

Eileen gave her mother a glowing smile, then swept her train into the waiting car. Marie and Jean piled in next to her. Up front Verna sat next to their father, Claude Brabin. Once everyone was in place, he saluted his wife, then tooted the horn.

'Off we go then, taking my daughter to be married.'

Claude pulled out onto Patrick Street and headed towards Elizabeth Street, tooting the horn every block or so.

'Where did you get the car, Dad?' Eileen asked.

'Borrowed it off a friend.'

Marie leaned in and whispered, 'Someone he met at the horses probably.'

'What kind is it?' Jean asked.

'An Austin. Runs beautifully. I might get one myself when things pick up again.' He patted the dash.

Jean pursed her lips.

'Why you needed all of us as bridesmaids I don't know!' Jean tugged at the lavender taffeta of her skirt. 'Marie and Verna would have been perfectly acceptable.'

'You're my baby sister, Jean,' Eileen said. 'How could I not include you? And underneath that cranky exterior, I know you'd do anything for me.'

'Just don't ask me to babysit when you start popping out children!'

Eileen laughed. 'I'll name the baby after you – then you'll have to help out!'

'Jean's just grumpy because she hates to dress up. She's

always far happier when she's in her nurses' outfit,' Marie teased. 'Your frock is unbelievably beautiful, Eileen. I'm so glad you decided to have a proper wedding. I remember being absolutely heartbroken when you talked about only having a simple thing with that Eric person. That was a lucky escape, wasn't it?'

Eileen had forgotten about her plans with Eric. Buying an off-white velvet dinner gown, which would be useful afterwards, keeping the wedding breakfast small... she had told herself it was because a man must feel silly all dressed up in front of too many people, but she couldn't wait to see Wilf in his suit, with half of Hobart watching. He had told her how proud he would be to stand up beside her and share their love with her friends and family. Now she realised her wish for a small, no fuss ceremony with Eric was yet another indication of her instincts warning her against the match.

'I suppose it was.'

Eric had left all the marriage plans to her, but this time she and Wilf had discussed every detail. The dress was to be a surprise though. Eileen had ordered samples from David Jones in Sydney, thinking she might choose a white broderie-Anglaise or organdie, but when they arrived, she had immediately fallen in love with a magnolia satin embossed with the faintest rose-leaf brocade. She had the material sent to her friend Joan Fish, then posted a letter with her measurements. By the time she and Wilf arrived in Hobart, having picked up Wilf's mother in Sydney on the way, all that remained to be done was the fitting and final detail work. Joan had surprised her with a beautiful perle d'or rose headdress to attach to the veil. She had also made the bridesmaids dresses, in lavender, with a row of tiny buttons down the bodice and a royal purple ribbon around the waist, with floral headpieces in the same colour combination. Jean kept tugging at everything.

'Leave it alone,' Verna ordered. 'You look very calm for someone who's about to be married, Eileen.'

'I feel very calm. Wilf is such a kind person, and we get on so well. I know we'll be happy.'

'It seems rather rushed,' Jean said.

'Oh, but we've known each other over four years,' Eileen said calmly. 'It may have only become romantic recently, but I have admired him for a long time.'

Marie patted Eileen's hand whilst also elbowing Jean. Growing up with three sisters, she had developed many skills, and dealing with two siblings simultaneously was one of them.

'It's war time, silly,' Marie scolded Jean. 'Rushed is normal. Who knows what might happen? There was an article in The Mercury only yesterday saying Japan might try to take strategic positions in the Pacific. You don't suppose that could mean New Britain, do you?'

Eileen felt a strange sensation, like an ice-cold finger running down her spine.

'The article also said it was probably just propaganda...' Jean said. 'I think "noise to drive away the dragon" was the phrase they used, which I thought was a rather colourful expression. The Japanese are trying to intimidate Britain and America. They don't have the capability for going to war, according to the article.'

Claude's voice boomed from the front. 'Let's not talk about war. Today is my eldest daughter's special day. We'll only talk about happy things.'

For once, Eileen was relieved her father had intervened. She often butted heads with him, but the talk of Japan unsettled her stomach. Today was a joyful day, and she didn't want to think about the endless swirling rumours about the war. Besides, she knew the constant conflict with her father wore out her mother, whose health was always fragile. She had vowed as she reached adulthood that she would not put Elsa through that anymore.

As they drove along Elizabeth Street, Claude continued to toot the horn. That and the white satin ribbon bedecking the car caused passers-by to offer sedate waves and smiles. Eileen thought of how this experience would be if the wedding were to happen in Rabaul. The school community would want to hold their own celebration. Her students would be terribly excited, no doubt making endless wreaths of beautiful frangipani and crotons, and the men would probably prepare hymns to sing, with their exquisite harmonies. They would cover her in flowers and weep with happiness, expressing their joy far more openly than Australians did, and there would be dancing and feasting. It would have been lovely to have a Rabaul wedding, but her family would have been heartbroken, since she was the first of the sisters to be married.

'I can't wait to hear Gladys Morris sing,' Marie gushed. 'She's become rather popular for performances around Hobart since you've been away, Eileen. You're lucky she's a school friend. It would be awfully difficult to get her to come otherwise.'

'I don't suppose I'll get to hear the song properly, since we'll be signing the register then.'

'And I can't believe you managed to book the Grotto tea rooms,' Marie continued. 'It's the most popular place for receptions! Their advertisements always say they enjoy a high-class clientele.'

'What a shame,' Jean said. In response to Marie's puzzled look, she continued, 'well, you won't be able to come in then, will you?'

'Haven't you two grown out of your bickering?' Verna snapped, and changed the subject before her sisters could start a row. 'You'll have a mother-in-law now. What's she like?'

Eileen gave the back of Verna's head a grateful smile, hoping her sister might catch it in the mirror. 'Oh, she's a delightful, gentle person. I can see where Wilf gets his kind nature from. She's already given us our gift, as she said she couldn't wait. The most beautiful tablecloths which she hand embroidered, and some lovely crochet work too. I think she is just so glad to see Wilf marry again.'

Jean frowned. 'Don't you feel his dead wife watching you?'

'Jean!' Marie exclaimed, at the same time as Claude announced they had arrived. He pulled the car to the curb and Verna hopped out of the front, whilst Jean and Marie climbed from the back. Then Claude reached in and offered his hand to Eileen. She hung her train over her arm and followed her sisters, who then took a minute to make sure everything was smoothed and in place.

Jean stood in front of Eileen, checking her headdress wasn't tilted. Eileen grabbed her wrist.

'Wilf's first wife Gladys was a lovely lady. She was very kind to me when I first arrived in Rabaul. I think she'd be pleased Wilf has found happiness again. So, if she is watching over me, I'm sure she's smiling.'

Jean nodded. 'You'll make a wonderful wife. I'm sorry I've been rude – you know how I hate dressing up.'

Verna was already halfway to the church door. Jean took her

place with Marie behind Eileen. Both picked up her train, taking a moment to arrange it to perfection. Once they were done, Claude looped Eileen's arm over his.

'Are you ready?'

Eileen looked down at her dress. It was beautiful, the fabric shimmering softly in the afternoon light, and she loved it so much. The church looked perfectly picturesque, with its white picket fence, diamond-paned panelling on the pitched roof and large gothic stained-glass windows.

'I'm ready.'

They walked along the tree-lined path to the arched front entrance. After a final flurry of arrangements, Verna took a step forward and gave the signal. Beethoven's Moonlight Sonata began playing on the organ. Eileen and Wilf had agreed that was far more appropriate for them than the bridal waltz.

As Eileen passed through the doorway, all eyes turned to her, but she saw only Wilf, looking dashing in his black tuxedo and crisp white shirt and bowtie. He was shorter than all three of his groomsmen, but then Eileen was far shorter than any of her sisters, so she thought that was quite suitable. She made her way up the aisle sedately, although she had to fight the temptation to do a little skip.

Light from the stained-glass windows fell across the men waiting at the altar, so that for a long moment Wilf was washed in a wavering blue light, like moonlight on the ocean at Talili Bay. Then a shadow must have passed over the sun, because the light dropped away and for a brief instant his face was drained of colour, almost skeletal in its paleness. Eileen felt a cold stabbing in her chest, but then the light returned, bathing Wilf with gold and red, and the ominous sensation was gone.

When she reached Wilf's side, Eileen gave Claude a kiss and he took his place in the front row with her mother, Elsa. Wilf whispered under his breath, 'You look radiant, my darling.'

His eyes sparkled so, it reminded her of the fireflies in the jungle.

As the pastor began the Methodist ceremony, Wilf whispered, 'Do they ever have volcanic eruptions in Hobart?'

Eileen suppressed a giggle then whispered, as the pastor gave them a disapproving look. 'No, I think we're quite safe here.'

Mid-February 1941. Conningham, Tasmania.

A friend had loaned the couple her cottage at Conningham for their honeymoon, so Wilf and Eileen spent a relaxing two weeks walking in the bush and on the beach, with Shelley for company. They had decided to bring the kelpie to Hobart with them and leave her with Marie in the short term since married life would mean a change of house and work situation. Eileen dreaded saying farewell to her pup when they returned to Rabaul, so she had convinced Wilf to let Shelley join them at the beach. Fortunately, the kelpie seemed to have changed her attitude to him since their arrival in Tasmania, following him around constantly, so he agreed without hesitation.

It was strange for both not to have the constant demands of running the Mission and the girls' school, but they set those thoughts aside and took pleasure in every one of the long, warm days of the Tasmanian summer. The holiday would be over soon enough and their responsibilities would resume. For now though, they could concentrate on each other.

On their first morning Wilf was sitting in the garden when Eileen brought out a tray of coffee. She placed it on the table and gave her new husband a kiss on the forehead.

'What's this? You've made coffee?'

Eileen poured him a cup and passed it over, then made up her own. She was just about to take a sip when Wilf leaned forward in his chair. 'Is that a bandicoot?'

At the end of the garden was a potato patch, which they had already raided once to make a delicious mash for their dinner. Amongst the leaves something was moving. Shelley became instantly alert but obeyed when Eileen ordered her inside the cottage. After making sure the door was securely latched, Eileen took Wilf's proffered hand and they crept closer.

There were two of the creatures, one foraging in the dirt with its snout, the other holding a potato in its paws. Wilf crouched down and peered closely.

'They look different from the ones in New Britain. The snout's longer, for a start. Tasmanian bandicoots! I wish I had my camera. They're so busy having their breakfast I could easily get a close up snap.'

He was right. The little creatures didn't seem at all aware humans were so close. Eileen crouched beside him and took his hand again.

'See how it's digging with its snout?' he continued. 'Our dear linguist friend Laurie Linggood told me that to dig that way is "to bandicoot". Most creatures would use their paws, but these little things do things a bit differently. Of course, in Rabaul they're more passionate about taro than potato. Probably because it's sweeter.'

'There are a lot of differences between Tasmania and

Rabaul,' Eileen said. Wilf glanced at her.

'Now that you're here with all your family and friends, and the cooler weather, do you wish you could stay?' He helped her stand and they returned to the table.

Eileen picked up her coffee and sipped it, thinking about her answer. 'I do love it here. I miss Hobart when I'm in Rabaul. I think about how beautiful it is, with Mt Wellington and the river. And I miss my family, although they drive me crazy sometimes.'

'I bet you enjoy having electricity and all the modern conveniences.'

She reached for the sugar and added another spoonful to her coffee. 'It's funny, you know. Those conveniences are nice, I won't deny it. To be able to buy meat that doesn't taste of ammonia is an utter luxury. And hot chips! But when I'm here it all feels a bit... much. We don't have half these things in Vunairima, but we manage. Everyone is usually so happy at the school, except at the end of the year of course, when they weep endlessly because their friends have gone home to the islands or New Ireland. And life just seems simpler. Dad's always got some drama or other going on, and there's all the constant talk of the men away at war in Europe. I'm glad war hasn't come to the islands.'

Wilf sipped his drink and pulled a face. 'You know, my darling sweetheart, I am trying, but I'm just not sure I'll get the hang of this coffee thing.' He put his cup down and his expression turned serious. 'I've been talking to Harold Page about the rumours that Japan might enter the war. I tend to avoid rumours, as you know, but Harold's brother has been in government, and he's part of the British War Committee now, so Harold hears things from reliable sources. Apparently, there's talk of the islands forming a kind of barrier to stop the Japanese coming to Australia. If that happens, we might be in the line of fire, sweetie.'

Eileen stood and began pacing. 'Oh, I hope not. That would be terrible. What would the Tolai do? How would we protect them?'

Wilf stood and took her in his arms. 'Don't worry yourself about that now. We're on our honeymoon. I must admit, the rumours are the real reason I thought we should bring Shelley to Tasmania with us. I didn't want to upset you with something that might not happen but I'm bringing it up now because I wondered... seeing you with all your family... would you rather we made our home here? Especially now you've had to give up your job to be married.'

Eileen looked up at him and took a deep breath. 'Wilf, my dearest, Hobart doesn't feel like home anymore. Our community is in Rabaul. I can still be part of the Lotu, helping the Tolai with gardening and small medical tasks, and I can preach, just like the other wives. I know you wouldn't want to leave your work either.'

He leaned in and kissed her deeply. 'You're right,' he said when they finally broke apart. 'It's my calling, not just a job. And if war does come to the islands, I couldn't abandon my Tolai friends.'

'Then it's decided. We finish our furlough and go home, just as we planned. I do wish you'd been honest with me about the reason you wanted Shelley to come with us! But you must understand, I don't intend to leave her here for long – once we've moved in together and sorted everything out, I couldn't bear to be away from her any longer.'

Wilf brushed one wild auburn curl from her face. 'I suspect, my darling, that if I wanted you or the pup to stay here, I wouldn't have the smallest chance of convincing you.'

'No, you wouldn't,' Eileen said and kissed him.

April to June 1941. Touring Tasmania.

After the holiday part of their furlough ended, all too quickly, Eileen and Wilf travelled Tasmania on Overseas deputation, giving lantern talks at many small towns. Eileen remembered Reverend Burton, the General Secretary, describing once how crucial these talks were to the Mission's work, as they encouraged Australian congregations to make donations of money and gifts. Gift boxes sent to the islands were always received with excitement, although their contents were ordinary, including soap and Eucalyptus oil, bandages, writing pads and so on. Still, they were the sort of things that were hard to come by in any sort of quantity in New Britain, so everyone gained a new appreciation of them. The only problem with the gift boxes was that they were passed around all the stations and schools, starting with those closest to Rabaul and making their way further out, so some of the circuits only received dregs. Percy Clark considered this something of an injustice, but Eileen saw it as a challenge to give her all in her talks while back in Tasmania, so Australian Methodists would be inspired to send more supplies.

Wilf had converted many of his photos into slides which they used to accompany their presentation. These were received with great interest, especially those showing the Tolai in their ceremonial dress for the Warataba, or with the huge woven baskets they used for fishing. Eileen was annoyed at the somewhat condescending questions of some folk, which reminded her of the superior attitude some plantation managers and civil administration staff held toward the natives of New Britain. In her experience, the Tolai were dignified, intelligent and true friends. Ia Lo was one of her dearest friends. But recognising the importance of her role as a representative of the Overseas Mission, Eileen always answered even the most dreadful questions calmly and kindly.

She and Wilf made a good team during these presentations, sharing the time and telling stories as a pair, their voices overlapping as each added new detail about life in the faraway Australian Mandated District of New Guinea. Their audience was interested not only in the work of the church overseas – both the preaching and the teaching, as Wilf joked – but the lifestyle of the natives. They particularly enjoyed hearing about things like festivals and superstitions. Eileen didn't like to focus too much on the magic practiced by the Tolai, something the missionaries worked hard to reduce through education, but for a Tasmanian audience this was one of the most fascinating aspects of what she spoke about.

If she downplayed it in her speeches, Eileen found there were always countless questions about it, so she spoke openly about the natives' belief in evil spirits, and how at the school their education taught them another way of seeing things. She liked to paint a picture of how, after the younger girls had been there for a term or so, they would play a game of running around the native huts laughing as they shouted the names of the evil spirits they no longer feared.

Wilf and Eileen both took pleasure in giving the talks, though it made them miss their friends and home in Rabaul. Those who came along frequently told them afterwards how enjoyable they had found the whole experience. Working was not the same as relaxing by the beach in Conningham, but at least they were together and that made everything perfect. Once they were done, they would be returning to Rabaul to establish a home together. Eileen had never been happier in her life.

Early July 1941. Onboard the *Macdhui*[1].

Eileen bent over the railing and vomited. Wilf could tell she had tried terribly hard to hold it in as he helped her along the deck. Given the choice, she would never have broken the bounds of propriety in this way, but the urge had come over her so suddenly she had not been able to stop herself.

'My darling, do what you must! I'll take you to lie down as soon as you can move.'

Wilf passed Eileen his handkerchief and she wiped her mouth. 'My stomach is churning, it feels like someone is squeezing my throat, and I'm hot all over. All I want is to lie down in my bed. I've never been so miserable in my life.'

They had come up on deck to watch the sunset, which had been spectacular, but Eileen had taken ill almost immediately. During their steamer trip across Bass Straight from Tasmania to Sydney the weather had been far rougher than this – they had experienced a good tossing about – but she had not been this ill. She usually travelled extremely well.

Wilf reached for her forehead, finding it warm to the touch. 'Is it something you ate? Did you have the prawns?' A hint of

---

[1] Due to the risk of Japanese interception, by mid-1941 shipping times were no longer published so it's impossible to pinpoint the exact date .

dread entered his voice, though he tried to hide it. His thoughts flashed back to Gladys' last days in Rabaul, and how helpless he had felt. 'Could it be a malaria flare up?'

Eileen reached for both his hands and clasped them together. 'It's not malaria, my dearest. Don't fret about that. I was going to wait a little longer, until I knew things were safe, to tell you...' Her face crumpled and she turned again, grasping the railing once more, but nothing came.

Staring at her back, Wilf's thoughts raced and a foolish grin lit up his face. 'A little longer... my sweetheart, you're not... are you?'

Eileen turned to him. 'Yes, Wilf, you're going to be a father.'

He pulled her into his arms and spun her around, laughing out loud. When he placed her down, she reeled a little. 'Oh, sweetie, I'm sorry! I didn't mean to add to your sickness.'

'No, it's fine. I'm okay. But I would like to lie down now.'

Wilf put an arm round her and led her to their cabin.

'How long have you known? Oh, my dear, did you know while we were in Sydney? All that running around we did visiting my family, and I made you come and visit Reverend Burton with me at head office. If I'd know I would have insisted you rest, instead of dragging you all over the place.'

'It's fine. I expected that sort of thing when I married the business manager. And I've only been certain the last few days.'

'We'll have to take you to see a doctor as soon as we get home. You're so tiny, my dearest. Can you really carry a baby?'

Eileen laughed. 'Wilf darling, women have been doing this since time began. I'm sure I'll manage. I've managed everything else so far.'

'I'm going to be a father!'

He hovered over her as she settled on the bed, then fetched her some water, and found a cool cloth for her brow. Finally, Eileen told him firmly that all she needed was rest. In no time she had drifted off to sleep, but Wilf was too excited himself to lie down. He made his way up to the deck.

Night had fallen and the ocean was an endless mass of darkness, with only a single broken beam of light from the moon revealing its cresting and falling. Wilf strolled along the deck, past small groups of travellers and couples seeking a romantic moment. Finally, he found a section of railing that offered complete quiet. Looking out at the unchanging sea, he offered a quiet prayer, then let his thoughts roam.

Netta had written in April that Laurie Mac was worried they would be away too long, and that he wasn't coping with his role as Chairman without Wilf there. Wilf didn't think that was because he was completely indispensable, nor that Mac was incapable of the job – he was a compassionate, thoughtful leader. No, this was more that Mac was still reasonably new to the role and relied on Wilf to find a path through some of the complexities.

And the work was becoming more difficult. In November last year the Australian War Cabinet had put forward the proposal that warships of the Netherlands East Indies should regularly visit Rabaul, as a disincentive to any military action, and this year they had begun moving troops in. At first, Wilf had missed the news, being on his honeymoon in the remote reaches of Tasmania, so he hadn't seen the announcement of the 'Malay barrier', a War Cabinet plan to send troops to Ambon, Timor and New Britain, and to reinforce those already in Singapore. The idea was that, should Japan enter the war, these forces would create a sort of early warning system to protect Australia from any moves south. But as a linguist, Wilf couldn't help noticing that these units, Sparrow Force, Lark Force and Gull Force, were all named after small, non-predatory birds. He hoped that was no reflection of their size or capabilities.

After the honeymoon, he had kept pace with events concerning New Britain in the paper, though Hobart's Mercury didn't always consider these relevant to local affairs. Laurie Linggood had posted him the *Pacific Islands Monthly* regularly, and these had been full of the news of the arrival of Lark Force in Rabaul. Advance forces began arriving in March and the main body of the company arrived on Anzac Day. *You won't know the place*, Laurie had warned. *Soldiers everywhere, digging trenches, taking over the clubs and filling the Regent when there's a film running.*

Japan had not yet entered the war, but speculation was growing in the Australian newspapers. Wilf thought all the signs were there that if they did, Rabaul was in their sights. For the last three years members of the Rabaul community who were from Japan had been claiming family illness and returning home. There should be nothing suspicious about that, but it had become more and more frequent. Perhaps more worrying, there had been a noticeable increase in Japanese ships arriving in Simpson Harbour in the last year. The sight of Japanese tourists moving around town, taking photos, had become common. But they weren't taking photos of the beautiful sights, like the harbour and the botanical gardens. Instead, Wilf had seen them photographing specific buildings, as well as warehouses and wharves.

Wilf and Eileen had talked about all of this often, but there had never been any question of returning to Rabaul, to their home. Now, knowing Eileen was pregnant, Wilf began to wonder whether that was the wisest choice. The news had shifted his perspective utterly. Eileen was a strong-willed, independent woman, deeply committed to the Tolai people. But if there was any risk of the Japanese coming to Rabaul, he would want not only her, but their child, to be as far away as possible. The problem would be convincing her of that. He chuckled to himself, thinking of some of the arguments he'd already lost.

They were on the final leg of their journey home. There was no going back now. But once they reached Rabaul, Wilf decided he would need to have some serious conversations about the future. The first would be with Harold Page, his friend, and the Assistant Administrator of the New Guinea District. Harold regularly attended the Rabaul church, sometimes acting as a lay preacher. He was a man of morals, and Wilf knew he'd get a straight answer from Harold. Then he would need to talk with Mac about the future of the Mission. Ensuring the safety of his wife and baby was the highest priority. Whether he would leave his job, his vocation, was another question altogether.

10 - The Army in Rabaul

Eileen and Wilf

Sunday 24ᵗʰ August 1941

> To secure Rabaul against attack would
> require a scale of defence beyond the
> resources at its disposal.

Secret army minute of 2nd August, 1941

Wilf and Eileen went home to Rabaul for a few happy, peaceful months. Many things had changed, but as newlyweds they paid little attention at first, so nothing intruded on their joy. The most immediate problem was that Tavurvur was awake again, spewing ash across the town regularly. But Laurie Linggood had unexpectedly had to bring his furlough forward due to a kidney stone, so the Raluana mission house was sitting empty, and Mac agreed that Wilf and Eileen, along with Wilf's younger sister Netta and her husband Ken, who were also suffering from the sulphurous fall out, could stay there until the Linggoods returned. With no teaching responsibilities, Eileen was happy to spend most of her time at Raluana, especially as Rabaul had dust everywhere and, according to Netta, was swarming with soldiers. Eileen and Wilf wanted to spend as much time together as possible, and they much preferred picnics and walks on the beach to going to the Cosmopolitan or the pictures, so their days in New Britain passed quietly at first.

Despite some gentle teasing, Wilf got on well with Netta and

Ken, and Eileen quickly became firm friends with them as well. Whilst Wilf and Ken were at work in Rabaul, when other Mission-related tasks didn't require their attention she and Netta would spend their time gardening and cooking together, chatting all the while.

The house in Raluana was the usual weatherboard with a corrugated iron roof, but with a wooden floor instead of a concrete slab. It was raised on concrete piles to keep the white ants out and consisted of four rooms and the usual wide veranda encircling the entire building. The house was arranged so the two bedrooms had the dining room between them. The bedrooms had mosquito net doors and beds with the usual mosquito nets over them. The office was a small, separate structure with white wooden walls like the bedrooms and kitchen. There was a large kitchen separated from the rest of the house by a bridge and a door, which could be locked to protect supplies such as the methylated spirits kept there for lighting the primus stove and lamps. Finally, there was a native hut housing train tracks and a model of the Flying Scotchman. Laurie Linggood was a model railway enthusiast, and whilst they had packed everything else away according to the usual requirements before their rushed trip to Australia, there hadn't been time to pack the Scotchman up.

There was a wide veranda with bamboo chairs and a chaise lounge; at one end was an enclosed space with a cast iron tub. Once a week, Eileen took great delight in having a luxurious bath, the warm water being carried from the kitchen in a bucket by the cook boy. She was starting to feel her body changing with the pregnancy, so found it a delight to lie in the water and chat to Netta, who sat on a cane chair nearby.

After a few blissful weeks of ignorance, Eileen decided it was time to find out about the changes that had happened while she and Wilf were away, a subject she had been avoiding as she didn't want her honeymoon happiness to dissolve. It turned out the increased volcanic activity was only the beginning of what had changed in New Britain. She quizzed Netta from her bath.

'Well, the army began arriving in February, although only in dribs and drabs at first. More came in March. When the Katoomba came in to the government wharves, some of the natives went out in their boats, and the soldiers started throwing Australian coins overboard, so they jumped in the water and dove for the coins. Here, lean forward and I'll scrub your back.'

Eileen did so, enjoying the luxury of being cared for as Netta kept up her story.

'In April there was the biggest number of troops yet. When they turned up in Simpson Harbour on Anzac Day there were lakatoi and schooners and canoes and all types in the water. Some of the natives even took fruit out to sell to the soldiers. I guess they thought they'd done rather well from the first lot so everyone who had a boat was out there. The soldiers took a while to disembark, but once they did, they paraded straight up from the wharf and along Malaguna Road, then down Mango Road and on to their camp. There was a band playing, and all the soldiers marched in unison. It was quite impressive! It was such a hot and humid day, well, you know what it can get like at that time of year, but they all had big smiles on their faces.'

Netta dropped the sponge in the water. 'They brought two big coastal guns with them and set them up at Praed Point. Then another lot arrived last weekend. But of course you and Wilf were in your happy bubble out here at Raluana, so you haven't been as aware of all of it. They've been digging trenches absolutely everywhere and getting the civilians to as well. It's rather strange. Oh, and the new Chinese school was opened in May. There was a lovely ceremony. And a concert at the picture theatre with some of the band from Lark Force forming a choir. Things have become quite lively around here!'

Eileen indicated she wanted to get out of the tub, so Netta held up a towel for her, then gave her privacy to get dressed. But new thoughts kept occurring to her and she kept talking, leaning up against the corrugated iron wall of the bathroom to be sure Eileen caught every detail.

'Oh, and they're talking about moving the administration to Lae, *again!* Although we know nothing ever comes of that. But I suppose with the volcanoes threatening to blow, and all the chatter of Japan, some people are getting nervous. But a lot don't think there's any real risk of an invasion.'

Eileen, now dressed, came out from the walled-in area. 'Cup of coffee?'

'Yes, please.'

Eileen started preparing the brew on the primus stove. Netta continued to fill her in about everything she knew about Lark Force.

'You said there was a band?'

'I didn't know an army company could have their own band, but they do. Most of them were in the Salvation Army together in Melbourne apparently, although there's one Yank, would you believe? They all signed up at the same time so they could stay together. Quite a lot of them come to the service on Sunday, so Ken and I can introduce you to them this weekend. I know! Since we have this lovely house at the moment, we should have the morning tea here after the service. What do you think? I think it's scheduled for Helen Pearson's but I'm sure she'd be happy to change.'

Eileen had finished laying out her brown and cream coffee set just as the pot began boiling.

'Oh, but that would mean we'd have to spend tomorrow making cakes and so on, and I really wanted to get on with making Christmas puddings. I promised Wilf last year he'd have a proper pudding for Christmas, not just something cobbled together at the last minute.'

'We've got months 'til Christmas!' Netta chose a cup and poured sugar cane syrup into it. 'We can do the pudding next weekend.'

Eileen took the pot off the stove and began serving the coffee. 'I don't have any glace cherries yet anyway,' she mused. 'Mum was sending them on the boat, so I guess pudding making can wait until they turn up.'

'It wouldn't be a proper pudding without cherries! It's settled then. Oh, you'll love Bill Harry, he's such a lovely chap. He's in intelligence, so he's basically a spy.'

They took the coffee out onto the veranda and Netta exclaimed as they were taking their seat,

'Oh, I've missed the most important bit of all the news. There was a major earth tremor at Vunairima in January. It knocked the Sisters' House off its foundations, and there was a fair amount of damage to the school. Did Jack tell you?'

'No!'

'It's a while ago now. He probably didn't realise you didn't know.'

Eileen leaned forward. 'Was anyone hurt?'

'No. No injuries. But it's probably why Mel Trevitt's gone to Australia. Their home was a mess.'

Eileen sat back, shocked. She really had missed out on the bush telegraph.

'Jean Shelton too, plus all their children. The Australian government organised it.'

'When was this?'

'Just before you returned. I was worried you'd stay in Australia too, with all the talk of Rabaul being in the firing line. I'm glad you didn't. There are so few women around. Of course, the government refused to pay for the evacuation. Apparently, they think there's no evidence of any threat, and it wasn't compulsory, but a lot of people went anyway. Probably because they were sick of all the sulphur in the air. I know I am!'

Eileen sipped her coffee and thought about the child she was carrying. Rabaul had changed an extraordinary amount in the six months of their absence. Her role here felt different too, now she was no longer teaching at Vunairima. As a Mission wife she still had responsibilities around basic medical care, and training native women in mothercraft and domestic duties. But it wasn't the same as being the head of the girls' school. Her connection to those she worked with was more distant and the positive benefits for those she taught far smaller. Her certainty that she would stay in Rabaul no matter what was beginning to evaporate, especially as the threat from the Japanese began to seem more realistic.

That Sunday, after the morning's service, which Howard Pearson conducted, many of the congregation accepted the Pearces' invitation to tea at Raluana. They stood in clumps or sat on blankets on the lawn, admiring the gorgeous view of the sea.

Today it was a dazzling aqua, matched in brightness by the brilliant azure of the sky. To their right the expanse of blue was unblemished, but to the left sulphurous clouds hung over Simpson Harbour and Rabaul. The occasional cauliflower burst from Tavurvur was visible, almost directly ahead.

As she offered a plate of copra cakes around, Eileen was silently trying to remind herself of the names belonging to the all-new faces. The tall soldier who looked like a movie star was James Thurst, the American bandsman. Near him was Arthur Gullidge, the bandleader, less handsome, but with a charismatic smile. Beside him was Wilf Trigg, another bandsman. Helping themselves to the treats, they thanked her profusely for the delicious spread.

'Thank you for bringing your lovely voices to the church,' Eileen responded. 'I was so impressed to hear the hymns this morning. The quality of the singing has improved immensely with an entire band of musicians coming along.'

'Not all the men are great singers,' Gullidge said with a smile, 'but they can certainly hold a tune. You can't play a horn in a band if you can't find the notes!'

'Did you make these?' Trigg said through a mouthful of copra cake.

'I did. The cook boy makes delicious native foods, but expecting the Tolai to make European food doesn't always end well. They're not used to our way of doing things. Wilf, that is, my husband Wilf, was extremely excited once to get hold of some eggs, because they're usually scarce, and his cook boy assured him he knew how to make a proper baked custard, with nutmeg and so on. Apparently, it came out looking perfect, but when Wilf took his first mouthful it wasn't nutmeg, it was a thick coating of black pepper! Luckily Wilf had no guests for dinner that day or it would have been a disaster.'

'Well, there's no culinary disaster today, Mrs Pearce,' Gullidge said with a smile, taking the opportunity to grab another.

'Although to tell you the truth, we're grateful to eat anything that's not out of a can,' Wilf Trigg added, taking one for himself. 'Canned meat. Canned veg. Canned bloody cheese... oh, pardon me.'

'I'm sure Mrs Pearce will forgive you for your swearing if you give us a musical interlude,' Gullidge said, smiling at Eileen. 'Trigg here takes his piano accordion with him everywhere. I'm sure it won't take much to convince him to play something for us. How about it, Trigg? Can you give us a rendition of *Maid of the Mountain* or *Lilac Time*?'

Trigg shrugged. 'As long as it's not the Little Hell march. I am so sick of that. No offense, Arthur, it's a great piece you've written, but we do it with every parade and every ceremonial occasion. It's never ending.'

'Little... Hell?' Eileen asked.

The men grinned at each other, then Wilf Trigg explained.

'It's what we call the company. We're the Second Twenty-Second, and one of our officers is a gambler. Apparently three twos is the lowest three of a kind you can get in poker, and sometimes it's just enough to win, but sometimes it's not. So if you get it, it's a dilemma – a kind of little hell.' He changed the subject. 'I hear you're from Tasmania, Mrs Pearce? I am too. The weather here is quite different, isn't it?'

'Absolutely. But you do get used to it.'

They chatted briefly about the medical issues of a tropical

climate, since Trigg's role involved first aid and Eileen had often had to treat minor problems during her time teaching. Then Eileen excused herself and kept circulating. When Netta grabbed her arm, the last few copra cakes on her plate nearly toppled.

'Eileen! I wanted to introduce you to Bill Harry.' She continued in a stage whisper, *'He's the spy I told you about.'*

Standing behind her, a tall man in army uniform laughed, then offered his hand to Eileen in greeting. The badge on his shirt was a purple and red diamond on a grey background. He noticed her glancing at it and explained it was the insignia of Lark Force.

'But I'm afraid I need to correct Mrs Allsop. I'm not a spy. It's important that I get a good picture of the lay of the land so our army have the best chance if the Japs do turn up. In fact, I'm off to the Baining Mountains this week with Reverend Poole to get a better understanding of the area.'

'Oh, the Bainings are lovely,' Eileen said. 'I've gone up there with the girls a number of times during our holidays.'

'Eileen was the head of the girls' school until her marriage,' Netta said. 'Here, let me take those around. You fill Mr Harry in on the Bainings.' She took the platter off Eileen and left the two to chat.

'Please, call me Bill. So, tell me about the Bainings.'

Wilf Trigg had pulled out his accordion and, to applause, began playing some lively songs. Eileen and Bill wandered a little further towards the cliff face and away from the music, looking out across the ocean as they chatted.

'Well, it's lovely there, but very isolated. From Vunairima, where the school was, it was a two or three day trek inland, but there are rest houses along the way. There are several villages up that way, and the villagers have spent less time with us Europeans, so you'll see more of their original way of dress and so on.'

'It sounds fascinating.'

Eileen nodded. 'What I find intriguing is that they always know when someone is coming. I'm not really sure how, but they have their own ways of communicating, with drums, I think. It surprised me the first time because the jungle is so dense, they couldn't possibly have seen us. But they welcomed us in the friendliest way, completely prepared for our arrival with a feast. They're such open, generous folk.'

'And did they do any traditional dances for you? I've been told the costumes can be quite spectacular.'

'Oh yes. The men decorated themselves most elaborately with large sections of fibre, dried banana leaves perhaps. I don't really remember what they were made of, but I can visualise them easily. They were stiffened and kept in shape on fine bamboo frames, painted with the blood of the dancers and their friends and sewn onto their skin with the fibre of stems of vines, threaded through bamboo needles. Unfortunately, blood poisoning is common as a result. Despite the danger of this, it's impossible to persuade them not to sew the decorations to their backs.'

Bill was interested in anything to do with the region, so she told him about the history of savage fights between the villages, and how that had decreased in recent years, although problems occasionally still arose. Like most Australians, he was intrigued to hear polygamy was traditional, and that there were stories of chiefs having up to sixty wives.

Eager to teach him the less sensational side of Tolai culture,

Eileen mentioned the native villagers had built and expanded a native hospital in the Bainings, which they were terribly proud of, refusing mission funds as it was for their people. She explained two Methodist sisters were in charge of the skilled work, but part of their role was to train up native doctor boys and girls, teaching them about preventative measures and treatments for common problems like granuloma, ulcers and malaria.

'Ring worm is a real problem in the hills, so it's best not to shake hands with people, and to wash your hands regularly, and of course the mosquitoes are particularly bad up there. But it's such a beautiful area.' Eileen glanced around. 'It's been lovely talking about this – I always love my time in the hills, but if you'll excuse me, I should continue my hostess duties.'

Bill thanked her warmly and she made her way to the kitchen to plate up the rainbow cake she had baked and iced the day before, a tribute to her old boss, Miss March, who had claimed it as her speciality. More and more her thoughts kept returning to her teaching and her students. She wasn't sure sitting at home with a baby was going to suit her terribly well. All this talk of her trips to the mountains hadn't helped.

At the end of term, there were always girls from New Ireland who stayed at the school, because to get home was a long canoe trip, and then an even longer trek. Miss March liked to take them on excursions to make their holidays more interesting, and Eileen had continued the tradition. She loved the peacefulness of hiking through the jungle. The inland country was all hills and valleys, but because the trees were so close together there was a strange illusion where the whole area looked almost completely flat. It was impossible to see the villages that were dotted through the Bainings because they were completely hidden by the dense jungle. As they climbed higher, they could see all the surrounding tree-covered hills, and it almost felt as though they were drifting in the sky themselves. Some days that sky was a dazzling blue, whilst on others it was misty, the air damp. Always, it felt like they had journeyed somewhere magical.

'You seem to be in your own world,' Netta's voice recalled her to reality. Eileen had become lost in her memories halfway through cutting the rainbow cake. 'What were you thinking about?'

Eileen gave a wry smile. 'How much I miss teaching.'

'It's such a stupid rule, having to give up work when we marry. I can't wait for the day it changes. Still, I guess after marriage it's not long before babies and then it's impossible to work.'

'If I have to, I'm sure I can find a way to do both,' Eileen said firmly. 'In war time I imagine we all learn to do things a little differently.'

Netta peered at her closely. 'If I have to... present tense. You're not... are you pregnant?'

'Oh darn, Wilf wanted us to tell you together.'

Netta gave a shriek, then drew Eileen into a hug. When she pulled back, she ran pinched fingers across her lips. 'I won't say a word. You and Wilf can tell Ken and I together and I'll pretend I had no idea. Trust me, I've spent a lifetime hiding things from my big brother. He'll never realise you've spilled the beans.'

She did a funny little dance. 'I'm going to be an aunt! When is it due?'

'Late January, next year.'

'What a wonderful way to start the new year. Hopefully this

blasted war will be over by then and it'll be a bit quieter around here. Then you can raise the baby like the natives do, running around with no clothes on, free as a bird. Oh, I'm terrible at keeping secrets. I'm going to go and tell Ken and congratulate Wilf!' She glanced over her shoulder at Eileen. 'Sorry!'

Wilf was never able to be annoyed with his high-spirited sister for long, and Eileen realised she couldn't either. She pondered what Netta had said. If the war continued, what would it be like raising a child in Rabaul? A year ago, she would have thought it would be a wonderful life. But now, with the army everywhere, building trenches and marching in regimented parades, the carefree spirit of the Gazelle Peninsula seemed to be slipping away.

Sunday 14th December 1941. Raluana.

'No passing heavy plates around in your condition,' Wilf admonished, taking the tray of biscuits away from Eileen. 'Please sweetie, you have to look after yourself. It'll be our turn soon to celebrate the arrival of our little baby, but you're going to need your strength.'

Today wasn't just the usual post-church morning tea. They were celebrating the baptism of Rodger and Kath Brown's new baby, Graham. Eileen had been disappointed to hear they had chosen the name Graham, because it was one she and Wilf had on their own list.

Wilf peered at her closely, noting the shadows under her eyes. She could probably say the same about him though. Sleep was hard to come by lately, with all the extra work, not to mention what he was hearing from Harold Page. Most of which he kept from Eileen, not wanting to cause her any stress.

'How are you feeling, my darling?' He placed one hand protectively on her belly.

'I'm fine.'

'Not finding the socialising too tiring?'

'No, it's lovely to catch up with everyone. The Salvation Army men are always so positive and cheery, no matter what. It was good to hear them play during the service this morning too. They've improved a lot since the fete in September when we raised money for the London Blitz recovery. That's the last time I really heard them playing something other than the usual parade marches.'

'That's because they've been allowed more chance to practice lately. I know Arthur's much happier because of it. Wilf Trigg too, although that's because they let him return to medical duties. He wasn't happy in the public works office.'

Wilf reached for the plate and Eileen moved to slap his hand away, then stopped, hopefully because she had realised he was not stealing cake, but taking it to offer it around.

'I'm pleased to hear that, because Bill Harry has offered to take us up to the 'drome and see the Wirraways this afternoon. What do you think?'

'That sounds wonderful!' Wilf recalled her excitement, only a few years ago, when she had seen Rabaul's first mail plane flying overhead. Now, they were simply part of the background to living here, but to see an army plane up close would be an exciting thing.

A little over an hour later, Wilf saw Eileen's face fall as her expectations of seeing terribly modern aircraft were shattered.

Wilf had driven her, Netta and Ken in his little car up to the tiny airfield on the hill behind Rabaul. It could barely be called an airfield, with one airstrip, and basic facilities. Its combined hangar and workshop was basically a large tin roof held up by four poles. They were not the only visitors to the area. Apparently, it was a popular outing for the white folk from town. Bill Harry met them at their car and led them to where all the Wirraways were parked in a row. They were tiny little things.

'Those are all we have to protect New Britain?' Eileen asked, dismayed. Bill Harry nodded.

'I'm afraid so.'

'What happened to the fortifications the US promised in October?' Ken asked.

'They never showed up,' Bill said.

'But these are only baby planes,' Eileen said. 'And there are so few of them. Only... eight?'

Wilf took her hand and squeezed it. 'Baby planes seems appropriate,' he said. 'They do look like cloth fixed together with safety pins. Not much better than nappies!'

'They're actually training craft,' Bill Harry told them. 'They're not designed for fighting. But they're what we've been given, so we have to make the most of them.'

'It shows how much the Australian government has thought about defence,' Ken added. 'Which is not at all, I'd say.'

'Well, General MacArthur has said Japan overextended themselves in China and won't go anywhere else until Spring of next year, so I guess they think there's no rush,' Netta said.

Bill Harry didn't respond, and Wilf didn't mention the private conversation they'd had. Since Japan had entered the war a week earlier, on the 7th of December, the rumours circulating around

Rabaul had gone into overdrive – that the Japanese army was poorly equipped, that if there was any real risk of invasion the Australian government would evacuate everyone, that the Americans would still come... There was enormous confusion around what was or wasn't happening, and what might happen. Bill couldn't speak openly about classified army intelligence, but he'd certainly implied that they shouldn't underestimate Japan.

The fact that Walter McNicoll and most of the administration had moved to Lae in November, after years of dithering around, was telling. In the end, the change of location for the capital had been swift, as though they had information that made timing a priority. Harold Page, as deputy administrator, had been left in charge of finalising the pack up, but whatever McNicoll knew, Harold had not been kept informed. That didn't mean he wasn't worried, and suspicious. He might be inexperienced at the top job, but he was committed to the people of Rabaul, and willing to fight for their safety. But without knowing what the risks were, he was in the difficult position of not knowing whether any given fight was necessary or not.

The party headed back to their cars. Eileen filled Netta in on everything to do with the pregnancy as they walked. Bill Harry had to get back to the army camp on Malaguna Road, so he bid them farewell and promised to visit again soon. As the others squeezed into the car, a look of concern settled on Netta's face.

'This pregnancy... you're such a tiny thing, Eileen. Do you think perhaps you should talk to the doctor?'

Eileen glanced at Wilf. 'We've already booked an x-ray of my pelvis, actually. Just to be safe.'

Wilf smiled and started the car, glad for the distraction from his darker thoughts about the future.

'The first picture of our beautiful baby! I can't wait to see it. He or she is going to bring so many changes to our lives.' His expression turned serious. 'Speaking of changes, I've been talking to Harold Page. He seems to think the threat from Japan should be taken seriously. They've just established a place up on Namanula Ridge for everyone to retreat to if there are air raids.' He frowned. 'Of course, Rabaul society being what it is, the area for the Europeans is higher up the hill than for the natives or Chinese, and they've built little huts which they've named after famous hotels, like the Savoy. They've even organised valet parking.'

'It's a refuge, for goodness' sake,' Ken said. 'If we're sheltering there, we won't be taking tea and wearing our best summer whites.'

Wilf shook his head. 'I'm afraid you're wrong there, Ken. Harold says they've drawn up rosters for afternoon teas if we must go to Refuge Gully. People here do like their comforts.'

'If war comes to Rabaul, I don't think we'll be able to be that civilised,' Eileen said.

'Well, apologies for bringing up such a topic. Let's change it.' Wilf slapped one hand on the steering wheel. 'I have something to cheer you up. I was having a chat to some lads from the army on Friday. Gunners. Lovely chaps. I helped them out with a little problem they had, and they invited me to pop by this afternoon. You're not too tired yet are you, dearest?' He glanced across at Eileen, who shook her head.

'Right-o then. Let's go.'

He steered the car down the hill and towards town, then parked at the beach closest to Malaguna Road. Aside from the usual natives weaving fishing baskets and repairing boats, it was surprisingly busy, but then there were a lot more men wandering around town than usual, including soldiers with time on their hands and a desperate need for distraction from endless waiting.

Eileen looped her arm through Wilf's and they shuffled along the sand together. Ken and Netta followed along behind. Men in the water were diving and whooping, whilst others ran along the beachfront, tossing what looked like a football to each other. A group of native boys had joined in with the sports, and by the sound of things they were winning. They certainly seemed able to run rings around the Australian soldiers, their bare feet better suited to the black lava sand typical of New Britain beaches.

At the end of the shore there was a cluster of square tents. Eileen pointed them out. 'What are they?'

Ken was the first to respond. 'The army put up a makeshift hospital. Just behind them is the army encampment on Malaguna Road, but Wilf Trigg said the medical officers wanted to keep things portable so they set up these tents instead of a base in a building. I don't know if it's the most sterile environment for medical practice, but it's not a bad location really. Pretty central.'

'Corporal Trigg says since McNicoll left for Lae they've started setting up Government House as the army hospital, so I think they'll probably take the tents down soon,' Wilf said. 'If there was an invasion the beach would be the first place in the line of fire I suppose, so not too safe for patients.'

They kept strolling and Eileen spotted two small groups of men kneeling behind what looked like a couple of clumps of rocks. There was another man running along the beach, holding something up on a bamboo pole. It was only as they got closer that she realised the object on the pole looked suspiciously like the model airplane Wilf kept in his office. She looked at her husband and raised one eyebrow.

'Is that what I think it is?'

'Amazing that it's still holding together, isn't it? I met some of the gunners on my lunch break the other day, and a young fellow named Keith was telling me they needed something for practice. Of course I thought of my plane, and Ainui quickly attached it to a pole so they could fly it around.'

They circled around so they could come up behind the men. The clumps of rocks were, in fact, two long, slim guns on wheeled frames, each camouflaged by grey hessian and some actual rocks. As the fellow with the pole ran back and forth, the kneeling men took turns swinging the guns around and aiming them at the moving object. Once someone had the tiny plane properly in their sights, they would say 'click'.

Netta started giggling.

'Why aren't they firing?' Eileen asked. 'Surely it's not much use to just pretend?'

They were standing close enough by now that her question was overheard and a slender, well-turned out chap came over.

'Captain David Selby at your service.' He offered his hand to Wilf and Ken. 'If I can explain, unfortunately one of our guns has a crack in its breech block, so we're not actually permitted to fire it. The lads are rather green though. We only got in last weekend, and they haven't had much experience. I thought some practice aiming and firing was important.'

He gave a rueful smile.

'Although of course, without the firing. Yesterday we had a go aiming at the mail plane when it was arriving, and again when it was leaving. That was quite good, because it gave the boys some idea of how fast it moves across the sky. But we have fifty-four militiamen, so once a week doesn't give everyone a chance to have a go. Fortunately, one of the civilians happened to have a model in his office...'

'That was me,' Wilf said. Selby clapped him on the shoulder.

'Good work! We're very grateful. Well, you can see we're making good use of it.' He waved at the lad with the pole, who was looking rather tired. 'Mind you, now they know what's involved, I doubt we'll get volunteers to be our duty pilot officer again. I might have to come up with some other system. Demerit points might work. What do you think of our camouflage? The lads are rather proud of it?'

'From a distance it does look like rocks,' Ken said. Selby smiled.

'I'll let them know. They'll be pleased. Some of them had seen the natives using planes in their dances so they were hoping to get their hands on one. Anyway, I'd better get back to them and give them some more pointers. Cheerio.'

Eileen and Wilf, Ken and Netta, watched the training for a while longer. The soldier with the pole appeared to be getting rather tired and swinging it around cavalierly.

'They seem to be rather careless with your model, Wilf,' Netta said. 'Aren't you worried it will be damaged?'

'I have every faith in Ainui's ability to craft something sturdy,' her brother responded. 'Besides, it survived a volcano eruption intact. I'm sure it can survive this.'

Later that evening, Eileen lay in bed with Wilf, uncertain whether to share the thoughts that were racing through her head. But they always talked through everything that was worrying them. It was better not to hold her fears in. Besides, he could sense that something was on her mind. 'What is it, my dearest?'

She searched for the words. 'It's all been rather... disheartening today. I thought the army was here to protect us but... those planes look so old. And the guns they had on the beach, if they're damaged, and the soldiers can't even fire them during their practice... how are they supposed to work properly?'

She thought about what Wilf had said about Refuge Gully, with its tea service and valet parking. 'Is anybody taking any of this seriously?'

Wilf raised her hand to his mouth and kissed it. 'You know what most people are like. As long as things are going their way they don't think too far ahead. Everyone's constantly saying the Japanese are poorly equipped too.'

'I can't imagine they could be more poorly equipped than us,' Eileen said with a sigh. 'Are they seriously going to defend Rabaul with paper planes and boys who've never fired a gun?'

Wilf turned to face her, his expression serious. 'Harold Page took me aside at the service this morning and told me McNicoll called a meeting of the executive council yesterday. Harold doesn't think they would have moved the civil administration to Lae unless invasion was a real threat. He's also heard from his brother that there was a meeting of the War Council in Australia at the start of this month, but he doesn't know the full details.'

Harold's brother was Earle Page, who had been Deputy Prime Minister of Australia twice, and Prime Minister briefly, until a new party leader was elected following the death of Lyons. He was still active in government.

'Of course, all mail is being reviewed now, so Earle couldn't say anything explicitly, but Harold feels there was a definite warning in his brother's letter.'

'What does this mean for us?'

'For the moment, I suppose we wait for more information. There are still so many questions. It's coming up to the busiest time of year, with Synod and the Warataba. I'll keep on with my job, but at the same time I'll keep my ear to the ground.'

He placed a hand carefully on Eileen's belly, which now had a definite swell to it. 'Would it be completely foolish to ask you not to worry? We wouldn't want to do anything to endanger our baby.'

At that moment Eileen felt a lurching movement. 'Did you feel that?'

Wilf shook his head.

'Our baby just moved.' She took his hand and repositioned it over the correct spot. A moment later there was a sharp kick. Wilf's face lit up with joy. He was so often at work that he missed these moments, so they were still special to him. Eileen knew them far too well. She couldn't wait for the baby to be born. Still, the excited look on Wilf's face at his child's acrobatics was worth her discomfort. They kissed, their worries forgotten for a while. But the shadow of that conversation would continue to grow in their thoughts in the months to come.

11 - Evacuation

Eileen and Wilf

11am, Monday 22nd December 1941. Rabaul.

> As long as I live I shall never forget the sight of that evacuation: the long line of weeping women with their husband's arms around them, streaming down the roads towards the harbour and the waiting boats, their children walking with them. We knew that the Japanese were close and we did not know if or when we would meet again. It was the worst day of our lives.

Eileen Brabin, Memoirs

Monday was a work day, and there was an awful lot to organise, even though it was just before the Christmas break, a time when business would normally be winding down as services and festivities flourished. Luckily, their residence was in the same building as the accountant's office, so Wilf was able to pop in to check on Eileen whenever he took a break. Mac had told him to spend whatever time he wanted with his wife today, so he spent the better part of the morning prioritising what could be set aside in order to free up his afternoon. He was determined to have an early dinner with Eileen before she had to report to the ship.

Six days ago, after much speculation, they had all been summoned to Queen Elizabeth Park, where the official notice of evacuation had been read out. Since they'd broadcast it on the radio just about every day since, Wilf wasn't sure what the purpose of the gathering had been, other than to impress on everyone the seriousness of it all. Which was odd, since the administration had spent months saying there was no evidence of any threat and that anyone who wanted to leave would have to do so at their own expense. Suddenly the matter had become urgent: so much so that the initial announcement on the 16th had been that all women and children must be ready to evacuate within twenty-four hours of the notice.

There was no talk of evacuating the men. They were told they would not be given an actual date, for fear of the information making it into the hands of the Japanese, which could result in an attack on the evacuees. Despite this, most people seemed to think the rushed timing was not about any real threat, but to ensure people had the least amount of time to complain about the conditions imposed.

Even though most of the European population had lived in Rabaul for years, each woman was only allowed thirty pounds of luggage. This was met with two responses. Some were angry or upset because they were expected to fit their entire household into a single trunk or suitcase. Others were not concerned, because they expected they would be returning in six months or so, when everything settled down.

Burns Philp, known to all as Beeps, was the company that owned the evacuation ships, the Macdhui and the Neptuna. Wilf had spent many years working closely with Beeps staff. Since he had been welcoming new missionaries or collecting old ones returned from leave for fourteen years now, smoothing the way with paperwork, customs and other necessaries, all on the Beeps wharf knew him well. Ping Hui, one of the clerks, had already let

Wilf know Eileen could pack a second trunk. It wasn't entirely against the rules, because there was an extra luggage allowance for children, even though their child wasn't, strictly speaking, a child yet.

Eileen had not been worried about that aspect of things. It was more concerning that she and Netta were going to be split up. They had become close in the last six months, but Netta had been classified as a 'single woman', since she didn't have children, much to Ken's bemusement. So she was being transported on the Neptuna, whilst Eileen would be travelling on the Macdhui with the mothers. Apparently eight months pregnant was close enough to having a child to count.

Despite the uproar about the short timeframe to prepare, the 'twenty-four hours to be ready' command had swiftly been shown to be impossible. Many families had to come in from the outlying areas, including New Ireland and the Duke of York Islands, and there was no conceivable way of making the journey so swiftly. No official date was ever given, but unofficial rumours suggested the evacuation would happen on the 22nd. Although that day had arrived, there were still travellers turning up. It seemed the ships would be leaving today regardless.

When Wilf entered the living room, Eileen was sitting on the couch, tugging at the sleeves of a pair of his pyjamas. She gave him a smile, but he could see the sadness in her eyes.

'What are you doing my dearest?'

'The packing was finished almost a week ago,' she waved at the two Camphorwood chests by the door, 'although with all the waiting to leave I kept fiddling around, taking things out and adding things in. Deciding what to take was almost impossible. And today the waiting has been completely unbearable, so I had to find something to do. I never did get round to fixing your pyjamas after Synod.'

Wilf grinned at the memory. He had travelled to Vatnabara with the other ministers and laymen for the church's most important meeting each year. On the first day the men had stolen the mattresses of Dora Wilson, Dorothy Beale and Mary Jenkins, the only women attending. So the women had retaliated by sewing all the sleeves and legs of their pyjamas together. But they had folded them all up so neatly, it was only when the men went to put them on that they found they were hobbled, falling over with tangled legs, or puzzled when arms wouldn't go into sleeves. Wilf had just snapped the stitches apart at the time.

'There were still threads everywhere.' Eileen pulled another one out. 'There, I think I'm done now.' She folded the pyjama top and placed it on the arm of the couch, then sat very still. Wilf rushed to her side, knowing Eileen was not one to cry or express fears, but recognising her stillness as a sign of inner turmoil. She didn't look at him initially, but finally she turned to face him.

'Who's going to look after you when I'm gone? You get lost in your books and forget to eat or do any chores.'

'Oh, my sweetie. You know To Waragit and To Lulu will keep the house running. They won't let me forget to eat.'

'But you've lost so much weight, and you've been having those terrible headaches.'

He lifted her hands and kissed them. 'That's because I've been worried about you and our darling baby. I'm so relieved to know you'll be safe in Hobart soon with your parents, without a care in the world but being a mother.'

Eileen gave him a steely gaze. 'You know I won't stop worrying about you until you can join me again, or I can come home and be with you.'

Wilf picked up a pack of cigarettes from the coffee table. 'Will you join me on the veranda, my darling?'

Eileen frowned. 'I don't want to encourage that awful habit.'

'It's just a terribly difficult time to give it up.' Wilf helped her up off the couch. He knew she hated being so ungainly, but he loved the sight of her belly. Until their marriage, he had thought his opportunity to be a father was well and truly behind him. Feeling the baby kick was one of the most exciting things he could imagine.

Since the accountant residences were in the centre of town, the veranda was much smaller than those at the mission houses, but they were still able to sit outside. Tavurvur's constant sulphurous belching had finally settled down, so the air quality was better than it had been for months. On the way outdoors, Wilf checked with To Waragit about lunch and was surprised to see Ia Lo standing in the kitchen. She was unpacking a basket of food and when she saw Wilf, she raised one finger to her lips. He gave a smile and a nod, then gave instructions for To Waragit to take the trunks down to the wharf as though there was no one else in the room. Then he hurried outside to where Eileen was just lowering herself into a chair.

'Lunch is almost ready, dearest, and then it will be time to go to the ship.' He lit up his cigarette with a sigh of relief and took a long drag. 'When you get to Sydney, if you're not too tired from the voyage Netta will help you make the arrangements to travel on to Hobart,' he said, puffing out smoke.

'I don't see why we couldn't have just made the booking now,' Eileen snapped. 'I want to get home to Hobart as quickly as possible. It worries me that I couldn't let my parents know I'm coming. Dad will be upset about that.'

'Just tell him it was orders from the Government,' Wilf took another drag, 'not wanting to alert the Japanese and so on. They don't want to risk the enemy bombing a ship full of civilians if they found out you were all on board.'

'I wish you'd give up the cigarettes!' Eileen snapped. Then her face fell. It was so unlike her to speak sharply, and Wilf knew she would be unhappy to have done so. But he was sure many other wives would be in tears at this point, and given her pregnancy, the usual high standards she held herself to could not apply. It had been such an emotional rollercoaster for his wife these last few months. Normally she was so strong and determined that even having to evacuate would do little to dent her composure. He butted out his cigarette, sat beside her and pulled her into an embrace, then held her hands as he spoke.

'There you go. No more cigarettes. I promise, I'll do my best to give them up. I really will.'

'I'm sorry, Wilf, my hormones are so terrible.'

The door to the veranda opened then, and Ia Lo stepped out with a tray of banana leaf parcels. Eileen's smile lit up her face.

'Ia Lo! You came! I thought you would have gone home by now.'

'I couldn't let you leave on your winawana without a proper goodbye. Look, I made you punapur.' She laid the food down on the table and began unwrapping the coconut-soaked taro.

'I'm going to miss your punapur so much,' Eileen said. 'There's nothing like this in Australia at all. How are the girls?'

They chatted for a while about the school. Most of the girls had gone home for the break and Ia Lo's face clouded as she mused on whether they would return in the new year. With all the European sister teachers leaving for Australia, and the possibility of war coming to New Britain, there was a lot of talk among the Tolai that it might be safer for the girls to stay with their families for a while.

'It would be terrible for their schooling to be disrupted,' Eileen said, 'but their safety is the most important thing. Yours too, Ia Lo. I know you've been committed to the school for a long time, but please promise me you'll go somewhere safe if it comes to it.'

Ia Lo promised. As they ate, their conversation moved on to the Chinese community in Rabaul. Reverend Mo Pui Sam, the minister for the Chinese Methodist Church, had confided in Laurie Mac at the offices, with Wilf in the room, about how fearful the Chinese people were that they were being overlooked in the evacuation. There was a great deal of bitterness and fear, he had said, that the Australian government had completely disregarded this part of the Rabaul population.

Wilf had kept this information from Eileen, but it soon became apparent she had worked it out. He should have known that would happen. Chinatown, with all its exotic fans and statues and colourful silk clothes, was one of Eileen's favourite places, and she still liked to go there even now, although walking any distance made her uncomfortable. Her fear for her Rabaul friends, whatever their background, was strong.

He remembered one thing that might ease her mind. 'Eileen, darling, I do have some good news. Harold Page managed to get permission for the nurses up at Namanula Hospital to evacuate if they want to.'

'I'm so glad. They've been looking after me so well with the pregnancy. It's good to know they'll be safe. Will they be on the ship?'

'Well, I haven't heard who has decided to leave and who might stay. Our own nurses are staying, as you know. It would be a relief to know there were nurses on the ship with you given it's not long now until our baby is due. But at least we know for sure Essie will be with you.'

Essie Linggood had nursing training, so Wilf and Laurie had decided she would look after Eileen on the voyage.

Wilf checked his watch and realised it was nearly time to report to the ship. He had arranged to take Eileen a little early, so she wouldn't have to wait in long queues, but he regretted that now as the time drew closer when they would have to say goodbye.

Ia Lo prepared to take her own leave, packing away the lunch remains. Eileen went into the house and came out with a bundle of fabric, which she offered to her friend. 'To make yourself some new dresses,' she said. 'And I'm so sorry – I was going to embroider you some handkerchiefs as well, but I didn't get time.'

Ia Lo reached into the net bag she had brought with her and pulled out the most beautiful cats eye shell, pure white and about half an inch across, the swirl at its centre perfectly formed. On the back, in its dark centre, were scratched the tiny letters 'I + E', for Ia Lo and Eileen, in careful script. Someone had bored a tiny hole into the shell and it hung on cord woven from grass. Eileen had sent such shells home to her family a few times, Wilf knew. He had seen a large one on the mantlepiece of the Brabin's house in Hobart when they travelled there for their wedding. This was a small one, but sometimes they could be three inches across.

Eileen ran her thumb over the letters then looked up at Ia Lo. 'You taught me Kuanua like a Tolai. You taught me to swim.'

Ia Lo grinned. 'Our girls, they tried to teach you but they were not so good. I'm a better teacher.'

'Yes... yes, you really are. The best. Promise me you'll look after the school and the girls. I've told them you should be in charge. Really, you have been since you were young. Jessie and I just pretended we were in charge.'

Ia Lo's eyes sparkled at the compliment, but Eileen's smile wavered. When she spoke, her voice was steady, but filled with emotion. 'I'm going to miss you so much. You've really looked after me.'

Ia Lo patted Eileen's stomach. 'I wish I could look after the bubba. But what you have told me about Hobart, it's far too cold for me. You'll be a wonderful mama. You have so much love in your heart.'

They hugged then. Wilf went into the house to give them a moment's privacy. The trunks were gone, he noticed. On their way to the ship. There was a small carry bag on the table still and Wilf checked it. Inside were all the papers Eileen would need for her voyage. An indemnity form acknowledging the danger of travel and the difficulty of evacuation in the event of hostilities. The 'permission to travel slip' he had queued over three hours for. Various forms for the bank, so Eileen would be able to have access to his salary in Australia. Writing a will hadn't been necessary for either of them because all staff had to create one before taking up a Mission post, but he had made sure Eileen packed a copy. Wilf and Eileen had both updated theirs on their way back to Rabaul after their marriage, lodging a copy with Reverend Burton at the Overseas Mission offices.

Though he had reassured Eileen that writing his will was only a precaution, he felt a strange reluctance to touch it, as though to do so would bring bad luck. Wilf was a careful man, not at all superstitious, but he had spent a lot of time around the Tolai, for whom superstition was embedded in their daily life. Looking at that piece of paper caused his stomach to churn.

Wilf bundled all the papers into the bag, mentally checking off the list of what was needed. Eileen stood in the doorway, her eyes bright as crystal. But she was not crying any more. Not his Eileen. She was a strong woman.

Outside, there was a tapping on the veranda as Ia Lo left, the sound of her cane on the wooden floor fading away to nothing.

It was a short distance from their residence and office on Mango Avenue to the wharf. Eileen refused to be driven, even though rain was threatening. The skies were grey and heavy as they walked slowly, partly because Eileen was carrying all the extra baby weight, and partly because she wanted to take in the sights and sounds of Rabaul one last time.

In the four years since the 1937 eruption, trees and plants had flourished, thriving on the rich volcanic soil. Months of outbursts had deposited some ash, and the sulphur-filled air had caused some dieback, but never to the same extent as on the weekend of the Trevitt's wedding, and ash deposits were quickly cleared away. Their corrosive effect on anything metal was a problem no matter how fast they were removed, with members of the army constantly finding their vehicles and weapons damaged. Arthur Gullidge had complained to Wilf that all the sulphur was causing the army band's silver-plated instruments to turn blue.

Some of the store walls had V for Victory posters. The shops were far busier than usual and Eileen asked Wilf what was going on. He told her the storekeepers had lowered their prices because they were worried they might have to pack everything up and leave, so there was a lot of impulse buying going on.

'Well, since we're only allowed thirty pounds of luggage, which doesn't even come close to taking what matters, it seems ridiculous to buy new things.'

Despite the early hour, there was a long queue at the wharf, with customs checking everyone's papers were in order. Husbands waited with wives, some talking earnestly, as though trying to share every last word that needed to be said. Others stood silently, their faces ghostly. Some wept. Children were subdued, for the most part, clinging to their fathers' hands, their usual ebullience gone in the strange mix of emotions and events.

Seeing Eileen's state no one quibbled when Wilf took her to the front of the queue. She passed Helen Pearson and her children standing with Nellie Simpson and her little baby. Nellie's face was tear streaked. She had travelled in from one of the most distant stations and had said her farewells to her husband Tom days before, so she had already experienced some of the loss the other wives had yet to encounter. Further down the line Syd Beazley's wife Beryl was talking with her husband and didn't notice Eileen and Wilf passing. Netta saw them coming though. She was waiting with Ken, neither talking, just holding hands in silence. When Eileen reached them, Netta embraced her.

'I'll see you in Sydney. I wish I could be on the same ship as you.' She glanced at her brother. 'Wilf tried so hard to organise it, but there are some limits to what he can fix! Travel safely, Eileen. My brother will kill me if anything happens to you!'

Ken earnestly wished Eileen a safe voyage and returned his attention to his wife.

Near the front of the line Laurie Mac's wife Daisy waited with her two boys. Daisy was with Jean Poole, who looked utterly exhausted and explained she'd had to travel in to Rabaul from Kalas by whatever means she could find because storms had turned the road to mud. Daisy was less of an obvious leader to the Mission family than Mrs Lewis had been, but she was a deeply caring woman. She greeted Eileen and Wilf warmly, but her focus was on Jean, who already seemed to be struggling with the sudden change of circumstances that had been thrust upon them all.

Wilf wished he could gather up every one of the women from the Mission, seeing their faces taut with anxiety and exhaustion, and take them to the front of the queue with Eileen, but he knew it would cause a great deal of anger amongst the plantation wives and civilian women, so he simply exchanged what reassuring words he could with each encounter, and continued toward the ship.

Near the head of the queue was Helen Huntley with her husband Bill and their infant son, and Ron Wayne with his wife Helen. Bill had been the manager of the plantation at Vunairima. He nodded to Wilf and greeted Eileen like a dear friend. He was older than most of the Mission folk and joked that working as the postmaster at Kokopo was his retirement job, although he wasn't yet fifty.

Going through the paperwork and signing yet another travel indemnity was a minor hiccup. By the time they finally reached the cabin, Eileen was exhausted. It was only a tiny room, and she would be sharing it with Essie Linggood and her little girl, Loloma, but it had the luxury of a seat and small table between the two single beds. Essie's son Bill was already in Australia with his grandparents, for which Eileen was grateful. Sharing with a school-aged boy would have added even more to her stress.

'It's smaller than other cabins,' Wilf said, 'but it means sharing with fewer people.'

'Did you arrange this, my darling?' she asked as she sat heavily on the bed. He helped her remove her shoes, then sat beside her.

'It always pays to be popular,' he said with a smile. His expression turned serious. 'I thought you might want somewhere to sit away from the crowds when the pregnancy makes you tired. I hope you won't be too mad, sweetie, but I've asked Essie Linggood to keep a close eye on you, to make sure you're not about to have our little baby on the ship! I'm sure she won't hover though.'

'I'll be fine. The baby's not due for weeks yet.'

Wilf placed a hand on her belly and smiled when he felt a kick. 'Our little one's awfully active. I can't help but worry, dearest. I know they said everything was fine at Namanula Hospital when you had your last check-up, but this is all so stressful.' He leaned down and talked to Eileen's bump. 'Now, my little one, I'm not going to be there when you're born, and I'm sorry about that, but I'll see you as soon as I possibly can. Hopefully all this fuss will come to nothing and your Mama will be able to return to Rabaul very soon.'

There was another kick. Wilf sat up and held his wife's hands. 'Our baby Jean or John is full of beans. I hope the little one won't wear you out too much when I can't be there. Oh my darling, I'm going to miss you so much.'

They sat in silence for a while, holding each other. It was almost impossible to find words under the circumstances.

They'd had a few late night, deep conversations, talking about the future, trying to plan for every conceivable eventuality. They had discussed baby names, deciding on John for a boy after Wilf's father, or Jean for a girl, after Eileen's sister. All the important discussions had already been had, or at least they hoped so.

And truly, what could you say at a time like this? Despite all Wilf's queries and connections, nobody knew how long they might be separated for, or what might happen over the next few months, although somehow the possibility of the Japanese invading had started to crystallise into a certainty in most people's minds in the last week.

Wilf was torn in two, wanting to protect his wife and baby, but also knowing what it would cost him to leave everyone he had worked with for so long. There had been an unspoken agreement at the last district meeting that the men would not abandon their duty, at least for now. But as the possibility of invasion coalesced into something more real, he knew he was not the only one wondering whether that was the right course. He also knew no one would think poorly of him if he chose to leave his post to look after his soon-to-be new family. He wanted to stay in his job, in his Rabaul home, with his wife by his side. But as fragments of information and half-truths filtered through the rumours, doubts were taking deeper roots. Duty or family – it was an impossible choice.

Wilf couldn't talk to Eileen about the fears that made his thoughts dull and heavy. More than anything, he wanted to keep her from the worries that kept him awake at night. He didn't mention the long conversation he'd had with Laurie Mac about what might transpire if the Japanese did invade. Publicly, Mac took the position that the missionaries could probably act as intermediaries, keeping the natives safe, if the Japanese took control of Rabaul. But privately, he had told Wilf he had no idea whether that was realistic or not. Anything they knew about the enemy was little more than guesswork.

The weight of this moment also silenced Wilf. What could you say when a farewell had been forced upon you suddenly? There was no place for ordinary conversation in this tiny cabin, when the future was a great uncertainty. Neither Wilf nor Eileen was fond of small talk anyway.

A sharp rap on the door startled them both.

'All ashore who aren't travelling,' came the cry.

Eileen clutched Wilf and they stared at each other.

'Come home to me,' she said, her voice croaky. Wilf nodded, not trusting his own voice. They said a brief prayer together, then he kissed the bump, murmuring of his love to the unborn babe.

'You stay well,' he said to his wife. 'I'll be so worried until I hear that our little one has arrived and that you're both well.'

They lingered on their final kiss, then they walked slowly up to the deck together, using Eileen's pregnancy as an excuse to take their time, stretching each moment as though they could turn it into an eternity. Despite this, the final moment came, the one where they would have to part. Wilf felt the warmth of Eileen's fingers in his, and touched her face, kissed her lips, tried to memorise her auburn hair and pale eyes with the dark ring around them.

'I love you so much,' he said.

'I love you more than I can ever say,' she replied.

He didn't want to let go. He held her hand, then kept reaching for it until only their fingertips were connected. When they let go, he felt he had lost something fragile. He kept looking back as he strode down the gangplank. Eileen stood by the railing, her tiny frame made even smaller by the vastness of the Macdhui.

Wilf blew her a kiss. In that instant, the dark skies overhead broke, and torrential rain fell.

10pm, Monday 22nd December 1941. Rabaul.

In the end, they were delayed. Everyone had expected the ships to sail in the afternoon, and the Neptuna did, but hours passed and the Macdhui didn't move. Eileen and Wilf spent half an hour staring at each other across the unbridgeable distance between ship and shore, but Eileen was sore and exhausted, so in the end Wilf called out that he would go to work and she must rest. Eileen thought it would be impossible to do so, knowing they were still in port and that she could walk off the ship and be back with Wilf in no time. But since the announcement of the evacuation she had barely slept, worrying for what the future might hold, and before that the quality of her sleep had been declining anyway, since it was almost impossible to find a comfortable position to lie in nowadays.

After their first shipboard dinner, Mel Trevitt came and told Eileen Wilf was at the dock once more. Though the rain was still pouring down, she went up to the deck and resumed her silent communion with Wilf at a distance. It was a terrible agony.

Nobody seemed to know what the delay was at first, but the truth spread from spark to fire once it was finally uncovered. A boat was on its way from Bougainville with more women and children needing to be evacuated. Word had come through that they were close so the ship's departure had been held up.

There was some dismay among the clusters of women on the deck of the *Macdhui* when they heard this. Eileen learned from the chatter that the ship was full to overflowing, with some cabins housing five families. Talking like a frantic group of galahs, everyone wondered where they would fit the new arrivals. Suddenly feeling guilty at only sharing with Essie and little Loloma, Eileen wondered if they would be asked to accommodate another person. There was room to unfold the upper bunks for two more. But the bush telegraph, or in this case the ship telegraph, swiftly shared the news that the music room was to be converted into a makeshift bunkhouse.

Essie brought Eileen a blanket to protect her from the wet, but knew better than to try to force her back to her cabin. Though the rain returned periodically, the air was its usual warm, humid cloak, so nobody felt chilled or too uncomfortable. Many of the children had gone to bed due to the late hour, but a few of the older ones still lingered to catch a last glimpse of their father.

As the night wore on, somebody's compassion must have come to the fore, because the men were allowed on board again for an hour or so. It was impossible to find any private space, Loloma being asleep in the cabin and the dining room, library and games room full to the brim with families and all their bundles, so Wilf and Eileen sat together on deck, watching the clouds converge and break apart in the skies above, allowing the occasional glimpse of the fragile moon. Every word and touch that passed between them felt equally fragile, as though they were reaching across a growing distance.

Finally, the men were ordered ashore once more at 10pm. By then, the clouds had massed again, hiding the moon and stars completely, so the only light was from the kerosene lanterns onboard and on the dock, where Wilf waited. He would not leave until the Macdhui had left the harbour. Eileen could still make out his face as he waited patiently, but a lantern resting on a barrel next to him cast its light up under his chin, creating shadows around his eyes and under his cheekbones until his beloved face was little more than a skeleton. She remembered a similar illusion on their wedding day, and fear settled in her stomach.

The families from the outlying areas finally arrived and were bundled on board, the crew working swiftly to find them whatever space remained. As midnight neared, the hustle of their arrival died down. A mist sprang up over the water. Crew did the rounds, urging the women to return to their cabins for departure, but it was a hopeless task. None of the waiting men had left the dock, and as the Macdhui finally began to pull away, the men moved as one to the next pier, a longer one that let them follow the ship's path until the last possible moment. There were some cries of goodbye, but mostly a strange silence fell.

Unable to follow their wives any further, the men remained at the end of the pier. Some raised their hands in a last farewell, whilst others just spoke with their eyes. Eileen stood at the railing, keeping her eyes fixed on the figure in white that she knew was Wilf, even if she couldn't make out his features anymore.

The Macdhui steamed towards the channel where Simpson Harbour connected with the ocean, the growing mist parting before them. They passed Dawapia, the Beehives in the centre of the Harbour, almost close enough to touch them.

Eileen thought about all the things she had left behind. She didn't mind about the household goods and clothing that wouldn't be needed at her parents', but she felt sudden regret at leaving the stones and shells she had collected from all the beautiful places she had visited. Then it struck her that she hadn't taken a copy of Wilf's pidgin hymn book. He had spent years preparing it, and it had finally been published on the Mission Press in October, just in time for Synod. He had worked closely with Laurie Linggood on the final wording and formatting, and with Isikel Mulas, the head printer, to get all the typeface done. It was a great achievement. She would have to get him to post one to her. He was so proud of it, and she had wanted to see his shy smile when she asked him to sign a copy for her, with his beautiful, ornate script.

Eileen pushed away the thought that she might not see his smile again for a long time.

The ship glided through the mist. Somewhere close behind her on the deck she heard a male voice cut through the tears and muted talk of the women. He spoke softly, probably to stop any fears spreading among the distraught passengers, but Eileen was close enough to catch his words.

'This fog's a blessing. It'll help us get out without being spotted by the Japs.'

Eileen cursed the fog though, because it was swiftly concealing her last sight of Rabaul, and of her darling husband. The men of the town grew smaller and smaller in the distance, mist curling up around the pier on which they stood, until all that could be seen were the faint, winking lights of their lanterns, like fireflies dancing in the jungle in the dying hours before dawn.

12 – A Terrible Christmas

Eileen

Thursday 25th December 1941. Onboard the *Macdhui*.

> But then they heard again the story of the birth of the Son of God; the story of the young mother Mary, exhausted, far from home, searching for a place to lie down. They listened with a new understanding.
>
> *Whereabouts Unknown*, Margaret Reeson, p. 93.

When Essie Linggood came to collect her for the Christmas morning service, Eileen nearly told her to go away in the sharpest of terms. She thought it was the scruffy-looking ship's doctor who kept 'checking in' on her every morning. Eileen was determined she would never let the grubby man examine her, but he didn't seem inclined to anyway; he simply poked his head in each day and asked if she was well. He was probably worried the company might be liable if she gave birth prematurely on the ship and something went wrong, as he certainly didn't seem interested in providing good medical care.

When she realised it was Essie, not the doctor, she was more polite, but still reluctant to join the festivities.

'Can you let me in?' Essie called. 'I left my key behind.'

'Just give me a moment,' Eileen said. 'I'm a bit slow this morning.'

'I can understand that,' Essie called, but even with her voice muffled her cheery tone sounded rather forced.

Eileen had barely been awake when Essie and Loloma left to have breakfast, and had missed it herself, unable to drag herself from bed. It wasn't just the physical heaviness of pregnancy. It felt like there was a weight in her heart, or in her soul, that made sleep a welcome oblivion. She had always been an early riser, wanting to get on with her duties, but during this dreadful voyage each day offered nothing but the constant noise of slightly frantic children and the weighty sadness of women who had lost their homes and husbands in one swift blow.

Finally, Eileen got the door open. Essie hurried in, her face registering dismay that Eileen wasn't yet dressed.

'Good morning,' Essie said. 'I'm sorry if I dragged you out of bed, but I thought you would want to attend the service.' She peered at Eileen, concerned. 'I didn't see you at breakfast. It's important to keep your strength up. We'll make sure you get a good feed at lunch, shall we? It's going to be a Christmas feast.'

This was not the Christmas Eileen had planned. As promised, she'd made Wilf a pudding months ago, so it would have plenty of time to cure, but she wasn't there to share it with him. Christmas in Vunairima was similar to birthdays in that the girls from the school and the boys from George Brown College who hadn't gone home for the holidays would start singing hymns and carols at the first light of dawn. Eileen had always joked about how terrible this was, but when a screaming baby and a shouting toddler pulled her from her sleep this morning, she realised she would give anything to be woken by the sweet harmonies of the impromptu Christmas choir.

Eileen gave herself a quick sponge bath in the tiny ensuite that she could barely fit her bulk into, using the water a purser had brought earlier. Finally, she opened the door, hoping Essie wouldn't expect her to be cheerful as well as present.

'Let's get you dressed,' Essie said, helping Eileen into one of her cotton dresses. 'The service is starting soon. I know you won't want to miss it.'

Eileen wanted to contradict her, but she had never railed against the obligations of being a missionary teacher and later wife. One had to do one's work to the best of one's ability, for the good of others and to further the teachings of the church. She knew she would have to make an appearance.

Almost ready, she gave her hair a quick brush and slipped on her shoes. They were a bit tight because her feet had swelled dreadfully with the pregnancy. Then she let Essie hurry her out the door.

Eileen had never been one to allow herself to be dragged along by others, but today she didn't have the energy to protest. Essie led her to the music room, which had been cleared of its makeshift beds and filled with chairs, although there was still bedding crumpled against the walls. The room was already crowded, but Helen Pearson quickly gave up her chair for Eileen and went to find another one. Not all of the two hundred and fifty or so women and children on the ship were attending the service, but enough that seating was in high demand.

The ship's Chaplain had tried to come up with a service that was suitable for the array of backgrounds of the women on the ship, so it had none of the specific hallmarks of the Methodist Christmas service Eileen was used to. Given the number of different missions in Rabaul, including Catholic and Seventh Day Adventist, that was not surprising, but it saddened her. When the Chaplain told the Christmas story, Eileen noticed a few women glanced her way, and at the other pregnant women in the room.

The story of a woman forced to leave her home and have a child in a land far away held special resonance.

Eileen was pleased to discover the Chaplain had at least selected his hymns from the Methodist hymn book. They finished the service with one of the prettiest ones, 'Little children, wake and listen.'

As they sung of angels rejoicing in the birth of Jesus, her hands went unconsciously to her belly. The baby, which had been kicking frantically during the sermon, seemed to be soothed by the music. Eileen felt a deep sadness that her child was being born into a world at war. She sent up a silent prayer that circumstances would allow the infant to be reunited with their father before too long.

Knowing the hymn well, Eileen was singing it without too much thought, until she realised what she was singing during the fourth verse, about the words of the angels.

> 'Words to bring us greater gladness,
> Though our hearts from care are free;
> Words to chase away our sadness,
> Howe'er sad our lot may be!'

A lump formed in her throat and she couldn't finish. Around her, she saw other women reacting in the same way, their eyes bright with unshed tears. She sent up a silent prayer that this sadness would be gone by next Christmas. It was an emotion she didn't have much time for, preferring to set aside despondency and get on with work.

After the service, word quickly spread that there would be a special visitor at lunch time, with gifts for the children. The women from the Methodist Mission took their children to have a rest before the excitement and agreed to meet in the dining room for lunch, but it was clear they were going to be going through the motions. The pain of parting was too recent.

Eileen lay on her bed and wondered how she could make her excuses to avoid the Christmas lunch. Growing up as the oldest of four girls, she had developed a will of steel early on. But when it came time, Essie was not to be persuaded.

'You missed breakfast, and I promised Wilf I would look after you. Consider this a medical order. At least have some turkey. A good bit of meat to strengthen your blood.' Her forced smile slipped. 'I know how difficult this is for you, Eileen. For all of us. But truly, it's important for you to stay strong. Giving birth is hard work. Even if you're not feeling festive, it's important you have something healthy to eat.'

Christmas lunch was as much of a nightmare as Eileen had imagined. The ship had made an effort at a festive atmosphere, with a tree in one corner and streamers hung along all the walls. The silverware was polished to a high shine, and there was plenty of traditional food. Roast turkey and potatoes, vegetables, gravy and mint sauce. Although she was not in the mood for festivities, Eileen was rather hungry, so she ate everything she was served.

Around her the wives talked about their plans when they arrived in Australia. Barely a week ago they had all been celebrating the Christening of baby Graham Brown, sharing food and conversation easily. The sense of being a small but close community had been strong. But at the end of this voyage, they were going to travel to homes as far apart as Tasmania and Western Australia and it was already apparent the group was splintering, with those based in Sydney discussing arrangements to meet regularly, a discussion the others could not take part in.

Eileen realised she would be the only one from the Mission based in Hobart. At least she would have her family for support as she waited to return to Rabaul. Her mother was excited about the arrival of the baby and glad Eileen would be home so she could help with caring for it.

Occasionally someone asked Eileen a direct question or attempted to draw her into the conversation. She responded politely, but for the most part she stayed a quiet observer, noticing how some women were too bright and cheerful, while others could barely hide their bewildered sadness.

Kath Brown seemed equally withdrawn, only becoming animated when she picked up two-month-old Graham and chatted to him. She looked exhausted, her face drawn, and shadowy hollows beneath her eyes making her appear lost. Eileen wondered if that would be her reality soon, caring for a newborn without her husband by her side.

'Do you want to hold him?' Kath asked, in response to Eileen's gaze.

'Oh no, no.' Eileen's response was swift, and it took her a moment to realise why. Staring at the infant boy had reminded her of a memory long locked away, of her younger brother Roland. He had been two years younger than her, the only boy in the family. Roland had fallen on a metal hoop when he was seven, developed septicaemia, and died. His loss had changed her family forever, especially her father.

Seeing Kath's face fall, Eileen searched for an excuse. 'I'm just so awkward and tired at this stage of the pregnancy. I'd be worried I'd drop him.'

Kath nodded, understanding in her eyes. 'Sometimes I worry I'll drop him too,' she confided.

Little Loloma Linggood, born just after the eruption of '37 and now four and a half years old, seemed to be fascinated by baby Graham. She interrupted their exchange to stare at him, then wandered away from their table for a few minutes to stare at the hanging streamers. Kath and Eileen fell into a companionable silence.

Eileen hadn't thought of Roland in years, but it didn't take her long to realise it wasn't just the sight of Graham that had brought him to mind. She'd read in the Pacific Islands Monthly years before of a little girl called Rosemary, the daughter of an Anglican missionary family, who had fallen from the balcony at their house and broken her arm. Like Roland, she had been healing well, then a later article explained she had taken ill and died from septicaemia. The pointless loss, so like Roland's death, had stayed with Eileen ever since.

She tried to shake those memories away. Her thoughts seemed to dwell on death far too much recently.

It wasn't long before Loloma returned from her wandering. She picked a piece of carrot off her mother's plate and munched it, then turned to Kath Brown and asked to touch the baby. Once Kath gave her permission, Loloma's chubby little hand reached out to stroke his forehead and rosy cheeks.

Eileen and Wilf had talked about having several children. The sight of the little girl admiring the baby made Eileen long for the future they had planned, which was becoming harder to picture the further the *Macdhui* sailed from Rabaul.

'Is there a baby in your tummy too?' Loloma's question pulled Eileen out of her bittersweet thoughts.

'Yes, there is.'

Loloma's tiny hand reached out and patted the bump. 'Hello,

baby.' She looked up again, her eyes big and round. 'What's the baby's name?'

'We don't know yet. If it's a boy it will be John, and if it's a girl it will be Jean.'

Loloma nodded solemnly. She seemed to immediately decide the baby was a girl, and her next question caused Eileen to gasp. 'Did she have to leave her Daddy behind too? I had to leave my Daddy behind. It made Mummy sad.'

The lump in her throat made it hard for Eileen to answer immediately. As she tried to gather her thoughts to form a reply, Essie came over and knelt beside her daughter.

'Loloma, I think there's a special visitor arriving. Would you like to see?'

The little girl nodded eagerly. She was old enough to know exactly who that special visitor would be, and young enough not to wonder how he might have landed his sleigh on a ship in the middle of the ocean. Essie gave Eileen a comforting look and led the child away. Eileen's thoughts turned again to the tragedy of the little missionary girl who'd died. Some might tell her it was safer to raise a child in Tasmania, with better medical facilities and so on, but Roland's death had taught her otherwise.

Santa took the form of Lofty, the ship's steward, bedecked in a red suit, pillowed stomach and cotton wool beard. Lofty was a cheerful gentleman who would often break into a tap dance to lighten the spirits of the women and children for whom this voyage was not a joyful holiday, but a terrible parting. He had confided in some of the Mission women that he used to work in the theatre in his younger days, and he was an excellent tap dancer. But not today. Santa did not tap dance. Still, his warm, ebullient manner meant that in no time at all he was surrounded by an enormous gaggle of children of all ages.

'They had everything ready for the annual children's Christmas party at the New Guinea Club,' Essie confided to Eileen, leaning in so the children wouldn't hear, 'so they just loaded up all the gifts and food onto the ship.'

Santa Claus gave out stocking after stocking, and soon the energy in the room changed as toddlers and older children started running around, energised by sweets, flying their model airplanes through the air or swinging little dolls around by the arms. Others grew impatient waiting for their turn with Santa and began whining or crying loudly.

At the Methodist Mission table many of the children were less than a year old, so the women took it in turns to return to their cabins to feed fractious babies. The noise and the fake cheer were becoming unbearable to Eileen and she began to look for the right moment to make her departure. Finally, dessert began to arrive.

One of the ship's crew, in crisp pants and jacket, placed a jug of steaming custard on the table, and a moment later someone else slid a china bowl in front of Eileen. Inside was a large slice of Christmas pudding.

'Doesn't that look delicious?' Daisy Mac said. Eileen found she couldn't look up or respond. All of this was wrong. She was supposed to have attended the service in Rabaul, with Laurie Mac presiding. She should be the one serving dessert to all the guests at the Raluana mission house now, having spent the morning working cheerfully side by side with Essie to make sure everyone got a feast. Wilf should be sitting next to her, telling her what he thought of her Christmas pudding now he finally got to taste one she could prepare properly.

'Excuse me,' she managed. 'I need to... I'm not feeling well.' Eileen stood and was about to leave when a thought came to her. She reached for the bowl of pudding.

'I'll finish this in my cabin,' she told Essie, and hurried out. It was simply a ruse to stop Essie following her to make sure she was alright. There was no way she could return to her cabin; the thought of the tiny room enclosing her was unbearable. She needed space. She wanted to stroll through the gardens and jungle surrounding Vunairima, where she could breathe the fresh air and cool her swollen ankles at the nearby beach.

Since all the Christmas festivities were still ongoing, Eileen had the deck to herself apart from a few crewmen, who were busy about their tasks. She stood at the railing and looked over the sea, the pudding bowl still in her hand. They had been onboard three days but they hadn't left tropical climes yet, so the air was still warm. The sea and the sky were both brilliant blue, stretching to meet each other with nothing to mar their topaz hue. Not a single cloud broke the sweeping expanse, only the dazzling white of the sun, its rays sweeping across the sea, flickering glints breaking the surface.

It was a glorious day, bright and brilliant, yet Eileen felt it would have been far more appropriate if it were overcast and grey. For most of the time so far, the rain had been unrelenting, but they were moving from the Pacific climate's wet season to Australia's dry season with every day. She remembered her first arrival in Rabaul, five and a half years ago. She had been filled with excitement and possibility. A new life in a new land awaited. This journey was a strange, sombre contrast, the future clouded and unknown.

Returning home to Hobart should have filled her with joy.

She truly loved its familiar streets, beautiful old buildings and the reassuring presence of Mount Wellington always in the background. And seeing her family again would be comforting in these odd times. But all she could feel was loss. She had become used to an entirely different lifestyle in the tropics, one that was in many ways far more laid back and authentic than she had ever known. Where she had found her place, as a teacher at the school, as a lay preacher in the church and in caring for the Tolai people. She had people who respected what she did there, as well as dear friends like Ia Lo. And she had found love, and a future, with Wilf. They had started a family together. She had expected him to be by her side every day from now on.

'This isn't really Christmas,' she said, but her voice sounded lost rather than angry, a pathetic wisp of sound that drifted away on the breeze. With a sharp movement, she flung the pudding, bowl and all, away from her, watching it hit the water and sink without a trace.

Wilf

Thursday 25th December 1941. Raluana.

```
In an arid tropic region, there's
another missing legion
Who sailed away in answer to Old Old
England's call
But much to our disgust, we were
landed in the dust,
In a pumice stricken dump, they call
RABAUL
And here we sit and wait, resigned
unto our fate,
Wondering what the future holds in
```

```
store:
Whether those in High Command will
release us from this Land
And let us see a little bit of War!
```

The Missing Legion, Anonymous poem
published in the Cobram Courier,
Wednesday 3 December, 1941, p. 3

Life was much quieter with all the women gone. Six months ago, the European civilian population had been over four thousand, but with the administration's move to Lae and the evacuation of the women and children there were barely two hundred left. Natives with homes in distant villages had also disappeared, returning to their families.

Life had become more restricted too, with regular air raid drills and lush gardens torn up to dig split trenches. Businesses had less stock than usual, so some things were hard to come by. Japanese planes had been seen overhead since early December. Most people had ignored them initially, but they were increasing in frequency and now accompanied by the sound of sirens. For those in town this meant a trek up to Refuge Gully. Many saw this as a waste of time because it was never followed by anything except an all-clear signal. Harold Page and the Air Raid Warden, Nobby Clark, regularly made the point that although the planes were no doubt doing recon, one day soon the sirens would signal something more serious. By unspoken consensus, the Europeans stopped wearing their dazzling white pants and shirts, opting for darker colours so they wouldn't stand out from a distance.

Amongst the changes in Rabaul, one made the missionary men uncomfortable. Any Japanese men in the civilian population had been rounded up and sent to Australia as prisoners. Their wives were left to fend for themselves. Where possible, the mission tried to provide support to them, but they found they had to do this discreetly because of strong anti-Japanese sentiment. This was partly fuelled by anger at propaganda broadcasts from Tokyo many could pick up on their radios. Such broadcasts were aimed, according to Page, at breaking the morale of those living in the islands.

Terrible rumours fuelled the collective uncertainty and anxiety. The worst was that grave markers were being prepared by Chinese craftsmen for all of Lark Force. Such rumours spoke volumes about the growing fears of the young soldiers. With little factual information available – even to the army, according to Bill Harry – people were agitated and fearful, but had no clear idea of where to aim their anger. With added responsibilities, the soldiers had no idle days. The Salvation Army bandsmen still attended Sunday services at the Methodist church in Rabaul, but Arthur Gullidge, Wilf Trigg and other musicians rarely dropped by Wilf's office any more for a chat. They were medical orderlies first and bandsmen second now. The training and preparation for their official, rather than ceremonial, role suddenly became more intense.

On Christmas morning, a line of attendees were trailing into the church when Wilf arrived. He had found it unusually difficult to get out of bed. After years of bachelorhood, he had found great joy in waking to see Eileen lying beside him each morning. She had only been gone a few days and the ache of her absence had not lessened by even the smallest amount.

Wilf had given the houseboys the day off so breakfast was his own responsibility, but he had checked the butcher's cabinet with dismay. There were no eggs or meat, the last of the bread was a hard, mouldy lump, and there was little else that could be called food. Finally, he'd settled for some sliced paw paw and a cup of tea. At least lunch would be a decent meal.

As Wilf made his way into the church, he glanced up at the sign that hung over the doorway. It was infinitely familiar to him, but today the words seemed to burn into his thoughts.

> *I shall pass through this world but once. If there is any goodness I can do or any kindness I can show, let me do it now for I shall not pass this way again.*

Howard Pearson conducted the Christmas service, with Mac leading the prayers for the safety of their families far away at sea. Wilf found his mind drifting during Howard's sermon, as he pondered what doing good meant when war was bearing down on their little community. What would be the greatest good? To stay in Rabaul, and try to lessen the impact of the coming storm? Or to be a husband and father to those who depended on him? Everyone who worked for the mission would probably have to ask themselves this question one final time, very soon. They had all discussed their duty, but the threat had seemed distant and unreal. Now it loomed closer. After evacuating the women and children, the next step would be to evacuate the male civilians. When that order was given, would they have a choice whether to go or to stay? And if they did, if leaving wasn't mandatory, what would be the right thing to do?

In this strange, uncertain environment, no one expected much from Christmas lunch. Since the day the women left, all the men had been dejected. They missed their families and found little motivation for the household management tasks that now fell to them on top of their usual jobs. Fortunately, with all the delays before they left, the wives had prepared a variety of foods, or instructed houseboys in what to prepare, and lunch turned out to be a large, traditional spread, with some uniquely tropical touches. Alongside the small roast fowl, a rare treat in Rabaul, there were roast potatoes basted in coconut oil and baked vegetables drizzled with coconut milk, which made them deliciously creamy. And of course they ate outdoors, the table set up on the veranda since that was the only space where so many could enjoy a meal together.

As Chairman, Laurie Mac was the most senior staff member present at Raluana for their lunch, but he gave up his role as host to Margaret Harris, one of the Methodist nurses from the Stewart Hospital. She took to the role with gusto, doling out tasks and lifting everyone's spirits with her stories. Margaret had caught a boat from Vunairima with other women and children for the evacuation, but they had arrived late at night on the 22nd to find the ships had sailed without them. Still, she managed to turn even this problematical turn of events into an exciting sailing adventure with – hopefully – a positive final outcome. They had been told a flight was being organised to take the stragglers to Australia, although exactly when was shrouded in mystery.

Another group of families had arrived on the *Ambon* early this morning. They had been given rooms at the different hotels in town. The group discussed the likelihood of these women and children also being on the flight, whenever it might be. After a while Margaret, seeing thoughts turning to the weight of an uncertain future, steered the conversation back to absent families, and what their plans were when they reached Australia.

With eleven at the table, including Wilf and Ken Allsop, missionaries John Poole, Laurie Linggood and Rodger Brown, laymen Ron Wayne and Bill Huntley, as well as nurses Mavis

Green and Jean Christopher (known as Chris), with Mac and Margaret presiding, there was plenty to talk about. Everyone missed their families immensely. Talking about them seemed to bring them closer, and the conversation went on in this way throughout the meal as people wondered how they were faring on the seas, recalled recent funny incidents involving their children and so on.

Laurie, who had not long returned from Australia after his kidney stone problem, was in full health again. Since the Raluana House was his responsibility, he made sure the food and drinks kept flowing. He joked that he missed his model trains as much as his children and wife, since they had decided to leave the train set in Australia with the possibility of invasion looming. Even the Scotchman had been packed up. The mention of invasion changed the mood again, so Laurie declared he was going to serve up the pudding. Then he begged Mavis and Chris to show him how to heat it, and requested they make the custard, which brought a round of laughter.

'*You're* going to serve up dessert? Honestly Laurie, how are you eating at all with Essie gone?' Ron joked.

'Better give credit where credit's due,' Ken said, as the nurses went off to the kitchen. 'Laurie's house boy is keeping him well fed.'

'I hope you've got eggs for the custard,' Wilf said and Laurie looked stricken, clearly uncertain whether he did. 'And nutmeg,' Wilf continued. He regaled them all with the pepper-coated custard story. By the time Chris and Mavis returned with dessert, the festive mood had been restored.

Margaret Harris had disappeared into the kitchen as well, and she brought out a bottle of brandy. When Mavis placed the pudding on the table, she doused it in alcohol.

'Who's got some matches?'

'Wilf?' Mac asked. Wilf threw his arms in the air.

'Not me! I've given up smoking. I promised Eileen.'

'Good on you,' Ron said, and handed over a box of matches. 'I couldn't handle all the stress without my ciggies.'

Margaret lit the pudding and it blazed up, blue and orange flames flickering. Its surface shone golden with the liquid, while the fruit glistened like little gems. Everyone exclaimed with delight.

'This is Eileen's work, isn't it?' Ken asked. Wilf nodded.

'She promised me a pudding this year.' He didn't add that she'd expected to be there to share it with him for their first Christmas as a married couple. He could see from everyone's faces that they were thinking similar thoughts. This morning, before the service, they should have enjoyed watching their children's faces light up when they opened their stockings. Without the evacuation, they would probably all be sitting out on the lawn now, since the added numbers of wives and children would have made even the veranda too small. There would have been babies wriggling in woven baskets and children zooming around on the lawn.

The flames died away, and Margaret Harris did the honours, slicing the pudding and passing it out.

'Doesn't look like there'll be leftovers,' Laurie Linggood said as the last piece hit a plate, leaving only crumbs and stray cherries on the serving dish.

'Oh, Eileen made a second one,' Wilf said. 'She knows what you vultures are like.'

He didn't say that she'd prepared for a Christmas luncheon

with numerous families, rather than a miserable collection of lone men.

'We can have that one on New Year's,' Mac said. 'Another chance to celebrate.'

They were just about to dig into their pudding when they heard the distant scream of the air raid sirens. Everyone snatched up their plates and raced outside.

'If it's a false alarm I say we go back and finish dessert,' Rodger Brown said. 'I haven't had pudding in months, with the pregnancy and the new baby and all.'

When they reached the cliff that looked out towards Praed Point, it was clear this was not a rehearsal. A Japanese recon plane was circling over Rabaul.

'Into the trenches, men,' Mac said, and they ran to the split trench at the rear of the house. Bill Huntley struggled to keep up with the others. When he finally climbed into the trench beside them he gasped out, between shuddering breaths,

'It's hard to run on a full stomach.'

'Of course it is, Bill,' Laurie Linggood said with a smile. Glancing around, they realised that every one of them except Rodger Brown had brought their bowls with them, and they burst out laughing. Rodger looked dismayed, until Ken passed his over.

'Sounds like you were more deprived than me,' he said. 'Netta helped Eileen on pudding day and she's not one to follow the conventions, so we've been eating Christmas pudding all month.'

'Eileen is a great cook,' Mac said through a mouthful.

'She is,' Wilf said. 'I'll have to tell her it was so popular, even an air raid couldn't stop us eating it.'

Laurie Linggood waited until they were all finished eating,

then his face turned serious. 'I don't mean to dampen the mood, but did anyone notice the flashes of light when we were looking out over the harbour?' A few of them said they had. 'It was morse code,' Laurie went on. 'I didn't catch the message, since we were so busy running our pudding relay, but it was definitely letters.'

Mac frowned. 'Word around town's been that some of the German residents might have been passing information to the Japanese. Possibly even some of the German missionaries. I didn't want to believe it. But war changes everything. And it's come to Rabaul. We know the Japanese and Germans are allies. I guess I just didn't expect people we've worked beside for years to choose that alliance over long-term friendships.'

Bill Huntley nodded. 'I hate adding to rumours. There have been far too many of them lately, and I don't think they've been helping. But one of the natives told me they'd seen a new flag on one of the German missions up in the hills. They drew me a picture of the symbol on it. It was a swastika.'

'I may be naive,' Chris said, 'but how can missionaries side with the Nazis?'

'How can anyone do what they do during war?' Mac said. Everyone nodded or murmured their agreement at this. Mac tilted his head. 'Do you hear that?'

The group looked around and smiled.

'Silence,' Wilf said. The air raid was over.

'Well,' Laurie said, scraping the last of the custard from his plate, 'I guess that means we could return to the veranda, but since this is the last of the pudding, is there really any point? It's terribly comfortable in a split trench this time of year.'

'Wilf Trigg told me the soldiers call running to the trenches the hundred-yard foot race,' Wilf said.

'Well, if we put some pudding in the trench, I'm sure Laurie will win every time,' Mac joked.

Margaret Harris collected their dishes before they all climbed out of the trenches. The nurses went up to the house, leaving the men at the cliff's edge, gazing out over the glistening harbour and the familiar streets of Rabaul.

'Well, no matter what happens, today's been a great day,' Ken Allsop said, to general agreement. 'You've all lifted my spirits, I can tell you.'

'She's a beautiful town, isn't she?' Ron Wayne said. Again, his companions agreed. Even from this distance they could make out the sweeping trees over Mango Avenue. Wilf wanted the peaceful, happy mood to remain intact, so he didn't speak out loud, but he couldn't help thinking of the eruption of 1937, and the accompanying thunderstorms and flooding. With the town engulfed in ash and floods, destroying roads and roofs, there had been so much damage. It had taken a long for life and growth to return. The events that threatened them this time were being brought by men, not natural forces. In some ways that made them more terrifying, but no less unpredictable.

I hope the storm passes us over this time, he thought. But he suspected they were right in its path.

13 - The Time Before

Eileen

30th December 1941 – 2nd January 1942. Sydney.

```
Old year and new: Allied Recovery In 1941

The rush of events has been so tumul-
tuous that the end of the year pro-
vides an opportunity to look back, to
get the actual happenings in their
proper perspective, and to contrast
the present position with that of
twelve months ago.

Notwithstanding the inexorable ap-
proach of war to our Own shores, the
year closes with the Allies in a very
much better position than that of
last January. There is still a great
cleft between promise and fulfilment,
and in some ways the menaces have
sharply increased; but the positive
gains have been considerable and the
long-ranged factors now have a better
chance of working in our favour.
```

Stephen H. Roberts, Challis Professor of History, University of Sydney
The Sydney Morning Herald, Wednesday 31st December 1941, p. 6

When the scruffy doctor presented Eileen with an account for ten shillings for his daily intrusion on her morning, she nearly threw it back in his face, wanting to shout that he had done nothing at all, and she would never have let him try. But she was determined to put the voyage behind her without any fuss, so she placed the money in an envelope and gave it to Lofty, the steward, to pass on. She wished she could have given the money to Lofty instead, for all the times he had broken into a spontaneous tap dance to entertain them all, but unresolved questions around finances prevented her giving him his own tip.

With all the excitement and complications of the last year, Eileen had never had the chance to cash her retirement bonus, and she would have to talk to Reverend Burton at head office to see if the cheque was even still valid. Wilf's income was also going to have to be split between two households for an unknown period. Under the circumstances, Eileen wondered whether a return to work might be necessary. She didn't want to be dependent on her father, whose own income tended to be somewhat unreliable. Wilf would be surprised, because he was keen for her to stay at home with the baby, but needs must and so on.

Life on the *Macdhui* had become easier after Boxing Day, when many women and children had left the ship in Townsville, most to catch the train to Brisbane. Eileen had hoped they would dock at the same time as the *Neptuna*, so she could see Netta, but somehow the other ship was now a day behind them. Despite the ship being blacked out at night throughout the entire voyage, there had been no sightings of Japanese planes or boats that Eileen was aware of, although she suspected if there had been Essie Linggood would have kept the information from her. Eileen hated being coddled.

On arrival in Sydney, they went through customs, a much slower and more tedious process than in Rabaul, where Wilf's knowledge and diplomacy always facilitated the process. Finally standing on the Sydney wharf, those Mission wives who had remained on the ship after Queensland found Reverend John Burton himself there to greet them. Most took it as a good sign that their husbands would be taken care of if the Chairman himself was taking an interest in the wives' immediate future.

Burton, or at least his secretary, had made all the arrangements for Eileen's camphorwood chests to be sent on to Hobart, leaving her with only what was necessary for the next few weeks. Back in Rabaul, Eileen had planned to travel on to Hobart immediately on reaching Sydney, since the baby was not due until mid-January, but she had been experiencing pain over the last few days. A conversation with Kath Brown convinced her this might be an indication the baby was not far away, so when Reverend Burton took one look at her and suggested she stay at George Brown College in Haberfield until the birth, she found herself agreeing. Wilf's final remonstrations that she look after herself weighed heavily on her mind. She was too tired to fight for something just because it had previously seemed like the right thing to do.

On arrival at the college she realised she had inadvertently sent all her books on to Hobart with the trunks. She was most put out when they wouldn't open the library for her to select something to read, since it was after 6pm. Fortunately Miss Greenfield, one of the staff members she'd first met during her training in 1936, insisted on catering to her every whim, so the next morning the college librarian came to offer a personal consultation, then returned with a small stack of reading matter – but not until after Eileen had written to Wilf about the library closure, rather put out by the refusal. She was happy to live without electricity or go camping in the Baining Mountains and sleep on a woven mat, but going without reading matter was a step too far.

A radiogram was sent, at the Mission's expense, to inform Eileen's family of her change of plans. Since she was in Australia now the ban on communications around travel plans didn't apply, although Reverend Burton had made it clear none of the wives were to talk about anything to do with Rabaul that could reach the wrong ears and place their husbands at risk.

Mrs Margetts, the college house mother, was concerned about the false contractions Eileen was experiencing, insisting it would be safest if she took to her bed whilst they made all the arrangements for her forthcoming hospitalisation. That was how Eileen found herself lying in the Queen of Tonga's bed at the training College on New Year's Eve, a glass of fresh milk within arm's reach on the bedside table. Her dinner consisted of two boiled eggs as an entrée, then roast chicken with stuffing, and vegetables. The pampering regime apparently included providing all the foods that were hard to come by in New Britain, the glass of milk being a particular luxury, according to Miss Greenfield.

'We're in drought,' she explained. 'Water's being rationed. They've threatened to ration milk too, but it hasn't quite happened yet. Finding the bed comfortable?'

Eileen nodded as Miss Greenfield fussed around her.

'Why is it called the Queen of Tonga's bed?' This had been the subject of much debate during Eileen's training, when a tour of the college had revealed the immense, ornately carved bed in a guest room. 'Is it a metaphor?'

Miss Greenfield laughed. 'Oh no! No, the Queen of Tonga is very real. She visits the college occasionally and she's rather a large lady, so the bed was made especially for her. You're a tiny woman yourself, Mrs Pearce, but with the baby, Mrs Margetts thought you would be more comfortable with plenty of space. Did you enjoy your dinner?'

She eyed the leftovers on the bedside table.

'It was delicious, but I just can't fit much in lately. I suppose there's no room for my stomach anymore.'

Miss Greenfield swept up the dirty dishes. 'Well, it won't be long until that baby makes its way into the world. My sisters have seven between them, so I know the signs. A quiet New Year's for you tonight then. Although it's quiet all round really, with the blackouts. I don't suppose you've seen much of that, having only been back a couple of days.'

Eileen shook her head. Miss Greenfield put the dishes down and took a seat next to the bed.

'The city is like a war zone. Everyone's put up blackout curtains. There are sandbags and trenches, and rationing. Oh, the rationing has been difficult, but we wanted to get some good food into you after your long trip so we didn't let it stop us! People are fearful that the Japanese might reach Australia.'

Crossing her legs, she bounced the top one excitedly. 'How do you celebrate New Year's Eve in Rabaul? I mean, normally. I see so many people trained to travel overseas here, but I've never had the chance to go myself.'

For the Mission folk there was often a concert and supper, with maybe some subdued celebrations, but Eileen thought about the talks she and Wilf had given in Tasmania. The audience always loved to hear about the Tolai people, so that's what she decided would be most interesting.

'It's a big day for the Christian Tolai. They hold a special service in their native church until late at night or even early morning. At the service, they confess all the sins they have committed that year, that they can remember. When they run out of sins, they use their imagination to help think of some more.'

'Goodness!'

Eileen smiled, the memory bringing delight. 'When that fails them, they begin to confess all the sins of everyone they know – real or otherwise, I believe. They don't like to be outdone.'

The two women laughed. Eileen hadn't felt such lightness of spirit since she had boarded the *Macdhui*. But the mood dissipated as quickly as it had come as she wondered how her Tolai friends were spending this New Year's Eve. Were they celebrating, or had they fled to the hills? And what changes would the new year bring? Would the girls return for another term at the college at Vunairima, or would their education be put on hold? The papers were full of discussion of the strategic importance of New Britain for the Japanese, so it was becoming more difficult to dismiss the possibility of an invasion.

'Oh, I forgot to tell you,' Miss Greenfield said, 'Netta Allsop rang the College telephone.' The telephone was a new addition since Eileen's training days. 'She's planning to visit tomorrow.'

Eileen was glad. It would be good to be able to talk about Wilf, and Ken. Whilst everyone was looking after her wonderfully, they were avoiding any topics that might upset her. The restrictions made her want to scream.

In the end, Eileen only got to enjoy the luxury of the Queen of Tonga's bed for another twenty-four hours. Her contractions began properly late on New Year's Day, after Netta's visit. They had talked for hours about life in Rabaul, wondering what Ken and Wilf were up to. Both were still new brides so to spend the festive season away from their husbands was almost unbearable.

At first Eileen wasn't sure she was experiencing proper contractions, since she'd been having similar pain for a week or so by now, but they grew and grew in intensity until, in the middle of the night, she agreed it was time to travel to the hospital. Mrs Margetts immediately organised her into the Waverley Memorial Methodist Hospital, where all the best care and attention were provided during the birth. Mrs Margetts had assured Eileen there was to be no expense nor effort spared, with the Mission Board covering everything.

By mid-morning on January 2nd, Eileen lay in a bed far smaller than the Queen of Tonga's, in a two-bed ward, and a nurse placed her newborn little girl into her arms. The room had two large windows, both open to the Sydney summer. Outside, a beautiful garden provided a soothing balm for her sleepless state as she fed the baby for the first time. A strange, raucous cry from outside startled the infant, who began screaming.

'What was that?' Eileen said, alarmed. She hadn't realised how on edge the events of the last few weeks had made her, but the scream jangled her to her core.

'That's old Percy, I'd say,' the nurse said. 'One of the peacocks. There are two of them that wander around. The other one's Petunia. They do like to sing a lot. I'm sure they won't stay outside your window the whole time.'

She helped Eileen reattach the crying baby, and silence descended once more, apart from a whispering breeze outdoors.

'She's not a bad size for a premmie,' the nurse continued. 'Have you thought of a name?'

Eileen looked down at the tiny baby, who was drinking

contentedly. Wilf had pretended not to care, but she knew how much he wanted a girl. She would have to send him a cable as soon as possible to let him know he had a daughter. In their conversation about names, they had decided on Jean, and of course Elsa, after Eileen's mother if it was a girl. But holding her in her arms, Eileen felt a new impulse. As she spoke, she didn't remember where she'd come across the name before, she only felt it seemed right.

'Rosemary,' she said. 'Her name is Rosemary Elsa Jean.'

Wilf

Wednesday 7th January 1942. Rabaul.

```
In this strange, terrible world war
there is a place for everyone, man
and woman, old and young, hale and
halt; service in a thousand forms is
open. There is no room now for the
dilettante, the weakling, for the
shirker, or the sluggard. The mine,
the factory, the dockyard, the salt
sea waves, the fields to till, the
home, the hospital, the chair of the
scientist, the pulpit of the preacher
- from the highest to the humblest
tasks, all are of equal honour; all
have their part to play. The enemies
ranged against us, coalesced and
combined against us, have asked for
total war. Let us make sure they get it.
```

Winston Churchill, 30 December 1941

Wilf sat at the table on the veranda, fighting the urge to light up a cigarette. His dirty dinner dishes were pushed to one side. Benri, the houseboy, had never returned to work after the New Year's holiday, probably because he was scared by the invasion rumours, so Wilf would have to deal with the dishes himself. But first, he had to write to Eileen. He tapped the paper with his pen, wondering how to capture the week just passed with mere words. The highs and lows of emotions, the growing reality of the threat to Rabaul; it had all come into sharp focus.

On the morning of the thirtieth, all the missionary men had crowded into Wilf's office first thing, to listen to Churchill's New Year's speech, the consensus afterwards being that it was rather invigorating. On New Year's Eve there had been a thoroughly entertaining impromptu concert at Anzac Hall, with all the Salvation Army bandsmen contributing items together and separately, including Wilf Trigg with his accordion. It had been wonderful to catch up with them again, since their duties kept them away from Sunday services all too often now. The address during the midnight service had focused on the Mission's caring responsibilities. Overall, the end of 1941 had been inspiring, if subdued.

Then on New Year's Day, Mac, Wilf and most of the local mission men had driven out to Vunairima, where they were joined by the nurses from Stewart Hospital. Being at Vunairima made Eileen's absence achingly obvious. Everywhere he looked he felt his wife's presence, on the veranda of the Sisters' House, where they had dined together in the romantic lamplight, and in the garden, where they had strolled so many times during his visits, their conversations wide-ranging and stimulating. Her second Christmas pudding was the dessert for the meal, with everyone again commenting on her cooking expertise. Dorothy Beale, who had worked closely with Eileen during her time at the girls' school, was eager to know if Wilf had any news yet about the baby. He had to explain it wasn't due for another few weeks.

When the men drove back to Rabaul that evening, they were surprised to find Percy Clark waiting for them, having made his way in from Kavieng. It had been too far for him to travel for the luncheon, yet he had unexpectedly made the longer journey all the way to town. As the other men dispersed, Percy went into the Chairman's office with Mac. A short while later Mac came out, his face giving away little, and told Wilf that Percy had resigned. He asked for Wilf's assistance to organise the relevant paperwork and transport of all his possessions to Australia. Since Wilf had known Mac for a long time, he could tell the Chairman was not pleased by this unexpected staffing change. Mac had previously called a planning meeting for the fifth of January, which all the missionaries had promised to attend, with the intention of discussing the future of the Mission. Percy had jumped the gun with his decision.

Wilf's loyalty was to the Mission, always, but Percy's decision shook him. The rock-solid foundation of their work in New Britain seemed to be crumbling as the threat of invasion drew nearer. Both Tom Simpson and Howard Pearson had expressed doubts privately to Wilf about whether staying was the right thing to do. Tom had questioned whether the expectation they all had, that after the invasion the Japanese would allow their work to continue, might be inaccurate.

Wilf picked up the letter he'd received from Eileen last Sunday. She'd written it just after she arrived in Australia, so there was no news of the baby yet. Responding to her news gave his whirling thoughts something simple to focus on, before he tackled the more complex question of what to tell her about recent events. Usually, he would speak freely with her. She had a backbone of steel, and a common-sense worldview to match. But he didn't want to cause her any stress when the birth was only a few weeks away. And there was the issue of censorship.

Eileen was safe in Sydney, being cared for at George Brown College, which was an enormous relief, although it saddened him that he wasn't the one looking after her. After expressing his gladness at her situation, he reassured her that he had, in fact, given up smoking, because she'd spent quite a bit of time remonstrating him about that on their last day together. It felt like their first proper argument, to read how upset she was about the habit. It distressed him that he couldn't reassure her face to face.

He decided to give her a scant outline of the week that was, starting with the bombing raid on Sunday.

Sunday morning I got up about 8am and was just going down for mail when the car arrived with Ken who informed me that the plane was delayed – about 10.30am we were sitting talking when we heard planes coming over, it happened to be a squad of Japs and they came over and left their visiting cards at Rapinaiki. During Sunday we had alerts, but didn't get any more bombs till night. We were just about to start church when the alarm went and we went scurrying to our dugout. This time he dropped a few near the top drome. So we had a quiet Sunday.

It sounded innocuous on the page, but the truth was, Sunday had left him deeply shaken. Air raids were commonplace now, but the planes flying overhead had always been, according to Bill Harry, reconnaissance. On Sunday, he and Ken had seen the planes, extremely high, counting sixteen of them moving in perfect formation.

'It's like a school of tiny fish,' Ken commented. By the time the sirens began they were already racing to the slit trench. Then there was an echoing boom followed by a whistling sound, and another one a short while later.

'Sounds like the boys on the beach are getting to fire their anti-aircraft guns finally,' Wilf said.

'I hope the crack in the gun doesn't cause any problems.'

'Do you think they have a chance of hitting those planes? They're pretty high up.'

'Probably not,' Ken said. 'But I bet they're glad to finally see some action.'

There was silence for a few minutes. Both men expected the all-clear to sound, as it usually did, but then a huge explosion echoed around them. They looked at each other, both registering shock, but before they could speak another explosion jarred their hearing, then another and another.

'We're being bombed,' Ken said between blasts. After weeks of seeing planes at a distance, war had suddenly arrived in Rabaul.

While the bombs were exploding there seemed no end to the terrible noise, but it was all over quickly. Later that afternoon, Harold Page dropped into Wilf's office and filled him and Mac in on what had happened. The Japanese pilots had released about forty bombs over the Lakunai airdrome, which was the one closest to Matupi Island. Only three had hit the runway, with many more landing in the harbour, killing scores of fish, which floated to the surface.

'The natives were reluctant to collect them,' Page said, and

Wilf knew that was because so many had died trying to collect fish floating in the harbour during the 1937 eruption. The Tolai didn't forget. But the worst part of that first bombing was that about half the bombs had landed squarely on Rapindik native hospital, and the native compound next to it. Page estimated about fifteen natives had died and a similar number had terrible injuries, because the bombs had released deadly shrapnel, severing limbs or puncturing eyes. The missionaries' noble idea of protecting the natives from the Japanese suddenly seemed naive in the face of such destruction.

Wilf debated with himself whether he would write about the fallout of the bombs, but was torn, so moved on to Monday, trying to keep his tone light.

> *Monday morning we had planned a district committee meeting and were just about to start when we got word that there was likely to be a raid so we all piled into the cars and went up to Refuge Valley where we had our meeting, or at least part of it, for as soon as the all clear was sounded we came back to the office. Monday afternoon we continued. The meeting finished up around 5.30pm having talked a lot but done very little else.*

More bombs had been dropped shortly after they called a halt to the meeting, but none had hit anything important. Still, the ear-shattering sounds, which Wilf thought he would never get used to, and the possibility of indiscriminate death from above, brought a new anxiety to daily activities. But what had been more disturbing about Monday, and the continuation of the meeting on Tuesday, had been the topic of conversation.

Mac had set aside all the usual business to focus on preparations for invasion. He encouraged everyone to parcel up household goods and organise with Wilf to send them to

Australia, just in case. There was a long, intense discussion about which native preachers might be ready to take over ministering on each circuit, and how to prepare them to do so. The question of why the Australian missionaries might not be able to continue their work wasn't discussed.

Until now they had all been determined it was their duty to stay. Reverend Burton, in his position as head of the Overseas Mission in Australia, had always taken the progressive view that the missionaries' role was to ensure the natives weren't exploited by the Europeans in Rabaul, and to prepare them for a life coping with modern society. He took the Mission's responsibility for the Australian Mandated Territory and its citizens seriously. Obviously thinking along these lines, someone had suggested that if the missionaries acted as go-betweens, encouraging the natives to cooperate with the Japanese, the invaders might appreciate these efforts and send the church men home. Wilf could tell the younger men, at least, considered this unrealistic. The thought that it might be better to leave before things reached that eventuality lingered over the rest of the discussion.

Mac advised them all he was writing to the Board about their families, a topic of constant worry for them all.

'Whatever happens, I want their assurance that your wives and children will be looked after, financially, as well as emotionally and spiritually.'

Whatever happens.

The unspoken possibilities behind these words made Wilf's breath catch. Most of the older men didn't seem to read anything into them, but Tom Simpson was clearly shaken by the ominous suggestion they contained. Wilf was relieved to realise he was not the only one feeling less than confident an invading force might act as they expected.

The meeting went on for two days, and at the end of Tuesday, after a discussion of the various possible outcomes of an invasion, they agreed to continue with the circuit work for now. The men continued to hope for the best, their faith and sense of vocation strong. They expressed confidence that the Japanese, if they did take over, would treat them with respect, at the very least, as men of the cloth. Wilf's faith wasn't wavering, but his father had been a carpenter and a builder, so common sense was strong in his family. It worried him that they really didn't know how the Japanese might behave towards the missionary men. He wasn't sure they could assume people from a different culture might regard the Christian church in the same way as Australians.

Yesterday, Harold Page had stayed in the office after the meeting and quietly told Wilf and Mac he was looking at avenues for evacuation of all civilians left in Rabaul.

'I just need permission from the government,' he assured them. His words were confident, but his shoulders slumped and his eyes darted around the room as he spoke.

After Page had left, Mac sat down with Wilf, his expression serious. 'I want you to box up any vital documents. Financial books, deeds for the churches, that sort of thing. I don't want to send them to Australia, because hopefully we'll be able to get back to business as usual before too long. I'm sure it's just a question of whether the Americans get here before or after the Japanese. But just in case... I want to be prepared to bury the legal papers. Wrap them well then go to Chinatown and get a steel box that's watertight.'

'Where are you going to bury them?'

'I'm thinking Kalas might be safer than here.' Wilf agreed. It was isolated and hard to reach. 'And can you get this in the post? It's the letter to John Burton. I've broached the subject of us heading to Australia for a while – just until it's safe to return. I know some of the men are having doubts, and I don't want to force them into anything.'

After posting the letter, Wilf had spent the rest of Tuesday and much of yesterday packing and sorting, papers for Mac, and household goods for the missionaries. It was good to have such menial tasks to do, because his concentration for anything more complex was non-existent. He mentioned his work briefly in the letter, but decided to finish on the most reassuring note he could. As he wrote, it occurred to him that the bombings might make the news in Australia, so he decided to include a little more detail. Eileen would see straight through the reassurances otherwise and worry about what he was not telling her.

This afternoon I have spent the whole afternoon in the office. And tonight I'm just trying to let you know what we have been doing. I do hope you will not be too worried over the air raids Darling – There isn't any need to be Dearie – we go into our holes as soon as we hear they are coming and should be quite O.K. So far there have been very few casualties – most of them, in fact all except a couple, being on Sunday morning when there were a dozen natives killed and 22 other natives injured. Well Sweetest, that completes my diary and I'm sure there isn't much else to write about.

He signed the letter with his swooping, elaborate signature, then sealed the envelope. Packing up, he went inside and placed the letter on the kitchen table, ready for posting tomorrow.

Wilf was shaving the next morning when he heard a car door slam, then feet pounding across the veranda. His heart lurched.

He hurried outside. Ken was standing there, grinning like a fool.

'I expect a jolly good tip for this. Brought around a radiogram that just came through for you.'

After everything that had happened this week, Wilf was reluctant to take it, but then he noticed the envelope was torn. Ken's grin suddenly made sense.

'Not bad news?'

'No, definitely not bad news.'

Still, Wilf's hand was shaking as he took the envelope and slid the radiogram out.

'Baby Rosemary born 2nd Jan. Both healthy. Letter soon xx'

Wilf looked up at his brother-in-law. 'What do you say we have a special lunch today? A celebration. I'm a father!'

Raluana Lane

14 – Unbearable Waiting

Eileen

10am, Tuesday 20th January 1942. Sydney.

> We in Australia have a special responsibility for these people. As Australian Methodists the responsibility is still more immediate, for these people are our own peculiar charge, and none other is working amongst them. If we do not help them they will not be helped… […] It is required of us that we be faithful, and thus we shall see rise in majesty and in power a truly Christian Church in a land that was once stained dully purple with human blood.

John Burton Wear, *Our Task in Papua*, 1926, p. 124

Perhaps it wasn't the best idea to take a baby in a basket on public transport, but there really hadn't been any other option. Eileen couldn't have left Rosemary in her Auntie Nell's care for the morning. There was the complicated issue of feeding, and Auntie Nell and her family had done so much for her already, she really didn't want to ask for this additional favour. Though their house was a tidy, three-bed weatherboard, it was very small, and she was constantly aware of imposing on her relatives' comfortable life with a noisy infant. Eileen had also absorbed the Tolai women's attitude to babies, so she didn't see any real difficulty in carrying Rosemary with her wherever she went.

The ferry from Manly into Sydney had caused Eileen unease, and initially she hadn't been able to work out why. The war posters on the walls didn't worry her: similar ones had appeared in Rabaul months ago. Someone nearby had been talking loudly about the possibility that the Japanese might sneak into the harbour with a submarine, an idea Eileen thought absurd. Sunny Sydney, even with its sandbags and 'loose lips' posters, seemed so far from the growing dangers in Rabaul, she couldn't imagine war coming here.

The risks were real in the place she had left behind. After they reached Sydney, Jean Shelton had told her a Japanese ship was spotted shortly after they left Simpson Harbour, causing terror to ripple through the ship like a bushfire. Although the ship was blacked out and hopefully almost invisible, they had all been ordered to stay inside, and Jean had described the women huddled in the dark, barely breathing, waiting for the danger to pass. Eileen, ensconced in her cabin, had been unaware, and Essie had obviously kept the information from her.

As the ferry made its picturesque journey across Sydney harbour, sunlight glinting on the gentle waves, Eileen was delighted to see the Harbour Bridge, with its sweeping arc. She realised then, it was the very normalcy of the day, and her enjoyment of it, that disturbed her. Wilf's experience must be terribly different. There had been reports in the papers that Rabaul was being bombed regularly. She'd only received one letter from her husband, dated the 7th, where he had written about the bombs. His rather casual mention of the deaths of a number of natives had been a clear sign that he was minimising the truth, because he would have been deeply upset by this, as was she.

It was frustrating to feel so worn out after the birth. Auntie Nell was understanding, feeding her liver and tongue and other fortifying meats that were still available despite rationing, to strengthen her blood. Having lived with limited meat for so long, Eileen did not enjoy the experience, but she knew her aunt was trying to do the right thing. Baby Rosemary barely slept either, and Eileen didn't want to disturb her aunt, so she spent much of the night trying to coax her newborn to sleep, or at least not to wail. The last two and a half weeks had passed in a dispiriting blur.

Now though, Rosemary was settling into better sleep patterns, which meant Eileen was starting to be able to think again. She wanted to travel home to Hobart once the baby was old enough, so there were arrangements to be finalised. The Overseas Mission Office in Castlereagh Street was her destination. She had last been there with Wilf during their furlough last year, although they had been staying with Wilf's parents then so the first leg of her journey had been different. As the business manager for Rabaul, Wilf had had many matters to discuss with Reverend Burton, but for Eileen it had only been a social call. Today was different. In her bag, alongside a change of nappies, Eileen had all the paperwork she and Wilf had completed, as well as other, more general papers Wilf had asked her to deliver.

Once the ferry docked at its destination, Eileen caught the train from Circular Quay, leaving the dazzling blue of Sydney Harbour for the dark of the underground tunnels. This part of the trip was much quicker, and she soon emerged from Museum Station, with its stately tilework, into the green expanse of Hyde Park. Here she was on familiar ground and quickly made her way to the Overseas Mission offices. Reverend Burton was waiting for her.

'Eileen, so good to see you!'

'And you, John.' He'd insisted on first names during their last visit. John's round face lit up when he saw the baby. 'You've brought little Rosemary with you! Bring her into my office so I can have a good look at Wilf's little one.'

John instructed Miss Harris, his secretary, to fetch tea. He led Eileen into his inner sanctum, swiftly gathering the scattered papers that covered his desk into a ragged pile, which he pushed to one side.

'Here, let me help you with that,' he said, taking the baby's basket and placing it where the papers had been. Rosemary had slept through most of the travel, perhaps soothed by the steady movement of the ferry, then the train, but now her basket was still, she immediately woke up. Unperturbed by the face that loomed over her, she watched John Burton for a moment, then gave a funny gurgling sound.

'Well, I believe she takes after Wilf rather than you,' John said, letting the infant grasp his finger. 'There's a rather serious expression on her face that reminds me of him when he needs to talk to one of the missionaries about their poor account keeping. It's a shame she hasn't got your lovely red hair, but then if she did, she might be something of a handful.' Realising what he'd said, he gave Eileen a wink. 'Not that I'm saying you were a handful. Far from it! But you do know your own mind. Which was perfect for a headmistress.'

'Red hair or not, she's a busy little thing already,' Eileen told him. John retrieved his hand and went round the desk to take his seat, gesturing for Eileen to sit also. Feeling it would be a bit odd to have the carry basket between them, Eileen went to lift it down, but as soon as she picked it up Rosemary started grisling.

'I think she wants to be at the centre of events,' John said with a smile. 'Leave her there. We'll put the tea things on the side.'

As if summoned by those words, Miss Harris returned with a pot and cups, as well as a plate of home-made biscuits. 'Despite the rationing, we have managed a little treat,' she said with a smile, pouring their refreshments. Once she left, Eileen drew out all the paperwork, personal and Mission-related, and handed it over. John spent several minutes going through it, nodding and asking the occasional question.

'I was hoping you might answer my questions,' Eileen said abruptly. 'It's been nearly a month since I left and I've only had one letter. Do you know what's happening? The newspapers seem to be short on facts and long on drama.'

John put the forms down and steepled his fingers. 'That's their modus operandi. My apologies, I hadn't thought you might be waiting on news. Normally, a month wouldn't see many changes, but that can't be said of these strange times. I have been in touch with Laurie Mac a few times since your return. The men are all well, I can assure you of that. Everything has been calm and they seem determined to stay. They believe they can act as intermediaries between the Tolai and the Japanese, hopefully protecting our flock from the ravages of war.'

'Do you think that's really...' Before Eileen could finish her thought, Rosemary let out a wailing cry. Eileen went to pick her up, but the baby found her own fist and began sucking on it, her distress immediately gone. John pushed on.

'Mac has asked that we allow wives to draw a monthly stipend and the board has approved that, so I will get you to do some more paperwork while you're here.' He abruptly changed topic, probably hoping she would not read anything in his body language, but Eileen was an astute woman. She wondered if Mac's request had arisen from worry about what would happen to the families if the missionaries were interned or killed. 'Oh, and Miss Harris tells me your retiring cheque was never cashed.'

'I intended to cash it as soon as we arrived in Australia last year, but what with the wedding and honeymoon, and then travelling around doing our talks, I suppose I never got around to it.'

John searched through the pile of papers on his desk and drew out an envelope, along with a form.

'That's the paperwork for drawing an allowance. If you can fill that out now, we'll get it organised as quickly as possible. In the envelope is a new cheque for the retiring allowance. Just tear up the old one. It's been cancelled at this end.'

Eileen spent a few minutes filling out the form, thinking as she always did how messy her signature looked compared to Wilf's beautiful, swirling letters. Once she had returned it, John turned the conversation to church work in Rabaul as they drank their tea.

'I've been hearing wonderful things from Ia Lo about the school. The students continue to reach a higher standard year after year. You laid a wonderful foundation with your work, and since taking over from you, Ia Lo has continued in that vein. We're grateful for your recommendation.'

'She's perfect for the position,' Eileen said. 'The girls adore her and she has a real gift for teaching. I don't think she's capable of *not* teaching! And she's one of the most sensible people I know.' She took a sip of her tea but left her biscuit untouched.

Thoughts of Ia Lo brought a heaviness behind her eyes. Not quite tears, more simple sadness. 'Saying goodbye to her was terribly hard. I worry about her safety.'

'As do we all,' John said. 'I pray every day for all our men and nursing sisters as well.'

'So do I.'

The baby started stirring in her basket again. A moment later she scrunched up her face.

'If you need a private room for some time there's an office next door that's empty,' John said as the infant let out a wail. 'Babies don't like to wait to have their needs met. It's a long time ago now for me, having infants in the house, but one doesn't forget.'

'Thank you. That's probably wise.' They both stood.

'Are you headed to Hobart soon?' John asked as Eileen gathered her things.

'I think I'll be at my aunt's another week or two, then I've been invited to stay at the Cleverdons' if necessary, depending on when I can get on the boat across Bass Strait.'

Rosemary Jean began screaming. Eileen seized her bag and looped her arm through the basket. 'I'd better get her sorted,' she said, and hurried to the door. John stepped out from behind his desk, another envelope in his hand.

'It would have been dreadful if I'd forgotten this. It was addressed to the hospital, but since you'd already left, they sent it back to us.' He held out a letter. Eileen's heart started pounding as she recognised Wilf's graceful hand. 'One last thing Eileen. I want to assure you that the Board and I are keeping a close eye on events in New Britain. Wilf's safety, and the safety of every one of our men, is our highest priority.'

'Thank you,' Eileen said. Rosemary was becoming increasingly distressed. Eileen took the letter and pushed it into the depths of her bag. She wondered what the board could actually do if the situation deteriorated, but pushed the thought aside. Stopping Rosemary's screams was her highest priority. Her concerns, and the letter, would have to wait.

Wilf

Noon, Tuesday 20th January 1942. Rabaul.

'Are you sure that's everything?' Mac asked as Wilf locked the steel box. 'All the legal papers? No, forget I asked. You've always been meticulous and thorough. I'm just nervous.'

'I know,' Wilf said. 'I'm dying for a smoke myself, but I promised Eileen. I must tell you, Mac, there was a bit of room left so I've put my letters from Eileen and Netta in there too. I didn't think you'd mind.'

'Of course not. I only wish I'd thought of it. I gave mine to Akuila for safekeeping.'

'He'll guard them with his life,' Wilf said. He'd known the native minister a long time and if anyone embodied Christian values of integrity and responsibility, Akuila To Ngaru was such a man.

Mac came and stood beside Wilf. 'Are you sure you won't come to Kalas with us?'

'I've kept this office running since 1927. I don't think I should stop now. Besides, you know how the men like to drop in for a chat. If I'm not here, what will they do?'

Mac clapped him on the back. 'Everyone trusts you, Wilf. You'll keep the morale up for those that are left.'

'I hope so.'

There was a tap at the door, and Bill Harry entered. 'Hi, Wilf, Mac. Just thought I'd check in since everything's so unsteady.'

'It's good to see you, Bill. How are the lads in the army coping?' Wilf asked him.

'They're a mixed bunch. Some of them are looking forward to seeing some action. They've been getting pretty bored with all the waiting. Those are the lads that were disappointed to find they weren't being shipped to Europe, after their training. They're convinced they'll clean up if the Japs turn up. Others are pretty downhearted. What about at your end?'

'I'd say it's the same,' Wilf said. 'The last fortnight has brought the reality a bit closer to home, hasn't it? Everyone's anxious and no one has enough information.'

Mac chimed in. 'It looked possible we could all evacuate on the Malaita, but at the time everyone thought their duties here outweighed the risks. Our commitment to our work is a core part of our values, and of course Churchill's speech at New Year's really underlined that. Since then, with the increase in flyovers and the Japanese propaganda we're picking up on the radio, it's impossible not to have doubts, I suppose. We're not blind to the dangers. We sent the wives and children who are part of Reverend Sam's church out to Vunakabi a few days ago.'

Bill lowered his voice, glancing at the door. 'I can't say anything about what's happening, of course. In the normal run of things, you'd expect some back-up to be sent when you're a small company, or at least plans for escape to be put in place. But it wouldn't be wrong to say some of the lads are feeling like they've been *given away* by the Government.' He inclined his head to emphasise the point and continued. 'With the *Herstein* in the harbour, it might not be a bad idea to make enquiries about passage to Australia for anyone with the doubts you mention.'

Wilf felt a knot of anxiety in his chest. Bill Harry was in army intelligence, so any warning from him was worth taking note of, no matter how oblique. If he was reading it correctly, at least some of the army were feeling abandoned by the Australian Government. A similar sentiment had begun making the rounds amongst the civilians. Bitterness towards the administration was becoming more common in conversations, often targeted at Harold Page, since anyone higher than him had moved to Lae, and Walter McNicoll, his boss, was apparently seriously unwell.

But Harold Page took his responsibilities seriously, to the extent that he was weighed down by them. He had already spent half of last Friday exchanging telegrams with the administrators of the External Territories in Canberra, requesting all remaining civilians be evacuated on the *Herstein*. The ship had come in bringing more military equipment, then started taking on a load of copra, Rabaul's prime export and, in wartime, a key ingredient in munitions production. So far Harold's requests had come to nothing. He'd reported after the quarterly meeting on Sunday night that the unsympathetic response from Australia had been to keep loading copra.

Wilf passed this information on to Bill. 'Harold's been making enquiries, but he hasn't been given permission so far.'

'Sometimes waiting for permission isn't the quickest way to get something done,' Bill said. Wilf didn't think the point could be any clearer. Bill was warning them the time to leave was now.

Mac tapped the steel box that still sat on Wilf's desk. 'We've been planning for all contingencies. I'm taking some things up to Kalas, just in case. Thanks for your advice, Bill. We might need to call another meeting once I'm back to see whether people are changing their minds about evacuating.' Bill nodded emphatically. 'I don't suppose you can tell us any news from the army?' Mac continued.

'I'm afraid not,' said Bill. 'But it's probably wise to get any important documents away. Just don't take too long returning. I'd hate to see the *Herstein* leave before you can look at evacuation options. Sometimes the window of opportunity doesn't stay open for long. What about you, Wilf? Are you heading to the hills too?'

'No, someone's got to be here in case there are important communications, or one of the missionaries turns up from the outer territories, like Percy Clark did the other week.'

Mac looked at his watch. 'Nearly twelve-thirty already. Well, I'd better get going. I have to pick up Laurie from Raluana before we head out of town.'

'Don't forget to call that meeting,' Bill said, and left with a farewell salute.

'Wilf, could you take the box out to the car? I just want to check my desk. I'm sure there's a letter for John Poole from his wife that I should be taking with me.'

They hurried in opposite directions. Wilf had just placed the steel box on the tray of the utility when Mac returned. A moment later the air raid sirens sounded. Before they could make any decisions, Bill came running up.

'I just ran into one of the other men. This one's not a patrol. Can you get to Refuge Gully straight away? Both of you?'

Mac and Wilf looked at each other and jumped into the truck. A moment later they were hurtling down Mango Avenue toward

Namanula Hill. They were barely ahead of other traffic, and by the time they pulled into the Gully with a scattering of dirt and stones, they could see a stream of vehicles coming up the hill. Leaving the utility unlocked, they raced to the top trenches. Diving in, they still had a good view of the action because it was all happening high in the sky. Although the enemy planes flew against a backdrop of grey clouds, beams from the midday sun lit up their wings, making flashes of light as they tilted and turned.

This morning two of the Wirraways had been patrolling, but now the Mission men counted seven taking to the sky. It was a cheering sight to see all the Australian planes ready to act. Well, nearly all. Wilf remembered from the visit to the 'drome a little over a month ago that there should have been eight. There was one missing.

A moment later it became apparent this didn't matter in the slightest as the air filled with Japanese fighters flying in rapidly from the west. Wilf stopped counting at thirty, his heart plunging when he recognised them as swift, highly manoeuvrable Zeros. They split into groups and swooped towards the Wirraways, intent on their prey. Then there was a puff of white smoke from an enemy plane, followed by a bright flash, and one of the Wirraways plummeted from the sky. Another was surrounded by several fighters, which harried it like magpies chasing a lark, forcing it to the ground. The air began to fill with smoke. The irritating buzz of engines combined with booming explosions and repetitious gunfire until the endless pounding was unbearable.

Refugees from the town were still running toward the trenches, but as the drama overhead unfolded some of them stopped, their faces frozen in fear or awe. But only for a moment.

The danger was too obvious for people to forget themselves entirely. Men dove for the trench around Wilf and Mac. Wilf noticed hardly any natives or Chinese residents had made their way to the Gully. They had probably taken to the jungle.

Another flash of fire caught Wilf's attention and a second later another Wirraway was shot down. A fourth practically fell from the sky, although whether from fire or some other issue it wasn't clear, and a fifth was pursued by half a dozen Zeros, diving and landing somewhere beyond the watchers' line of sight.

Within minutes not a single Wirraway was still airborne. From Refuge Gully they could see only one heading towards the nearby Lakunai airdrome, wings tilting precariously. As it descended, they saw a tiny figure falling from the plane, until its descent was halted by a parachute. A Japanese fighter was nearby, strafing the air around the escaping pilot unceasingly. Wilf prayed the falling man would make it to the ground without being hit or his parachute destroyed.

The stillness that followed brought no relief. Wilf was sure he was not the only one trying to absorb the terrible meaning of the sudden loss of virtually all the Australian planes. Thirty aircraft against eight was more than disheartening. Had everyone underestimated the force of the Japanese army?

Although the gunfire had ceased, the droning of the Zeros hadn't, and as the men in the trenches started to find their voices, that droning grew louder.

'I'll be blowed,' someone said. 'There are more of 'em.'

Aircraft appeared from all directions. Many of them were larger carrier craft, less manoeuvrable than the ones that had taken out the Wirraways, but still swift, alongside more fighters. Some headed south, no doubt to the second airdrome at

Vunakanau. The air was filled with fast-moving planes, black against the cloudless sky, zipping in all directions at once. There were easily a hundred of them, and once they were close enough, they started dropping bomb after bomb.

Not all the bombs exploded, but those that did created enough noise that the Rabaul civilians watching from their refuge had to hold their hands over their ears constantly. Lark Force were obviously in position, because there was some fire from the gun emplacements on the beach, and continuous fire from the anti-aircraft battery on the side of the North Daughter, one of the volcanoes, but they seemed to be having no luck.

'If they keep firing, our blokes are bound to hit something eventually,' one of the nearby men said with laconic Aussie humour, but no one laughed.

Mac leaned in towards Wilf, speaking when he could through the tremendous noise. 'I don't think I'll be heading to Kalas today. But if this isn't the invasion, it can only be a day or so away. When this is over, I want you to talk to Page. I don't care whether Canberra gives permission or not, we need to get our men on the *Herstein*.'

A cheer went up from someone near them, then another, the celebration spreading like a wave through the trench. One of the Japanese planes was falling from the sky in a death spiral, smoke billowing from it. It crash-landed on the side of Matupit, rather too close for comfort, and swiftly became a pyre.

Wilf leaned closer so Mac could hear him over the cheers. 'I'll talk to him this afternoon.' His words were cut off by a tremendous boom. It came from the direction of the harbour. Almost immediately black smoke began pouring into the air. At first, they couldn't see what was happening through the churning blackness.

'That wasn't the *Herstein* was it?' Mac asked.

'It's not on the right wharf,' Wilf said. 'I think it was the *Westralia*. Her hold's full of coal so that'd explain the smoke.' He turned to look behind them. 'They're going for Lakunai now,' he continued, as a swathe of bombers peeled off and headed to the end of the harbour where Refuge Gully was. For a moment, the possibility that they might be bombed where they sheltered loomed large, but Wilf was right. Like wasps released from the nest, they swirled around the airport. Then some began dropping their bombs, whilst others began using guns to strafe the coconut trees nearby. It seemed their goal was simply to destroy anything they possibly could.

There were only a few dive bombers still circling Simpson Harbour. Around Wilf, everyone was watching the swarms of aircraft to the southwest, or nearby, over Lakunai. The harbour was covered by dense smoke, making it impossible for the planes to target anything close to the centre of town.

The raid seemed to go on forever, but barely forty-five minutes later every single enemy craft turned and flew away, leaving an echoing silence and clouds of smoke. It took another ten minutes for the all-clear to sound.

Wilf and Mac headed to Mango Avenue in the utility, talking through the logistics of getting all the missionaries evacuated. Some, like Dan Oakes, Rodger Brown and Tom Simpson, were a long way away, so getting them into town before the *Herstein* left might not be an option. They hadn't reached any conclusions by the time they pulled into the church office. Harold Page was waiting for them at the front door.

Harold regularly took part in Methodist services and

meetings and had a close relationship with Mac, Wilf and the other Rabaul staff.

'I'm glad to see you're both okay,' he greeted his friends, his face grim. 'I'm sending a message out to all civilians, but I wanted to let you know personally. I'm recommending people head out of town. I'm getting nothing back from Canberra. We're on our own, so I have to make decisions for everyone's safety. I think the best bet is to head south to Kokopo. Hopefully, we can organise some way of being picked up from the south.'

'The rain might be a problem,' Mac said, looking up. The grey clouds had become far denser during their drive down from the valley, and no doubt it would begin pouring down soon. 'I was actually heading up to Kalas this afternoon, but if the rain hits it'll be impossible to get through.' He glanced at Wilf. 'Harold, do you think we should act sooner? Rather than heading south and trying to get away from there, can't we just talk to the captain of the *Herstein*? There'd be plenty of room to get the civilians out.'

Harold shook his head. 'An hour ago, that would have been my plan. I guess you didn't see what happened. Three bombers hit the *Herstein* squarely. The copra in the hold caught alight and she's burning like a bonfire. The *Herstein*'s going nowhere.'

15 - Invasion

Wilf

Noon, 22ⁿᵈ January 1942. Rabaul to Kokopo to the Warangoi River

```
Some of the premises on which the War
Cabinet  appears  to  be  working  at
present are:

Long-term  planning  will  bring  ulti-
mate  Allied  victory  in  the  various
theatres of world war. But an essen-
tial of long-term planning is that it
must make immediate provision for the
holding  of  bases  essential  for  the
execution  of  plans  worked  out  that
involves, until the Allied war poten-
tial  in  manpower  and  equipment  is
fully achieved, the immediate concen-
tration  of  maximum  possible  Allied
strength  at  the  vital  points  where
maximum  immediate  danger  exists  for
the  Allied  cause.  At  present  the
south-west  Pacific  is  chief  among
those points.
```

The Sydney Morning Herald, 26 January 1942, p. 4

By the time this article was published, Lark Force was defeated: captured or scattered and fighting for their survival.

Nobody knew what to do.

The wait was almost over, that was clear. Invasion was imminent. Yesterday had been a bizarre mix of endless, scurrying preparation and unbearable waiting. Today felt like the heavy stillness before wild weather finally breaks, when the sky is so ponderous and dark you almost wish for the downpour and lightning, simply to end the prolonged suspense.

People did strange things in their anxiety. There was generous behaviour, such as yesterday morning, when those storekeepers who hadn't left Rabaul opened up and allowed everyone to take whatever they wanted. Wilf wasn't sure of the logic – was it a purely altruistic act, to support those who would have scant access to supplies soon, or did they want their goods in the hands of their fellow citizens rather than the hands of the enemy?

There were also those whose anxiety made them turn on others. Wilf had spent last night at Refuge Gully again, along with most of the other Europeans, but where previous stays had had a feeling of camaraderie and something like adventure, last night had seen extended bitter tirades against the army, the government, the administration and anyone else who could be blamed for the impending disaster.

Perhaps the most inexplicable of all were the acts of the army. That was not merely Wilf's assessment – speaking to Bill Harry yesterday had confirmed his sense that they didn't have a strong plan, even though Bill was as circumspect as usual. Units seemed to be moving all over the place. They had decamped from their barracks on Malaguna Road yesterday, although they hadn't seemed to take many supplies with them. Then last night they had demolished the Vunakanau airstrip, having planted mines earlier. Bill had warned Wilf there would be a series of explosions before the invasion, since the army didn't want their equipment, however old it might be, to be taken by the Japanese.

In the last twenty-four hours it had become hard to tell which explosions were caused by the army, and which from the endless bombing raids. Since the beginning of January these raids had swiftly increased in number, with less reprieve between them. After last night's demolition at Vunakanau, Japanese fighters had taken their turn this morning, scorching the airdrome with every kind of gunfire and bomb they had, based on the range of sounds. From deep booms to the rat-a-tat of machine guns, all accompanied by the endless drone and mosquito whine of planes, as the airdrome was pounded over and over.

The noise was constant and jarring, made worse by the ever-present sirens that caused an automatic spike in stress. Wilf thought he would never get used to the air-raid warning, because it signalled fearful destruction. To top it off, Tavurvur was active again, spewing smoke and rumbling with unease, and it looked like a storm would hit this afternoon. Nature was adding to the chaos.

This morning Nobby Clark had dropped by the office, looking for Laurie Mac. But after the delay caused by the raid on the 20th, Mac had resumed his plan and left for Kalas the following morning, along with Laurie Linggood and Howard Pearson, leaving Wilf in charge. Mac was planning to head to Vunairima first to get the Mission nurses to safety, then make his way to the hills to hide the vital documents. What he did after that would depend on what was happening in Rabaul.

With Mac unavailable, Nobby gave Wilf the message from Army Intelligence that all civilians should 'resume normal duties'.

'Resume normal duties? With all this noise and craziness?

They've got to be joking! I can't breathe for the tension,' Wilf had said.

'I know. It's ridiculous. They seem to think we're stupid. That we won't work out it's all about to go to hell. I think the only thing to do is head to the Gully and leave the army to do their job and deal with the Japs. But we don't have official directives yet.'

After a morning spent running to and from the split-trenches, Wilf was starting to think heading up to Refuge Gully would at least be more stable, when Harold Page arrived at his office, with Harry Townsend, the Treasurer of the Administration, in tow. Wilf had been reading his copy of the Pidgin hymn book he had translated when they entered.

'Wilf, how can you work at a time like this?'

Wilf shrugged. He closed the book and tucked it away in one of the drawers of his desk.

'Rabaul's done for,' Harold said, cutting straight to the heart of the matter. 'The Japs will be here by tomorrow. I tried, Wilf. I tried to organise evacuation for the civilians. I got nowhere. Those bastards sitting comfortably in Canberra decided copra was more important than men. So now we have a choice. We can go up to the Gully and wait to be taken prisoner, or we can head out of town and hope for rescue.'

Wilf looked at Harry, who had a canvas backpack across his shoulders, then at Harold.

'What's the likelihood of that?'

'Pretty good, I think. I organised for Keith McCarthy to set up food dumps and he's in the process of getting hold of boats from plantation owners, to evacuate whoever he can along the coast. We stand a chance of being picked up if we get out of town. If we stay here there's a likelihood we'll get caught up in the fighting, and I'm not keen to be collateral damage.'

'We've tried to tell anyone we meet,' Harry chimed in, 'but some of them think we should stay put. They're worried if they get caught escaping things might go badly for them, or they're keen on following orders.'

Harold grimaced.

'I spent a lot of time following orders. Lot of good it did me. I should have got everyone out on the Herstein weeks ago, without waiting for permission. I've had it with orders.'

Harry patted his arm.

'Me too, mate, me too.'

'So, what do you think, Wilf?'

Where did his responsibilities lie? With the Mission? They had packed up and hidden the most important documents. Everything else was replaceable. And if the outlying missionaries, Tom and Dan, had any sense, they would stay away from Rabaul if the Japanese took over. With the Nurses? Mac had already taken them to safety. With the natives? Most had left town, and the native ministers and teachers – Akulia To Pui, Isimel, and all the other men of leadership in the different regions – had reassured Mac they would continue the good work of the Lotu, no matter what happened. Wilf was also beginning to wonder if staying to protect the Tolai was a kind of foolish arrogance. The people of New Britain were far better equipped to evade the Japanese than any of the missionaries or other Australians. And assuming the Japanese would place greater store on the opinions of the men of the church than on those of the New Britain natives was based on no evidence whatsoever.

His mind made up, Wilf sat at his desk and pulled open one of the drawers. Inside was the telegram he'd received from

Eileen about baby Rosemary's birth, as well as the x-ray image taken when Eileen was pregnant. He slid them both into an envelope, which he folded carefully and placed in his shirt pocket. He left the Tolai hymn book he had spent so many hours translating. When the world was being turned upside down, his thoughts were of his wife and child, not his work.

'Let's go,' he said.

Since Mac had taken one of the utilities and the other was out at Vunairima, only the little mission car remained, but when Wilf tried to start it, the engine wouldn't turn over. Checking under the hood, he saw a fine coating of volcano ash and knew it would need a good clean out to be functional. They didn't have time for that.

'Looks like we're walking,' Harry said.

When they reached Malaguna Road, they ran into Ron Wayne. Harold Page knew Ron well, since both were active members of the Methodist church. Ron was also a firm fixture in Rabaul's civil administration, which meant he encountered Page professionally too. Due to his abilities with Pidgin, a position had been created for him as Court interpreter, to offer support to natives facing the colonists' legal system. Ron was heading up to the Gully but was easily persuaded to join them on the trek out of town.

The town was busy with troops, many of them making preparations along Malaguna Road where bombs had been stockpiled after they were unloaded from the Herstein. Wilf saw one of the Salvation Army bandsmen putting stretchers against a wall and went over to get a sense of what was going on.

'James, how are you?'

James, the only American in the band, was a tall, handsome

charismatic man. 'Wilf, good to see you. What are you up to?'

'We're heading south.'

'Very wise. It's all about to go to hell in a handbasket, my friend. Get as far away from here as you can.'

Wilf nodded towards the munition piles. 'What's going on?'

James' face turned grim. He looked around before answering in a low voice.

'They're going to blow the lot. They don't want the Japs getting their hands on it all. They're planning to blow up comms and vehicles too. I've never seen anything like it.' He leaned in a little, his voice becoming even softer. 'Colonel Scanlan doesn't seem to have a clear idea what he's doing. Blowing everything up tells me he thinks we're not going to be able to put up a fight, but when someone asked him about preparing for guerrilla warfare, you know, setting up food and hides in the jungle, he blasted them for their defeatist attitude. He's got everyone running around like... what's that phrase you Aussies like to use about chickens?'

'Running around like headless chooks,' Wilf offered. James nodded.

'That's the one. Anyways, I think you're doing the right thing. Don't just wait around.' He offered his hand. Wilf shook it. 'I wish you luck my friend.'

Wilf joined Harold, Harry and Ron, filling them in on what he'd learned.

'Well, that just confirms it,' Harold said. 'We keep heading south until we come across one of Keith's boats and can get off this island.'

They resumed their journey, taking the main road south towards Raluana. It wasn't long before the black clouds broke and they were trudging through a torrential downpour, but they continued on regardless. Slightly more than three hours later, they reached Raluana. The Mission station was empty, Laurie Linggood having gone to Kalas with Mac, but Wilf knew his way around, since he had spent time there when he and Eileen returned from their honeymoon.

As he passed the bathtub on the veranda, he smiled to himself, remembering how much Eileen had loved the luxury of it. Then he thought about his little girl, baby Rosemary, and how she would be nearly three weeks old. He had missed those magic first few weeks. The smile slipped from his face.

There was no sign of the houseboys, but a loaf of bread sat in the butcher's box, free of mould, so Wilf put together a simple afternoon tea and carried it out to the veranda, where the men were resting their aching feet. Ron was facing the harbour, and he was the first to notice a ship sailing past them, on its way to St George's Channel.

'What's that?'

The men all peered at it.

'Looks like the Malaita,' Harold said. 'She wasn't in port at lunchtime. She must have come in, the captain must have taken one look at things, and sailed straight out again.'

'Do you reckon she had some empty cabins?' Harry asked. Harold nodded.

They watched the Malaita steam through directly past Raluana Point, moving at speed, despite the bucketing rain. The silence was heavy with lost possibility, until Harry broke it.

'Shit.'

No one could think of anything more to add. The expletive summed up their thoughts completely. Harold stood up, brushing breadcrumbs off his pants.

'Well, we missed that opportunity, but there'll be boats coming in down the coast. Let's get going.'

'Shouldn't we wait 'til the rain stops?' Ron asked. Wilf, clearing the table, smiled at Ron.

'Have you ever known a tropical storm to stop this fast?'

'True. Let's get going.'

Wilf took the remains of their food to the kitchen, doing a quick search for anything to take on their trek. He filled a backpack with supplies, then joined the others on the veranda, just as an enormous cracking filled the air, followed by a sound like thunder, echoing in their ear drums. Another crack-boom reverberated around them, then another, the sound going on and on, like a series of fireworks, but far deeper in pitch. Across the bay, they saw smoke rising over Rabaul in an expanding line. Wilf tried to make out the familiar lay of the streets through the swirling clouds.

'That's Malaguna Road. They're blowing the ammunition dump.'

The noise increased, and moments later the smoke took on a different quality, with new colours surging upwards. It was hard to tell what was happening at first, but as the smoke rose higher, leaving clear patches at road level, it became apparent there were gaps in the street line where there hadn't been before.

'They've blown up some of the buildings along the road.' Wilf couldn't hide his dismay. He had walked that street for close to fifteen years. It was as familiar to him as his childhood home. It suddenly struck him that not only were all the people of Rabaul at risk. The town was going to suffer too. Even if the Americans arrived swiftly to free them, there would be extensive damage.

'I hope they gave everyone plenty of warning,' Ron said. 'The army's been so secretive, people could have been walking around with no idea what was about to happen.'

More of the smoke drifted away, and they saw movement in the centre of town. Trucks were heading down from Namanula Hill towards Mango Avenue, whilst others were curving in from the ruins of the native hospital at Rapindik, where temporary medical tents had been set up after the hospital was bombed.

'Evacuating the hospitals?' Harold surmised.

'It'd make sense,' Harry said.

When the trucks reached the junction at the end of Malaguna Road, they peeled off to the south.

'We should get on the road,' Harry said urgently. 'If they're coming this way, we can get a lift to Kokopo.'

The men hauled their bags over their shoulders and left the Mission House. Wilf turned to look one last time at the lawns, the beautiful garden, the wide veranda. Standing in the heavy rain, he nevertheless saw the wide green spaces as he often had, bathed in soft sunlight. He could almost hear the echo of laughter from all the picnics and morning teas he had attended here over the years. Times of joy, friendship and communion, when they had shared good food and company, with the shimmering peacock colours of the harbour as the extraordinary backdrop. When would they have the chance to gather again in safety and fellowship?

Ron called to him to hurry up and Wilf rushed to join the others.

The convoy of trucks reached them half an hour later, having halted twice to clear the road of trees that must have been brought down by the rain or the explosions. The trucks in front had red crosses hastily painted on the side, or ragged flags painted with the same cross hanging off the top of their buckets. Their drivers ignored the men by the side of the road, driving on through the rain with care. It was only as the tail end of the convoy approached that a truck stopped. Wilf recognised Jon Lerew, the Squadron leader of the RAAF pilots, in the passenger seat.

'Harold Page!' Lerew called out, waving the men over. 'This is where you've got to. I'm afraid there are a lot of people up at Refuge Gully unhappy with you mate. They think you're abandoning them.'

'I tried to get the message out to head to Kokopo. There are supposed to be boats coming to pick us up. Keith McCarthy's organising it.'

'Don't know if that message got through. But it's too late to go back now. I managed to convince Scanlan to let us evacuate, so we can take you south if you like. Jump in.'

Wilf recognised some of the men in the truck, pilots from the squadron, and a few of the young lads who had practiced so diligently with his model plane on the beach. Some exchanged names and pleasantries.

'Geoff Lempriere,' one of them offered his hand. 'You're Wilf Pearce, right? A friend of Bill Harry's?'

'Yes. Is he safe?'

'He's headed up to the hills. I work in intelligence too. Well, I did. They've just blown up half the comms back there, so how I'm supposed to get any intelligence now I don't know.'

'How come everyone's leaving town?' Harold asked.

'I think old Scanlan's feeling guilty,' Geoff mused. 'After the attack two days ago that wiped out all our planes, he told 24

Squadron to get out there with all available aircraft. What a joke. There were two Wirraways left, but they were worse than useless, and a Hudson. There were pilots who were in a really bad way, so Jon contacted Port Moresby and asked permission to evacuate them on the Hudson. You know what they said?'

The listeners shook their heads.

'Keep the squadron combat ready. What a joke. No planes, men in pieces... so Jon and I sent a telegram back... Padre May helped us get the wording right. "Morituri vos Salutamus".'

'What does it mean?' Harry Townsend asked. Wilf translated.

'We who are about to die salute you. It's what the gladiators used to say in Ancient Rome.'

Geoff nodded. 'Didn't get much of a response at the time, but round lunchtime today Scanlan contacts Jon on the field radio and gives him permission to leave. None of the pilots are trained for field combat, and with their planes destroyed they're more of a liability than anything. So we're heading south. One of the men's gone ahead on a motorbike to look for a radio and organise a flying boat to come and get us.'

As the trucks rattled along the road the rain grew more intense, whilst the clouds grew ever darker. Tension became a palpable weight for the men huddled, knees drawn in tight against the weather, in the tray of the truck.

'Why don't they put the truck's lights on?' Ron asked Geoff, looking at the vehicle following them. The road curved continually so the lack of headlights seemed like a fool's choice.

'Don't want to be spotted by any planes,' he said. It made for dangerous travel, especially as the afternoon waned. They passed through Kokopo, continuing along the coast road for a while longer in the growing dusk. Wilf, on the left side of the vehicle, had a good view of the ocean and the road behind them, so he saw some trucks leave the convoy at Raluana. He asked Geoff what that was about.

'That'll be David Selby, taking reinforcements to Y Company.'

'There are soldiers based at Raluana?' It seemed like a kind of sacrilege to Wilf. They hadn't seen anything during their rest break, but then the layout of the Mission house and its garden made it feel like a secluded piece of paradise so that wasn't surprising.

'The beach there would make a good landing point. Scanlan's trying to cover all bases.'

'Without enough men,' someone scoffed.

As night fell properly, and the storm grew in intensity, their progress slowed again. Wilf had a good view of Simpson Harbour as they followed the curving coastal road. In the growing darkness, Tavurvur's glowing peak became more noticeable. The earlier eruptive bursts had lessened but ash continued spewing into the air now and then. An orange glow crowned her summit, vivid against the black, casting its flame colours onto the underside of the storm clouds.

The noise of the earlier explosions was long gone, leaving only the persistent drumming of the rain on the truck. Most of the men had been subdued into silence. There was a strange peacefulness about their journey, until yelling and screams tore through the air. A minute later there were loud creaks and crunches, followed by the sound of palm trees breaking and the thumping and bangs of something large tumbling through the jungle.

The truck stopped. Lerew jumped from the passenger seat and hurried down the dark road to find out what was going on.

He was gone about ten minutes, and when he returned there were half a dozen men with him.

'Make room boys,' he called out. 'One of the trucks has gone off the road. Everyone managed to get out without injury, but we had to divide them up between the other trucks.'

There was some grumbling from the men in the truck tray, but Lerew gave them a hard look and they fell silent. Those at the back held out their hands to pull the new men up, and everyone shuffled up to fit them in.

After this accident, the truck slowed even more.

'I could walk faster than this,' someone muttered.

'Yeah, but would you want to?'

'Not bloody likely.'

Not long after, a distant buzz heralded an influx of Japanese recon planes. Shortly after that, the trucks turned off onto the road leading through the jungle to the southern plantations. This new road was barely wide enough for the vehicles. The going was extremely slow and rough. It was close to midnight when they stopped again. Lerew leapt out and banged the side of the first truck.

'We're going on foot from here,' he announced. 'Grab anything you brought with you, then we need to dismantle the trucks. We don't want to leave anything useful behind.'

He had a quick word to Geoff Lempriere, who set off down the convoy line repeating this message. Everyone climbed down from the trucks. A few men set to work on them, lifting the bonnets and removing parts of the engine, whilst others hovered around the fuel tanks. Jon Lerew organised the remaining refugees into small groups as they arrived from the more distant trucks. It was easy to see most of the men had military training, because they moved swiftly and followed orders without question.

It was a short distance from where they left the trucks to a sudden drop off, where a river raged below, heavy from the storm. Lerew shone a torch, keeping the path of the beam low despite the dense tree cover overhead.

'How the hell are we going to cross that?' came a voice through the darkness. Even with only the meagre torchlight it was clear the wide, flooded watercourse posed a challenge.

At various points in their service in New Britain, each of the Methodist missionaries would go on patrol, hiking through whichever region they were allocated, to understand the people and places encompassed by their circuit. Since he was the Business Manager, and based in Rabaul, Wilf wasn't required to do this with the same regularity, for which he was grateful. At forty-two, long hikes through hilly, dense jungle were more exhausting than they used to be, although he did still enjoy visiting the hill country for the Warataba and other special occasions. But he had explored this region in his early days in New Britain, and read every patrol report that came in, so his knowledge was current, and more than most in the party. The longest any of them had been in the country was ten months, and many had done no more exploration than climbing the volcanoes or a short trip to the Baining Mountains. He stepped forward to speak to Lerew.

'This is the Warangoi River. There's a point upriver where it narrows and there are vines we can use to swing across, but it's several hours' walk from here.'

Some of the men nearby swore at this. Lerew didn't bother to silence them.

'Alright, let's take a short rest break. Brookes, Lempriere, Page, a word. We need to work out a plan of action. The rest of you, try and catch some kip. We need to get as far away from Rabaul as possible, so we'll be pushing on tonight.'

Wilf and Ron sat with their backs against a giant Irima tree. Ron closed his eyes and was snoring in less than a minute. The tree reminded Wilf of his first non-work-related conversation with Eileen, the day she arrived, in 1936. The dedication service had just finished, and everyone was standing on the lawn in front of the Rabaul church. Miss Brabin was wandering the edges of the area, admiring the plants, so Wilf joined her and asked if she'd like to know what the various plants were. Her eagerness was genuine, he could tell, as he pointed out various flowers and trees, giving them their Kuanua names as well as their European ones.

'Where you'll be teaching is actually named after a tree,' he told her. '"Vunairima" basically means a cluster of irima trees.'

Her blue eyes lit up. 'It sounds beautiful there.'

'It is. Some of the names don't quite capture the beauty of a place though – they're more descriptive. "Raluana" basically means 'the bulge', in the dialect of that area, and if you look at the map it's a little bulge on the coastline.' Eileen laughed. Wilf continued. 'But when you go there, the view is extraordinary. It's probably my favourite place in New Britain.'

The memory made his thoughts stray into less happy places. What was happening in Raluana now? Were the army facing an enemy, or was it still quiet?

'Kuskus Wilf? Talatala Ron?' A voice whispered through the darkness. 'Do you need help?'

A young Tolai man stepped out of the foliage.

'Jona!' Wilf stood and clasped the man's hands in greeting. 'I am so glad to see you. Are your family safe?'

'Yes, Kuskus. But many are running from Rabaul. There are far too many balus flying and it sounds as if Rabalanakaia is angry again, but the smoke comes from the town, not from the mountains.'

'They're the explosions of war.'

'Some of our people have been killed. They left their bodies in the street.'

Wilf shut his eyes for a moment.

'It pains my heart to hear that,' he told his Tolai friend. Suddenly he felt ashamed for leaving town. Men were dying, probably in pain and fear. He should be there to give them comfort. 'It should be us who are asking if you need help.'

Jona waved one arm at the river. 'Do you wish to cross? Pellei is here and we have oaga.'

Wilf glanced around at all the waiting men.

'Everyone here wants to cross. There are too many.'

'No problem. We will do this for our Kuskus, who brought us the Lotu.'

Wilf reached out and clasped both Jona's hands again.

'Thank you, my friend.'

Lerew was delighted to learn of this option, expecting it to save them the time and effort of an upstream trek, but in the end, it took two hours for Jona and Pellei to transport all the men across the river in their tiny canoe. The rushing water made it impossible to go straight across, so each small group had to be taken downstream and left at the beach where the Warangoi met the sea, allowing them to begin their trek on the other side of the bank.

Wilf and Ron waited until last. They farewelled the Tolai men with words of extreme gratitude. Jona held onto Wilf's hands for a long time.

'You must use great adep. Be careful,' he used English to be sure Wilf understood. 'We go upriver, home to Rabata now. Maybe we will need to move deeper into the jungle, but if you need help, we will find a way.'

Then Jona and Pellei slipped away.

The party struggled on through the night, leaving the beach behind. Progress through the jungle was slow and torturous. Though the rain had stopped, there was no moon to give them light. There was a track, but it was poorly made, with undergrowth that needed to be cleared frequently. Worse, from Wilf's point of view, was the behaviour of some of the civilian men of the party, whom he recognised as plantation managers. Whilst the soldiers and RAAF trekked on without complaint for the most part, helping anyone who struggled, a few of the civilians seemed to have the attitude that anyone who slowed them down was putting their survival at risk. They began making dismissive comments if someone slipped or trailed behind, and refused to offer any assistance. As the night wore on their behaviour became increasingly hostile. Wilf deliberately distanced himself from them. There had long been a cold distance between plantation managers and the Methodist Mission, because the managers thought the Methodists were stirring up trouble by working towards the future autonomy of the locals.

Everyone was relieved to arrive at a plantation in the darkest hours of the night, but Lerew only allowed them a quick break.

'If we don't get south fast enough, we won't be evacuated,' he told everyone. Then he divided the group in two, ordering about a hundred of the young, fit soldiers to follow him. The remaining fifty were civilians and older men, as well as the artillery men, most of whom looked like teenagers. As the military group moved off, someone could be heard saying, 'it's a good thing we're leaving the chocos behind.'

Wilf tapped one of the young men on the shoulder. 'Keith, is it?' he asked. The lad nodded, then recognition lit up his face.

'You're the missionary who gave us the plane to practise with, right?'

'That's right. Keith, I'm curious, why was that soldier saying something about chocos?'

Keith's face scrunched up for a moment. 'They're talking about us. The young gunners, the guys who are part of the militia. They don't think we're proper soldiers. They reckon we're made of chocolate, so chocos. Because they think we'll melt away at the first sign of trouble.' He looked around at the party. 'To be honest, I'm kind of mixed up about this. I feel like we are running away, but what good would we do there? They blew up all the anti-aircraft weapons. We've got no way of fighting them. We wouldn't stand a chance.'

Another man strode past them, calling over his shoulder, 'We never stood a chance in the first place, kid. Not enough weapons, and the ones we did have were last used in the Trojan war. The Japs' planes are modern as anything.'

Wilf and Keith continued in silence. The track was almost invisible, only possible to follow because others were tramping through it before them. It was arduous work, in the black of the warm night, with jungle looming on all sides. At times water coursed over the path, making it slippery. Men fell over often, with the occasional injury as a result, luckily nothing serious. But it was a clear taste of what was to come. They crossed a second river hours after passing the Warangoi, this time using hanging vines. Keith, young and fit, made it across easily, but Wilf felt his arms shaking afterwards. He was too used to office life.

Most of the time they paid little attention to the sparse conversation around them, concentrating on the difficulty of finding their steps and pushing through foliage. When they heard some curses, they paid more attention. Someone was lying on the ground ahead, half blocking the way. As they neared, Wilf realised it was Harold Page.

'Harold!' Wilf rushed to his side. 'What happened?'

'One of the men pushed me out of the way. Well, more of a shove. I was going too slow for him.'

'Are you hurt?'

'Twisted my ankle a bit.'

'Military or civilian?'

'Civilian.'

As Wilf reached out to help Harold up, he felt a sharp jolt in his back, and toppled over next to Harold.

'That's coz you're useless.' One of the plantation managers loomed over both men. 'You never stood up for us,' he glared at Page, 'and you're not the boss of us now. So get out of the way, you fat bastard. We don't need the likes of you slowing us down.' The man leered, then spat, his spittle landing square on Harold's cheek. Then he turned and sped away.

Wilf helped Harold up. They both stood there watching the retreating backs of the civilians.

'Shouldn't we get going?' Keith asked, his voice high pitched.

'You keep going, Keith,' Wilf said, his voice reassuring. 'We'll catch up.'

The young gunner gave them a brisk salute and joined the trail of men. Harold took a step and sighed.

'Well, that hurts. I'm not going to be able to do this, Wilf. I'm too unfit and now I've done my ankle.'

'I don't want to do this, Harold. Not if those are our travel companions.'

Without another word, they both turned and began walking the way they had come. A short time later they ran into Ron, then Harry Townsend. Both men reported seeing similar behaviour, and both were equally disgusted. Ron, like Wilf, also knew how tough the going would be. Their progress would only get worse as men fell sick with beri beri or tropical ulcers, and injuries were easy to come by in such unfriendly terrain. Years before Wilf had developed ulcers on both hands, so he knew how debilitating they were.

'Tol's a long way away. We'll get dysentery in no time, and the mozzies are thick on the ground,' Ron said. Wilf agreed.

'If we had a guide, to help us find food and water, we might stand a chance, but I've trekked these jungles enough to know it'd be a punishing journey. And with this many mozzies around, we'll be sick with malaria in no time. I brought some Atabrin, but it won't be enough.'

Harold looked defeated. 'I thought we'd find boats before now,' he said. 'If the only pick up is Tol, I don't think I'll make it.'

It didn't take long for them to decide returning to Rabaul might be their best option.

'Maybe we'll find one of your civilian boats along the way,' Wilf reassured him.

By dawn, they had reached the Warangoi again. Exhausted, having trekked with little reprieve since noon the day before, they decided to camp there, near the river mouth.

'We'd be more comfortable if we used the trucks for shelter,' Harry Townsend said.

'Too stuffed, mate,' Ron replied. Harold's ankle had swollen severely – he had barely made it this far. They agreed to return to the trucks the following day and camp there, which is what they did. Fortunately, there was food and even blankets in the trucks, so they were in a decent position.

'What day is it? I've lost track,' Harry said much later in the day, after they'd slept and eaten.

'It's the twenty-third of January.' Wilf gazed off into the distance. 'My baby girl is three weeks old today.'

That afternoon their conversation ran in circles about what might happen. What was occurring in Rabaul? Had it fallen? Someone was likely to come along with a boat sometime in the next week, but would it be ally or enemy? If it was the Japanese, should they hide or try their luck, hoping they'd be treated well?

'There are conventions around these things,' Harold told them. 'We'd be prisoners of war. At least we'd get food and medical treatment and so on. We've been lucky with what we found in the trucks, but it's not going to last long.'

They hoped the first boat that came past would be one of Keith McCarthy's, to evacuate those who'd fled town, but agreed that if it was the Japanese, they would surrender.

4th February 1942. The mouth of the Warangoi River.

It was more than a week later that a boat arrived at the beach at the mouth of the Warangoi River, on February 4th, by Wilf's estimation. The Japanese flag flew from its side. Wilf, Ron, Harold and Harry walked down the beach with their arms up in surrender. A small tender was sent for them, with several Japanese soldiers in khaki shorts, carrying bayonets. Shouting in their own language, they waved the men aboard, one hitting Harold Page in the head with the butt of his rifle when he had trouble climbing in, causing his scalp to bleed. The shouting and hitting were repeated when they climbed onto the larger boat.

Once on board, they were greeted by a bespectacled Japanese man who spoke to them in English.

'You are prisoners of General Noda. Rabaul is in the hands of the Imperial Japanese Army. You will be returned there and placed in confinement. You are fortunate you surrendered. All those who don't will not be shown the mercy of the Japanese army.'

He broke into Japanese, and the men were dragged to an open hatch. They were thrown down into a hold crowded with Australian men. At first Wilf didn't recognise any of them, but then someone called out his name. It was the young 'choco', Keith.

'Wilf. Am I glad to see you!' Keith shook his head. 'You saved yourself a long trip for nothing! By the time we got to Tol plantation the Japanese weren't far behind us. There was a sign there that said we should surrender to the Japanese, so about twenty of us went down to the beach and when they arrived, we gave ourselves up. The others were brought in later.'

'What did Lerew do?'

'All the RAAF men got away.'

'So what happened to the men who didn't surrender?'

Keith's energy dropped.

'I don't know, but I don't think it was good. They took all our tags and things off everyone when we surrendered. Then this morning, they took all the men they'd brought back who hadn't surrendered, tied them up in pairs and led them away. A bunch of soldiers went with them. They took their rifles, Wilf, with the bayonets on. When they returned, there wasn't a single Australian with them, and they were all laughing and joking. Some of them mimed that they were going to stab us with their bayonets. They wouldn't do that, would they? We surrendered.'

Wilf and Harold Page looked at each other. A trail of blood ran down the side of Harold's face from the earlier brutality. Wilf could see in Harold's eyes he was thinking the same thing. Their assumption they would be treated well as prisoners of war was very likely incorrect. Every decision they made – to leave town, to return, to surrender – had been based on too little information. Now, they were going to discover the reality.

16 – Lack of News

Eileen

Wednesday 28th January 1942. Manly, Sydney

> The attitude of those with near rel-
> atives in our Garrison at Rabaul is
> becoming bitter and hostile at the
> lack of news of their sons, brothers
> and husbands, and of the feeling that
> is being created that although some-
> thing could be done to assist them,
> nothing is being attempted.

Frank Forde to Prime Minister Curtin

Eileen snatched up the Sydney Morning Herald, scanning the front page for news. Any news. There had been little information, but since last Wednesday it had been apparent Rabaul was under serious attack. First there had been reports of a large-scale air raid on military installations and 'the aerodrome': presumably the RAAF one, since the papers were focused on the army. Mention of further air attacks two days later had said these were a prelude to the landing of Japanese troops. Rabaul had been under constant, serious fire.

But of greatest concern was that on the 23rd, the papers had reported 'radio silence' since 4pm the day before, with speculation that the Australian forces may have destroyed their own radios. Although Deputy Prime Minister Forde made an official statement that evacuation had occurred, Eileen wondered how true that was, since, if there was radio silence, nobody could actually know what was going on. Forde also said they presumed a Japanese landing had occurred. A separate article about the evacuation of women and children by plane had stated that such evacuations occurred 'before the Japanese landings took place'.

So, although there had been no clear statement, it seemed likely the Japanese had occupied Rabaul since at least last Saturday. An article on the 26th had also made a brief mention of Japanese ships in Simpson Harbour. Eileen was sick of it. All the articles focused on the risks to Australia, the defence of Australia, the gasbagging of politicians, and, worst of all, discussion of doing what was right for 'the war machine', a term she hated. Not only was there nothing specific about the town she considered home, but there was no apparent concern for its inhabitants, like Wilf, whom she missed with all her heart.

Scanning the paper again, Eileen read that Allied aircraft were now bombing Rabaul and had taken out two... no, three ships in the harbour. She thought about the villagers that lived around Simpson Harbour and wondered what had happened to them. Had they got away to safety? Wilf's office – and their home – was so close to the harbour. But of course, he wouldn't still be at work, she chided herself. The town had been evacuated, according to an article she'd read on the 23rd, although whether this was civilians or soldiers, or both, had not been mentioned. They wouldn't evacuate the army and leave behind the civilians though.

Auntie Nell entered the kitchen, her eyes full of concern. She brushed a loose strand of greying hair off her face and gestured with a hand gnarled from arthritis. 'Take a seat, dear. I'll make you a pot of coffee while you read your paper. Is baby Rosemary still asleep?'

'I should hope so! She was up three times during the night. She's running me ragged.' Eileen sat and spread out the paper, flicking through for more mention of Rabaul.

Auntie Nell lit the stove and blew out the match. 'They do settle down after the first month or so. She's a little live wire though, especially for such a tiny thing.'

'She was like that from the first day! When the babies were brought to their mothers to be fed on the long trolley at the hospital, they put Rosemary down side by side with the other babies when they left the nursery, but by the time she reached me she always worked herself upside down.'

With the kettle on the stove, Auntie Nell sat down kitty-corner from Eileen, who closed the paper and folded it with a slap.

'Any more information today?'

'No. There's so little detail, Auntie Nell. All I know comes from reading between the lines. They're not saying anything about what's really happening.'

'They probably don't know much yet. I'm sure there'll be more information soon. At least they did say the town was evacuated.'

'Yes, but to where? Was it everybody, or were some captured?' Her eyes fell on the front page. 'Oh, will you look at that! Mr Churchill is saying Britain and the United States are sending reinforcements and arms "by the best routes" to increase Australia's security and that they've been reinforcing troops in Malaya. It's a bit late! You should have seen the army in Rabaul. Half a dozen planes, broken equipment, a lot of the soldiers terribly young, with no experience. They could have used reinforcements and arms months ago!'

Auntie Nell reached for Eileen's hand. 'It must be so frustrating not knowing. Perhaps you could talk to Reverend Burton. He might have received more information.'

'Netta went to see him yesterday, before she came here.' She was interrupted by the whistle of the kettle. Nell hurried to finish the drinks. 'He didn't want to tell her anything, but you know how Netta is. She can charm anything out of anyone. Apparently, he recently finished a letter to Laurie Mac – he's the Chairman of the district in New Britain – where he said our native ministers might have to take over the church's work. Netta says he mentioned the possibility Wilf and the others might be interred.'

Nell poured the coffee and placed a cup in front of Eileen. 'Why did he say that? Does he know something?'

'Netta didn't think so. He was probably just talking about all the possibilities. He said he told Laurie Mac it was up to the missionaries to decide whether to evacuate. That it would be a matter for their own conscience.'

Nell closed her eyes momentarily. 'Well, you've already told me they won't abandon their congregations.'

'But how come nobody knows anything?' Eileen asked. 'I was sure John Burton would have more information. The papers are so vague. Surely the politicians must know something? But then, why would Curtin travel to Western Australia, at the exact time Rabaul was being invaded, if he knew that was going on?'

She took a sip of her coffee and for a moment she remembered sitting on the veranda with Wilf, joking that he should convert to coffee from his perennial tea-drinking habit. A surge of emotion nearly crushed her. Then a cry came from the other room.

'All the politicians seem to be interested in is protecting their own reputations or making deals with business,' she said as she stood up, slapping the paper with one hand. 'Otherwise, they would have evacuated Wilf and the other civilians weeks ago.' She picked up her coffee cup and drained it, then banged it down on the table. Rosemary was wailing without pause now. Eileen straightened her spine. 'Well, not knowing what's going on doesn't stop the work that needs doing.' And she hurried from the room to care for the baby.

Saturday 28 February 1942. Hobart.

Dear Eileen,

Not good news I'm afraid. I've been meaning to write since I found out but I've been flat out with the Emergency Services so do forgive me. Everyone's in such a flap about a possible invasion. As you know they've started up a New Guinea association here in Sydney. It's terribly good for communication, when there is any.

Anyway, at today's meeting you'll never guess who attended – Gil Platten! He had the most extraordinary story of his escape from New Ireland. But he didn't know anything about Wilf or Ken or any of the other men I'm afraid. Or any detail about what happened in Rabaul when the Japanese arrived, other than that he saw a skyful of planes beforehand.

You'll be pleased to know he did say a lot of the natives were building huts in the jungle to hide. They're calling the invasion the great confusion. Mostly they're getting as far away as possible from it. Reverend Burton says our native ministers will be looking after them.

No news on Ia Lo though. I'm sure she would have made it home. Mr Mac would have shut down the school at the first whiff of danger.

Now, about that. I'm so sorry, Eileen, but there was a lot of bombing. It seems George Brown College and Stewart Hospital are destroyed. That news came through at the NSW church conference. Apparently, our own bombers got a good view of the area and there's nothing left. So that means the girls' school is gone as well.

Did I mention I went to see John Burton again? Still no news, but he said missionaries from other areas have escaped and made it to Australia. Wilf knows the mountains so well, and he has a lot of friends among the natives. I'm sure he's on his way home right now. He and Ken will have all sorts of amazing tales to tell us when they get here.

How's little Rosemary Jean? Knowing you, you'll be carrying the baby on one hip while you build your house singlehandedly! I do worry about you alone down there in Hobart though. At least here in Sydney there are a bunch of us evacuees to support each other.

That's all I can think of for now. Let me know when you find that perfect block of land. Wilf will be so proud of you, having a lovely new home to come home to. He can grow his roses. I don't know about you growing tropical flowers when you get to Hobart though – it's terribly cold there isn't it? Ken and I will come visit in the summer, when it's a bit warmer and we can all forget this horrible mess.

Lots of love

From Netta

Eileen folded the letter and slipped it in her handbag. She had been reading it to pass the time, but there was still no sign of the real estate agent. He was fifteen minutes late now. Well, this was all open land, so she would just wander around herself until he got here. She ventured onto the block, which sloped gently at first, then with a sharper incline. If she was to buy here and build, the house would probably need to be single story at the front and double at the back. It was the perfect suburb, walking distance to town, not far from her parents' home and the New Town Methodist Church. There were lots of leafy, well-established large trees too.

Even though this was the second time she had read the letter, the emotions it raised were as fresh and shocking as the first time. To think that the entire compound at Vunairima was destroyed. The beautiful crotons around the cemetery flattened, the sacred burial sites pitted and broken. The stately Sisters' House, where she had lived for so many years, now only a pile of rubble. Where choirs had sung in joy far too early in the morning, the ground would be scorched. The hall, which had been filled with heavy concentration when the students sat their exams, or joy and excitement and frangipanis when newly ordained ministers married their freshly graduated wives, would be gone.

Eileen thrust those thoughts away. They were too painful to dwell on, her imagination too vivid. She pushed aside too the frustration that arose from still more lack of news. It was the constant in her life these last two months, no matter where she turned, whether writing to John Burton and the Overseas Mission Board or even to the Department for External Territories. Netta's efforts were meeting with dead ends as well. No one knew more than the basic details. News reports were almost non-existent and so short on facts as to be laughable.

They seemed to get even basic information about the layout of Rabaul and the Gazelle Peninsula wrong.

Netta was right about one thing. Eileen's determination was not dulled by motherhood. If anything, it was made more acute. A few weeks of living with her parents and caring for a newborn had been enough to make her want to pursue her plan of returning to work. She adored her baby, but Eileen needed the intellectual stimulation and socialisation that teaching provided. And more importantly, she was obstinate about having a house for Wilf to come home to. Whatever he was going through now, he would need somewhere safe and stable to recover when he finally reached Australia.

Eileen strode across the block. It was extremely large, and being sold off in several separate parcels. She eyed the lay of the land carefully, her gardening experience at the forefront as she considered which area would be best to establish a greenhouse, fruit trees and vegetable beds. At the girls' school they had grown most of what they needed, and she planned to put those skills to good use here. Presumably once the war was over they would do away with coupons, and the shortages would end, but it was never a bad thing to be able to support yourself.

A creek ran along the block at its lowest point, before the land rose again steeply. In the distance she could see a farmhouse on the hill, but no other houses. If this area had been part of the farm originally, the soil would be well developed, perfect for growing, although nothing would ever have the virulent magic of the volcanic soil around Vunairima and Rabaul. Still, growing their own food would be easy, although not the only solution to building a future.

Wilf didn't want her to go back to work, but his plan to

support her while she cared for the baby was well and truly in pieces. She was lucky in a way; she had a family to come home to, unlike some of the other wives. The Mission Board were going to continue to pay part of Wilf's salary, enough to live off whilst she was at her parents. And she had her retirement money, and Wilf's savings. Buying this land would take a chunk of that, so she would have to work to save enough to do the actual building. Her father thought prices would come down after the war so that would be a better time to buy, but then when Wilf came home, they'd be living with her parents. That would never do.

An old roadster pulled in on the little lane. Finally, the real estate agent had arrived. Eileen made her way back up the hill, where he greeted her without apology for his lateness, offering a handshake.

'Mr Austin, from A. A. Austin and Co, at your service. Have you had a look around? What do you think, Miss Pearce?'

'It's Mrs, thank you,' Eileen said in her best headmistress voice, without taking his hand. They walked slowly a little way down the hill as she ran him through several questions so he would understand she was not some foolish young woman. Finally, he managed to turn the conversation to the topic that was clearly concerning him.

'And your husband isn't able to be here today?'

'He's currently in New Britain,' Eileen said.

'And where is that?'

'In the Pacific.'

'The name's familiar. New Britain. Where have I heard it before? Was there something in the news recently?

'Yes, there was.' Eileen waited for further questions about a faraway exotic place that was facing war, but there were none forthcoming. Really, she should be used to that reaction by now. Very few Australians showed any interest in what was happening in Rabaul. They were far more concerned about the threat of invasion on Australian soil, and the conditions impacting their lives, such as rationing and blackouts. And the limited news meant most people had little real awareness that Australians were caught up in the Japanese invasion. Most didn't even know New Britain was Australian Mandated Territory.

His next questions showed his true concern. Business as usual. 'Is he working there? I assume his income would be underwriting the mortgage?'

'If I decide to buy this land, I will be paying in full. In cash.'

The truth was, she didn't have the full amount, but she was put out by Mr Austin's lack of interest in Wilf's whereabouts. She knew it was an irrational thing to pique her, but she was tired of having to explain every little thing about Rabaul to uncaring strangers.

'Very good. Yes, very good. Each of these blocks is an acre and there are four altogether. You can see the posts with the ribbons tied around them that mark the width of each block. I don't suppose you're interested in more than one?' He swept his arm out, indicating the broad sweep of land.

'I think one will meet our needs. Where is the rear boundary of the land, that way?' She pointed down the hill.

Mr Austin rubbed his hands together. 'Have you gone down there?' Eileen murmured in the affirmative. 'Did you see the creek? That's basically the boundary of the block – well the far side of it. I have some paperwork here if you'd like to show your husband a map before he makes a decision.'

'Thank you.' Eileen took the proffered sheet and examined it closely. She pointed at the third block from Augusta Road. 'I think this one will do nicely. I'll put in a formal offer in writing, of course.'

'That's excellent. It's nice to meet a customer who knows her own mind.' His tone suggested otherwise. They moved towards the road. As they neared Mr Austin's car, he stopped walking abruptly.

'Oh, I should let you know of a rare opportunity that comes with this land. I was going to use it as a selling point, but I think we're beyond that, aren't we?' He gave a little laugh. 'Anyway, this laneway doesn't have an official name yet, so if you want to purchase here you could choose what it's called. I do have other interested parties of course, but...'

'How would that work?'

'I have the paperwork at my office,' Mr Austin said. 'I can give it to you to complete, and all you need to do is submit it to Hobart Council. I suppose it would be a decision you would need to give a lot of thought to. It really is a unique opportunity.'

Eileen looked down the sweep of the hill.

'I wouldn't have to give it any thought at all,' she said. Mr Austin peered at her curiously.

There were two places in New Britain that would be engraved in her heart forever. The first was Vunairima, with its gracious gardens and beautiful beaches, where she had made fast friends with Jessie March, Ia Lo, Dorothy Beale, and Mel Trevitt. Where she had taught, coming into her own as a teacher and later headmistress, enjoying the enthusiasm and joy of so many bright young women. Where she had learned skills such as grass weaving and baking food in a fire pit. And most precious of all, where Wilf had proposed to her. But Netta's letter had marred her thoughts of Vunairima. When she tried to picture it now, all she could see was ash, grey and engulfing, like the aftermath of the volcano.

Besides, the layout of this block was all wrong. Vunairima was largely flat. Whilst there were no majestic harbour views here, only a tiny creek, Eileen was sure Wilf would agree with her that the sloping hill was more like the spot where they had lived for a few brief but gloriously happy months, after they returned from their honeymoon. It occurred to her that their first wedding anniversary was only a few days away. So much had changed in twelve months. Wilf's absence was a hollow in her heart, but if she could find a way to create a little piece of paradise here, perhaps next year they would be able to recreate those contented, settled times.

Verandas were not necessarily a wise move with a Tasmanian winter, but Eileen thought it might be a good idea to build a sunroom at the rear of the house. Wilf would be able to rest and enjoy the warmth of the sunlight as he looked out over the gardens, while he recovered from whatever hardships he had endured.

'If I might ask, what name would you give it?' Mr Austin finally asked, clearly unable to endure not knowing. Eileen met his eyes, but her gaze was still on a distant place, with an outdoor bath and a tropical garden that had seen many happy picnics.

'Raluana Lane,' she said.

Late April 1942. Hobart.

Life found a kind of routine, although the uncertainty that hovered over every day made it difficult to settle to anything.

Rosemary Jean was growing fast. Eileen's father Claude purchased a camera so they could take a photograph of her each month. That way Wilf wouldn't miss out on seeing the rapid changes in his daughter. Eileen had given up writing letters because every single one was returned stamped with 'service suspended'. Instead, every few days she kept a journal about the baby or about her plans for their house and future in a small notebook.

Netta wrote to her about the meetings of the New Guinea society. The missionary wives in Sydney seemed largely to have put their lives on hold, expecting the war to end soon. Most were planning to return to New Britain as soon as circumstances allowed. Netta found it amusing, but also sad, that they were knitting jumpers and scarves for their missing husbands.

'As if they will need woollies in Rabaul!' she had said in her last letter. But Eileen understood the impulse to prepare whatever treats and luxuries they could for men who might have experienced extreme hardship. Wasn't she doing the same thing, but on a larger scale, with her plans for a large house and bright sunroom?

The regular newspapers continued to report little. Eileen had never noticed before how they spun stories out of one or two threads of truth, and a whole skein of guesswork or poor research. It maddened her, when she wanted cold hard facts. She tried going to the pictures to see the newsreels, but they were no better. When they did mention Rabaul they focused solely on the brave Allied soldiers who were bombing Japanese encampments.

Claude only tried to hide her copy of Pacific Islands Monthly once.

'Don't you dare hide anything from me!' she had fumed. 'I'm not a child anymore.'

He handed it over with a sigh. The March edition reported civilians were believed to have escaped into the jungle, but as usual there was no detail about where this information came from or who those civilians might be. It was deeply maddening. When the April issue arrived, Eileen's breath was taken away by an article written by Reverend Rodger Brown, who had made it back to Australia. She read it through rapidly, her heart beating double time, thinking Rodger knew Wilf and the others, so would surely have some concrete news. But it soon became apparent that because he had begun his escape so far from Rabaul, all he knew about events there were more rumours.

Even with her sisters and parents to support her, Eileen felt a keen sense of isolation. They couldn't begin to understand the fear that nestled in her chest constantly, not just for Wilf, but for the other missionaries, and all the Tolai people that she knew and loved. She barely thought about her Mango Street home, probably occupied now by Japanese soldiers. Nothing that she had left behind was worth a passing thought, aside from photos. She had one snap Wilf had taken in the gardens at Vunairima, when Shelley, bless her little soul, had been jumping up. But Wilf had been an avid photographer, and most of his photos had been left in a box in their house, to her deep regret. She particularly regretted having left the x ray of baby Rosemary, but she hoped it was bringing Wilf some comfort, wherever he was.

Whenever she prayed, Eileen asked that Wilf be able to get away from the invaders. Her head told her he would put his duty above his personal freedom – he had always run himself to exhaustion for the good of the Methodist Mission. But her heart wanted to believe he would take any help offered by the Tolai, who would be able to guide him safely through the jungle to a place where he could be rescued and brought safely back to Australia. If Gil Platten and Rodger Brown had made it home, it was only a matter of time until the others did.

Raluana Lane

17 - Prisoners

Wilf

Mid-February 1942. Malaguna Rd Camp, Rabaul.

```
This melancholy state: you are in the
power of the enemy. You owe your life
to his humanity, your daily bread to
his compassion. You must obey his or-
ders, await his pleasure, possess
your soul in patience. The days are
long, hours crawl like paralytic cen-
tipedes. Moreover, the whole atmos-
phere of prison is odious. You feel
a constant humiliation in being
fenced in by wire, watched by armed
men, and webbed about by a tangle of
regulations and restrictions.
```

Winston Churchill, A Roving Commission

'Civilian number hyaku yon ju, please to report.'

Wilf glanced at Syd Beazley, who stood next to him. Syd had been at the camp when Wilf and Ron Wayne arrived, with Jack Trevitt arriving a few days later. None of the other missionaries had appeared amongst the daily new arrivals. The Japanese were trawling the outlying areas constantly for escapees, and had put up signs saying those who didn't surrender would be executed.

Syd nodded reassuringly, and on his left, Jack murmured, 'We're here for you Wilf.'

Breaking from the muster line, Wilf shuffled over to Captain Harada, bowing low. Every prisoner learned immediately on arrival to do this, or face a beating. Harada held a small book out to him and barked something in Japanese. Kawaguchi, the translator, whom the prisoners had nicknamed 'Puss in Boots' because he wore boots far too large for his tiny frame, spoke with an American accent.

'Our honourable captain wants to know if this is you?' Harada had the book open to the title page and was jabbing at a line of text.

Translated by E.W. Pearce.

It was the Pidgin hymn book Wilf had spent so many years on. The one he had left in his desk drawer. Other prisoners had told him that the Japanese had held numerous bonfires in the first days of occupation, burning endless books and papers, but clearly his hymn book had survived the pyre.

'Yes, that's me.'

Kawaguchi translated, and received a stream of words in response. 'Captain Harada has an important job for you. This book says you are fluent in pidgin. You will become translator for the native people.'

As jobs went, it sounded like a better option than what he was currently doing, which was working at the wharves unloading supplies from every Japanese ship that arrived. With his slight build, Wilf had never been strong, and at forty-two he struggled far more than many of the young soldiers, although he suspected their poor diet would soon be a great leveller of everyone's strength. He had only been in the camp a few weeks, but he knew he had lost several pounds already. A handful of rice and a cup of soup that, if you were lucky, contained a piece of vegetable, twice a day, was not conducive to good health.

Rumours flew through the camp like flies on meat, so Wilf

knew the invaders were treating the islanders better than any other racial group. The Chinese were being subjected to terrible brutality and the Australian soldiers with deep contempt, although Australian civilians less so. But for the most part the Tolai were not receiving the brunt of the ill treatment, as long as they complied with demands for food and other assistance. Some had even joined the Kempei Tai, the Japanese police force.

Kawaguchi translated another speech by Harada. 'When natives are caught defying the orders of the Imperial Japanese Army, or when they steal food from our hardworking men, they will be placed on trial. You will act as trial translator, so they understand what they have done and what punishment they will receive.'

Wilf looked at Harada, who did not meet his eyes. Then he turned and glanced at Jack and Syd, both of whom couldn't hide their expressions of horror. Jack gave the slightest nod, perhaps acknowledging what was about to come. Anyone who knew Wilf would know such a task would be absolutely abhorrent to him. Many of the Tolai were family to him. No other member of the Mission had ever been given the special honorific 'Kuskus'.

The thought of having any role in the punishment of native people was not to be considered, whatever the cost. And there would be a cost. Even after only a few weeks, Wilf had seen more brutality by Japanese soldiers than he could bear. When the highest-ranking army officer had argued that officers should not be taking part in work parties according to the Geneva Convention, everyone watching was certain he would be executed on the spot. Given the palpable sense of the threat, the fact that he wasn't had been more surprising than if he had.

Japanese soldiers regularly screamed at prisoners, or

threatened them with their bayonets, their words not understood but their actions and smiles conveying their intentions clearly. Even the slightest infractions, such as being late to muster in the morning or not following an order quickly enough, resulted in torrents of verbal abuse and threats, or a beating.

What weighed most on Wilf's mind as he prepared to speak though were the reports by some of the men who had arrived at the camp recently. Soldiers surrendered when they realised the conditions in the jungle were beyond their abilities to survive. Some had witnessed executions of fellow Australians, by shooting or bayonet. What Wilf couldn't fathom was that the Japanese seemed to think the highest honour was to execute someone with a sword: a sign of respect for the victim. He was terrified of the possibility, but he had lived his life according to his faith and his principles. Now was a time of trial.

'I won't do it,' he said, his voice calm and quiet. Kawaguchi stared at him. 'Please translate what I have said,' Wilf insisted, still speaking softly.

Kawaguchi spoke to Captain Harada, who responded briefly, without flying into a rage as Wilf had seen other Japanese soldiers do at the slightest defiance. 'He asks why?'

'The people of New Britain are my friends,' Wilf said. 'To be a part of their suffering or death is not something I can do.'

The two Japanese men spoke to each other at length. Harada peered closely at Wilf, who saw a fierce intelligence and what might be compassion in the soldier's eyes. Behind him, the other prisoners, still standing in their muster line up, seemed to collectively be holding their breath. Finally, the little translator spoke directly to Wilf, not projecting his voice for the watching prisoners as he usually did.

'Captain Harada considers you have made a noble decision.' Wilf released a breath he didn't realise he had been holding. Then Kawaguchi continued. 'He sees you are a man of education, as he is. So he knows you will understand such a refusal cannot go unpunished. There must be discipline.'

Harada waved at a couple of nearby soldiers and spoke in rapid fire Japanese. The men stepped forward and one of them forced Wilf's arms behind his back while the other waved his bayonet at him. Wilf would have gone with them willingly but they seemed determined to drag him between them.

At one end of the Malaguna Road prison camp, which had been Lark Force's barracks before the invasion, a pole made from part of a coconut tree trunk had been erected recently, with several Australian soldiers forced to dig the hole for it. There had been speculation amongst the captives about its purpose. They were about to find out.

One of the soldiers stripped Wilf of his shirt, dropping it in the dirt. The other forced him to his knees, pushing him backwards so he was against the pole. A third approached with rope and with the one who had stripped him wrenched Wilf's arms behind him, causing agonising pain in his shoulders, then tied his hands together with the rope, pulling the knots as tight as possible.

Once he was in position, Harada spoke to the watching prisoners, with Kawaguchi translating. 'This is the punishment for those who defy the wishes of the Imperial Japanese army. His punishment is just. Anyone caught helping prisoner one hundred forty will be shot.'

A few minutes later the prisoners were dismissed, and

dispersed to have their breakfast of a single handful of rice, before a day of hard labour at the wharves, or, for a smaller number, camp duties such as digging latrines and preparing meals. Wilf was left alone in the morning heat. Work parties formed, each accompanied by a group of soldiers, shuffling in lines out of the camp.

The burning strain in his shoulders was already unbearable. Wilf wondered how long he would be left in this position. He bowed his head and prayed for courage to bear this burden, which he had taken on himself to save his Tolai friends.

'Wilf.'

A whisper broke his silent prayer. Looking up, he saw a work party stopped a few feet away. It was the group he normally went out with, which included Syd, Jack and several members of the Salvation Army band. Ron Wayne was talking to the accompanying soldiers, which was why they had stopped. As Ron continued to speak rapidly and loudly, keeping the Japanese focused on him, Jack Trevitt edged a foot closer.

'We'll look after you,' Jack whispered. 'Steal extra food at the wharves.'

The Mission men had seen this happening regularly over the last few weeks. Whenever the cargo they were unloading contained valuable supplies such as jam or butter, members of Lark Force would find a way to conceal small amounts in secret places. Pockets were too obvious, but heels of shoes, for those who still had shoes, stood up to inspection. Though the thieves were generous in sharing their gains, there was never enough to go far, and getting caught meant a beating.

'Don't,' Wilf said. He kept his head still and his mouth mostly closed, not wanting to attract attention. 'My shirt.'

The shirt was still lying on the ground. Jack nodded. 'I'll keep it safe for you.' He started to step out of line, leaning down to grab the garment, but as he did so, one of the soldiers stepped towards him and hit him in the head with the butt of his weapon, shouting something in Japanese. With a look of apology to Wilf, Jack fell into line and the work party was marched out.

Hours later, when the pain in his shoulders had overtaken his whole body and Wilf could no longer tell what hurt and what didn't, the camp's principal translator and Kawaguchi's superior, Matsui, marched up to him. By now Wilf was desperately thirsty, his tongue swollen and his head throbbing with heat and dehydration. Matsui had more expression when he spoke English than Kawaguchi did; the men had already taken to calling him the dive bomber because his pitch could change from low to quite high with English words he wasn't sure of.

'You are lucky man,' Matsui said in his gravelly voice. 'If Major Matsuda see you defy, he get men to put ants on you, maybe beat you. Colonel Harada, he think you show spirit of Samurai. You do your punishment with bravery, you earn respect. One of the men say you want your shirt.'

Matsui went and picked up the shirt, searching through the pockets. He found a white envelope in the breast pocket. 'Is this why?'

Wilf had endured his torture for most of the day. He felt slightly delirious and knew he was probably suffering from heatstroke, as well as sunburn. Sharp pains seized his gut regularly, the first signs of dysentery. But none of that mattered compared to the pain of seeing that envelope in the Japanese soldier's hands. He felt growing despair, watching the man draw out its contents. Having farewelled his wife, seen his home destroyed and his community shattered, this was all he had left.

'This is your baby?' Matsui asked, looking at the photo of the x-ray. Wilf nodded. Next, the Japanese man read the telegram. 'You are new father?' Again, Wilf nodded. 'Rosemary,' Matsui said. 'Is this a boy or girl name?'

'Girl,' Wilf managed through dry lips and swollen tongue. 'I have a daughter.'

Matsui smiled. 'I have a daughter too. Her name Ayaka. It means sweet smelling flower.'

'Rosemary is a kind of sweet-smelling plant,' Wilf gasped.

Matsui tucked the telegram and x-ray image back into the envelope. 'There are many fireflies in the garden near here,' he said. The change of topic confused Wilf. 'In our culture, we say they are spirit of Samurai, after they are free from their earthly body. You will not be firefly yet. I keep these safe for you.' He returned the envelope to the shirt and spoke again.

'Being translator is an easier job than on wharves. You could make life easier for yourself, but you make noble choice. Captain Harada, he respect that. But he would still make you do what he wants. Now another man say he do translating. Lon Wayne say he translate for courts in Rabaul before, he will do again. You will do hard work on wharves.'

Matsui turned to leave. Wilf became lost in his thoughts. He would have to thank Ron for volunteering in his place, if he had the opportunity. Ron may have just saved his life, since a second refusal could have resulted in Wilf's death. Although the day was not over yet.

'One thing more,' Matsui said, turning suddenly. Wilf drew in his breath, waiting for some other terrible pronouncement. Maybe this torture wasn't the end of what was to happen to him.

Matsui bowed, then dropped the shirt on the ground.

'Congratulations on your baby.'

10 March 1942. The Regent Theatre, Rabaul.

Despite the physical injuries and illness that resulted from his defiance, Wilf was to realise later as he lay in the camp hospital how lucky he had been. Based on what he learned from his friends in the camp, his experience, which didn't include being beaten or otherwise physically attacked, was minor compared to what others faced.

Bert Morgan, one of the Salvation Army bandsmen who had regularly attended Methodist services and knew Wilf well, had taken on the role of finding medical supplies and feeding the sick so Wilf saw him daily while he was in the hospital. Bert worked out that if he spoke fast, he could get away with telling Wilf things the Japanese would not pick up on, since they were not fluent in English. In this way, he was able to tell Wilf that his shirt, with its precious photo and telegram, had been tucked safely away in the hut, awaiting his return.

Altogether, Wilf spent two and a half weeks in the camp hospital, suffering the effects of heatstroke and dehydration, as well as coming down with a terrible bout of malaria combined with dysentery. He was unconscious, then delirious, much of the time. The Japanese doctor, Fushita, did nothing for him, only inspecting him occasionally and writing careful notes on his clipboard. He didn't receive any prescribed medicine, only what Bert could sneak in to him.

The day Wilf was released from hospital, which he calculated would have been about the fifth of March, Bert told him three men had been brought into the camp that morning, two of them dangerously ill with dysentery. Bert had expected to be caring for those men but to his horror, and the shock of every Prisoner of War and civilian internee, they were executed on the parade ground during muster as the Australians were made to watch.

'Major Matsuda did it himself. I'll never forget the sight,' Bert said, visibly shaken. 'The blood... They got some natives to take them away afterwards. Their death was public, but they're not the only ones.'

'I know,' Wilf said. 'The past few weeks I've seen them taking away soldiers with terrible injuries, or the ones who are sick after weeks in the jungle. They pull them from their beds and take them away. They never return.'

When he gave Bert the names of some of the missing patients, it seemed no one in the camp had seen them either. Wilf wondered how close he had come to a similar fate.

The term 'recovered' applied rather loosely by the time Wilf returned to his usual bed in one of the huts. Malnourishment made it impossible to regain his health in any meaningful way, but at least the malarial fever was gone, thanks to Bert somehow finding Atebrin and sneaking it in. The dysentery was more persistent. It took a long time for the blood in his stools to disappear.

Getting moving in the morning was extremely difficult, and he was grateful for the trick Henry McLellan, known as Mac, had developed. He had been recognised as the officer in charge by the Japanese, who called him MacCrum, to the Australian prisoner's hilarity. They had placed him in charge of managing roll call, or tenko. Mac had been distressed by the punishment the Japanese were swift to bring down on anyone who was late, even if they were in hospital or on the toilet with the runs and unable to shift. So when the guards discovered the numbers weren't correct, Mac would say he had miscounted, and start all over again, which allowed latecomers to sneak in. This saved Wilf a beating several times.

Two and a half weeks brought a lot of changes. Many more soldiers had been captured and brought in, making conditions increasingly crowded in the small cluster of huts. Wilf was saddened to see some of the missionaries from the outlying areas were now at the camp, including Dan Oakes and John Shelton. His hope that they might have escaped was shattered, and his heart was heavy when he saw that Dan Oakes had suffered a terrible head injury during the invasion, which left him somewhat confused. There was no sign of Laurie Mac, Laurie Linggood, Howard Pearson, John Poole, or Ken Allsop, who had all been at Kalas, or Tom Simpson, who had also been in the outlying regions. Wilf hoped their absence meant they had got away, although he longed to be able to talk to Ken about Eileen, and his sister Netta. The pain of missing them never lessened.

The mood in the camp had changed as well. There had been a degree of hope at first: an expectation that rescue would be imminent. With each passing day that hope dwindled to a tiny flicker. Overlaying the dread that came from the changing moods and unexpected brutality of the Japanese soldiers, was a real fear of the internees being killed by their own people. Allied raids had become a regular event, with bombs falling in the prison camp regularly. Luckily no one had died from the bombs, but death seemed to be a growing presence from other quarters.

Stan French, one of the Salvation Army bandsmen, died while Wilf was in hospital, of injuries received during the invasion. He was not the only one. Deaths both within and outside the camp were commonplace. Word reached them of many public executions in Rabaul, particularly amongst the Chinese. The Japanese were targeting community leaders, no doubt to shatter any resistance.

Wilf worried about Reverend Po Mui Sam and the other Chinese Methodists, as well as the native leaders of the Methodist church: Akulia and the various pastor teachers who had promised to keep the Lotu alive if anything happened to the Australian missionaries. It was becoming increasingly apparent the Japanese were not giving any special treatment to Christians. Possibly the opposite.

'We need to get you well,' Gullidge had whispered to Wilf five days ago, as they huddled together in the hut just before lights out. 'And we have a plan to do that. Arthur and Lex Fraser came up with it.'

Since the plan involved once more defying the Japanese, it made Wilf queasy, but he didn't want to disappoint his friends, who were determined to do this for him. If he was punished a second time, he was unlikely to be treated so leniently. But the full force of Arthur Gullidge's inspiring personality, and the risks the bandsmen were willing to take to do this for him, overcame his fears.

It had all begun when Lex was asked by a Japanese soldier named Kishida to create sheet music for army songs. Lex convinced the man he needed Arthur's help, and the pair were released from work duty for days to do the job. When they discovered this also meant extra rations, they wondered how they could share their luck with their mates. Then the Japanese announced they had set up what they called a minseibu for Rabaul, which the men worked out was their name for administrative infrastructure. They planned to hold a night of celebration to formally mark the event.

Since Kishida oversaw entertainment, he naturally asked Lex and Arthur to put together music for the night. They saw the perfect opportunity to help those in the camp who would benefit the most from extra rations, so the band was a mix of actual bandsmen, and those whose musical abilities were not so... well developed.

Which was why Wilf found himself sitting on the small stage at the Regent Theatre, a clarinet in his lap. Though he had protested that others needed the food more than he, Arthur was determined to help his friend.

'This is going to be a fancier event than last time,' Arthur had told Wilf as they unloaded crates on the wharf the day he explained the plan. Wilf didn't fail to notice Arthur was taking the greater weight of their burden each time they picked up another crate.

'Last time?' Wilf gave him a blank look.

'Right! That was just after you went into sick bay. They were celebrating invading Singapore, and they spent the night marching a lot, singing songs and drinking. When they're happy, they seem to like their sake a lot, so we'll get away with this – no worries!'

So far, they had. There had been endless rehearsals in the last few days, and Wilf's main task had been to stop his hands shaking, purse his lips, and turn the page on the music whenever the real musicians did. Arthur praised his passable pretence of playing the baritone clarinet that had previously belonged to Stan French, the fallen bandsman.

'Just remember,' Arthur said over and over, 'don't ever actually blow into the instrument.'

In return, Wilf received extra rations. These were increasing in portion size each time, since Arthur had convinced Kishida that musicians can't play well on an empty stomach. The success of the evening depended on the musicians being well fed, he argued.

'Failure doesn't seem to be an option for these men,' Arthur confided. 'No "she'll be right" attitude. If things don't go perfectly, they suffer for it.'

Wilf was not the only ring-in. Others who, like Wilf, were ill, but no longer ill enough to be hospitalised, found themselves hiding in plain sight amongst the band members.

The chairs that usually filled the space when it functioned as a cinema had been placed around the edge of the hall, alongside tables laden with food and small ceramic bottles and sake cups. There appeared to be more sake than food. The Japanese attendees were all high-ranking officers, who were usually rigid and strait-laced in the dealings with the POW camp, so it was surprising to see the sake flowing like a river.

At first Arthur played it safe, with a couple of sets of Japanese army music, which were received with many smiles. But as their audience being boisterous and loose-limbed, their dancing taking on an unusual fluidity, he began to slip in some Australian songs, played in a jazz style so they were virtually unrecognisable to anyone less familiar with them.

Wilf's heart pounded at speed as he mimed along to Waltzing Matilda, but the Japanese officers danced with as much enjoyment as they had the earlier Japanese marching songs. Whenever there was a break in the music they would come over to the band, huge smiles on their faces, and speak in Japanese. Despite his experience learning languages, Wilf could only pick up a word here and there, but he understood they were pleased with the songs.

The musicians were given frequent breaks, during which they were fed platters of sliced fish and fresh fruit. Wilf hadn't eaten anything fresh in a month and a half. He savoured the sweetness, the juiciness, the flavours that seemed almost overpowering after eating only rice. He was concerned his belly would pay for it later, but with the other prisoners, he took whatever was on offer, uncertain when he might get the chance again.

Later in the evening, Arthur asked them to turn to Rule Britannia, and Wilf almost couldn't breathe as they started the song in an upbeat tempo. Surely their captors couldn't fail to recognise it and mete out swift punishment? Sure enough, halfway through, there was a shout, then another one. Scuffling broke out. The music died like a deflating bagpipe. Terror taking hold of him, Wilf accidentally blew into the clarinet, an awful squeaking sound that clearly wasn't the work of a practiced musician. Complete silence fell.

A moment later the shouting began again, combined with scuffling and frenzied movements in the main part of the theatre. Arthur cast a worried look at Wilf. Was their ruse blown? Then he raised his cornet to his lips with a devil-may-care grin and launched back into the British National Anthem. The others swiftly joined him and the moment passed.

Since he didn't actually have to concentrate on playing, Wilf was able to see what was really going on. The noise had nothing to do with the band being caught out. An officer who was falling-down drunk was aiming blows at a young Asian looking woman standing next to him. He landed a few, but others quickly intervened. Someone slapped him in the face, then yelled at him. Then he was dragged from the hall. The dancing and conversation resumed, with another guest bowing to the young woman and sweeping her out into the centre of the room.

The bandsmen had been surprised to see young women walking through the town when they went to their first rehearsal. Wilf hadn't recognised any of them as being from the Chinese community. Lex had asked Kishida, who had explained with apparent discomfort only that they were there for the soldiers. Whether they had travelled to Rabaul voluntarily or through coercion Lex had been unable to discover.

After the successful insertion of Rule Britannia into the proceedings, Arthur was emboldened. They played Advanced Australia Fair in their final set, with a rapid ragtime feel, and by now their audience was too busy dancing and playing unfamiliar drinking games to notice what the music was, as long as it continued. Wilf no longer felt deep anxiety when they played Australian songs. Although his own defiance had cost him, he was pleased that nothing had cowed the bandsmen's Australian spirit.

As they neared the end of the song, Kishida approached Gullidge, his eyes narrowed with suspicion. But just as he tapped the bandmaster on the shoulder there was yet another disruption, this time far louder than mere shouting. An enormous bang was followed by cries of shock as the doors to the Regent Theatre were flung inward, one falling forward off its hinges, as a truck plunged into the hall. Its momentum was slowed by its collision with the doors, and a moment later it halted, just before it would hit several dancing couples. They lunged back, eyes wide with horror. The truck's horn sounded for a long moment.

Arthur gestured to the men to keep playing. As they finished the song, the drunken lout who had been removed earlier was pulled from the truck. With quiet efficiency several men dragged him from the hall, while others lifted the doors upright and someone reversed the truck out of the theatre. In a matter of minutes, it was as though the disruption had never happened. By this time the band had moved on to a new song.

When they finished this one, to loud applause from their audience, Kishida approached Arthur and held up one finger. Arthur turned to his bandsmen.

'Okay men, it's time to call it a night. Let's play Auld Lang Syne.'

They launched into the New Year's standard, and they'd barely played the first line when they noticed a strange thing. All the Japanese officers and their dates had stopped dancing. They all turned to face the band. Wilf felt a deep sense of dread. Drawing the clarinet a tiny distance away from his mouth he muttered softly, 'What have we done?'

Next to him, Wilf Trigg used a break in the music to mutter, 'Just keep playing. Too late now.'

Wilf resumed his miming, but he watched the faces of their audience closely. A moment later he was astonished to realise some of them were openly weeping. Others had placed their arms around whoever was next to them, male or female, and were swaying a little. They stayed that way, their expressions wistful, for the entire song. When it ended, they bowed to the band, a sign of unexpected respect, and the night ended.

Packing up their instruments, the bandsmen discussed what it had meant.

'Clearly they know Auld Lang Syne as well,' James Thurst said in his American accent. 'Who knew?'

'It's good to know it makes them sentimental,' one of the other musicians commented. 'Might come in handy later.'

A few of the other men nodded. Any leverage to prevent punishment was worth holding on to.

'Well, back to starvation rations,' someone said. 'It's been a good wicket. Let's hope they have something else to celebrate soon.'

'As long as it's not the invasion of Australia,' another man said. It might have been meant as a joke, but the faces of those around him fell. The hope that their families were safe kept many of them going. To think otherwise was unbearable.

'What's going on there?' someone asked, and they all turned to see Kishida speaking animatedly to Arthur. Wilf worried that their choice of music was going to land them in hot water. But Kishida was smiling.

The conversation over, Arthur came and spoke to the men. 'Great work today, lads, especially since we haven't rehearsed in months.'

'I've had a few other things on my plate,' someone joked, and laughter erupted.

'Kishida says Major Matsuda was pleased with the entertainment,' Arthur continued. 'He's going to let us take all the instruments to the camp.' There were cheers all round, and some men patted each other on the back. Anything to pass the time and lift morale would be welcomed. Arthur held up his hand for silence. He had a huge grin as he delivered the final piece of good news.

'Even the piano.'

18 - The Montevideo Maru

Wilf

Evening, Saturday 20th June 1942. Malaguna Rd Camp, Rabaul.

There were few things in the Malaguna Road camp that the prisoners placed any worth on anymore. Most of their possessions had been stripped from them. Only a few days after the minseibu celebrations, their captors realised the musical instruments were boosting morale too much and removed them. Little else remained. The prisoners' clothes were in tatters, shirts long ago abandoned and shoes a rare commodity. Even their lives were shown to be disposable at every juncture.

A little over a fortnight ago news had come that the Japanese had even executed an eleven-year-old boy, the stepson of plantation owner Ted Harvey. Ted, his wife, and young Richard had been accused of spying. Word had it that Japanese soldiers had played football with the young lad during his parents' trial, then shown no concern about loading him on a truck with his parents to be shot nearby at the overflowing POW graveyard at the Malay Hole, just out of town. If they could execute a child under such circumstances, no one held any remaining illusions that their own life might be spared.

One of the things that retained value in the internees' eyes was food. Since the Navy had taken over management of the camp at the end of April, supplies had reduced greatly. Ships came in far less frequently, and those that did had weapons and ammunition more often than anything edible. Over the months of their internment, more and more prisoners had been brought in, including Laurie Mac, Howard Pearson, John Poole, Laurie Linggood and Ken Allsop. Mac brought a rare piece of good news; the four Methodist nursing sisters were still at Vunapope and although they had been terrorised, they had been safe from physical attack – at least so far.

There were well over a thousand men crammed into the former army barracks now. Meals were often just a ball of rice. Soup that had once had vegetables in it was little more than water. For Wilf and the men who had attended the minseibu celebrations, the memory of fish and fruit seemed a fantastical dream. The ever-reducing rations provoked fear in some, who thought there was a corresponding increase in ill prisoners being taken away, never to return.

This morning Ron Wayne had been one of those taken away, even though he was as healthy as anyone else in the camp, which was to say, underweight, exhausted, and suffering from regular bouts of dysentery or beri beri. The missionary men mourned their lay pastor, having little energy to speculate on any other reason for his disappearance, so his return at the end of the day was been a surprise.

Ron's news was the first positive thing they had known in a long time.

'I know you've all been worried about me. They took me to the Catholic mission at Vunapope, to act as an interpreter. They were buying vegetables grown in the gardens there. And you'll never believe it. I got to see our nurses. Mavis, Chris, Dorothy Beale and Dora were all there. They look like they're doing ok.

Pretty skinny, but then we all know what that's like.'

He reached into his shorts pocket and produced a first aid kit, soap, and needles and thread.

'Thank you, Lord,' John Poole said. Such simple supplies, but desperately needed. Early on, soap and toothpaste had been easy to find since the Japanese seemed extremely focused on cleanliness, but once the Navy took over the camp, all supplies became scarcer. By now every available piece of unused land had been turned into a benjo hole, so the entire camp had the permanent miasma of human waste in the air. Anyone who valued cleanliness had to settle for less than basic standards. A bar of soap might has well be a lump of gold now to the desperate men.

'That's not all,' Ron said, keeping his voice low. Howard Pearson was keeping an eye out for approaching soldiers, since plenty of beatings had taught them to be beyond cautious.

'I saw Ainui.' He held out a parcel wrapped in a banana leaf to Wilf, keeping his hand palm downwards so it wasn't too obvious. 'He asked after you, Kuskus. The natives heard you'd been ill a while back. They've been worried about you. He asked me to give you this and said you must stay well.' His eyes became shadowed. 'He had other news. A rumour has come in that Tom Simpson may have been executed. Ainui heard he was being brought in to Rabaul and there was an incident. He tried to protect a young soldier and... It sounds like it was quick, at least.' He shook his head and fell silent, looking around before dropping the parcel into Wilf's waiting hand.

Despite its constant presence, the reality of death often went unsaid in the camp, because the truth could bring suffering and fear, and there was room for neither. Their captors didn't understand depression and treated it with as much brutality as defiance. A quick death could mean a bullet, or beheading, but no one wanted to find out which.

Wilf received the offering of Tolai food and unwrapped it with care. Inside the banana leaf was a serving of punapur, rich with coconut milk. The sight was terrifying, because if they were caught with it, they would be punished, and Ainui executed if it was discovered he had sent it. In his role as interpreter for the Tolai, Ron Wayne had seen natives executed with regularity, for the smallest infractions. Passing food to the prisoners merited a beheading, whilst talking to them could lead to being bayoneted to death.

At first, when Ron had witnessed Japanese 'justice', he had told the others, needing to share the burden that weighed on his soul. But lately only his haunted eyes spoke of the growing number of deaths of Tolai and Chinese carried out by the Japanese. No one doubted the truth of his stories. Laurie and the others who had been at Kalas had been severely beaten when they surrendered, though it had taken a while for them to admit to that humiliation, and Wilf had experienced his own torture. They knew casual violence was always a heartbeat away.

Wilf looked around at the hollow cheeks of his fellow missionaries, and their desperate eyes. He didn't want to place them at risk, but a blessing like this might never come again. And he wanted to honour Ainui's bravery by treating this unexpected gift with suitable reverence.

'I wish we could use this to conduct a proper service,' he said with a nod to Mac. 'If there's ever been a more precious body of Christ, I don't know when. But the evidence is safer destroyed...' He shrugged and began breaking off pieces of the punapur, passing them out to everyone he could.

'Save some for yourself Wilf,' Ron said. 'If I ever run into Ainui again and have to tell him you didn't get any it'll be more than my life's worth.' His wry smile was a little crooked. Wilf passed a piece to Dan Oakes, leaving only smears of taro on the leaf.

'Pardon my manners,' he said in his most dignified voice, 'but I'm under orders. And you know what Ainui's like. He used to run my office with an iron fist.' Wilf licked the leaf clean, savouring the sweetness. There was barely enough to taste it properly, and it only served to make his stomach growl, but he treasured the flavour, nonetheless.

Even more valuable than food, because it was often in short supply, was sleep. The prisoners were woken for tenko daily at 5am, regardless of whether there had been allied raids the night before, and there often were. Some of the men in Lark Force were convinced they'd be killed by Australian bombs.

'First they forgot to give us decent weapons, then they abandoned us, and soon they'll bomb us to bits,' was a common refrain. But malnutrition and the inability to get proper sleep were more likely to kill them by degrees, Wilf thought.

4am, Monday 22nd June 1942. Malaguna Rd Camp, Rabaul.

They that go down to the sea in ships, and occupy
their business in great waters;
These men see the works of the Lord, and his wonders
in the deep.
For at his word the stormy wind ariseth, which lifteth
up the waves thereof.
They are carried up to the heaven, and down again to

the deep;
their soul melteth away because of the trouble.
They reel to and fro, and stagger like a drunken man,
and are at their wit's end.
So when they cry unto the Lord in their trouble, he
delivereth them out of their distress.
For he maketh the storm to cease, so that the waves
thereof are still.
Then are they glad, because they are at rest; and so he
bringeth them unto the haven where they should be.

Psalm 107, verses 23 to 26

A loud bang startled Wilf awake. In his half-asleep state, it took his brain a moment to process the shouting outside the hut. He'd picked up a lot of Japanese by now. They were calling for tenko. But that couldn't be right. It felt far too early. Matsui's familiar cry rang out.

'Hurry, all men come with running.'

Around him, everyone scrambled out of bed. More orders were shouted from the door of the hut. A few men looked to Wilf to translate.

'They're saying to bring any possessions,' he said. This was it. There had been rumours for a month or more that they might be taken to Japan, because the lack of supplies and overcrowding were becoming a real problem. But most prisoners hadn't taken this seriously.

All Wilf had left after six months was the envelope with the x ray and telegram. Unlike many of the soldiers, he had never stopped wearing his shirt, leaving it out each night to dry, and the envelope still sat in the breast pocket. He had nothing else to pack.

Once they stood on the parade ground the men were separated into groups of fifty, with much shoving and shouting.

When Matsui passed nearby, Wilf quietly asked him what was happening.

'You go now to paradise.'

The words sent a chill down Wilf's spine. But then Matsui spoke again. 'Soon we invade Australia, then you go home, but for now, you go to beautiful island of Hainan, work hard.'

He moved on, leaving Wilf to whisper the information to those around him. Within minutes all those standing on the parade ground knew what was happening.

Mac McLellan took his usual time counting the men to allow for the stragglers. As he called out their numbers and waited for their response, there was some shouting near one of the huts. The whisper ran through the standing men like wildfire.

'The officers aren't coming with us. They've barricaded them in their huts.'

Several men received a rifle butt to the head or kidneys for speaking, but most had become inured to such casual violence and still passed on the information. They didn't speculate about why the officers weren't coming with them. Any possible answer might be too horrible to speak out loud.

In the end they were kept standing for hours. Once roll call was over there was no clear reason for the wait, but they were not surprised by it. Then one by one, the groups of fifty were moved from the camp in a slow, staggering parade.

Wilf's legs were swollen from beri beri, making every step painful, and he could see others around him who could barely put one foot in front of the other. He wondered how they could possibly do hard labour once they reached Japan.

As he passed near one of the huts still containing the officers, he heard someone call out, 'Heads up, men. We tried to argue we should come with you, but they won't let us. See you in Japan.'

Then he heard the calm, deep tones of John May, the army Chaplain. He was reading the morning's psalm, as he did every day. The Japanese had not allowed any sort of Christian service or prayer at first, but eventually they had permitted John and the other ministers to take turns conducting a brief prayer service daily after tenko.

Wilf recognised the psalm as number one hundred and seven and he smiled at the choice, because he knew the beginning spoke of giving thanks to the Lord for redeeming people from the hands of their enemy. But May must have been reading it for a while, because as Wilf passed the hut, Syd Beazley and Jack Trevitt beside him, he heard verse twenty-three. 'They that go down to the sea in ships...'.

From the Malaguna Road camp to the wharves was only a short distance, but so many of the men were injured, sick or at the very least suffering from complete exhaustion, that their progress was deathly slow. They were surrounded by Japanese soldiers with machine guns, who forced them onward with occasional pushes or curses. Most of the Australians could do little more than shuffle, but they were not cowed. Despite the constant humiliations and violence, the Japanese had never broken the spirit of the men of Lark Force, the First Independent Company, who had been brought in from New Ireland, and the Rabaul civilians.

Native labourers and Chinese appeared at the side of the road, watching silently. Wilf recognised some of them, but not as many as he would have expected. He hoped that meant the church community had made their way to safety in the hills, or deep in the jungle. Any other possibility was terrible to contemplate. A young boy Wilf recognised as a member of the Catholic church community, Rudy Buckley, ran alongside the men as they made their way to the wharf.

'Bit of a change from our parade in Melbourne,' Arthur Gullidge said from the row in front of Wilf. 'Remember boys? Thousands of people turned out to see us. We were fit as could be from training, our uniforms fresh and new. They were standing by the roadside and on bridges, cheering for us.' His eyes shone.

'You'd written that great version of "We're off to see the wizard" from The Wizard of Oz,' James Thurst chimed in. 'Everyone loved it.'

Arthur nodded. 'Hold onto that memory lads. Someday, when this blasted war's over, there'll be another parade for us. We'll go home, and they'll call us heroes.'

His words had their intended impact. Wilf could see the soldiers and bandsmen nearby straighten their backs and lift their chins. Arthur had that effect on people.

Rabaul had changed so much in the five months since the invasion, Wilf felt a deep anguish as he stumbled past familiar buildings now dirty and unkempt, or pockmarked and damaged from bombing. Japanese soldiers swarmed everywhere, but he saw the town as it had once been, bustling with Tolai women making their way to the market, string bags full of fruit hanging from their heads, Chinese women strolling in bright silks, vans full of copra rattling walls and making the trees shiver as they passed by. A sharp shove recalled him from Rabaul that was, and as he glanced around, he experienced a strange sensation, a recognition that he was passing through a world he was no longer part of. A profound, heart-deep feeling of loss overcame him.

At the wharves, there was a small crowd to greet them, but no cheering, only solemn faces. Reverend Po Mui Sam stood as close as he dared to the ramp leading to the tender which would take them to the ship. When it was the missionaries' turn, Reverend Sam reached out to them one by one, taking their hands in his in the gesture of passing the peace.

'The Lord be with you,' he said to each of them, and each replied, 'and also with you.'

Just before Wilf stepped into the tender, he saw Ainui. Looking around, he made sure the Japanese guards were focused on getting men into the ship and took a step closer to his friend. Ainui reached out and clasped both Wilf's hands in his. He used the moment to pass something to Wilf.

'Return to us, Kuskus,' Ainui said. There was no time for any other words. A soldier lunged at them both, chasing Ainui away with gestures of his bayonet. Wilf climbed into the tender that would transport them to the Montevideo Maru, his hurried movements causing him to bang one swollen leg on the edge. Pain reverberated through his entire body. Only once that had died away, and after a cautious check for watchers, was he able to look at what Ainui had passed to him. It was a string of shell money.

'That's their money, isn't it?' one of the nearby soldiers asked. 'The natives? That won't buy you anything in Japan.'

Wilf shrugged. He didn't tell the man the shells weren't for Japan. For the Tolai, the shells weren't just a form of money. They were sacred. These shells were tabu, the greatest gift Ainui could have given him. Tabu was a crucial part of Tolai burial ceremonies, placed in the grave with the deceased. Without tabu, they believed, you wouldn't be able to reach heaven.

2am, Wednesday 1st July 1942. Onboard the Montevideo Maru.

> Patrolling northwest of Bojeador as before. Dove at dawn, surfaced at dusk. At 2216 sighted a darkened ship to southward at first, due to bearing on which sighted, believed him to be on northerly course, but after a few minutes observation it was evident he was on a westerly course, and going at high speed. Put on all engines and worked up to full power, proceeding to westward in attempt to get ahead of him. For an hour and a half we couldn't make a nickel. This fellow was really going, making at least 17 knots and probably a bit more, as he appeared to be zigzagging. At this time it looked a bit hopeless, but determined to hang on in the hope he would slow down or change course towards us. His range at this time was estimated at around 13,000 yards. Sure enough, about midnight he slowed to about 12 knots. After that it was easy.

Logbook of the USS Sturgeon, 30 June 1942

Sleep never came willingly in the hold of the Montevideo Maru. Mostly when they were locked in for the night the hundreds of men crowded in together could hope only for the drifting, strange half-waking state where reality blurred for a while. The lucky ones were able to squat with their backs against the hull of the ship, or against the dividers between holds. During the day this was impossible because of the heat radiating from the metal, but at night the residual warmth helped prevent little-used limbs from seizing.

They were only given a ball of rice and small cup of water every few days, so dehydration and starvation were swiftly stripping them of any remaining strength. Some could barely hold themselves upright, but it was impossible to lie down. There were too many of them. Legs curled against their chests, they huddled together, not for warmth, because the heat was never ending, the air stifling, but for comfort. To feel that they were still human, even amidst the darkness and filth.

During the day, the brave or foolhardy could use makeshift wooden benjos hung off the side of the ship, taking their lives in their hands to empty their bowels during the brief hours when they were allowed topside. But many now couldn't even climb the ladder out of the hold, their limbs dangerously weak. Holding their weight off the side of the ship, where any sudden lurch could lead them to drown, was an impossibility. The hold was awash with urine and faeces from those too weak to try.

After eight days, death was a familiar companion. Those who had been seriously ill when they came onboard died quietly, or screaming from the agony of gut pain or infection, or worst of all, calling softly for their mothers in the loneliest hours of the night. Their bodies were moved as far as possible from the living, piled on top of each other in a miserable attempt to create more space. In the heat, they quickly began to stink, adding a strangely sweet odour to the rotting smell of beri beri in infected limbs, and the stench of human waste.

The Methodist ministers did whatever they could to offer comfort to both the dying and the living, as did the other religious men amongst the internees. Too many times, each of them knew the deep sadness of holding the hand of someone as he slipped into unconscious and finally death. Their prayers echoed hollowly in the black hold.

Tonight, Wilf hadn't even tried to sleep. Although the stench and the moaning had not changed, he felt as if the air was charged. He'd sensed a variation in the thrum of the engines a few hours ago, a deepening of tone that told him they had slowed, but it offered him no serenity.

It was so dark he could see nothing, so when someone called his name, he couldn't tell who it was.

'Wilf?'

'Here... I'm here,' he kept talking so the person could find him. A moment later he felt something bump his arm. He reached into the black and found reaching fingers, which he embraced in the traditional Tolai two-handed greeting.

'It's me... Keith,' the voice said, sounding terribly young. 'We walked together the day of the invasion.'

'Of course. I remember. You were a gunner on the beach.'

'I'm afraid, Wilf. What's going to happen to us?'

Wilf squeezed the hand he couldn't see.

'The war has to end soon,' he murmured. 'They'll take us to Japan, and we'll spend some time there, then the Americans and the Brits will win, and we'll go home.'

'I'm not supposed to be here.' Keith's voice was husky with dehydration and regret. 'I lied, when I signed up. I was only seventeen, but I said I was eighteen.'

'You wanted to do your bit.'

'Yeah. I didn't want to be a hero though. I just wanted to keep Australia safe. But I didn't know it would be so... horrible. I don't want to go to Japan. I want to go home.'

'I know.' Wilf's words were swallowed by a terrifying volley of sound. First there was a distant boom, followed instantly by an unbearable reverberation through the hull. Around them, men awoke instantly, swearing, calling out.

'What was that?' Now Keith's words held deep fear.

There were more sounds, growing louder and louder. The rush of water, the clangs and creaks of distant metal and, most terrifying of all, distant screams.

Around Wilf, the missionary men had woken. He recognised their voices in the dark.

'What's going on?' Dan Oakes, his English accent standing out amongst the volley of Australian speech.

'I think we've been hit by some kind of bomb.' Laurie Linggood, his voice devoid of its usual spark of humour.

'Is this the end?' John Poole, the youngest of the missionaries, sounding less like the confident minister he had become and more like the young probationer he had been when he arrived.

'She'll go down fast,' Syd Beazley, the man who had built so many churches and houses, and trained so many young men in building, was practical as always.

'We need to get the hatch open, get as many men as we can out,' Howard Pearson, always good in a crisis, always thinking of others, like when he took Wilf's place as driver during the volcano eruption.

'It'll be locked,' Ron Wayne, practical, level-headed, a straight shooter. 'They always lock it at night.'

'We need to sing,' Arthur Gullidge, the bandmaster who inspired his men, keeping their spirits up no matter what. His comment met with a few protests. 'No, no – listen to me.

Remember the minseibu celebration Wilf? When we played Auld Lang Syne?'

'They got all sentimental,' Wilf said. 'The song means as much to them as it does to us. It might be our only chance. Appeal to their humanity.'

Arthur started them off, and the others joined in. Around them there were angry comments at first, but word quickly spread of the reason for the song, and the men in the hold joined their voices to the chorus, some more tunefully than others.

With the terrible sounds of a dying ship, it was hard to know at first whether their attempt would work, but then they heard the familiar whine of the lock being turned. The hatch opened, falling away with a clunk, and moonlight streamed down into the hold, washing over the desperate faces of hundreds of men looking up in hopes of salvation.

The singing died away as men surged for the ladder. Their movement reminded Wilf of rats falling on a piece of meat and he turned away. Desperation does terrible things to men, he thought. Some were shouting for help. Others were deathly quiet, frozen in place, too weak or fearful to move.

In the dim light, Wilf caught Syd Beazley's eyes, and saw his own fears reflected there. Syd was a tradesman, like Wilf's father. He had probably guessed, as Wilf had, that sentimental song or not, the Japanese would only open the hold if it wouldn't place them at risk from the desperate prisoners. It would have been the last thing they did as they abandoned the ship.

Wilf could see Keith next to him now, his face pale, eyes wide. Keith's tremulous voice sounded terribly young. 'Should I try and reach the ladder?'

Wilf reached for the boy's hand, then shook his head. 'There won't be time.'

Keith nodded. His grip on Wilf's hand tightened. 'Will it hurt?'

Wilf wanted to reassure him, but there was no room for lies in their dismal prison. 'It will be quick.'

None of the missionaries moved to flee. The ship was starting to tilt now. By unspoken agreement they moved towards the bulwark that was deeper in the water, away from the fleeing men.

Calmly, Mac led them in the Lord's Prayer.

'Our Father, who art in heaven...' As he spoke, his voice straining to be heard amongst the horrendous sounds of the dying ship, and dying men, other men drew near, men Wilf recognised from Methodist services in Rabaul. '... for Thine is the kingdom, the power and the glory, forever and ever.'

'Amen.'

A flicker of panic sparked in Wilf's heart as the prayer ended. He could see the same fear in the faces of the men around him. But Mac, their leader, kept smiling as the tilt of the ship increased, making it impossible to stand.

'See you in paradise,' Mac said, reaching out to clasp the hands of those closest to him.

Wilf's thoughts flashed to the ruins of Rabaul, the destruction of Vunairima, the bloodstained beaches of Raluana. Paradise was gone, ground to dust by the machinery of war. For a moment he knew only pure terror. This was the end.

Then he fixed his thoughts on his baby daughter. He prayed with everything in him for a future filled with peace for Rosemary Jean, the child he'd never know. He thought of the life he had lived, a life of service, to the Mission, to the Tolai, to his faith. It had been a life well lived. He pictured his darling wife, her blue eyes sparkling with intelligence, her auburn hair warning of the fire within, and prayed for that fire to carry her forward, beyond grief, to years where she might find happiness again.

In the dark of the hold, men were screaming and sobbing. The sound of breaking metal and rushing water made it impossible to speak. Bodies pressed against bodies. Thought became impossible, prayer reduced to wordless faith, a silent communion with eternity.

When water rushed in through the open hutch, panic and love fought within Wilf in his last moments.

Love won.

19 – A Kind of Amnesia

Eileen

Tuesday 11th September 1945. New Town, Hobart.

To be strong in dull and dreary duty is about the hardest task a man can face. It is a noble thing to be brave in tragic moments, but perhaps there is something even nobler than that. It is to be brave and glad and strong and tender when the sky is grey and when the road is dreary. It is in such seasons—and they form nine-tenths of life— that he who waits on God will show his strength.

Reverend Howard Pearson, personal diary

Despite the endless uncertainty, waiting for Wilf to return home, Eileen's life found a certain level. Though she had missed out on buying the land in Raluana Lane in 1942, her naming suggestion had been accepted, so it felt like fate when the same block came up for sale again in 1945. She was determined to be the successful bidder this time. Although her mother's help with Rosemary had been a godsend, she was tired of her father's attempts to control her life so staying with her parents was increasingly difficult. With the four of them, and Shelley, who she had reclaimed from Marie, living together, things were very crowded too. They had lived in many houses, from grand to less so depending on Claude's wavering fortunes. Their current accommodations were definitely of the less spacious kind.

It had been a strange few years, overlaid by constant uncertainty and an emotion that hovered between grief and hope. The only way to cope was to move forward, she had decided, but she knew she had lost some part of herself with all the waiting, a part that would only be restored when Wilf returned to her. She tried not to dwell on what he might have suffered, and how he might be changed.

Nor did she think about the future beyond his return. She missed the relaxed life and beautiful gardens of New Britain, but she knew things would have changed beyond recognition with the Japanese occupation. Still, the land and the people there were incredibly resilient, as she'd seen after the eruption of 1937. It had been almost unbelievable how swiftly everything had recovered.

War left its mark in a different way, though. Some things were gone forever. The Neptuna and the Macdhui had both been destroyed by Japanese bombs, as had the entire compound at Vunairima. Finding a future would mean letting go of many familiar, loved parts of her past.

Once Rosemary was old enough, weaned and able to walk, Eileen went on Overseas Missions deputation for the Methodist Church, travelling through Tasmania and saying in the homes of ministers and their wives, or elders or members of churches. While women looked after Rosemary, she took services and addressed meetings.

She remembered little of those days though; she found herself suffering a kind of amnesia for the duration of the war. She had little recollection now of any of the places she and Rosemary visited or the people she met. Only this week she had run into someone in Hobart who had asked her, 'Do you remember when you stayed at our place at Sheffield?' But she had no recollection of having ever seen them before or been in that town.

Occasionally she caught brief glimpses of memories, such as a home with a big apple orchard at Franklin on the Huon River. She had seen the apples being wrapped in tissue paper and packed in wooden cases for export. She remembered a lovely sheep dog that enjoyed apples and was permitted to eat those that fell under the trees but preferred the best fruit from the packing shed, watching for that door to be left open so she could steal them from the cases.

Another partial memory was of walking to a meeting at Waratah, near Ulverstone on the north-west coast. The party she had been with had paused on a bridge, and one of the two ministers had exclaimed 'it is a wide evening'. She had thought at the time it was an apt description for the clear night, the sky full of stars and a big, bright moon. Looking back, she saw clearly that it had reminded her of moments on the beach in Vunairima with Wilf, the same moon gazing down implacably.

Having done the tour, which reminded her what it felt like to do something worthwhile, she had decided it was time to return to teaching. Netta, who wrote to her regularly, had informed her many of the mission wives still had their lives on hold, relying on the pension the Overseas Missions board provided to survive. But Eileen had always valued self-reliance, and the pension they gave her wasn't enough for her to save to build the house for Wilf.

So she'd obtained a teaching position at Clemes College, despite the disapproval of some in the community who thought she should stay at home, raising Rosemary. There was a desperate shortage of teachers, with so many men and women away in the army or the navy or lost overseas, and local women busy in the land army. And Eileen was driven to play her part.

Rosemary was glad to be cared for by Eileen's mother Elsa. She was a gregarious child, happy with anyone who'd listen to her stories and chatter, and likely to wander off at a moment's notice if she found an open gate, looking for new friends to talk to. Having noticed people changed their clothes before going out, Rosemary had taken off down the street more than once in the nude. In New Britain, this would have been the natural way of things, but here it was more of a problem. Luckily, Shelley was terribly protective of the little girl, accompanying her on her wanderings.

The wait was nearly over, Eileen knew. Her father had told her about the bombing of Hiroshima, and the Japanese army's subsequent decision to surrender. Both Netta and John Burton had written to her saying the Methodist nurses, Dorothy Beale and the others, had been found in Japan, where they had been held as prisoners for three years. Reverend Burton had reassured her in his letter that they expected to hear any day that Wilf and the others had also been found in a Japanese camp. This news made her even more determined to begin building a house for Wilf. He would need stability and comfort.

Burton had also encouraged her to write to Wilf care of the Red Cross, because as soon as the men were located, he would make sure letters got through to them. Eileen hadn't managed to write yet. Between her teaching responsibilities and caring for Rosemary, spare time was especially difficult to grasp hold of. She would rather tell Wilf everything when she saw him anyway. The still, quiet voice inside her that whispered to stoke her doubt and fear played no part in her decision.

During the week, Eileen rose early and shared breakfast with Elsa. Claude, who was working night shifts as a compositor at the

Mercury, usually woke in time to farewell her before she cycled to school. He'd often leave the day's paper on the hallstand, having obtained a print hot off the presses on the way home, but Eileen had long ago stopped reading the news. Since the early days of the invasion, nothing had improved in terms of quality of information.

It was hard to get moving this morning. Eileen had been having the most awful nightmares for months, and they were increasing in frequency despite the hopeful news from John Burton. The nightmares were always the same. She was back in Rabaul, walking along Tunnel Hill Road with a familiar sense of urgency, like the day of the volcano eruption, but then she found herself stumbling instead inside a dark underground tunnel with many branching forks, searching endlessly for Wilf and the other missing men. The tunnels went on for miles and miles, and as she shuffled along, she became more and more frantic, until a deep, terrible sense of loss settled in her heart. The nightmare had visited her again last night, leaving her unsettled and oddly fearful.

Claude was late waking, rubbing his eyes as he passed Eileen in the hallway. 'Have a good day,' he said wearily, delivering his usual follow up. 'Keep those girls in line.' He entered the kitchen just as Eileen's eyes fell on the headline of the paper. 'Morning, love,' Claude said from the other room, no doubt giving his wife a kiss on the forehead.

Eileen stood frozen.

```
Grim story of Japanese savagery in
the islands.
```

'You were in late last night,' Elsa said. She sounded as though she were speaking from miles away. Eileen's head started thrumming.

    `Murder, Cannibalism.`

'We had a big story come in late that needed setting,' Claude said.

As Eileen scanned the article, the word 'missionaries' jumped from the page. Beneath it were the words 'decapitated' and 'bayoneted'.

Silence in the kitchen. Then, 'oh, damn,' from Claude, and his steps pounded across the wooden floor, strangely muffled by the cloud that engulfed Eileen's senses. He appeared suddenly in the doorway just as Eileen reached for the paper.

'It might be best if you don't...' Claude reached to take it before her. She snatched it up. 'Eileen, give that to me. It's not about the Methodist men. You don't need to read it.'

'Yes, I do,' she said, each word distinct. 'Don't you dare try and protect me.'

Elsa appeared in the doorway behind Claude as Eileen unfolded the paper and began reading.

'What's in the article?' Elsa asked her husband. His voice was soft as he replied.

'We're getting more information about what the Japanese have done to Australian soldiers and prisoners.'

'Oh, Claude.'

Eileen barely registered their exchange as she read the graphic account of violence against Australians and natives in the Pacific Islands. Massacres at the Tol and Waitavolo plantations, both places she had visited. Medical experiments on prisoners and natives. It was clear Christians were subject to as much brutality as anyone. Then the end of the article... native women raped and murdered. Her knees buckled.

'Ia Lo!' She sank to the floor, still clutching the paper. Elsa rushed to kneel by her side.

'Eileen, come and sit down. I'll make you another cup of tea.'

As though sensing her mother's distress, Rosemary Jean started screaming from the bedroom she shared with Eileen. Elsa glanced at Claude, then stood and hurried away to calm the baby. Eileen noticed another headline and continued to read. The second article provided more detail about the massacre at Tol, suggesting a hundred and fifty Australians evacuating from Rabaul had been caught and slaughtered.

'It's not your men,' Claude said as he offered a hand to help her up. 'Everything they found with the bodies was Army issue. I read the original wire. It's not him, Eileen.'

She let her father help her stand, leaving the paper lying on the floor. 'But it could be,' she said. Then in an instant a shutter seemed to come down over her eyes. 'I have to get to work.'

Elsa came into the hallway with Rosemary on her hip. Eileen reached for her daughter and gave her a kiss on the little girl's chubby cheek. For the first time in three years, seeing Wilf's dear features on her little girl didn't bring her comfort.

'I have to get to work,' she repeated.

23rd October 1945. Clemes College, Hobart.

The one remains, the many change and pass,
Heaven's light for ever shines; earth's shadows fly;
Life, like a dome of many-colour'd glass,
Stains the white radiance of eternity,
Until death tramples it to fragments.

Adonais, 48-52, Percy Bysshe Shelley

English was one of Eileen's favourite subjects to teach. Not grammar, the bones of language. Though absolutely necessary, it did not encourage her to inspire her pupils. It was poetry and literature, the soul of language, that she embraced. Today they were working on a poem by Shelley. To begin, each girl had read a stanza, one after the other. Now they were discussing themes.

'Adonais is an elegy for Keats,' Eileen lectured. 'Shelley admired the other poet, and was distressed at the way Keats was attacked by reviewers. He believed this drove him to his death.'

Her eyes fell on stanza fifty-one.

Here pause: these graves are all too young as yet/ To have outgrown the sorrow which consign'd/Its charge to each.

A chill ran up her spine. Eileen shook her head and continued. 'But look closely at the poem. Does Shelley mourn Keats' passing?' She looked around the room. Several girls put their hands up.

'Olive?'

'Miss, I think he's jealous. He wants to die too.'

'Which part of the poem tells you that?'

A fluent reader, Olive found the stanza and gave it expression.

'Thy hopes are gone before: from all things here they have departed: thou shouldst now depart!'

Eileen stared out the window, the words calling to her like a siren's song. Why had she chosen this poem today? It was not the recommended text, but at the last minute she'd changed her mind about which page the girls should turn to.

'Miss?' Olive's plaintive tone recalled her to herself.

'Good work, Olive. Shelley asks us not to weep, because he sees death as freedom, a chance to become one with Spirit in

Eternity. He alludes to life as darkness, a stain, and wishes to travel beyond it. Think of the ending of poem... "I am borne darkly, fearfully, afar; Whilst, burning through the inmost veil of Heaven, The soul of Adonais, like a star, Beacons from the abode where the Eternals are.'"

Her own words echoed in her head. Where the Eternals are. Why did everything feel so heavy with meaning today? It was only a poem. Again, she forced herself to be present, and realised all the girls had turned their attention to the classroom door. They had a visitor.

'Mrs Clemes?' The principal's wife had an odd expression on her face. Eileen jumped, shame washing like heat over her face at being found to be so distracted during class.

'Girls, please take an early recess. Mrs Pearce, if you could come with me.'

Mrs Clemes led the way through the stately school, to the private sitting room attached to the principal's office. There was no sign of Mr Clemes. The room was beautifully appointed, with an elegant velvet sofa and small round coffee table laden with an elegant, hand-painted tea set.

'Now, I know you prefer coffee over tea,' Mrs Clemes said, her voice strangely gentle, without the usual no-nonsense brusqueness that Eileen appreciated, 'but I think tea is the better option today.'

She poured from the pot, then without asking, opened the sugar bowl and, using a tiny, scalloped silver spoon, placed two heaped scoops of sugar in the tea. Eileen felt herself growing cold. Mrs Clemes knew she didn't take sugar. Numbly she accepted the warm drink.

The principal's wife waited until she had taken several sips before she spoke again. There was no small talk. 'I have had a phone call from your father. He's on his way to the school.'

Eileen felt like a child being supervised with her first hot drink as Mrs Clemes watched her sipping the tea, waiting to speak again until the cup had been returned to the little table. Then she moved to sit next to Eileen on the sofa. Time seemed to telescope, and Eileen wished that this moment before would go on forever, because she knew with absolute certainty, as though it had happened many times, exactly what was about to be said.

'A telegram arrived at your house this morning,' Mrs Clemes said. Eileen found herself staring at the other woman's wool skirt, a dark green plaid, and thinking how terribly impractical it would be in the heat of Rabaul. 'I'm so sorry, Eileen.'

No more befores, Eileen decided. She had to move on to afters.

'Wilf's dead, isn't he?'

She met Mrs Clemes' eyes. The other woman nodded, then reached out and drew Eileen into her arms. Eileen didn't sob. She could feel nothing, in that first moment. Nothing at all. Then something like relief flooded over her, swiftly followed by terrible shame. But not knowing had been unbearable. Three years of waiting, wondering, hoping, her life suspended in a bubble of unknowing, had been unbelievable torture. And no one had understood. To them Rabaul was a distant, exotic, strange place where events happened to people not like them.

Eileen's chest felt tight and her throat constricted. She couldn't speak if she wanted to. None of this was real.

Then her mind unfroze, and questions threatened to drown her. How had he died? Had he been tortured? When had he been captured? Had he been able to continue preaching and sharing the Lotu with their congregation in Rabaul? What would she do now?

What would she tell Rosemary Jean?

Afterwards Eileen had no idea how long Mrs Clemes held her. Time disappeared, leaving only the tiniest spark of pain that would grow to a burning flame in the days to come.

A knock on the door broke the moment. Mrs Clemes went to open it, letting Claude into her sitting room. He sat with Eileen, taking her hands.

'Elsa has taken Rosemary Jean to the botanical gardens. I had a call from John Burton,' he told her. 'They found Wilf's name on a list in Tokyo, along with all the other Methodist missionaries. They were being taken on a ship, the Montevideo Maru, to a prison camp in Japan.' He squeezed her hands. 'The ship was torpedoed by an American submarine.'

Eileen gasped.

'There were no survivors.'

Eileen broke from her father and went to the window overlooking the school gardens. She knew Claude and Mrs Clemes would be watching her, but she couldn't bear to face them. Emotions she couldn't even name overwhelmed her. Overhead only a few clouds marred the eternity of blue sky.

'I am borne darkly, fearfully, afar,' she murmured. She bowed her head, and her eyes fell on the roses in the garden. Where were Wilf's roses now? Did they still bloom in the garden on Malaguna Road? He'd been so proud to be able to grow them in a tropical climate. What had been the impact of war on all the places they loved so much?

Eileen turned back to the room. 'I suppose we should go and collect Rosemary.'

Claude nodded.

That evening, Eileen watched Rosemary sleep in the bed they shared. Always practical, Eileen had decided to tell her daughter her father was not coming home, knowing the little girl had no memory of Wilf. In her usual curious way, Rosemary had simply asked, 'Will I get a new father then?' Eileen hadn't been able to answer her.

Watching the three-year-old sleep, she recognised Wilf's smile in the gentle, unconscious curl of her lips. Here, at least, was a little part of her husband. Eileen had been able to bring so little home with her, only two trunks. Most of Wilf's possessions had been left behind. They had held such foolish hopes that he would be able to evacuate soon as well. His camphorwood chest sat at the end of the bed, and Eileen knelt in front of it. When she opened it, the familiar, oddly sweet smell instantly transported her to her travels to and from Rabaul.

A pair of China serving dishes, white with blue ornamentation, nestled amongst linen fancy work that she had prepared for her glory box. They had been Wilf's before their marriage, and Eileen had been keeping them for the time when she could serve Wilf a home-cooked meal in their new house. There were a few photos she'd brought home with her, and a few letters from their courtship. The one on top was stamped January 1942. It didn't look familiar.

Eileen lifted it out, her finger tracing her name and address, written as always with elaborate flourishes. Turning it over, she saw E.W. Pearce as sender. When had she received it? It was addressed to the Waverley Memorial Hospital.

The answer came in a flash. John Burton had given it to her, that day in the Mission Offices in Sydney. She'd put it in

Rosemary Jean's nappy bag and forgotten about it. Somehow it had ended up in Wilf's chest.

Her eyesight blurred, a weight behind them, as she stared at Wilf's beautiful, familiar handwriting. His letters had always been full of such love and humour. Could she bear to hear his voice now, alive on the page?

Eileen raised the envelope and sniffed it, hoping beyond hope she would smell his familiar scent – the hated cigarettes, that she had made such an awful fuss over, traces of ink from his ever-stained fingers, and the fragrance of roses that he always carried with him. But there was only the musty, slightly sweet aroma of camphorwood.

Her finger trembled at the edge of the envelope flap. Her eyes burned with unshed tears.

She couldn't do it.

Eileen slipped the letter back into the trunk unopened.

371

Epilogue

Rosemary

September 1994

We utterly deny all outward wars and strife and fightings with outward weapons, for any end or under any pretence whatsoever. And this is our testimony to the whole world.

From A Declaration to Charles II, 1661
These are the principles of the Quaker church.

Eileen's end was peaceful. Her gardening tools were still outside the front door. Something had distracted her before putting them away. She had gone inside, and sat in the chair that overlooked her large, lush garden. As the late afternoon sun cast its last golden glow across the room, she slipped away.

In her later years Eileen had embraced Quakerism, with its core principles of simplicity and peace, so her funeral was held in the Quaker style, with simple hymns and a gentle silence into which people could testify about her life. Her sisters, five children and many grandchildren attended.

Afterwards, Eileen's house was packed up, her things distributed amongst the family. Rosemary Jean received Wilf's camphorwood chest, along with the piano bought with compensation money after Wilf's death. Since she had nowhere to put it, she passed the piano on to her eldest daughter. The camphorwood chest sat at the end of her bed, a reminder of a past she knew little about. Rosemary didn't remember her early years, when Eileen had spoken openly about Wilf. Once Eileen remarried, she stopped talking about him, putting the past behind her.

A month after Eileen's death, Rabaul made the news. On the 19th of September, Vulcan and Tavurvur erupted once more, killing five people and causing eighty thousand more to evacuate. The town was buried in metres of ash that set like cement, destroying gardens, trees and buildings alike.

Rosemary knew the barest outline of her father's story – that he had been captured in Rabaul during the Japanese invasion, and that he had been on the Montevideo Maru when it was sunk. Seeing mention of Rabaul piqued her curiosity. She opened Wilf's chest.

Inside was a crumpled, yellowed wedding dress. When she pulled it out, the train was pitted with moth holes. There were the vestiges of a brocaded pattern but it was hard to make out on the old satin. Tiny buttons ran down the bodice. It would once have been beautiful.

Underneath the dress was a bundle of letters. Rosemary drew them out and opened them, one by one. Most were in her mother's familiar writing. But when she reached the bottom of the pile there were a scant few in another hand, written with beautifully formed, elaborate letters. Her heart nearly stopped when she saw the signature on them.

Wilf.

The very last letter was unopened, the envelope still sealed. It was addressed to E. Pearce, in the same ornate script. Hands trembling, Rosemary Jean slipped her finger under and released the flap. She drew the letter out, noticing how its fold was as crisp as the day, long ago, when it had been placed in there.

Why had Eileen never opened the letter? She had always told Rosemary she didn't know if Wilf knew he had a baby daughter. But this was dated almost a week after Rosemary's birth.

Rosemary began to read.

8th January 1942. Rabaul.

My Own Darling Eileen and baby Jean,

What a thrill it was Duckie to get yours and Mr Burton's radios this AM telling that our little daughter had arrived and you were both well. How thankful I am darling and to say I'm thrilled and delighted is just putting it mildly – It's just impossible to explain how I feel dearest and all I want now is to get this war over so that we can come together again and I can see my little baby Jean – I noticed you said Rosemary in the radio Sweetest, do you want us to use that name? Gee it's lovely darling to think I have two little girls waiting for me in Sydney and I'd give the world, if I owned it, to be with you both at the present moment. I do hope everything will go well with you both now Duckie. Do look after yourself Sweetheart and take great care of our baby. I'm anxious now to get the mail to hear what you think of our baby and to hear all about her. When she was born etc.

It was lovely of you Dearest to give me a bonny baby girl and I do hope she will prove a big joy and comfort to us both.

Well precious, I could go on writing all night I feel so joyful and so relieved that everything has turned out so well – but that wouldn't do and I'll probably have more to say after I get your letter telling me all about it. So I had better get a move on with my mail, but I just had to write and say how pleased and thankful I am. What's it like to be a mother Sweetie?

Well I suppose you are anxious to know just how I have been filling in my time sweetheart and so I had better bring my diary up to date and then I think I'll leave this note and finish it off tomorrow.

After I finished off writing to you last night Duckie I went straight off to bed. This morning I got up at the usual time and spent the whole morning in the office – spent quite a few minutes ringing up people to let them know the wonderful news. Dorothy Holmes is the only one from Vunairima who has heard the news so far and she suggests that she be given the job to take you on to Tasmania. She is very thrilled. Mac went out to Malaboga today and I gave him a radio to send to you as he went out – However he forgot it and rang me from Kokopo so I had to send a boy round and lost a couple of hours – I do hope you have received it Dearest. This afternoon I spent in the office and on accounts – At 5.30 pm Mac came back and brought us some pineapples and paw paws which we were very pleased to get for there hasn't been any tug at all, all week. And now tonight Dearest here I am working on mail - and that brings my diary right up to date. Well we've had a free day today – no Air raid – It was thought that they were coming over this morning but they didn't come, so we haven't had to go scurrying for the dugouts.

I do hope that you are feeling OK Dearest and that you are as thrilled as I am. Gee sweetheart, I'd love to see our baby girlie – It's wonderful to know that everything has gone so well and I do pray that things will continue to go well with you both. Do look after yourself sweetheart and take great care of my baby.

And now Darling, I'll have to leave you and write to the families, but I'll finish this note off tomorrow, anyhow pet, it's time you were asleep so here's a great big kiss and cuddle for yourself and an extra special kiss for my baby Jean. Goodnight Sweetie.

Well here I am again Sweetheart – it's midday

Friday and now I must get this letter finished off for the mail is sure to close this afternoon.

There isn't much to write about Darling, we have had a very wet morning and so I haven't ventured out, but have spent the whole morning working on my books and the air mail.

Well Pet, I think I have told you all there is to write about. Do look after yourself Sweetie and also look after my little daughter. It's a great thrill to know that I have a wee baby daughter – Gee I wish I could pop in and see you both – Still it won't be long Sweetheart before we are together again – I do pray Darling that God will be very near to you and Bless you and keep us all from harm and danger. I am quite well Sweetie and still sticking to my resolution. So please don't worry Sweetheart.

All my love to you my own Darling precious wife and baby and a great big kiss and cuddle for you both from your loving husband.

Wilf

Author's Epilogue

> It has now been ascertained the Japanese Navy Department officially informed the Tokio [sic] Prisoner of War Information Bureau on 6th June, 1943, that the S.S. "Montevideo Maru" sailed from Rabaul on approximately 22nd June, 1942, carrying 845 prisoners of war and 208 civilians, and that this ship was during its voyage torpedoed near Luzon with a total loss of the prisoners of war and internees embarked at Rabaul.
>
> Statement by the Minister for External Territories in the House of Representatives on Friday, 5th October, 1945

In the many years since the events described in this story, there have been numerous theories put forward about the fate of the Australian civilians and men of Lark Force. Whilst the official account is that everyone died when the Montevideo Maru sunk, other ideas have been proposed. One is that most died within the hull of the ship, but not everyone was trapped inside. A survivor of the sinking, one of the Japanese crew members, has stated there were prisoners in the water after the sinking, who were not rescued but left to drown. Although I've tried to track down the original interview, I haven't been successful so I can't comment on the veracity of this.

One author has dismissed this claim because the Japanese sailor reported the Australians singing 'Auld Lang Syne', which he says they wouldn't have done. However, survivors of the camps have stated they worked out this song made the Japanese more sentimental, and less likely to issue punishments. For men floating in the sea on debris, perhaps they hoped the song would encourage the Japanese to rescue them. Ultimately, there were no Australian survivors so the truth will never be known.

Another theory is that those men over the age of 45 were placed on a separate ship, which left Simpson Harbour, executed its passengers, then returned empty. The only thing apparently supporting this is that there was another ship in the harbour at the time. There are no clear reports of it leaving and returning. Thirdly, there is the theory that many of the prisoners were placed in one of the many tunnels dug into the hills around Rabaul by the Japanese during the three years of their occupation, with the tunnel then being blown up. Finally, there is a suggestion the Methodist Mission men were taken to Mioko Island, then executed.

Some have objected that the prisoners were actually not on the ship when it left Rabaul. However, given all the officers and women were deported to Japan a week later, where they lived out the rest of the war working in camps, it would seem odd if the Japanese had *not* shipped out the lower ranking men and civilians as they said. It would also make little sense for them to send the Montevideo Maru to Japan with no passengers or cargo.

Unfortunately, the accounts of native and Asian witnesses were not given much credence at the time due to colonialist attitudes and it is now too long ago to get a true picture of what they witnessed, which might have provided more details. However, Reverend John May and others reported seeing the men leave the camp on the date in question, and at least two witnesses, Reverend Mo Pui Sam and Tolai child Rudy Buckley, reported seeing the men arriving at the wharf and boarding the ship.

Some have even claimed the Montevideo Maru never existed. However, even prior to its discovery in April 2023, historical records clearly refuted this, establishing the ship's existence and ownership, as well as showing its ultimate fate: the bombing and sinking of the ship by the USS Sturgeon.

Part of the reason so many alternatives have been proposed is that several versions of the nominal roll, with the names of those supposedly on the Montevideo Maru, exist. Amongst these different versions, some contain the names of men known to have been executed elsewhere, so the suggestion is that the roll was used to cover up multiple executions with a more 'humane' death at a time when the Japanese were being tried for terrible crimes, including beheadings and cannibalism. It is also possible that multiple documents were combined through bureaucratic 'efficiencies' that inadvertently hid their separate origins.

However, the original roll found in Tokyo, which went missing for a long time, has re-emerged and doesn't appear to have these additional names. The practice of the Japanese army would have been to ensure great accuracy in their record keeping, so the roll can probably be taken as a true record of those who boarded the Montevideo Maru.

Since there has never been a formal inquiry into the fate of the Australians captured during the fall of Rabaul, the veracity of any of these alternate claims has never been considered. My opinion is that many Australians died when the Montevideo Maru was sunk, but that some names were added to the list to cover up previous executions. However, since the Australian government has never undertaken a full and proper inquiry the truth remains elusive.

Ultimately, as the grandchild of one of the civilians, all these possibilities are horrendous to consider. The wish to know the truth never goes away though. More than anything I would like to see a proper enquiry. The discovery of the Montevideo Maru in 2023 is only the beginning of a much needed process of truth telling. The fog of speculation obscures the loss and pain of many, many families.

This pain is a consequence of the death of over a thousand men who didn't have to die, and only did so because of bureaucratic bungling and the casual attitude to sacrifice of those in charge during war. But the events of 1942 were also only the beginning of a deeper, far more lasting sorrow. For many, many families, the loss of their husbands, sons, brothers, uncles, and children, saw their lives swerve onto a far different path.

Numerous accounts, including *A Very Long War* and *Whereabouts Unknown* by Margaret Reeson, *He's Not Coming Home* by Gillian Nikakis, and *Yours Sincerely, Tom* by Margaret Henderson, speak of the long-term effects on families who faced years of uncertainty, lack of support and, finally, a devastating loss. Wives were institutionalised or committed suicide, children were placed in homes or with extended families. Many lived with grief and depression as their constant companion. The aftershocks of the sinking of the *Montevideo Maru* have echoed down through generations.

Lost on the Montevideo Maru

The official numbers released by the Australia government at the time of those who died on the Montevideo Maru were 208 civilians, and 845 military personnel (1053 in total). However, just as this book was in the final stages of preparation for publication, further information was found that revealed those counted as 'military personnel' included 36 civilians who were volunteer members of the New Guinea Volunteer Rifles (NGVR). This puts the actual death count at 809 military personnel and 244 civilians. This explains why in our research we struggled to find the record for Ken Allsop. We knew he was a civilian, but he was not listed amongst the civilian dead.

The first figure puts the civilian deaths at under 20% of the total, whilst the second puts it at 23% - almost a quarter of those who died. One can only speculate as to why the government of the time chose to influence perceptions around the number of civilian deaths. Their failure to provide the means for civilian men to evacuate Rabaul before the invasion may have been a factor.

Amongst the 1053 civilians and soldiers lost on the Montevideo Maru (double the number of Australians lost in the Vietnam War) were the following who are part of this story:

Wilf Pearce – originally employed as an accountant, he was quickly promoted to business manager of the Methodist Mission in Rabaul

Laurie (Mac) MacArthur – Chairman of the Methodist Mission in Rabaul

Laurie Linggood – missionary

Howard Pearson – missionary

John Poole - missionary

Dan Oakes – missionary

Herbert Shelton – missionary

Tom Simpson – missionary. Officially numbered amongst those on the ships, but some accounts suggest he was killed by the Japanese earlier for trying to help an Australian soldier

Jack Trevitt – Principal of George Brown College

Syd Beazley – carpenter and trade teacher of the Methodist Mission

Ken Allsop – former employee of the Methodist Mission

Ron Wayne – former employee of the Methodist Mission

Harold Page – Deputy administrator of Rabaul and brother to former Deputy Prime Minister of Australia, Earle Page

Arthur Gullidge – Salvation Army Bandsmaster

Wilf Trigg – Salvation Army Deputy Bandmaster

James Thurst – Salvation Army Bandsman

Keith Trigg – the young gunner

The Fates of Others

Osea Lige and other church leaders from the islands – many of the ministers and lay preachers worked hard to keep the Lotu alive amongst their villages. The Japanese responded with extreme brutality, which was chronicled later in war crime trials, and left whole villages to die by stripping them of food and resources. Those who survived, including Osea Lige, rebuilt the church community after the Japanese surrendered, and it thrives in New Britain today.

Ainui and Pilip – Mission employees who worked closely with Wilf, there is no information available about Ainui or Pilip's fate. Many Tolai were executed, or starved to death, under Japanese rule. I can only hope they were not amongst them.

Ia Lo – Eileen's friend and fellow teacher returned to her village during the invasion. My sister and I spent months trying to find any trace of her after that point, fearful she might have died during Japanese occupation. We were greatly relieved to find that when Gil Platten returned to Rabaul in 1945, he mentioned seeing Ia Lo alive and well.

Rodger Brown (missionary) and Gil Platten (missionary) – both successfully escaped Rabaul and returned to Australia. Rodger Brown later wrote a book entitled Talatala, where he reflected on living with survivor's guilt for the rest of his life.

Bill Harry – the young soldier attached to Australian intelligence successfully escaped the Japanese and returned to Australia.

John May – the army Chaplain who read a psalm as the soldiers and civilians were evacuating was transported to Japan on the *Naruto Maru* a week later and held as a prisoner until the end of the war. He returned to Australia in 1945 and devoted time to contacting the wives of the Methodist missionaries, to answer their questions about their husbands' time as internees. He died in Hobart at the age of 95.

Bill Huntley – the former manager of the Mission plantation at Vunairima initially escaped, but on 29th August 1942 he was captured by the Japanese and executed for having a radio set.

Dorothy Beale, Jean (Chris) Christopher, Mavis Green and Dora Wilson – the Methodist Mission nurses, whose safety was a factor in the missionaries choosing not to evacuate, were sent to Japan on the *Naruto Maru* a week after the *Montevideo Maru* left Rabaul. They spent the rest of the war in a prison camp, and after the Japanese surrendered, returned home safely in 1945.

Information about the lives of the wives and children who evacuated just before Christmas 1941 is contained in Margaret Reeson's book, *A Very Long War*.

Glossary

Balaguan	Kuanua for feast
balus	airplane – actually the Kuanua word for pigeon
Beeps Store	Burns Philp
WRC	Carpenter's
	The two companies that dominated most Rabaul shipping and commerce at the time of the story
Benjo hole	a latrine – essentially a hole in the ground dug by the prisoners
besom	broom
gurias	Tolai word for earthquakes. guriu – earthquake – guria – plural
hyaku yon ju	one hundred and forty (Japanese)
job bilong mari	women's work – including cooking
kaia	Tolai word for supernatural spirits inhabiting natural features. There are thousands of spirits, but the most powerful inhabit volcanoes
kaluana	green coconut to drink out of – very refreshing, sweet, effervescent
kau kau	similar to sweet potato - starchy
Kempei tai	Japanese military police. Trained in interrogation – full power arrest of civilians and military
Kuskus	a special name given to Wilf by the Tolai, it means 'Father'
lakatoi	boat, large enough for 20+ men, with crab claw sail and little shelter on the deck
lik lik	somewhat ambiguous quantity of something, eg 'lik lik long way' could be a few hours to a few days walk

Lotu	Mission Christianity
luluai	local headman
Marama	name for white married ladies
maski	no matter (how long it takes) – ie laid back about time
oaga	canoe
over the eight	drunk
sisita	name for missionary sisters (teachers and nurses)
Talatala	name for European Minister/male missionary
Talatala Marmaravut	'Assistant minister', Indigenous ministers
the Malay Hole	town dump
Rakaia	the king spirit who inhabits Vulcan, one of Rabaul's four main volcanoes
tabu	shell money. Also used for special occasions. For example, only tabu can bring you to heaven. Tabu is paid as a bride price to a woman's family and to her church community when she is married.
puri puri	to use sorcery, for example, to make another ill
tenko	roll call, held twice daily in the prison camp – prisoners were lined up and made to stand for extended periods, regardless of their health or the weather
Warataba	Thank offering – the annual collection given by villages to the Methodist Mission to enable them to continue their work

Research Sources

Australian Broadcasting Corporation	2010	Sisters of War [film], ABC Australia.
British Pathe	1937	Volcano erupts in Papua New Guinea 1937 [film], https://www.britishpathe.com/video/ VLVAC5UP1LOY9CAJQNJOCTEUKT94Q-VOLCANO-ERUPTS-IN-PAPUA-NEW-GUINEA/query/rabaul
Bruce Gamble	2014	Darkest Hour: The True Story of Lark Force at Rabaul, Zenith Press
Bruce Gamble	2014	Invasion Rabaul, Zenith Press
Dudley Carter	2004	*Escape from Rabaul 1942: Diary of Dudley Carter, 2/22nd Battn. AIF*, Coulson, Helen (ed.), self-published, Echuca, Vic.
Gayle Thwaites (Ed.)	2017	*When the war came: New Guinea Islands 1942*, Papua New Guinea Association of Australia, Roseville, NSW.
Gil Platten	n.d.	'Problems of mission work in south New Ireland', hand typed notes
Gillian Nikakis	2005	*He's not coming home*, Lothian Books, South Melbourne.
Gordon Thomas	2012	*Prisoners in Rabaul: Civilians in Captivity 1942-1945*, Australian Military History Publications, Loftus NSW
(Gunner) David Bloomfield	2001	*Escaping capture in New Britain: The fate of 'Lark Force' – 1942*, self-published.
Imamura Hitoshi	1945	*The tenor of my life*, private manuscript
John Wear Burton	1926	*Our task in Papua*, The Epworth Press, London.
Judy Nunn	2004	*Pacific*, Random House, Sydney
Kathryn Spurling	2017	*Abandoned and sacrificed: the tragedy of the Montevideo Maru*, New Holland Publishers, Sydney.
Lex McAulay	2007	*We who are about to die: the story of John Lerew – A hero of Rabaul, 1942*, Banner Books, Hervey Bay, Qld.
Lindsay Cox	2003	*Brave and true: From blue to khaki: the band of the 2/22nd battalion*, The Salvation Army Australia, Southern Territory

Lisa Mariah as told by Raynor Barber	2006	*Touched by war - Memoirs of a Beaufighter pilot*, Australian Military History Publications, Loftus NSW
Margaret L Henderson	2000	*Yours sincerely, Tom*, self-published.
Margaret Reeson	1993	*Whereabouts unknown: The story of those who disappeared after the fall of Rabaul in 1942 – and the women who waited*, Albatross Books, Sutherland, NSW
Margaret Reeson	2000	*A very long war*, Melbourne University Press, Melbourne
Margaret Spencer	1967	*Doctor's wife in Rabaul*, The Trinity Press, London
McMurria affidavit		1st Lt James A. McMurria Affidavit regarding medical experiments and executions at Rabaul Tunnel Hill POW Camp, http://www.mansell.com/pow_resources/camplists/other/rabaul/mcmurria_affidavit_rabaul.html RG 331 Box 943 Rabaul Reports; NARA #7 IMG_0029 et al
Mrs E Linggood	? 1945	*New Britain: Three missionary studies*, originally prepared for the Victorian Women's Methodist Mission. Dedicated to the memory of the men who lost their lives on the "Montevideo Maru"
Neville Threlfall	1975	*One hundred years in the islands: The Methodist/United Church in the New Guinea islands region 1875-1976*, The United Church, New Guinea Islands Region, Rabaul, PNG
Neville Threlfall	2012	*Mangroves, coconuts and frangipani*, Gosford City Council, Gosford.
Patsy Adam-Smith	1997	*Australian Prisoners of War*, Penguin Books, Ringwood. 2nd edn.
Peter Stone	1994	*Hostages to freedom: The fall of Rabaul*, Oceans Enterprises, Yarram.
Rodger Brown	2001	*Talatala: An Australian missionary couple in PNG before, during and after the war*, Self-published. Edited by Margaret Henderson
RW Johnson & NA Threlfall	1985	*Volcano Town*, Robert Brown and Associates, Bathurst, Australia.

Ryoko Adachi & Andrew McKay	2005	*Shadows of War*, Indra Publishing, Briar Hill, VIC Aust
Sarah Chinnery	1998	*Malaguna Road: the Papua and New Guinea Diaries of Sarah Chinnery*, The National Library of Australia, Canberra, ACT.
Schindler Video Productions	2010	*The Fall of Rabaul*
Schindler Video Productions	2009	*The Tragedy of the Montevideo Maru*
	n.d.	*The Methodist School Hymnal*, Wesleyan Methodist Sunday School Department, Ludgate Circus, London (this edition has an epigraph gifting it in 1926)
Newspaper sources		The Brisbane Telegraph The Canberra Times The Kalgoorlie Miner (WA) The Methodist The Missionary Review The Mercury The Melbourne Herald The Sydney Herald Sun
Other sources		Documents from the era were obtained from: The State Library of Victoria Trove (online) The Pacific Manuscript Bureau

I am deeply greatly to the following people for their invaluable contributions to this manuscript:

Joss Larkins	Research assistant and provider of coffee
Angela Slatter	Editor and mentor
Christine Gordon	UC Synod Assembly Archivist
Deanna Moore	UC Synod Archives Research Assistant
Greta Thomas	State Library of Tasmania – Archive Service

Karen Woolford	Archivist, Wesley Heritage Hobart
Kate Forsyth	Mentor
Lisa Mariah	Research Assistant
Margaret Reeson	Author of several books about the impact of the events in Rabaul on the Mission survivors
Moira	Office manager, UC Synod and Training School
Neville Threlfall	Author of a number of excellent books about the Methodist Mission in Rabaul
Warren and David Roden	Archive volunteers, UC Synod and Training School

Miss Jessie March's Rainbow Cake

¼ lb. butter

½ lb. sugar

3 eggs

½ cup milk

½ lb. flour sifted with 2 teaspoons cream of tartar and 1 teaspoon carbonate soda

1 dessertspoon cocoa

cochineal

vanilla

Beat butter and sugar to a cream; add egg yolks and beat again. Stiffly whisk the egg whites and fold them into the mixture. Lastly sift in the flour mixture and blend thoroughly. Divide mixture into three parts—put one part plain, flavoured with vanilla, into a greased sandwich tin; tint the second with cochineal to make a delicate pink; and add cocoa to the third part. Spread both coloured parts into separate buttered sandwich tins the same size as the first, and bake in a moderate oven until cooked. Put together when cold with lemon cheese or icing. Ice all over.